T0354602

LIBRAN'S LOCH

Abbygail Donaldson

author<small>HOUSE</small>®

AuthorHouse™
1663 Liberty Drive
Bloomington, IN 47403
www.authorhouse.com
Phone: 1-800-839-8640

First published by AuthorHouse 11/30/2011

ISBN: 978-1-4678-8586-7 (sc)
ISBN: 978-1-4678-7937-8 (e)

Printed in the United States of America

I dedicate this book to:

My patient and supportive husband and children, who endured my estrangement during the many months it took to research and write this book.

To our dear friend Jason for his support, technical advice and keen eye for detail during the review.

To the enthralling and eminent Professor Brian Cox, and to 'Dr Who' and David Tennant for inspiring me to return to my lifelong passion for science and time travel.

INTRODUCTION

MY INTEREST IN SCIENCE BEGAN with the Apollo moon landing back in 1969, when I was only three and too young to appreciate, the monumental importance and global excitement generated by those historic first steps which stirred up the lunar dust that day. I confess that my initial interest was aroused more by my father's unusual fixation with the series of boring black and white images on our TV screen, than the event itself. That is, until my Father, clearly irritated by my incessant questions, refused my Mother's gentle suggestion that perhaps it was well past my bedtime. "No Margaret. ....This is something the bairn needs to see and remember, ...something she can tell her children about, ...the day man stood on the moon!".. and he was absolutely right. Albeit, it was years later when I fully began to appreciate the gift he gave me that evening, it was, without doubt, a pivotal event which left a lasting impression on me, and inspired me to take on what others would discard as impossible, high risk challenges.

Over the years, I came to realise the true importance of experience, how it influences our lives and how it can, at times, bring down the walls of established beliefs and knowledge and expose some truths that perhaps were better left hidden. At the time, no one had any idea of the true impact that the moon landing would have, not just on the lives of those astronauts, but on each one of us. Not since

1492 and the discovery that the world was not flat, had man's beliefs and superstitions been so dramatically shaken.

Then, thirty years later, as the Greenwich clock and the penny weighted balances and cogs within the mechanics of Big Ben, clicked and ticked their way towards the new Millennium, who amongst us didn't feel the trepidation instilled in us by centuries of prophecies and superstitions, that the world would suddenly fall into chaos and end. Yet, we are still here. We have survived more than a decade since its passing, proving that not all beliefs or superstitions are right. So why do we need them?

Some of them are based on practical experience and hold reliable practical advantages, like planting seeds during a full moon to increase the chances of successful seed germination. At the time this belief or rule was laid down, man had a very limited understanding of why the moon influenced our tides and our crops, so, in the absence of a provable scientific explanation, we accepted this rule on the basis of its reliability to produce expected results.

Similarly, over the centuries, scientific theory has been judged by the successful and reliable results it produces. For instance, an apple falling from a tree, will always fall downwards towards the earth, due to the force of gravity acting upon it. However, as we continue to expand our knowledge of our planet and the Universe and develop technology capable of analysing key information in greater detail, or reconstructing cosmic events to test previous assumptions and theories against the new data, we are beginning to discover that some theories aren't as reliable as we first thought. It's not that these theories were ever flawed in my opinion, it is only that the context changed and more detail has become available for a more critical analysis to be conducted.

As Albert Einstein once said himself:

"To raise new questions, new possibilities, to regard old problems from a new angle, requires creative imagination and marks real advance in science."

So where do we go from here and what does this have to do with Libran's Loch?

Libran's Loch is a fictional adventure and the culmination of many years of ad hoc research into the topics of precognition and time travel. Contrary to Einstein's theory that time travel is only possible if you can travel faster than the speed of light, Libran's Loch looks at the possibility of time travel by other means, not involving a famous fictional blue box or a ship capable of warp drive. It examines the possible link between genetically suppressed precognitive abilities, thought projection and the theoretical frequency of electrical energy that underpins and connects everything in the Universe. In the story, I explore what could happen, if someone was able to tap into this theoretical frequency and not only receive precognitions or snapshots from future critical, stress beacons in their own life but to connect or project into those events in their future or their past. Like the electrical shock waves that radiate outwards from the epicentre of an earthquake, I believe that at critical moments in our life, we radiate what some might call an electrical distress signal or beacon to our past and future subconscious and into our surroundings, which we can tune into under opportune circumstances. It is my suggestion that these beacons might provide an explanation for the source of déjà-vu, precognition and post traumatic 'flashbacks'. It is my idea, that if thought waves know no time boundaries, and the distress signal is strong enough, we could at least project our thoughts into the past or the future, and if our minds are capable of performing this feat whose to say that given the right frequency and electrical conditions, our bodies could travel too?

Finally, I would just like to say this:

"Whatever the subject, if your instinct questions accepted theory, have the courage to ask your questions or to search for your own answers. You might be wrong or you might be right, but whatever the outcome you'll find the journey quite revelationary."

Abbygail Donaldson

CHAPTER 1

IT WAS AUGUST 1746, THIRTY years before the end of the transportation of British convicts to North America and the Pride of Leith, carrying her cargo of convicts and indentured servants, was within a week of her destination in Virginia. Lightening flashed like skeletal white fingers grasping at the eighteenth century ship rising high on the western Atlantic swell as it met the eastern sea board off the coast of America. The thick oily black thunder clouds growled angrily and emitted an ear splitting crack above the aft main mast. Heavy rain from the sudden summer storm lashed the sails and the deck from all directions as the Captain's command of "Stow the sail!" barely achieved a whisper through the roaring winds to his crew. The masts bowed and the wooden hull groaned and creaked under the powerful tides, as the ship dipped acutely in its descent once more, sending crew and passengers scurrying and sliding along the water drenched decks. The servants and prisoners beneath the gun deck, crossed themselves and muttered prayers of mercy, as they watched the ceiling timbers above their heads, bend and bow beneath the weight of the cannons that rolled and rocked within their tackle leashed carriages. Like wild animals ready to pounce, the shifting cannons pulled and stretched their thick black chains almost to the point of breaking, before another wave tipped the ship in the opposite direction and they moved back into place again.

Suddenly, the ship pitched to starboard, casting icy cold

sea water through the gun ports on to the crew, filling their mouths, noses and eyes with water and the gagging, burning taste of salt. Jacob the young, dark haired cabin boy lost his footing and came crashing down on to the wet deck, as another wave struck the hull and swept him effortlessly towards the far side of the ship. Scrabbling desperately and breathlessly, his delicate young fingers found the strong heavy metal links of the gun carriage chain and he hung on tightly, muttering phrases from the twenty third psalm. With his eyes shut, and coughing from the brine that burned his throat, he felt himself pushed towards the open gun port, expecting nothing but the sudden stomach churning sharp drop into the ocean and the life consuming descent down to the depths of Davey Jones' Locker. Suddenly, he felt the heavy iron clad grip of the stalwart ship's cook at the back of his collar and a slightly weightless sensation as he hovered for a moment before he was reeled in to safety.

"What's the Captain doing sending you in here in this storm? You'll be crushed like a quail's egg if you're swept under one of those monsters!" he exclaimed as he pointed to the grumbling fluid line of cannons rolling back and forth. "Get yourself back to the galley and hold fast til I return!"

"Yes, Sir!" spluttered the drenched and shivering fragile waif, as he slipped and slid past the cook to the steps down to the galley below.

Crawling carefully down the steps, he dodged the heavy swinging galley door and leapt inside, catching the door handle on its return and pulling it closed behind him. Below the galley, Jacob could hear the moans, cries and whimpers of the prisoners and indentured servants stowed in that half of the hold, and covered his ears to muffle their agony. Then as the ship listed again, the cacophony of clanging metal pans and utensils suspended above his head, drowned out their cries completely.

Captain Magnus McGregor crouched in quiet miserable contemplation, coveting his cramped and sheltered vantage point behind the stairs that led to the upper decks from the hold. Watching the wayward and desperate prisoners as they scrabbled and rolled in the filth and squalor, half starved and diseased by their confinement, Magnus hid in the shadows, masking the smell of the stench beneath his soiled and torn French Cravat. An aging former sea captain, Magnus was himself a prisoner en route for the colonies to begin his life sentence. A worthy vicious vagabond for the hangman's noose, he had narrowly avoided the gallows by virtue of his well paid and influential counsel in the court. Commuted from execution to transportation for his sins, Magnus thought about the savage new life he was about to face and the memories of his brutalised childhood that his revolting imprisonment had rekindled in his mind. Being the battered illegitimate child of a wife beating drunkard, Magnus was no stranger to the harsher, more brutal and impoverished social life style of Glaswegian unfortunates. Since his humble and dramatic youth, he had strived unmercilessly to reach the giddy political and social heights that he had, until recently enjoyed. Now, as a consequence of the very evil behaviour, which he had witnessed and despised in his youth, Magnus had been forcefully sucked back into the social cauldron he'd tried so hard to escape from.

With his bitter reputation preceding him, Magnus kept his back to the wall, wary of retaliation from those he had cheated and deceived in his recent past, and who now sat in chains only feet away, waiting to strike, waiting for retribution. As he watched their gnarled and fleshy hands stretching and pulling their chains taut with menace, Magnus imagined the links pulled tightly around his own neck but glared back fearlessly and unrepentant of their plight which he had caused. Gazing imperiously at the

3

squalor and pestilence that were now his courtiers, Magnus surveyed his dire realm and the malleable subjects within it. With nothing to do but to sit and rattle the mandatory rusty bling of his convicted status, Magnus began to meticulously plan his revenge against his accuser back home in Libran's Loch.

The ship suddenly pitched again starboard, as a huge wave rolled up and towered high over them, before crashing down and swamping the heavily listing deck. Sails and rigging ravelled and twisted catapulting blocks and pulleys into the crew, hurling them against masts or overboard into the ferocious waters beyond. Then, a solid beam supporting the gun deck let out an unearthly crack, as the splitting timber gave up its weighty burden and brought the cannon plummeting down on to the prisoners facing Magnus, crushing their bones and flesh as if they were paper.

"The devil looks after his own, they say!" yelled a wizened beggar skulking to Magnus' right, drawing his harsh and critical stare. "You mark my words!" he cackled with eyes twinkling fiery red.

"The devil took my soul a long time ago," sniped Magnus and the old beggar grinned before vanishing into the shadows.

Then feeling the chains around his feet slide loosely over the tilting deck, Magnus realised that the falling cannon had crashed through the housing that nested the chains, shattering the links to himself and the other prisoners. Taking full advantage of his new found liberty, Magnus crept stealthily up the wooden steps as more torrents of sea water cascaded through the entrance hatch, forcing him flat against the boards until the ship rose again and he was able to make his escape.

As more lightening lashed the main deck, Magnus peered out from his hiding place near the hatch entrance and marvelled at the luminous cloud barely half a mile away that lay ominously ahead of them at the edge of the storm. Lightening flashed eerily within the cloud, whilst the stormy waters calmed before it, almost fearful to flow within its boundaries.

"Captain we're taking on too much water down below! She'll capsize for sure if this storm doesn't stop soon!" yelled the First Mate.

"Steer ten degrees starboard and head into that cloud, Peterson!" ordered the Captain.

"Begging your pardon Sir, but we can't see what's in there?" queried the First Mate. "We don't know how far off course we are since the storm struck and there could be rocks or God knows what manner of things, in there."

"Do it, Mr Peterson!" commanded the Captain. "We stand a far greater risk remaining in this storm than we do heading into the cloud. The waters appear much calmer there and may provide temporary sanctuary whilst we take stock of the damage and make good our repairs!"

"Aye Aye, Sir!"

The First Mate did as he was bid and turned the wheel ten degrees, steering the ship towards the cloud. Once more the lightening lashed out its skeletal fingers, as if clawing at the ship's rigging to pull it back into the heart of the storm, but the hearty Scottish built ship drove on. As they neared the mysterious cloud, the roar of the winds dropped suddenly, to little more than a hush and the swell of the tide diminished to just a gentle lapping against the ship's hull. The crew suddenly stopped in their tracks, wary of the deathly luminescent calmness that now engulfed them. Then, a sudden almost expected crackle at the top of the mast turned all eyes upwards to cower in fear at the web of flickering blue light that spread from mast to mast and downwards towards the deck of the ship.

"What in God's good name…?" asked the Captain in mystified disbelief.

"I think it's St. Elmo's Fire, Sir, begging your pardon. Seen it once before when I was on night watch, Sir," replied the First Mate.

Suddenly, a large branch of blinding white light struck the master-at-arms on the main deck, attracted by the weaponry about his person. As the Captain and the rest of the crew stopped and stared, his hair and his beard, curled and twisted upwards, whilst his body juddered as if performing some bizarre navy jig. The crew began to laugh heartily, sickeningly clapping in time with the jolts, naïve of the nerves that were being fried in his body with every second of contact. Only when his eyes rolled backwards into his head, and his teeth clamped hard together in a fixed agonised expression, did the laughing stop. With eyes widened in horror, the crew watched as the lightening, now fully discharged, disappeared and the well rounded meaty master-at-arms crashed down upon the deck, dead. With faint wisps of smoke drifting around him and the vague sweet smell of roasted meat wafting from his body, the crew dropped their weapons in fear and stood in guilt laden silence as the Captain approached. Clearing a way through the circle of men that surrounded the body, Captain Jameson ventured close to the corpse. Wrapping his kerchief around his hand and carefully cupping the handle of his sword, he warily touched the sailor's left leg with the blade and jumped as the leg suddenly twitched. The crew jumped back a pace and watched as the residue charge, no thicker than a pencil, leapt onto the sword and the Captain felt its pulse, only briefly, before discarding his weapon in haste.

"Do not touch the body!" he commanded. "Lest you share his fate!"

"Aye aye Sir," chorused the crew grimly.

"Peterson, have the body covered with sacking until we get out of this storm. Then, hopefully, we can attend to his remains with dignity."

"Aye aye Sir," Peterson replied.

"Oh and have two of the crew prepare the burial sack…. He was quite a rotund chap, so they will require extra sacking to get the job done."

"Aye aye Sir," nodded Peterson. "Finlay! Barton! Fetch the sacking!"

"Aye Sir," they chorused.

"You're on funeral duties," ordered Peterson as the Captain bowed his head before returning to the helm.

Meanwhile, as the unarmed crew encircled the corpse, Magnus and the other escaped prisoners crept silently on to the main deck and waited for someone to lead the charge. Looking around the deck, Magnus spied the recently discarded weapons, like manner from heaven and dobbed a mischievous salute of gratitude to his weatherly benefactor and grinned.

"Grab the weapons quietly," whispered Magnus to the prisoners behind him. "Then when I give the command, we strike and take over the ship!"

The prisoners, foul smelling from the weeks of cramped incarceration in the hold, breathed their first breath of fresh air before lowering on to their bellies like serpents and slithering across the wet deck towards their prey. Magnus carefully slid over the rail on to the outside of the ship and beckoned to three others to follow him. Hanging precariously from the wooden rail with their feet sliding carefully along the top edges of the gun doors, Magnus and his followers made their way towards the quarter deck aft of the main mast. Then pulling himself up the rigging and over the rail again, Magnus landed softly on the quarter deck and crept behind the captain. Sliding the short sword from its sheath and observing that the other prisoners were in place around the main deck ready to pounce, Magnus threw his left arm around the captain's neck and raised his right arm carrying the sword.

"Now men!"

In an instant, armed with the discarded weapons, the prisoners turned on the crew and held them at gun point awaiting further orders from their newly self-appointed leader.

"You'll all hang for this, mark my words!" bellowed the captain.

"Only if we reach land!" declared Magnus. "But in case you haven't noticed Captain, there's a particularly nasty storm to our aft, and a heavy fog across our bow. And, if I'm not mistaken, Peterson, I could have sworn that I heard you state so succinctly that we're lost! Yes?"

Peterson stumbled as the prisoner standing behind him, pushed the barrel of the loaded pistol into the centre of his back.

"I asked you a question!" barked Magnus.

Peterson looked quickly at the captain who nodded carefully, before replying, "Aye ,Sir!"

"Now then, Captain, I would like to propose a bargain!"

"I don't bargain and I don't parley!" snapped the captain. ".. particularly not with prisoners, pirates and dishonourable former captains!"

"Aaah, so my fame precedes me! I'm flattered you've taken due note of my achievements!" sneered Magnus.

"I've taken no more note than I would any potential threat aboard my ship!" replied the captain.

"Hmmn, "sighed Magnus pensively. Then he turned to a slight, and gaunt looking prisoner to his left. "You! What's your name?"

"Craven, Sir!" he replied.

"Right, Craven. Bind the Captain and bring him into the cabin! The rest of you, bind your prisoners and bring them to the quarter deck! The Captain may not want to bargain, but let's see if his underpaid crew are more prudent!"

A chorus of, "Aye aye Captain!" echoed around the prisoners as Craven lashed the Captain's wrists and bound them tightly before leading him into the Captain's cabin behind Magnus.

"You'll never get away with this!" snapped Captain Jameson.

Magnus walked around the Captain's table, and stood with his back silhouetted against the ghoulish green glow beyond the windows, that now shrouded the entire ship.

"And why do you think I was discharged from my position Captain?" asked Magnus.

"The Admiralty felt that you were a significant risk!" he responded snootily.

"To who? To you? To my crew? No, I was a risk to them! They felt threatened by the volume and severity of their own misdeeds which I was privy to! The more I knew, the bigger the threat I became, yet, they needed me to carry out their dirty work! I played their game, pirating their own ships' cargo to line their private purse, that is, until they double-crossed me!" he bawled slamming his fist down hard on the table.

"You lie Sir! You defame their honour!" replied the Captain.

"I think not Sir! I have guested in many of their powerful households and learned of many other schemes of their malpractice and mis-appropriation of coin to their benefaction!" Magnus growled. Then lowering his voice to a gleeful sneer he continued," Their big mistake was to under-estimate my many skills," he continued. "As additional

9

insurance, I charmed and bedded many of their valuable virginal daughters too!" he gloated. "As I recall, their thighs were pale like milk, sweet and yielding to the thrusts of my ambition! One wrong word in the right ear refuting their precious chastity and I'll bring their lifelong plans for influential marital alliances crashing down around their ears!"

"Good God, man! Know you no shame, no dishonour so base, to defile the innocent with your diseased intentions and contrived blackmail?" remarked the Captain in disgust.

"You flatter me Sir, with my accomplishments and I do confess to your piety that I did no such action under sufferance. I did, indeed, indulge my lusts and delighted in the pleasure and gratifications from such sweet torture." Then taking a deep sniff of the air, like a blood hound picking up a scent, his eyes glinted evilly and he sighed," Mmm, I sense the smell of adultery about you, Sir or are you such a dandy to flaunt your perfume so blatantly? I think I shall imminently enjoy the intimate realms of the mistress who was once yours solely to conquer. What say you Jameson?"

Captain Jameson stood to attention as tiny panic and guilt loaded beads of perspiration appeared on his brow.

"I am an honourable gentleman and loyal husband! How dare you slur me with allegations that could only exist in your depraved soul! You scoundrel Sir! I demand satisfaction!" yelled Captain Jameson.

"Oh you shall have it! But first I shall take mine!" commanded Magnus. "Craven!" he yelled.

"Aye Sir?"

"Open yonder chest, and tell me what you find there!"

"Aye Sir!"

Craven could see the long, deep, hand carved, dark oak chest that stood at the far side of the cabin and trotted over to it. Holding his acquired sword to the Captain's throat, Magnus grinned, his eyes filled with sadistic delight, as Craven lifted the heavy chest lid. The bright blue/green eyes sparkled with tears of fear out of the darkness, her heart pounding as she sensed her imminent fate. Reaching down into the chest, Craven suddenly yelled and jumped backwards, cradling his bloody wrist.

"She bit me Sir! The viper bit me!"

Magnus lowered his sword and strode across to the chest intrigued. He loved women who were filled with anger and fire, their boiling temperament heightened his passions. The more they resisted him, the more he craved them.

Approaching the chest, Magnus offered his hand in an almost gentlemanly fashion to the frightened young gypsy hidden in its depths.

"Fear not," he whispered seductively, his voice dark and sweet like Jamaican Rum. "I will set you free," he smiled. "I wish only to feast my eyes on your beauty, and to provide you with more befitting accommodation."

Slowly from the depths of the darkness, a swarthy slender hand emerged and reached up to his, and he saw her bewitching blue/green eyes for the first time. As she ascended gracefully to her feet, Magnus took in the beauty of her glossy and wavy raven black hair and her flame red softly parted lips. Helping her out of the chest, Magnus watched as she shook her tousled curls and smouldered in the luminescent half light of the cabin. Shaking the dust covered layers of her voluminous skirts and taming the frills that framed her pounding chest and bare shoulders, the gypsy shot an angry glance at her rope bound master. As she turned her face, Magnus saw the red, purple and green bruising on her upper cheek and instantly his anger flared. Recalling the battering of his fragile mother, he took the

11

gypsy's face in his hand and examined the bruising as she fidgeted uneasily.

"Did your master do this?" Magnus fumed.

The gypsy stared into his dark soulless eyes and saw her reflections floating out of the blackness to greet her. Gesturing to Magnus that she was unable to speak, she then jabbed her accusatory finger in the Captain's direction. Magnus glared angrily at her pompous uniformed master.

"Craven?" he bellowed.

"Yes Sir?"

"Leave us. The Captain and I have business to attend to!" commanded Magnus as he leered at Jameson.

"Aye, Sir! What will I tell the others?"

"Tell them to ready the launch! Those crew that do not switch their allegiance will be set adrift and left to the mercy of the storm!"

"Understood, Sir!" replied Craven as he retreated through the cabin door, leaving behind the bound Captain, his mute gypsy mistress and Magnus.

Once the cabin door was closed, Magnus approached the Captain and grabbing him by the shoulders, flung him face down on the end of the table. Then unbinding his hands and rebinding each one to either leg of the table he left the Captain bound and prostrate as he approached the injured gypsy.

Grateful of her apparent rescue from her abusive master she threw herself down at Magnus' feet. Stooping and taking her hand, he led her to the table to face the purveyor of her misery.

"You're free," he said. "Free to do what you will," he said as she stroked his aging face and stubbled chin. "What would you have me do with him?" Magnus asked gesturing towards the captain.

Grabbing hold of Magnus' hand and pressing it to her

stomach, he felt the movement and distortion of her swollen belly and let out a raucous laugh.

"Well, well Captain! So much for the honourable loyal husband that you swore to a moment ago! Your falsehood is confirmed and your guilt is manifest! Your mistress, Sir, is carrying your bastard!"

The Captain pulled and twisted on his ropes, trying to free himself.

"What would you have me do?" asked Magnus smiling gleefully at the gypsy, waiting for her direction.

The gypsy beckoned to Magnus to hand over his sword, and surprisingly he did so, mesmerised by the fire of vengeance in her eyes. Then, taking the sword and wandering round to the Captain's end of the table, Magnus stood silently, waiting for the inevitable.

"What's she going to do?" yelled Captain Jameson. "Stop her!"

"I am not feminine and understand not the ways of a woman scorned and defiled so intimately!" grinned Magnus. "She alone knows the price of her present ruination!"

The pain was swift and searing, and the Captain let out an agonising scream of terror as the point of the blade pierced his body below his spine and thrust further and further inside, until the hilt prevented the blade from travelling any further. As she twisted the blade inside the Captain, Magnus could see the wildness in her eyes and the satisfaction of her revenge glowing beneath her facial bruises. Magnus felt excited by her fire and her power as she wielded the sword like a baton of justice. Strange gagging sounds came from the captain's mouth as he coughed a pool of blood on to the table.

Carefully approaching the gypsy from behind, he softly lay his older rougher hands on her bare shoulders and breathed in the exotic scented oils from her hair, before slowly gliding his hands down each of her arms. The gypsy shivered as if a cold serpent had crawled over her body and tensed nervously as Magnus' hands came to rest over hers on the hilt of the sword.

"I believe he is dying. Your job is done," he whispered seductively in her ear as he carefully removed the sword from the Captain's body.

As her anger tempered, she realised the true extent of her actions. The Captain would be dead soon and that would make her a murderess, destined to hang when they eventually made port. Magnus' strategy hadn't freed her at all. He had instead, turned her instantly into his very malleable slave. Not only was her soul damned to hell, but her body was forever damned to serve this devil's whims and desires. Trembling with shock and fear, she backed away breathlessly and sought refuge in the darkness. With the Captain's blood still on his hands, Magnus stepped into the shadows stalking the gypsy as she backed up against the wall of the cabin. Having no place left to run, she pressed her back against the wall as the malevolent, victorious former captain advanced towards her. Her blue/green eyes flashed in the darkness and she held her breath uncertain of his intent. Slowly, he raised the bloody blade to her lips, painting them gently with Jameson's blood. As the luminescent green light from the windows cast an eerie green glow across her blood stained face, there was a sudden cutting of fabric as Magnus brought the sharp blade edge down through the bodice of her dress, like a hot knife through butter. The fabric fell away on either side of the blade and Magnus grinned lecherously as her abundant breasts burst free from their restraints and hung provocatively beneath the now loose folds of material.

Outside the cabin door, Craven heard the sound of clattering metal as the sword fell to floor and he listened intently to his master's moans of sadistic, satisfaction whilst the gypsy shed silent tears and prayed for merciful release.

As blood poured from the Captain's mortally wounded body on to the floor at his feet and the pain of his wounds gave way to the welcome numbness and tranquillity of death, Magnus gasped with pleasure and groaned huskily, "I will set you free."

Smothering her blood covered mouth with his, Magnus caressed her supple soft neck with his rough bare hands before suddenly clamping them tightly around her throat. Clawing wildly and ineffectively at his vice like grip, the gypsy struggled to breathe. Then, as he removed his mouth from her lips and took one last look at her tantalising eyes, he gave her neck one firm last hard sudden twist, and heard the stomach turning snap of the vertebrae and she was free, unto death.

Suddenly, Magnus heard the hammering on the cabin door.

"What is it?" he yelled.

"The launch is ready Sir!" shouted Craven.

Stepping away from the gypsy, Magnus watched contented as her now lifeless pregnant body slid to the floor and whispered, "Pity, she showed potential." Then turning his back on both corpses and straightening his attire, unremorseful, he strode across to the door, opened it and stepped out on to the quarter deck.

"The launch is ready Sir," repeated Craven.

"Good!" he replied. Then walking up and down in front of the bound crew he made his announcement.

"Captain Jameson is dead!"

The crew looked at each other, horrified but unsurprised.

"Be assured, he did not die at my hands but his manner

of dispatch from this world was well suited to his misdeeds! Those who wish to join him should step forward now!"

The crew stared at each other and stood fast, whilst Magnus nodded in acknowledgement.

"Take them down to the launch!" ordered Magnus.

"But we have chosen to serve you!" protested the confused first mate.

Magnus stopped and turned back towards his objector.

"Only a fool would trust a crew so easily turned and our supplies will last far longer with fewer mouths onboard!" he retorted as a single shot was heard and the first mate dropped to his knees, the victim of Magnus' decisive smoking pistol.

"Are there any more objections?" asked Magnus.

There was no response.

"Keep the first six crew men and place the rest onboard the launch with some water and supplies! Their fate now lies in the hands of the storm!"

"Aye aye Sir!" chorused the new substitute crew.

"Those six will train the rest!"

As the prisoners loaded the former crew into the launch, a web of white lightening reached out and engulfed the ship as the green mist glowed eerily all about them. Striking at the rope and pulleys that kept the launch in place, the bolt of lightening severed the rope, causing the wooden boat to drop suddenly and decisively, discarding all onboard into the strangely still waters below. More flashes struck the weapons held by the prisoners, causing them to fall again on to the deck at their feet as they cowered in fear at the mist's electrifying wrath. Suddenly the entire ship's hull began to creak and squeal as if the very life of the ship was being torn away. Fascinated, Magnus stood his ground as his prisoner crew ran here and there in a terrified frenzy, fearful of where the lightening would strike next. Looking forward towards the bowsprit, Magnus thought he saw the ship begin to ripple before his eyes as an invisible wave of energy struck the ship. As the energy advanced slowly but smoothly towards him, Magnus gazed transfixed as the ship, the rigging and everyone onboard began to disappear in its wake. Knowing that he could not escape it and unsure of its purpose, he closed his eyes and willed himself to survive this strange phenomenon.

For an indeterminate amount of time, Magnus stood alone, engulfed in silence until he suddenly felt the wetness of heavy rain hit his skin. Opening his eyes cautiously but curiously, he realised he was still onboard the ship. Gradually, those members of his crew whom he had observed towards the centre of the main deck, re-materialised along with the rest of the ship. The lightening and the green mist had vanished and was now replaced by a heavy warm rain, uncharacteristic of the western Atlantic. Then, gazing far out to sea ahead of the ship, Magnus squinted bewildered at the bizarre landscape that lay on the horizon.

"Fetch me the Captain's spyglass!" Ordered Magnus as he observed Craven stumbling nearby.

"Aye aye Sir!"

Within a minute, Craven returned and handed the spyglass to Magnus who extended it to its optimum length. Then peering through the eyepiece at the horizon, he adjusted the lens.

"Begging your pardon Sir, but where are we?"

Silently, Magnus scanned the metal cargo ships and luxury yachts in the distant harbour, and the hundreds of odd looking buildings along the bay. Rubbing his tired eyes he squinted again through the eyepiece of the spyglass as several fin shaped small orange sails appeared, and Magnus vaguely recalled where he had seen these small, dark wooden junk boats before.

"The place is unfamiliar to me," Magnus replied. "But I've seen these boats before."

"Have we reached Virginia Sir?" asked Craven.

"I don't believe so."

Suddenly, there was an almighty rumble and roar in the sky high above their heads and as they looked up, and saw the underbelly and descending undercarriage of the passenger plane, on its approach to Hong Kong airport. Terrified by the massive metal dragon in the sky, everyone except Magnus, dived face down on to the deck.

"What is it Sir?"

Magnus stood in awe at the wonders of modern technology that lay ahead of them. On the deck of the nearest junk ship, he could see the oriental crew staring as curiously at their ship, as Magnus stared at them.

"Jameson took us further off course than he thought!" concluded Magnus.

"Do you know where we are, Sir? Are we in hell?" asked Craven.

Behind them came the sudden blast of a ship's horn and the garbled bellow of mandarin commands as the ferry passed close by them, sending out a large wake that rocked their ship from side to side. As the crew of the Pride of Leith rose again to their feet, they stood and blinked at the crowd of ferry passengers who rushed towards the rail to take photographs of their ship. Looking at each other speechless, Magnus finished his sentence.

"No, we're not in hell! I'm sure that these were once the Hong Kong Islands, though they appear to have changed considerably since my last visit."

As Craven stood bewildered by the modern ships and buildings on the island, a couple of American tourists pushed their way to the front of the crowd peering over the ferry rail. Frank, a stocky businessman from Manhattan pulled his delicate wife beside him and pointed his digital cine camera at Magnus. Then as the Pride of Leith neared the ferry, Frank yelled across at the bemused 18th century crew.

"Hi there! Can you smile for the kids back home!"

Magnus and Craven exchanged puzzled expressions, unfamiliar with the strange dialect of the oddly dressed couple bearing the flashing silver box. Believing the box to be some odd kind of weapon, Magnus pulled out his pistol and fired his shot. For a second, the crowd cheered with delight, thinking the ship, the crew and the gunfire were part of some incredible and elaborate, maritime display. Then the camera flew out of Frank's hands and shattered into pieces on the deck, the still hot shot rolling amongst its debris.

Picking up the lead shot between his fingers, Frank's face turned red.

"Gee honey, mind your blood pressure! You know what the doctor said!" remarked his wife.

"Shut up, Ellen," he snapped before turning on Magnus. "You asshole! That camera cost be $900! I hope you have insurance and legal cover, cos you're gonna need it!"

Magnus raised an eyebrow and turned to look at Craven, puzzled.

"What's the matter hot shot? Cat got your tongue? Or are you just as much an asshole as you look in that outfit!" added Frank bitterly.

As Magnus scowled and scratched his head in puzzlement, Craven turned to him bewildered by this bizarre turn of events, and said,

"Begging your pardon Sir, I think we <u>are</u> in hell!"

CHAPTER 2

LIZ, WAS A YOUNG, TWENTY-SOMETHING single woman, living alone in a small village in the North East of England. She wasn't, what she would describe as, a 'supermodel' with her size 12 clothes and moderate height, and she certainly didn't have any strong desires for designer clothes and handbags. Her paltry salary from the call centre wouldn't have stood for it. Nevertheless, by anyone else's standards, she was a true, natural beauty, with her long natural wavy blond hair, silky cream complexion and stunning crystal blue eyes.

Life, until this point, had in Liz's mind, been a quarter century filled with nothing but monotonous, predictability and disappointing non-events, and showed little sign of changing. From Monday to Friday she pounded the commuter treadmill to her job in the city call centre several miles away, ticking off the days, hours and minutes until the weekend came around again. Every day at the call centre seemed like any other, with the same faces routinely arriving at their desks, trading information on the latest soap opera episodes or the latest celebrity magazine gossip, or whether or not the latest football transferee was worth their extortionate fees. Liz would arrive every morning at about 8:00 am and grab a quick cup of hot black coffee before sitting at her customer interchange portal, and plugging herself into the telephony system. Under starter's orders, she'd wait and watch for the red light to flash on her console to tell her that her first caller was on the line. Then, she'd press her receiver button and greet the caller with her overly lengthy cheery salutation before hearing what they had to say. But as the day wore on and her nerves became more and more frazzled from hours of auditory torment, her former cheery salutation invariably deteriorated into something more reminiscent of a sombre valediction, with some callers hanging up long before the, 'How can I help you?' finale.

She'd only taken the job initially as a temporary measure until something better came along, but eight years down the line, there she was, still at the same desk feeling less like a unique individual and more like a faceless cog in a massive human engine. Sometimes when the lines were quiet, Liz would sit and stare out of the second floor window and daydream of adventures that would take her far away from her mandatory monotony. Sometimes, she'd imagine her fantasy hero flying through the windows at the end of a helicopter rope ladder, pleading with her to leave the tedium of her present life and fly away with him into the sunset. At, home, she would spend night after night dreaming of her favourite actor, imagining him turning up at her front door one day, asking for help and role playing how she would react. Would she: faint with shock; invite him in for a cuppa or allow him to seduce her in the most tasteful and romantic way? Often the latter was her personal preference, and she'd imagine how it would feel to be in his arms.

"Hey Liz!" whispered her friend Karen from across the desk. "Get a life, girl!"

"What?" Liz replied.

"You're daydreaming again," said Karen.

Liz sighed, and adjusted her headset.

"Can you blame me?" she asked. "The only excitement I get in life these days, is when there's a power cut at home and I have to dig out the candles," she sighed.

"I know what you mean," nodded her friend. "Have you got anything nice planned for the weekend?"

"Well, I have a difficult decision to make."

"And what's that?"

"Whether to watch TV or read my book," Liz replied.

"Wow! That's a tough one!" teased her friend.

"How about you?"

"Oh, you know," sighed Karen feigning disinterest. "Same old…"

"Yeh. Me too!"

Although she appreciated the reliable income and security that came with the job, she never quite saw herself as someone who could truly fit in there. Frequently she had days where she felt more like a square peg in a round hole, than a team player, craving the courage to take a risk, to leave the comfort of her sedentary life and make a new career for herself, somewhere out there, beyond the clocking in machine. A job that would stretch and stimulate her mind, excite her imagination as well as fulfil her life long dream to travel the world and experience the cultures she'd only ever read about or watched on TV. But, another Monday morning would arrive, the alarm clock would buzz and the cycle of routine and mindless monotony would begin again. Weekends and holidays became her only precious opportunities for escape and a chance to save her individuality and her sanity. But even then, she lacked the courage to try the untried, to sample anything new, in case her expectations were dashed or she was left, humiliated. As the years went by, the fear of disappointment, rejection and broken dreams, compounded. She began to resent the routine and security that made her mundane life possible, but which she lacked the courage to change. Frustrated and annoyed by her own cowardly resignation, she turned to the escapism of her private night time world of dreams, to fulfil the latent desires that seemed so far beyond her reach in the real world.

The week dragged by, as it usually did, with its predictable routine of commuting delays and dismal weather, until finally, Friday evening arrived.

Settling down in her armchair, and wrapped in her thick, fleecy dressing gown, she clutched a steaming cup of hot chocolate, she pointed the silver remote at the screen and watched expectantly as the movie title flashed up on the screen. Blissfully unaware of the events already unfolding, in which she would play an important and intrinsic role, she pressed the 'play' button to begin her journey of indulgent escapism.

More than an hour passed, and as the action packed film accelerated towards its inevitable climax, she watched her favourite actor, fly suddenly backwards across the room as a zap of electricity sent him crashing into the opposite wall before falling to the floor. Liz huffed, imagining herself in the actor's shoes.

"Yeh, I know how that feels," she muttered, as she compared the action on the TV screen with the memory it triggered in her head. 'Been there, done it, got the T-shirt', she thought to herself remembering the accident from her distant childhood. Sighing at the recollection and allowing the resurgent resentment at what had happened to take over, she drifted into the detailed events of that disastrous school day.

The image of the school laboratory began to form in her mind. She could see the many tall and heavy mahogany laboratory tables lined up in neat regimental rows in front of the rolling blackboard on the far wall. She could see too, the many grey plasticised gas taps and white power sockets that broke the straight line visual symmetry of the table rows, like the vertical blips on a hospital heart monitor.

Around her she could see the diagrammatic and colourful representations of the periodic table of elements, engine combustion and clinical human anatomy, pinned up at intervals around the laboratory walls. She remembered too the prickliness of the red wool cardigan beneath her school blazer, which often rubbed against the back of her neck, as she bent over her exercise book and meticulously transcribed the notes from the blackboard.

"Electrical energy is never lost...........we just haven't been able to develop devices which are 100% energy efficient. In reality, when you plug something in and switch it on, you're probably losing about 5% electricity which is converted to the heat you can feel from the wires or plug, if they've been left on for some time," If you are using batteries, the same thing happens. The batteries get warm and eventually, the power in the cell diminishes to such a low level, that it is no longer of practical use even though there is energy still present."

Liz was there in her mind. She could quite plainly see the middle aged physics teacher as he stood in his Harris Tweed jacket, behind his desk and faced the class of silent, compliant and, for the most part, attentive young teenage pupils.

"Today, we're going to carry out an experiment to demonstrate how we can conduct electricity through us. I want you all to form a circle and hold hands with the person on either side of you."

"Oh yeh," sneered Gordon, the class exhibitionist. "I've done this before at my other school.........Pathetic!....... Pins and needles. I get more of a kick from the static shocks in our local supermarket..."

"Look, Gordon. If you don't want to take part, you can go and stand outside in the corridor or do detention........it's your choice! But I'm not going to take any of your nonsense today......do you understand?"

Gordon glared at the teacher.

"I said, Do you understand?"

"Yes."

"Yes what?"

"Yes Sir!"

"Okay class. Now I need two volunteers....one to hold the positive crocodile clamp coming out of the power-pack.......and one to hold the negative clamp.....Any volunteers?"

The physics teacher, who was grey haired and perhaps not far off retirement, reminded Liz of the typical university boffins she saw regularly on TV... Apart from his jacket patched with corduroy at the elbows, he wore faded dark green corduroy trousers and a well worn and slightly dull white shirt adorned with a typically wide, loud coloured nylon kipper tie. Typical that is, for the 1970's. He scanned the class for a gullible victim, but no one raised their hand.

"No volunteers??"

"I'll hold one end, if you like, Sir," said Liz. " If somebody else holds the other end," she added. "I'm not chicken....... Why don't one of you lads hold the other one?" She asked, scanning the boys' faces, but there was a stony silence. "No? I thought so. Gutless! Totally gutless!" she sniped.

"She does have a point," agreed the physics teacher. "I can assure you, there's nothing to be afraid of," he insisted and paused, hoping that one of the boys would step up to the challenge. "Right, well, if there's no volunteers amongst you lads, then, I'll decide. Stephen, come to the front."

Stephen was a short, quiet boy with lank, greasy hair, who fairly recently had begun to exhibit the early signs of his adolescence, with an unfortunate array of small but inflamed red spots all over his pale white face. He had a distinctly pungent odour about him too, and Liz couldn't help but think that, if there was ever a worthy candidate to thoroughly test the effectiveness of an anti body odour remedy or acne cream, he was it. Liz cringed as he came towards her…..her nose flinched and her lips pursed as she came within ground zero of his acrid aroma. Then, handing Liz and Stephen the appropriate crocodile clamps as the rest of the group reluctantly held each other's hands, the teacher switched on the power pack.

Almost as soon as the power was switched on, several hands released their grip and the human chain was broken.

"You need to keep hold of each other's hands or you'll break the circuit," reminded their teacher. "You'll just feel a slight tingle…..nothing painful," he added reassuringly. "So, hold hands again and I'll switch on the power for a count of ten, then you can let go….Alright?"

Tentatively, the class reformed the circle and the teacher flicked the switch again. Again, several hands released their grip and the circuit was broken.

In frustration by her classmate's cowardice to perform the simple experiment, and naively, eagerly curious to know what it would feel like to experience the electricity surging through her body, Liz had an idea.

"Sir? If everyone is so scared of the clamps, why don't I hold both of them and then they can hold on to my arms?"

The teacher nodded unthinking of the consequences that her suggested action would have. In her ignorance of how electrical circuits worked, Liz had failed to consider that the electrical current would take the shortest path through her body to the other crocodile clamp. Holding both the positive and negative clamps in her hands, Liz was about to complete her own human circuit.

The class reformed the circle for a third time with Liz holding on to both clamps whilst Stephen on her left side and her best friend Julie on her right side, held on to her wrists. Still oblivious to the apparent consequences of Liz's actions, the physics teacher flicked the switch on the power pack one last time.

The response was so instantaneous that nobody had time to react evasively. There was no pain, no tingle, in fact they all felt nothing, except for Liz. As the jolt of the electrical volts surged through her body, an incredible invisible force like a sudden strong gust of wind, instantly lifted her off the ground and repelled her backwards twelve feet or so across the laboratory, clearing two stools that lay in her path. As the force of the electrical blast, raised her heart and adrenaline rate, time and events suddenly slowed down, almost to a halt. In that moment, that extended the passage of time between one second and another, a vision appeared in her mind. It was a face of quite a handsome young man, she thought, but nobody that she knew. He had dark hair and rich brown and gold enigmatic eyes tinged with sadness. He was talking to her. Distracted by everything that was happening to her, Liz struggled to hear his words. Then, before any of the conversation had a chance to register in her mind, the vision ended and the stranger's face disappeared. Who was he, she asked herself, before the memory of his face slipped away from her into the distant dark vaults of her subconscious.

She didn't feel as if she was being thrown across the room, it felt more like she was floating gently backwards through the air. She felt no pain, no force as she observed the frozen expressions of horror on the faces of her classmates, before descending to the ground with the silence and grace of an angel, but as she made contact with the floor, time clicked on. The invisible force that had moved her so delicately through the air, now exerted its electrical wrath on her, ripping her apart from her head down to her feet. Tears of laughter and extreme sadness ran simultaneously down her cheeks as her classmates stood transfixed by her bizarre visual display of split emotional extremes outwardly expressing the polarised inner turmoil occurring throughout her entire body. All eyes watched Liz as she sat on the floor laughing and crying simultaneously, amazed that she was still alive!

Still unaware of her resultant cellular transformation, Liz recalled the curious reactions of her classmates and how they had never spoken about what happened from that day onwards. Was it their guilt at their act of cowardice that bound their silence, she wondered. Or was it perhaps their fear of the draconian physics teacher's wrath, if they breathed a word of the incident that gagged their normally conspiritous and vicious tongues? No one ever told her, but their subsequent reticence towards her, and their wariness of close proximity spoke volumes of the fear and suspicion she instilled them. She, the victim of their past taunts, who had shamed them with her boldness and courage, had faced death and defied it. She was no longer someone to be slighted, she was someone to be kept at a distance until her normality could be safely determined.

Recalling her isolation and loneliness following the event, and the occasional whispered jibes of, "Let's see you fly then", or "Can you climb walls yet?" Liz frowned. She remembered how cruel they'd been and how she'd prayed for them to forget, cruelty that became compounded by a second incident weeks later. As her mind wandered forward in time, she recalled the second event that had sealed her fate in their eyes and minds, and which destroyed their belief forever that she was anything other than 'extraordinary'.

It was almost three months later, when the topic of electrical conductivity was raised again for revision before their end of term exams. Their teacher brought out the Van de Graff generator......that weapon of hilarious electro-static consequence. All that week, since it had been announced during their previous physics lesson, her classmates had chattered incessantly about how they imagined each other would look when they stood at the generator. Yet, on that afternoon, when again, a volunteer was sought, no one stepped forward. All eyes turned uneasily but expectantly towards Liz. How harmful could this be, she thought. At least this experiment was well documented and assured a relatively safe hair-raising outcome.

"Alright, I'll do it! You're such a bunch of cowards!" said Liz frowning.

"Yeh, right," retorted Gordon from the centre of the class.

Liz remembered getting up from her laboratory stool at the back of the class and strolling down towards the Van de Graff generator, which had been placed next to the teacher's desk.

"Take your shoes off and step on to the stand," said her teacher. "Now hold your right index finger near the generator......closer.....closer.....until it's about two centimetres away from the dome. That's it!.......Now stay there.....don't move," he continued.

Standing behind his desk, the physics teacher addressed the whole class and explained how the Van de Graff generator worked.

"As Liz is standing there......a charge is accumulating in her body. The large-radius sphere of a Van de Graff generator can accumulate and hold a considerable negative charge before an arc is discharged into your body.…..Shortly, you will see an arc of light jump from the generator into Liz's finger.….. When this happens, because the two negative charges will repel each other, and because each single strand of hair will become negatively charged, Liz's hair will stand up as each strand of hair tries to repel another."

The whole class watched, unimpressed as Liz stood patiently on the stand seemingly un-reactive and disappointingly unaffected. She could feel the electrical energy tugging at her finger, pulling her towards the metal dome like a magnet. It took all of her concentration to keep her finger just at the right distance from the generator. Staring into her convex reflection in the highly polished dome, she could see quite clearly that her hair was not reacting at all and continued to lie limply around her shoulders. Bitterly disappointed by the experiment's apparent failure she drew the teacher's attention at a convenient pause in his dialogue.

"How long does it take Sir?" she asked after five minutes.

"Just a few minutes.…….Stay where you are.…….We'll give you another couple of minutes.……Try not to touch the dome."

With that, the teacher carried on addressing the class for a further twenty minutes, in relation to what he wanted them to study for their homework. Agitated that she too needed to take some essential notes, but couldn't as long as she was stuck in her current predicament, Liz began to fidget.

"On the subject of homework.……..Helen, can you collect all the homework books from the class please and bring them down to my desk?"

"Yes Sir."

Helen was a tall, athletic looking girl who, not

surprisingly due to her height, was the 'goal shooter' for the school netball team. She always sat on the back row close to Liz, to avoid blocking anyone's view of the blackboard. Quickly and quietly she wandered around the laboratory taking all the homework books that were handed to her, before heading towards the teacher's desk at the front of the room. To reach the desk she had to pass behind the generator and Liz, who was still being charged up on the stand. As Helen came closer to Liz, a sudden strong arc of solid white lightening shot out from Liz's left upper arm and struck Helen's left shoulder four feet away. For three or four seconds, the lightening held both girls in its grip and Helen screamed, dropping all the exercise books she was carrying. Liz felt the sharp deep pain in her upper arm, as though someone had stabbed her with a long cold knife. Gasps of surprise and horror echoed around the laboratory.

"You're hurting me!" screamed Helen. "Stop it!"

"I'm not doing anything!" Liz replied, wincing with the piercing sharp pain. "I can't stop it!"

"Liz, touch the dome!...... Earth yourself NOW!" yelled her teacher.

No sooner was it said, than Liz did as she was commanded and made contact with the silver dome. Instantly, the lightening stopped and the entire class stared at Liz, stunned into silence once again.

"It's you!......You're a freak!" jeered Gordon.

"I'm not! I didn't do anything!" pleaded Liz.

"Yes you did! Look what happened the last time!"

"It's not Liz's fault.......It's my fault," confessed her teacher. "I left Liz and the generator to charge up for too long. I'm surprised though, that the generator didn't discharge a smaller arc a lot sooner......Either the generator is faulty........and the school has had it for a few years now.... or someone must have altered the settings."

"Why didn't my hair stand on end Sir?" Liz asked.

"I don't know," shrugged the bemused teacher. "Are you both okay?" he asked."

"Yes Sir," replied Liz and Helen, in unison, as they each rubbed their arms.

"Then return to your seats please."

"Yes Sir."

"Freak!" hissed Gordon, as Liz passed by the end of his table.

Liz dropped her head as she felt the pressure to cry welling up inside her. Why had the experiment gone wrong, she asked herself? Was there something wrong with the machine, like her teacher suggested or was he just trying to protect her? Clearly something wasn't right. Had she changed in some way since the first accident? She wasn't sure. Maybe it was nothing more than just an unfortunate coincidence and perhaps the generator was faulty. Whatever the reason, just like the aftermath from the previous incident, Liz found herself isolated again, by the chilling and cruel unspoken vow of silence from her peers. Once again, she was guilty until proven un-weird and for weeks afterwards, while the two incidents were still fresh in their memories, her classmates viewed her with increased vigilance and caution.

After a few months, following a significant period of uneventful normality on her part, when their memories and attitudes had begun to fade, she found herself once more welcomed back into the fold.

She never did find out whether the generator was to blame on that occasion, as the school quickly disposed of it and funded a replacement. As for the human chain experiment, an instruction, either as a result of a third party verbal indiscretion or their physics teacher's confession out of fear of a parental confrontation of his questionable actions in relation to pupil safety, a notice was issued to all staff. In it, it stated that, 'under no circumstances was the experiment ever to be conducted in school again'. Consequently, the mystery surrounding how and why the incidents occurred, remained un-investigated and unsolved, much to the delight of the school's conspiracy theorists who ensured that the events quickly joined the ranks of the other school myths. Never openly discussed, the incidents were only ever recounted in drifting whispers behind library bookcases or in huddled bunches of first year pupils eager to learn of their school's notorious past.

Heaving a huge sigh as the memories faded into the recesses of her mind whilst the movie credits rolled on the television screen in front of her, Liz nodded in gratitude to the moral lesson of her reflection on those events. Specifically, they reminded her that perhaps she should count her blessings after all and perhaps being extraordinary or a famous person was not such a good idea.

Picking up the now empty cup of hot chocolate and returning it to the kitchen, she wondered why she had never reflected on her life in quite that way before and, why, after so long in the vaults of her forgetfulness, these memories had emerged to haunt her now. Perhaps all she needed was a holiday, a pleasurable break from routine, that might put a positive spark back into her life, without any devastating, negative consequences, she concluded.

Blissfully unaware of the significance of her recollections and their link to the adventures that were yet to come, Liz switched off the ground floor lights and ascended the stairs to her bedroom. Climbing into bed, she closed her eyes and smiled a sad smile of reluctant acceptance of her calm if hum drum life and fell into a peaceful sleep.

CHAPTER 3

WEEKS PASSED BY AND THE apprehension she had felt that evening had long since slipped surreptitiously into her subconscious, as her daily routine rolled on reliably towards summer and the prospect of two weeks free time to indulge herself. Drawing the curtains to block out the late afternoon sun shining through the front window of her house, Liz snuggled down into her favourite armchair and read the final gripping chapters of the latest best seller she'd acquired. It was no literary masterpiece but she enjoyed its pleasant distraction as an escape from her routine loneliness. Avidly she trawled through the detailed, exciting narrative and action responsive dialogue to reach what she'd hoped would be an unpredictable, thought provoking ending, only to be left frustrated and disappointed when it failed to live up to her expectations. Sighing disappointedly, she closed the book and placed it on the coffee table in front of her.

Laying back against the arm of the chair, as the night began to close in, she lazily rested her eyes for a moment and thought of far away shores where the sand was warm beneath her feet and the cool sea breeze was a welcoming relief from the hot summer sun. Within moments, her heart rate had slowed and the active beta brain waves that had kept her awake, now mellowed into obscurity as she drifted off to sleep.

Feeling the heat of the sun against her skin and seeing its red glow beneath her eyelids, Liz surmised that she had fallen asleep and her conscious holiday thoughts had now transformed themselves into a very realistic and pleasant dream. The distinct smell of ozone tickled her nose as she heard the soft rushing sound of gentle waves lapping against the sloped sandy beach. She wasn't surprised by the realism of her dream as she often experienced her dreams in three dimensional, sensory stimulating technicolour before. She imagined that when she opened her eyes in her dream that she would be lying on a sun-bed in a bikini, gently tanning beneath a hot summer sun. She opened her eyes.

The light was blinding, and she immediately raised her arm in front of her face to protect her from the glare. This was a bit too bright for a dream she thought and looked down at herself to avoid the sun's glare. She wasn't wearing the bikini she'd imagined. She was wearing exactly the same soft brushed cotton pyjamas, fleecy dressing gown and fluffy slippers that she had been wearing when she was awake. Quickly, she began to sweat in the fierce midday sun and struggled to pull off her fleecy dressing gown that now clung to her sweat drenched pyjamas. Something was wrong here, she thought. This was a bit too lucid for her liking and urged herself to wake up by pressing her eyes tightly closed and opening them again. She was still there and rapidly overheating.

Maybe it was a trick of the light in her dream or just her own imagination, but something else was odd too. She could see through her hands and her legs. In fact, she could see through her entire body, just as though she was a mirage or a three dimensional hologram. She'd never had a dream like this before. She felt different too. Brushing her hand across the sand, she noticed that it didn't move. She could sense the grittiness of the trillions of grains beneath her fingertips, yet she couldn't touch them or influence them in any way. She tried to grab a handful of the sand, but all she was left holding was fresh air. This was really strange she thought and closed her eyes again as her hair flattened against her hot sweating brow. Desperately needing to cool down, she waded into the gently lapping waves before her until the water came up to her chest. Moving her hands ahead of her to balance her against the anticipated current, she suddenly stopped. She knew the water was there, she could see it, she could smell and almost taste its saltiness and she could sense it all around her yet it didn't appear to touch her. Though the waves came towards her, they passed straight through, as she offered no resistance at all to the current. Liz realised that the only wetness she was feeling was from her own internally produced perspiration. She had no influence what so ever on her surroundings and other than the heat from the sun and the coolness of the sea, they had no impact on her either.

Daring to wade out further into the sea, she gradually sank deeper and deeper in the surf, willing herself to sink below the clear blue / green waters off the Indonesian island. Able to breathe normally, she saw the rippling creamy sand of the sea bed, stretch out ahead of her into the distance. Schools of brightly coloured fish flitted here and there in unison, providing sudden visual rippling curtains of bright yellow, orange and blue in the open water just ahead. Gazing up above her, she could see the waves breaking over her head and imagined how divers must feel for the first time discovering this other beautiful and tranquil world beneath the sea. Turning around to wards the shore, she could see the sand gradually slope upwards towards the shallows, and watched as the current picked up the grains and small broken shells, churning them into creamy opaque clouds before crashing the contents back onto the beach.

Suddenly, she sensed something cold and powerful cutting through the peace and tranquillity towards her.

Frightened to move, her heart pounding wildly she dared to turn in the water to face the one phobia she never dreamt she'd ever have to face in reality. Convincing herself that this had to be a dream in which nothing seemed to touch her or affect her, she bravely turned again to face the open sea.

From a hundred yards or so through the water she saw the dark, menacing unrelenting feeding machine, ploughing its way towards her. Sensing her electrical frequency through the salty water, the shark advanced unwavering towards the signal of life and, more importantly to his voracious appetite, food. Unsure of how to out manoeuvre the shark, Liz froze to the spot in panic. As her heart rate and fear increased, so did the intensity of her signal and the shark rolled back its eyes and projected its deadly teeth ready for impact.

Screaming for all she was worth whilst her heart pounded violently in her chest, she held her arms in front of her face expecting certain pain and death, but there was nothing. There was no bite; no tearing of flesh and crushing of bone; no heart stopping pain, just a momentary icy chill and a sinister blackness that shot through her mind like a poisoned arrow carrying the singular command 'kill'. The shark, unstoppable, cutting through the water at a ramming velocity, passed straight through her completely, into the shallows beyond, crashing unexpectedly into the soft sand. Liz, held her breath, uncertain of what had just happened. Then, dropping her arms and muttering a hurried prayer of gratitude for the unquestionable miracle that had occurred she turned to see the clouds of churned up sand and thrashing fins as the confused shark chomped on the meatless dissatisfying sand.

Homing in on her signal, another shark ventured into the shallows, followed quickly by another, as the first shark regained its composure and turned towards its oddly evasive prey. Realising now, that they were all picking up her signal, she lured them towards the shallows and the unsuccessful first contender. Then, waiting until the very last moment when she could see the whites of their eyes, she dropped on to the sand and rolled sideways away from the impact zone as the attacking momentarily blinded shark pack launched at their similarly blinded oncoming relation, tearing him to pieces in a wild ferocious frenzy of gnashing teeth and clashing fins.

For several seconds she lay still with her eyes tightly closed, continuing to sense the coolness of the water around her, but then that coolness changed to a far colder chill as she wished herself awake and back home. The air was cold around her now and the smell of ozone was gone, replaced by the familiar perfume of vanilla that emanated from the small dish of pot pourri that sat in the centre of her coffee table. She had been dreaming, she thought as she opened her eyes again. She was at home in her living room, but not in quite the way she had expected. She was lying face down on the carpet, soaked through with perspiration and fear. Sitting up, she looked down at herself, as the last glimmering starlight of her projection disappeared.

Shaking with a new fear, the fear of realisation, she shivered trying to rationalise what had just happened to her. Picking at her clothes, she smelled their fabric and the remnants of salty ozone that lingered from her adventure. This hadn't been a dream at all, she thought. Feeling the stale cold sweat on her brow and the damp pyjamas sticking to her skin, she shivered and concluded that, somehow, she had either been hallucinating or she had somehow projected her thoughts to that place, but how? Why?

Thoughts and memories flashed through her mind as she searched frantically for answers. She wasn't taking any medication and she'd never in her life taken any recreational drugs that might have triggered this mind tricking hallucination, if that was what it was. Maybe I'm ill, she thought, with something like a tumour perhaps, whose pressure on her optic nerve might be the cause of her false, self manufactured visual and sensory delusions. Whatever theories she came up with to explain her current condition, they were just that, theories. Whatever had caused this, Liz knew she couldn't ignore it. She made up her mind that if it happened again, she would make an appointment with her doctor.

As she made the ascent to her bedroom and climbed under the cold crisp sheets, she braced herself against the chill and muttered softly to herself, "No sharks please. No monsters. Bring me a nice dream, an adventure or a fantasy," she sighed and closed her eyes softly.

As she slept, the adrenaline rush from her recent adventure, transmitted a powerful electrical pulse into the atmosphere, like an S.O.S. signalling for help. Travelling along the sub atomic frequency of the universal wavelength, Liz's signal radiated out beyond the perceived boundaries of her present to her distant future self. Finding a similar peak adrenaline signal of equivalent amplitude, her sub-consciousness latched on, the electrical connection was established and the physical exchange took place. As energy replaced energy and her future self traded places with her past, Liz felt the softness of her pillow replaced by the sharp rough stone of the mine conveyor belt and Liz opened her eyes to a new adventure.

Where am I and why is it so dark? Liz thought to herself. A faint smell of sea water filled the air around her, in what appeared to be a long, steep and humid tunnel. Not another crazy hallucination she thought as she adjusted her eyes to the darkness and surveyed her surroundings. The tunnel behind her sloped away into the darkness and she could just make out the sound of rushing water a few metres away. Her clothes were dripping wet and once again she shivered as the coldness penetrated her deeply. Ahead of her lay a dusty and dirty heavy duty conveyor belt that ran the full length of the tunnel. Rocks of various sizes and shapes surrounded her, hindering the pace of her escape from the rising water behind her. Every twenty feet or so, a small caged lamp shed an almost a halcyon glow along the tunnel, just bright enough to light the way. Embracing her fear and uncertainty she climbed slowly up the conveyor belt, her heart exhilarated by the sense of acute danger which now dominated her thoughts. With her senses heightened and her excitement rising, she wondered how she had got there and where she was going. Picking up one of the many small rocks just ahead of her, she turned it over and over in her hands. About eight inches long and rough to the touch, Liz sniffed it and noted its metallic odour. As she gazed around the shaft, she noticed the occasional streaks of what looked like silver, glistening within the range of the lamp light. A strange dull red glow was also present in the surrounding rocks and Liz deduced that she was in some kind of mineral mine that for some reason was now flooding quite quickly.

Looking down at herself, examining her appearance for any further clues, she could just make out that she was thankfully not wearing her pyjamas but was instead, wearing ill fitting jeans that were not her own and which were curiously men's jeans too. The soaking wet shirt that clung to her skin she deduced also belonged to a man from the way the shirt was buttoned and the extended length of the sleeves that had been rolled back to her wrists. Looking at her hands, she noticed that her wrists were a little sore and swollen, as well as appearing red and badly grazed, almost as if they had been previously bound tightly. Every second she sat on the conveyor belt revealed more and more of the perplexing mystery she now faced. Lifting up her head, she peered a short distance ahead, to see a figure sharing this journey with her. Turning around to look back down the tunnel towards her, Liz could just make out the handsome features of a slim built man in his thirties. This stranger looked at her with affectionate recognition as if he knew her, and appeared puzzled by her momentary calm stance. Perhaps, like her, he didn't know why he was here either.

"Come on.......When that last device blows, this shaft will flood pretty fast!...Come on!!!" he yelled at her.

Intrigued, she continued to climb, eager to learn more about her new companion and the dangerous situation she had now found herself in. Like her previous hallucination about the beach, this seemed very real to her but with one very important difference. She wasn't transparent this time and she could feel everything around her. Somehow this time, she was physically there, with cuts and bruises on her legs and arms to prove it. Her imagination raced wildly. Had her previous excursion in a transparent form been a tentative attempt at physical projection? Or was this something else entirely?

The ground began to shudder beneath her feet, causing the lamps to swing violently, smashing several of the bulbs in the process. Taking a deep breath, she reached forward and began to crawl over the rocks ahead of her on the conveyor belt. Just as she was within arms length of the stranger, the shaft shook with the impact of a not too distant explosion and the blinding light that followed lit up the whole shaft as Liz clapped her hands over her ears. The force of the blast ripped through the shaft, scattering the rocks in all directions, hurtling Liz and the stranger against the wall. There was a sudden rumbling sound and Liz realised in terror, that whatever had controlled the pace of the rising water before, was no longer present and a tidal wave of highly pressured water was heading straight for them.

"Liz, come on! We've got to get out of here NOW!" yelled the stranger.

The stranger waited patiently, despite the chaos and danger, unswerving in his resolve to get them both out of there alive. Reaching out his hand towards her, he looked beyond her to the rapidly rising water that was catching up with them. Liz struggled, slipping and sliding over the tumbling rocks when all of a sudden she felt the firm grip around her wrist. Frantically reaching out ahead of him with one hand, grasping on to anything that seemed stable and solid the stranger held firmly on to Liz, pulling her with him away from the impending danger that threatened to swamp them at any moment.

As she scrambled behind her rescuer she couldn't help but puzzle over the clear and simple fact that he knew her name. He knew who she was. Perhaps she had projected into a future version of herself, she thought, but who was he and why were they there, together? Whoever he was, he had a tantalising educated Scottish lilt to his voice, even when he yelled at her, and he was strong too. His grip on her wrist was decisive but not painful, even with the grazes and bruises. If she had been in any other situation than this, she wouldn't have blamed herself for thinking that perhaps, this was all her birthdays rolled into one. She had her excitement, danger and a real hero to boot! Her fantasy had bizarrely become her reality, or had it?

Another explosion ripped through the shaft, extinguishing most of the remaining lights and reducing the visibility even further. Through the darkness and dust that enveloped them now, Liz heard the voice again.

"Keep going Liz! We're nearly there!" gasped the stranger.

She fumbled her way behind him in the darkness as the roar of the wave crashed towards them.

"There's a ladder up ahead. Grab it quick! It should take us to the next level!" he yelled.

But his words came too late as the icy cold water submersed them. Gasping for air and fighting against the force of the water, the stranger grabbed desperately at the ladder. Gritting his teeth as every muscle in his arms strained agonisingly, he fought to pull Liz against the current towards him. Spluttering and gasping for air, she grasped on to his upper arm before grasping the ladder itself. Pulling her between him and the ladder to protect her against the force of the water, the stranger guided her upwards. Climbing closely behind her, Liz and the stranger began their vertical ascent to the upper level.

With wet feet sliding on the metal rungs, Liz climbed slowly and carefully from rung to rung as she heard the roaring water rushing along beneath them. After what seemed like forever, she paused to rest as the stranger climbed up beside her. In the darkness, she couldn't see his face even though it was barely a few inches away from her own but she sensed he was looking directly at her.

"Liz, stay with me.......I know you're confused.......... You said this would happen, "he continued." Try to remember......You know me......I'm Iain."

"I said this would happen?...I don't understand," queried Liz.

"You had a vision....of our escape......but there's no time to explain right now. I need you to trust me!"

The tunnel shook again, but this time, it wasn't an explosion. This was seismic. Fractures began to appear in the walls of the tunnel as Iain held on to Liz.

"Move!" yelled Iain.

"I can't see anything!"

"Keep climbing! This shaft could collapse at any time! For God's sake climb!"

Liz slid her hands up the handrails on either side of the ladder and pulled herself up on to the rungs. She looked upwards as she began to climb but, it was still too dark to see anything. She could feel the vibration of Iain ascending the ladder behind her, reassuring her that she was not alone in this terrifying hell. 'Keep climbing', she kept saying to herself in her head as each foot found its way on to the next rung and the next rung, higher and higher up the ladder. Iain followed close behind, careful to avoid Liz's feet just above his head. The sounds from the shaft below began to change, becoming a little distant as they now climbed further and further up a vertical escape tunnel leading to the higher level.

"We're in a connecting tunnel!" shouted Iain. "I reckon we've got about another thirty feet to climb until we reach the hatch!"

The shaft below them suddenly began to rumble and shake violently again, causing the ladder to creak disturbingly. Liz's feet slipped off the rung, leaving her suspended from the handrails. She held on tightly, treading air with her feet until she was able to find the nearest rung again with the toes of her shoes. Her heart was pounding fast.

"Are you alright?" shouted Iain, who had felt the ladder wobble as Liz slipped.

"I'm okay!"

Steadying herself again, she resumed her ascent cautiously, sliding her hands up the rails as she went. Rung after rung she climbed, wondering if they would ever come to an end. Then she began to feel the walls of the connecting tunnel closing around her.

"We should be getting close to the hatch now! Reach carefully above you as you climb……you should be able to feel the handle!"

Liz nervously lifted her left hand off the rail and reached

into the darkness above her head. Nothing. She climbed another rung and tried again. Her fingertips brushed against something hard.

"I think it's just above," she shouted down to Iain.

"Stay where you are, I'll climb up beside you!"

Liz felt Iain brush against her legs as he climbed up the final few rungs to reach the hatch. In the darkness, she could feel his warm breath against her face, as he stood level with her on the ladder. Reaching above his head, Iain could feel the round turning handle on the door of the hatch and tried to turn it. Holding his breath and exerting every ounce of strength he could muster, Iain pulled on the handle. He gasped and took a deep breath, before trying again. They could hear a faint grinding of metal, as the mechanism within the hatch door slowly began to move. Climbing up another rung, Iain pushed his shoulder hard against the hatch as he turned and pulled on the handle again.

"Liz, I want you to carefully reach up and push the hatch as hard as you can!"

"Okay!"

Climbing up until her head was touching the hatch door, she reached up and pushed. There was an eerie deep groan coming from the metal door, then suddenly it opened.

"Keep on pushing!"

They both pushed the heavy hatch door until it opened completely. A sudden rush of cool dusty air hit their faces as the light blinded them momentarily. Blearily, Liz pulled herself up through the hatch and sat on the floor of the upper corridor coughing and catching her breath, while Iain pulled himself up.

The corridor shook violently causing the hatch to clash down, narrowly missing Iain's ankles, which he managed to pull out of the way just in time.

"That was close." He sighed. "Right, where are we?"

Liz gazed around her at the broad corridor filled with equipment.

"I think it's a main access tunnel," she replied.

Iain scanned the corridor, looking for clues and a way out. Almost eighty metres away a small motorised maintenance cart stood idle against the wall.

"I think you're right. I think this must be in a main access tunnel.......not far from the main entrance. I recognise it from when they dragged me in here," he said. "Let's grab that cart and get out of here," he continued, pointing to the maintenance cart.

Dusting themselves down as they stood up, Liz and Iain could hear the sound of heavy boots heading in their direction. Without any further hesitation, they sped off in the direction of the cart, as a small patrol of three armed guards, approached the hatch.

"Shoot them!......Both of them!" yelled the leading guard as he took aim with his hand gun.

"Don't look back, Liz! Keep running!" shouted Iain.

The guards opened fire and several bullets whistled towards Liz and Iain as they approached the cart.

"Get behind the cart! I'll get in and try to start it!"

The first bullet missed her head by millimetres, impacting against the wall of the tunnel just in front of her, spraying out a cloud of dust. She ducked behind the cart as a second bullet whizzed above her back, missing her by a split second. Iain dived into the foot-well of the cart as a third bullet struck the side. Rummaging under the dashboard of the cart, his fingers located the starter motor's ignition wires and he yanked them free. Biting off the plastic coating of each wire to expose the copper underneath, he shouted to Liz.

"Get ready to jump in!"

The guards advanced towards the cart as Iain brushed

one of the bare wires against the other until the cart burst into life with a jolt.

"Get in and stay down!" he shouted.

Liz slipped into the passenger foot-well of the cart just as Iain pushed down the accelerator pedal with his right foot. Leaning low over the driver's seat he peered carefully over the back of the cart at the guards rushing down the tunnel. Another round of bullets shot towards them at lightening speed. Iain ducked and turned quickly to look ahead of them through the steering wheel. Crouched in the foot well, Liz spotted some containers of machine oil just behind the driver's seat. If she could only reach them, she could tip them out of the back of the cart, she thought. Peering carefully around the side of her seat, she saw the guards trying to catch up to them. In an instant, she slipped around the side of her seat and into the back of the cart, where there was a box filled with an assortment of oil containers and paint tins. Grabbing the oil canister nearest to her, she unscrewed its lid and poured the contents in different directions on to the tunnel floor behind the cart as they sped along. Approaching the start of the oil spillage, the guards came to a halt and resumed their aim on the speeding cart, before opening fire once more. Suddenly the mine shook again as a high velocity high powered electromagnetic pulse surged outwards from the heart of the mine. Liz watched in horror as the invisible wave rippled down the tunnel, engulfing the guards and then they were gone. Turning to look straight ahead of them, Liz could see the mine entrance beckoning and running figures escaping out into the daylight.

"Hurry Iain! It's catching up with us!"

"What is it? What's wrong?"

"I don't know! Just drive!"

Pumping the accelerator as hard as he could, Iain willed the maintenance cart to speed up, but with a maximum speed of twenty to thirty miles an hour, he knew they probably couldn't out run whatever it was, but he had to try.

Liz watched with horror as the rippling invisible wave swept towards them, distorting her view of their surroundings as it travelled along the access tunnel. Quickly looking over her shoulder at the mine entrance, she could see that they were almost there, but the wave of energy was accelerating faster than they were. As the tip of the cart reached the entrance, the invisible energy force lashed out to claim its last victims. Liz screamed as the wave rippled through them and then......

She opened her eyes wide and sat up in bed, gasping for breath. She was drenched in sweat again from head to foot and strangely, she could still taste the gritty seawater on her lips. She could still feel his presence, the heat of his breath and the faint odour of his sweat stained skin. She stroked her lips with her fingers and felt the dirt on her finger tips. Pulling back the bed sheets, she could see her dirty impression on the bed. That hadn't been a dream or a hallucination. Somehow she had been there, wherever 'there' was! Her arms and legs were still covered in dirt and bruises and yet she was back in her pyjamas. This was surreal.

Looking all around her, she reassured herself that she was still safely in her bed. It was early morning, with just the moonlight lighting her room as she rolled over in bed to look at her bedside clock. The luminous digits read: 3:21 am. She sighed heavily as her pounding heart began to slow down and stared up at the plain white ceiling almost afraid to close her eyes again. Shaking her head bewildered by her experience, she puzzled as to why she had found herself down a mine and why the guards had been pursuing them just before they disappeared into thin air.

Then she thought about the handsome stranger again. Iain, that was his name she recalled, as she closed her eyes once more, willing the face of the stranger to appear again. Who was he and how did he know her? It certainly seemed as if she was scheduled to meet him and discuss this vision of her future with him. More importantly, he had accepted that during that point in time, she had not been herself and easily accepted her odd behaviour. The experience had certainly seemed realistic enough. Could she have conceivably projected her thoughts into her future self? She puzzled over this as she pulled the duvet up to her chin. One positive nuance to be drawn from all this, was that she would soon meet this handsome stranger. Imagining the circumstances of their first meeting, she smiled and closed her eyes once more.

CHAPTER 4

IT WAS ALMOST 9 AM before the winter sun lifted its face above the horizon. Liz rested peacefully, safe and warm beneath her duvet. Three years ago, she had bought a small Victorian terraced house in a semi rural village several miles outside of Durham. She had spotted the house in a local newspaper, and identified it as an affordable opportunity to stretch her wings and establish her independence within a more tranquil setting compared to the rat race of the city, where she worked.

When she moved in, although it was clean and recently decorated, it had lacked that certain homeliness that she could look forward to at the end of the day. Since then, she had imposed her own personal style on the house, adding furniture, pictures and curiosities that she felt reflected her character and that of her Victorian home. Having lived with her family for so long, she had surprised herself at how quickly she had adapted to being alone. For three years she had relished the solitude when she returned home from her office job each evening and languished in her comfortable, simple and quiet surroundings. Now, as a result of her experiences during the previous evening and night, she now eagerly sought an opportunity to set forth towards a new and challenging life.

In the past three years, she had ventured out on a weekly basis to the local village pub 'The Jolly Drover's, and had established a new repertoire of friends who had accepted her for who she was. With her natural talent for solving problems and her uncanny ability for understanding their situations and making them feel completely at ease, Liz quickly acquired many new friends. After pouring out their woes and worries to Liz, it always seemed as if their problems weren't as worrying as they'd first thought. They would come away from the conversations feeling lighter, calmer and more objective about their situation. Liz, on the other hand, came away feeling like she had the burden of the world on her shoulders, but she didn't mind. The negative effect was only temporary and she liked helping and supporting her new friends.

As she sat up in bed and contemplated her plans for the day ahead, she decided that she wouldn't spend the next evening on her own, just in case she had any more hallucinations or adventures.

Entering the pub the following evening, she couldn't help but notice the serious discussions that were going on between the regulars seated at the bar.

"I'm tellin' ye. When she came out of that back room she was in floods of tears. I had to phone for a taxi to take her home!" said Roni the pub landlord. "So that's why I've booked them again," he added.

"What's up Roni?" she asked as she approached the bar.

"I've told him before, those two are a couple of con men just out to fleece people!" said Paul as he leaned against the bar in his jeans and sweatshirt and placed a now empty pint glass on the bar counter.

"Who?" asked Liz.

"Bill and Ben the psychic men!" replied Paul.

"That's a good'n," said John who was seated on a stool beside Liz.

"I've booked a couple of psychics for a 'Spiritual Exploration Evening'," said Roni.

"Aye! And the only spiritual exploration they'll be doing is to the bottom of a whisky glass!" laughed Paul.

"I don't believe in it myself," said John casually. "I once had my fortune told but none of it happened the way she said it would."

"What do you think Liz?" asked Roni, hoping for some support.

"I'm pretty open-minded on these kinds of things. I used to be quite cynical and sceptical, but I have to admit there have been things I've seen in my life which I just can't explain," she replied.

The regulars turned to look at Liz, curiously surprised and intrigued by her response.

"What do you mean?" asked Roni.

"You'd think I was nuts if I told you," she answered as she ordered her drink.

Now she really had their attention. Glass after glass were placed gently on the bar as the regulars listened intently.

"Ha' ye got one or two ghost stories?" asked Paul.

"I guess you could say that, but it's not just ghosts," she said. "I once saw a woman levitated three feet off the ground in a room full of witnesses. Now that was scary!"

"I bet! You wouldn't have seen me for dust if I'd been there!" said Roni shivering.

"What's up Ron, did somebody walk over your grave?" asked Paul grinning.

"Eee don't say that!" replied Roni edgily. "So what do you think about these psychics then, Liz?"

"I honestly don't know. I've never been to one of those psychic evenings and I can't really criticise when I do a bit of palm reading myself, just as a party piece of course. I don't know if I'm any good or not. Nobody's ever told me," replied Liz noticing their jaws dropped and their eyebrows raised.

"Now this has to be a wind-up!" said Paul.

"Honestly Paul, I can read palms," she said confidently.

"Get away! Really?" asked Roni, the pub manager. Liz nodded as she took a sip from her drink.

"You've never mentioned this before," remarked Dennis the barman returning from the kitchen with clean drip trays for the beer pumps.

"It's the first time I've heard you mention the subject. I don't exactly go around advertising the fact you know! Some people are very sensitive about this sort thing and I don't want to offend anyone," replied Liz. "It's not magic you know. Anyone can do it. There are tons of books on the subject that show you what the lines on your hand represent and how to read them. It's just like reading a book."

"Yeh, right….but just because I wear underpants on the outside of my trousers doesn't mean I can fly like Superman!" remarked Roni.

"What you get up to after hours Roni, is none of my business," she replied.

"You really walked into that one!" cheered Paul as the Regulars burst into laughter looking at Roni behind the bar. They all knew what Roni was like. He was the loveliest kind hearted man you ever wanted to meet, with a flamboyant style for special occasions which always had you laughing along with him. A man for all seasons, well……..at least for the party season….. Halloween; Christmas; New Years Eve, he loved to be the life and soul of any party or celebration, especially if it was for a good cause. There wasn't a month that went by, without Roni hosting some themed evening to raise funds for local charities. With his enthusiasm and almost child like excitement, you had to be pretty cold hearted to refuse his request for volunteers to assist him in his fund raising endeavours. Needless to say, it didn't take him long to recognise that he could have a new talent and attraction to reel in the customers.

"John, you're nearest. Why don't you ask Liz to read your palm?" asked Roni deeply interested in seeing a demonstration.

"I'm not really into that sort of thing," he replied.

"She won't bite you know," encouraged Roni.

"Go on. Have a go!" agreed Paul.

Reluctantly, John held out his right palm towards Liz and the bar suddenly fell silent. Liz took a deep breath.

"There's nothing like pressure is there fellas?" said Liz.

"Go on Liz, do your best!" said Roni supportively.

Gently taking John's hand in hers she carefully drew her fingers across his palm, scrutinising the lines closely. As she focussed on her connection to John, she explained what the lines meant on his hand.

It had been quite a while since she'd done any palm reading, but she soon got into the swing of it. Then, something happened, something that had never happened in all the years that she'd performed her 'party piece'. Snap shots of John's life popped into her conscious mind like an animated 3D photo album, showing her scenes from his past. Her head buzzed with the intricacies of his life.

"This line which crosses your palm near the top, that's your head line," she explained. "The one below that is your heart line. The more parallel they are in relation to each other, the more practical and rational a thinker you are, and the way yours are, you're quite clearly a problem solver. You seldom get pulled emotively into arguments or discussions, you tend to look at situations from a detached almost objective point of view, even when it involves family," she announced.

John looked at Liz closely without giving any indication of whether she was right or wrong, whilst the regulars sat eagerly waiting for more.

"This vertical line at the bottom of your palm cutting into the lower left side represents your career line which is all to do with money and finances. With the objectivity you have applied to your business you've been able to achieve a great many financial successes over the years, and this cross in the centre of that area of your palm which touches your career line, tells me that you're due to receive a large commission or bonus from a job you've recently completed," she said, as an image of John receiving the good news by phone popped into her mind. "Someone will phone you with the good news."

John nodded silently.

"Come on John, is she right?" asked Roni.

"As it happens I've just completed a contract and I'm expecting a phone call from my business partner to tell me how much bonus I've earned, seeing as I finished the job early," John declared.

"Wow! That was spot on!" admitted Paul.

The regulars standing at the bar lowered their glasses in awe.

"So does that mean you're good for a pint or two?" asked Paul curiously.

"You'll get quite a bit," whispered Liz to John discreetly.

"Yeh, and let's hope the tax man doesn't take a massive chunk of it!" said Roni.

A Mexican wave of nodding heads went up and down the bar, in agreement.

"That was brilliant Liz! Are you always that good?" asked Roni.

"Nobody tells me. Maybe I just struck lucky tonight,"

she replied, still coming to terms with the new level of ability she'd acquired.

"You call that luck.........Where's that paper?....If you pick a horse that's racing tomorrow, I'll back it!" announced Paul.

"I don't gamble," she said.

"You don't have to gamble........I'll place the bet."

"But that's personal gain.......and besides I might be wrong," she replied cautiously.

"Personal gain?...You wouldn't be gaining anything unless you backed the horse yourself, and it won."

"No. I see what she means," said Roni supportively. "If she was right, she'd be hassled to death to pick the next winner or come up with the jackpot numbers for the lottery......Then,....if she got it wrong.......she'd get lynched."

"It's just my party piece......I do it occasionally but never on a regular basis precisely because people want to exploit it. I read palms primarily to help people and I never take money for doing it. It just doesn't feel right......I'm grateful for having this 'gift', if you like....and I don't want to abuse it."

"But you could earn a good living at it," said Roni. "You could have a roaring trade!"

"That wouldn't be right........Besides, people can get funny about that sort of thing. I don't want any trouble landing on my door step."

"Okay then. If you don't want to do it for yourself...... how about doing it for the kids?" asked Roni.

"The kids?"

"Aye! What about helping the hospice?" asked Paul.

"The kid's cancer hospice...... just down the road," explained Roni.

Liz thought carefully for a moment. Roni had a point.

With her ability, she could help to raise valuable funds for those children. How could she refuse? She wanted to help, she knew she could help, but what would the consequences be?

"I get very nervous about performing. I've never done this sort of thing publicly before. What will people think about me? They'll think I'm some sort of freak? I don't think I could deal with being the source of ridicule or gossip! I'm not qualified either!" she pleaded.

"Do you think Bill and Ben are qualified to do what they do?" asked Paul rhetorically.

"I don't know," she replied.

"I don't think you'll have anything to worry about, do you Roni?" asked Paul.

"If people know that you're not getting anything out of it and the money raised is all going to charity, no one's going to give you a hard time are they?" asked Roni.

"Besides, we'll be here to support you. Any hassle and we'll be there like a shot!" said Paul supportively.

Thinking carefully for a moment, she began to realise that her reasons for not wanting to do this were more or less the same as her reasons for not taking a chance on anything new in her life. She lacked the confidence and the courage to be different, worrying more and more about what other people thought of her. She lacked the courage to take a chance, to put herself on the line. The difference was, this time she was being asked to take that chance to help somebody else.

She considered that maybe this was the critical first step she had to make if she was going to change her life for the better. For years she had hidden in the shadows afraid to be ostracised in the adult world, the way she had been when she was a child. Although nobody at school had ever spoken to her about the two incidents in the physics laboratory, it had taken a long time for her friends and classmates to accept her back into the fold. She never wanted to go through that isolation again. It was one thing enjoying ones own company by choice, it was another thing entirely to have solitude forced upon you, she thought. Still, if she wasn't prepared to take that first step, she knew deep inside that she wouldn't only be letting herself down this time, she'd be letting the children down too.

"Okay," she relented. "I'll do it……..on one condition."

"And that is?" asked Roni.

"Roni, you'll be my donation manager. You handle the money side of this and make sure the donations go into the charity box. I do not want the money passing through my hands."

"Sounds fine by me," he agreed. "How about, New Year's Eve?" he suggested.

"That's a cracking idea," added Paul. "There'll be loads of people wanting to know their future, …. and they'll be ……"

"Drunk, perhaps?" interrupted Liz.

"Does that matter?" Paul asked. "At least, you won't get a lot of hassle if you get something wrong, cos they probably won't remember it in the morning."

"He's got a point Liz," added Roni.

"And if anyone gives you a hard time, …. We'll sort them out! Right Roni?" said Paul encouragingly.

"Right!"

"Okay, I'll give it a try."

"What you going to call yourself?" asked Paul.

"I don't know."

"You've got to have a catchy stage name."

"I know," babbled Roni excitedly. "How about 'Astral Liz'?"

"You're kidding," said Paul. "That sounds like a name for a suppository!"

Liz blushed.

"Thanks Paul!" said Roni.

"How about 'Mystical Liz'?" suggested John.

"It's simple…..It's short…….and it's a mystery to me, how you were spot on with John," said Roni.

A chorus of agreement echoed along the bar, and raising their glasses in unison, the regulars cheered.

"Here's to Mystical Liz!"

"To Mystical Liz!"

CHAPTER 5

Liz arrived at The Jolly Drover's at about 8 o'clock to find a queue of men, as well as women, waiting for her to turn up. Thank goodness that this was just a 'one-off' for charity, she thought. There were at least fifteen people waiting to have their palms read. Fifteen people whose lives would be laid open before her, like watching soap operas on the television.........only these were real people ....bringing with them real emotional baggage and responsibility which Liz was going to have to cope with. Still, Roni was there, along with Dennis and the regulars. They'd make sure she was okay.

Roni came out into the bar to greet her.

"Thank God you're here!" he sighed.

"What's up?.....I can see there's a few people already waiting."

"Some have been waiting here since 6 o'clock."

"Why didn't you tell them I wasn't going to be here til eight?"

"I did,.....but they wanted to be here early.......to get a good seat.....Some of them had already heard rumours about how good you were."

"Great!..........I hope you know who's first then!........I don't want any fights on my hands!"

"I've got it sorted........I'll bring them to you."

Liz walked across to the alcove where a small round bar table had been covered with a large pink tablecloth underneath a smaller white one. There were two small bar stools placed at the table and standing in the centre of the table was a small folded piece of white card emblazoned with the word 'RESERVED' in black felt tip pen. Liz walked calmly up to the table and sat down. Placing her coat and bag on the floor beside her, she took a deep breath in…….. and slowly breathed out.

"Okay …….Roni, who's first?" she asked nervously.

One by one, Roni escorted his customers to the table, each one shouldering their own burdens and problems ……..each one seeking resolution in their lives. For some, there was happiness in loving relationships…….with future happiness and good careers well starred. For others ……it was the end of a turbulent year…..with dreams and hopes for a brighter future ahead. Some would attain their realistic goals whilst some faced further disappointment. Liz was careful, confidential and diplomatic, saying nothing negative and raising no false hopes with her readings, and offering direction, support and guidance where it was needed. As one reading was completed and that customer left the table with a lighter heart and their emotional burden lifted…….. another was ready to take their place.

In the far corner of the bar, next to the old black range, a curious dark haired stranger with rich brown and honey gold eyes, drank his pint of shandy and watched the steady procession of customers being led into the alcove to meet Liz. Suddenly a piper dressed in Battle Stewart tartan stood up in the centre of the pub, and despite the noisy hubbub of the News Years Eve revelry, the sound of the bagpipes gasping air bags were heard by everyone, as the piper prepared to play. Children attending the festivities with their parents, plugged their fingers in their ears as the bagpipes wheezed like an asthmatic elephant. The stranger smiled to hear the sound of his homeland, and made a resolution there and then, to make a return trip to his home village before the end of the next summer.

Rising from his seat, the stranger approached the bar and ordered another drink. As he waited to be served, he couldn't resist the temptation to stretch his neck and peer down on Liz with her latest client. Transfixed by her presence, the stranger didn't hear the voice from across the bar.

"That'll be £2.49."

"I think he's talking to you," said John who was standing next to the stranger.

The stranger turned, slightly startled.

"Sorry, I was miles away," he apologised.

"If you're interested," began Dennis. "She's very good. Haven't heard a bad word about her, all night. She's a canny lass too. She just lives here in the village."

"Does she," replied the stranger.

"You should have go," said Roni encouragingly. "All the proceeds go to charity you know."

"She did my palm the other night," said John. "And she was spot on. She said I would get news of a bonus, and 9 o'clock the next morning, sure enough I got the call."

"Go on, lad," said Roni smiling.

"Sorry, I can't," he sighed.

"Why, are you superstitious?"

"Something like that," he said. "But here's a couple of quid for your charity box anyway. Oh, and thanks again," he said downing the freshly poured shandy and placing the empty glass on the counter. "And have a Happy New Year!" he cheered, quickly glancing at Liz before making a hasty departure.

"What did I say?" asked Roni rhetorically. "He was off like a shot wasn't he?"

"I think he had his eyes on our Liz," said Dennis.

"Then why didn't he get his palm done?" asked Roni. "What better excuse would he have to break the ice with her?"

"Maybe he's just shy," said Dennis.

"Hmmn," sighed Roni as he moved up the bar to serve the next customer.

A freezing draft of air struck his face, as the dark haired stranger stepped out into the icy crisp winter's night. Then, as the piper struck up another tune, and the strains of 'Scotland The Brave' drifted out across the car park, the stranger took one last look at Liz through the windows smiling, and climbed into his car.

As the count down began for the approaching New Year, Liz was surprised at how quickly the four hours had passed. She was starting to get a headache from all the intense concentration and her mouth was parched from all the talking she'd had to do. She had never been a great talker and was more used to taking a back seat.......listening to what others had to say. Being the centre and origin of continuous conversation for four hours, took some getting used to. Fifteen palms and minds she had read in that time. She felt shattered. Sipping only on lime and soda, so that she could concentrate, Liz felt sadly isolated from the revelry as Big Ben on the wide screen television chimed midnight. She reconciled herself, that at least she would have a relatively clear head in the morning compared to most of Roni's customers, and if she hadn't come to the pub, she would have only been stuck in her flat alone, watching repeats of old movies and drowning her sorrows in a bottle of wine. Cheering 'Happy New Year' to her final client and noting that the charity boxes were stuffed full of five and ten pound notes for the hospice, Liz noticed a stranger heading in her direction. Dressed in jeans and a dark blue shirt, the young bleary eyed man swaggered towards her table. Unable to shout for Roni's assistance over the top of the noise in the bar, Liz stood behind her table uncertain what to do.

"Would you read my palm?" he asked.

"Well.........I was just about to pack up...."

"I need you to read my palm!" he insisted.

"I'm sorry, but I'm finished for the evening."

Leaning towards her, he pushed his hand out in front of her. Liz took a step backwards and noted the tension and desperation in the tone of his voice. Reluctantly and a little frightened of her client, she sat down again on her stool.

"Take a seat."

"I want you to act like you're reading my palm and I want you to listen very carefully," he demanded. "I have a gun, and you're going to do exactly what I ask you to do. When I say, we're going to get up and walk out of here." He instructed as he looked around the bar for any observers.

With that, the young man, who was in his mid to late thirties, sat down on the stool opposite Liz and held out both of his hands.

"Just your right hand, please." she said nervously. Then taking his hand in hers, she took a deep breath in......... and slowly breathed out.

Looking down at his hands, she could feel the toned muscular tissue beneath his skin. His hand was very square with a well padded palm and fingers, whilst each of the main lines across its centre, were well defined. She closed her eyes for a moment and focused.

She saw him wearing a black military style uniform standing on guard outside of a laboratory. The room looked like it was inside some kind of cave, due to the rough rocky surface of the walls behind the laboratory furniture. There was a horrible twisted faced man lying back in a reclining medical chair. Wires were attached to his head, his chest and his arms, and these wires were connected to what looked like a hospital Electro Cardio Graph machine. However, it didn't appear to be just monitoring his heart rate…It seemed to be monitoring his brain waves too. Beside the machine was a computer monitor which appeared to show images being transmitted from the man's brain waves. His eyes suddenly opened, and Liz could swear that he was looking directly at her as he salivated and grinned hideously. The guard saw another man inside the room, wearing a white medical coat. A gun was in his hand and he was pointing it at another man who lay motionless on the floor, covered in blood. Liz sat horrified at the scene that was being displayed before her. Then she noticed the images on the computer monitor and gasped. It was her village, her street, her home! Somehow this mad man was using this person to mentally stalk her.

Liz's mouth went suddenly dry. She wanted to pull herself away but, she knew if she did, she'd probably never find out what was going on or why somebody was watching her. As her heart began to pound anxiously, she took another deep breath and focussed on the screens. He was inside her house. He was climbing the stairs and now, he was in her bedroom watching her as she slept.

"That's her!" yelled the man in the white coat, as he pulled out a radio receiver from his pocket. "Eric, I'm emailing you the co-ordinates now. Take a small squad with you and make sure there are no witnesses!"

Liz dropped the soldier's hand as he pulled a small gun out of his jacket. Sounding suddenly surprisingly sober, the soldier pointed the gun at Liz.

"When I tell you, I went you to collect your things and leave. Any funny business and I won't hesitate to use this," he whispered firmly. "Now move."

Shaking nervously Liz rose from the table slowly and carefully picked up her belongings. Noticing Liz getting up from her table with a pale worried look on her face, Roni left Dennis behind the bar and went over to investigate. As he approached Liz through the crowd, he could see the look of fear in her eyes. "Is everything alright Liz?" asked Roni concerned.

Liz suddenly felt the sharp edge of the gun barrel in the centre of her back.

"Yeh, I'm okay Roni…….Just a bit tired. It's been a long evening, so I'm heading home."

"Are you sure you'll be alright, you don't look so good?" he asked.

"I'll be fine. It was a little bit stuffy in that corner. I'll be okay once I get some fresh air," she said.

"Sure?"

"I'm sure."

"Okay, thanks for all your hard work. Next time you're in, I'll let you know how much money you managed to raise for the hospice," said Roni suspiciously.

"Okay, see you. Bye!" she said, and made her way through the remaining people towards the door. Bemused, Roni watched as Liz departed, closely followed by the stranger.

"What's up Roni?" asked Dennis as Roni returned behind the bar.

"There was something very odd about that," he answered.

"About what?" asked Dennis.

"Liz."

"What about her?"

"That guy that just left, he went to see Liz to have his palm read. Then she suddenly got up, packed her things and that guy followed her. Something's up! I can smell trouble a mile off!" said Roni.

"If Liz needed our help, she would have asked," said Dennis.

"I don't know. There was something really odd about that guy, and I've never seen him in here before."

"He might be her new boyfriend," suggested Dennis.

"I don't think so. He didn't look her type."

"I'm sure she'll be alright," replied Dennis.

Liz buttoned up her coat as she stepped out into the dark and freezing car park. The late night sky was clear and filled with stars as Liz breathed in the cold, crisp air. Breathing out, her exhaled warm breath hung in the air as a small misty cloud, as she stamped her feet on the icy ground beneath her. The gun dug into her back again and she made her way slowly and carefully up towards the top of the car park.

"Where are we going?" she asked nervously.

"Just keep going along the old public footpath," he replied.

Liz did as she was told and made her way along the old railway track that had been converted into a public footpath. As they walked further along the path, the grassy bank rose up high on her left hand side, and the bare trees towered over her blocking out the moonlight. Knowing what his mission was, Liz walked slowly ahead of him, fearing that each step would be her last.

Suddenly her left foot slipped on the fluffy white frost crystals that covered the path like sprinkled sugar, knocking her right leg out from under her. Instantly, she fell to the ground, landing on her left hip.

"Aaagggh!" she cried out.

"Get up!" he ordered.

"I can't," she replied. "I think I've hurt my leg."

"Get up or I'll shoot you right here!" he commanded.

Shakily, she rolled over on to her knees and pushed herself up into a crawling position before attempting to stand up.

"Why do you want to shoot me?" she asked bravely. "I don't know what I've done!"

"Orders!" he said curtly.

"Orders? Whose orders? Why?" she asked. "Surely you can tell me why?"

"Shut up and move!" commanded the stranger sternly.

As she winced with the pain from her sore hip and limped slowly along the footpath, there was a sudden rustling sound in the bushes behind them. As the stranger turned sharply with his gun poised, a large mussel with bright sparkling eyes peered out from beneath the ferns before darting across the path and leaping over the dry stone wall into the meadow beyond. Thinking that this might be her only opportunity for escape, she dropped to the ground and kicked out both of her feet against the back of the stranger's lower legs. Rolling quickly across the path, Liz watched as the armed man came crashing down on the path, firing two shots as he fell. Whilst he lay on the ground, Liz jumped to her feet and ran as fast as she could along the darkened path back towards the pub, hoping and praying that the gunman couldn't see her.

Roni and Dennis were serving customers behind the bar when they heard the two gun shots.

"What was that?" asked Roni.

"It could have been fireworks. After all it is New Year!" said John, seated at the bar.

"They weren't fireworks," said Paul concerned. "I've been in the army. I'd know that sound anywhere. They were gunshots!"

"Gunshots!" exclaimed Roni alarmed. "For God's sake, Liz is out there somewhere! I knew there was going to be trouble!"

"What do you mean Roni?" asked Paul, picking up his jacket from the end of the bar.

"Liz left suddenly about five or ten minutes ago followed by a man, a stranger. She looked really worried," he replied.

"Christ! Why didn't you say something!" yelled Paul as he put on his jacket. "Phone the police!"

"What do I tell them?" asked Roni anxiously.

"Tell them you heard gun shots close by and tell them to get here quickly! Tell them about Liz!" yelled Paul as he dashed across the bar towards the door.

"Where's he going?" asked Paul's wife Helen. "What's happening?"

"We think Liz could be in trouble. Paul's gone to find out," said Dennis.

"Hang on Paul, I'm coming with you!" shouted Roni from behind the bar.

Together, Paul and Roni dashed out into the cold night air and headed out across the car park.

"Jeez it's cold enough out to freeze the wotsits off a brass monkey!" said Paul as they made it to the top of the car park, just as Liz came running towards them, gasping for breath.

"Bloody hell, Liz!........What's the matter? We heard the gunshots!"

"That guy, "she gasped breathlessly. "The one I read his palm.......he's back there, ...about two or three hundred yards down the footpath! ....He's got a gun! .....He was going to kill me!"

"I knew it!" exclaimed Roni. "I knew that guy was bad news the moment I set eyes on him!"

"Roni, take Liz inside!" ordered Paul.

"What are you going to do?" asked Roni concerned. "If he's got a gun, he might shoot you!"

"Nee chance! I've managed to dodge enemy fire before!" said Paul.

"Aye! But that was a canny while ago! You were younger and fitter then!"

"Look, just get her inside! I'll deal with this! Nobody threatens my friends with a gun, I don't care who they are!" shouted Paul as he sprinted off towards the footpath.

"Come on, pet. Let's get you safely indoors," said Roni placing his arm around her shoulders. "So what happened? Who is he? I could tell something was up. Why didn't you say anything?"

"He had a gun in my back. If I'd said anything, he was going to use it," Liz explained.

"In my pub?"

"I don't understand Roni. I don't know who he is and don't know why he wanted to kill me!"

"Could it have been mistaken identity?"

"I don't think so! When I held his hand, I saw something, like a vision. There was a laboratory with TV monitors. He had this horrible looking man wired up to a machine and this guy in a white lab coat was watching my house on the monitor. I think he was using that man's mind to find me. They came into my house Roni. They could see me asleep in bed!" she sobbed. "Why? Why do they want me? I never do anything or go anywhere! What have I done Roni? What have I done?"

"I haven't a clue, Liz!" replied Roni. "Come on. I'll take you upstairs to the flat and I'll put the kettle on…..There's nothing like a hot sweet cup of tea when you've had a nasty shock." He said comfortingly.

Liz nodded silently. She felt really cold and sick to her stomach. Even though she'd done nothing wrong, she felt guilty. Guilty that she'd led some mad gunman into Roni's pub, who could have shot anyone there at any time.

"Everything will be okay…….I'm sure it will," said Roni as he led Liz up the stairs to his flat above the bar and took her into his living room. "There now…..You sit down there on the sofa……I'll just go and put the kettle on…..I'll not be a minute."

Liz could hear the dulled hollow sound of Roni filling the plastic kettle with water and switching it on to boil. There was the distant sound of cupboard doors opening and the clinking of cups. Liz sat staring blankly at the pictures on Roni's living room wall as her heart pounded madly and her head throbbed. Any minute now, she'd wake up and find that this had all been just a very bad dream.

A few minutes later, Roni returned carrying two cups of tea.

"Here you go…..mind the cup's hot…….hot and sweet," he said as he handed one of the cups to Liz.

"Thanks Roni."

"Don't mention it pet…….It's the very least I can do. I've phoned the police and they should be here soon. Don't worry, we'll get it sorted out."

They both took hesitant sips from the cups and sat silently thinking for a moment.

"I just can't work it out Roni! Why me? What do I know that makes somebody want to kill me?" asked Liz.

"If you don't know the answer to that one, I'm damned sure I don't!" replied Roni puzzled.

Just at that moment, they heard heavy footsteps running up the stairs to the flat. It was Paul.

"Jeez Roni, you need a lift for them stairs, "he gasped. "It's like running up the north face of Everest."

"So what's happening?"

"I found that guy…..just where you said Liz……..He was lying on the ground, dead."

Liz clasped her hands over her mouth, horrified.

"Oh God, no! I killed him! I killed him Paul!"

"When I saw him, there was a huge pool of blood under his head. Looked to me like he'd come down heavily and cracked his skull open!"

"I killed him! Something startled him and when his back was turned, I kicked his legs out from under him and he fell like a rock! I didn't hang around after that!" confessed Liz.

"Crikey, I never knew you had it in you, Liz! I'm impressed!" remarked Paul.

"Paul!" snapped Roni.

"What? It's a clear case of self defence! If Liz hadn't acted quickly, she could have been the one lying on the ground with a bullet in her!" replied Paul.

Liz suddenly turned a ghastly shade of green and began to retch as she shot up from the chair and ran for Roni's bathroom.

"Have you phoned for an ambulance……..the police?" asked Paul.

"Aye. I've phoned for the police. They'll be here shortly," answered Roni. "What was he like, Paul?"

"Looked like a professional to me. What's goin' on?"

"Liz said someone's been watching her house. She said he wanted to kill her," replied Roni.

"Did she tell you why?"

"She doesn't know."

Liz eventually returned from the bathroom, with her face a deathly shade of grey.

"Roni? Fetch a cold flannel quick! …..I think she's going to pass out."

As Liz stood in the doorway of the living room, the last thing she saw was the look of acute concern on both Roni's and Paul's face, before everything turned fuzzy then black.

CHAPTER 6

WHEN LIZ OPENED HER EYES, the sun was just starting to rise in the sky. She lay staring up at the plain white ceiling above her, realising that this wasn't her bedroom or even her house. As her eyes adjusted to the unforgiving bright morning sunshine, she tried to recall how she had gotten there. Slowly she sat up still dressed in the clothes she'd worn during the previous evening. An uneasy feeling that something dreadful had happened, overcame her along with an overwhelming wave of nausea. Wherever she was, she needed the bathroom quickly! Jumping out of the bed Liz ran out of the room into Roni's bathroom. Suddenly, she heard a scramble of footsteps and voices in the hallway outside.

"Liz? Liz? Are you alright in there?"

"Yeh. I'm okay........I think."

"Fetch the doctor.......he's just downstairs with the police," she heard Roni mutter to someone. There was the sound of heavy feet on the stairs as Liz pulled herself up and washed her face and hands in the bathroom sink. Just as she opened the bathroom door Roni's sister Gillian came dashing up the stairs followed by a young fair haired man wearing a white shirt and suit trousers.

"Roni…..I've got Doctor Anderson here for Liz."

"Cheers pet," replied Roni as he shook the doctor's hand. "Thanks for coming out Doctor. This is Liz…..She passed out last night with the shock.......Then we put her to bed and she only woke up a few minutes ago."

"Let's go into the bedroom Liz, and I'll examine you there if that's okay?"

"Thanks Doctor," she replied as she followed Doctor Anderson into the bedroom. Then taking a small surgical torch from his bag, he shone it briefly into her eyes. Liz blinked several times.

"Well, you're eyes are okay......I'm just going to check your pulse then your chest."

With that, the doctor took a gentle hold of Liz's right wrist for a few seconds, before pulling out his stethoscope and placing it carefully against her chest.

"I want you to take a few deep breaths......" he said.

Liz did as she was asked by the doctor, as he moved the stethoscope to different areas of her chest and her back.

"You're pulse was quite fast.......but other than that,...... you're okay," he said. Then turning to Roni he said, "Make sure she takes it easy and drinks plenty of liquids to re-hydrate herself......I'm off to the hospital now."

"Cheers Doctor.......Any word on her attacker?"

The doctor gently took a hold of Roni's arm and pulled him to one side, just out of Liz's earshot.

"Dead I'm afraid. He suffered trauma to the base of the skull, consistent with a hard fall. He was already dead when I arrived. His body's on the way to the mortuary as we speak. Did you know him?"

"No. Neither did Liz."

"Just be careful how you break the news to her. She needs to be kept calm."

"Okay Doctor."

"Liz?"

"Yes, Doctor?"

"I've given Roni some sedatives for you..........I

recommend that you rest........Get plenty of sleep and drink some water..........Any problems.......just give me a call."

"Thanks Doctor."

With that, Doctor Anderson picked up his surgical bag and left.

"How are you feeling Liz?" asked Roni.

"Stunned.......shocked..........sick," she replied with her hands trembling.

"That's understandable."

"So what did the Doctor say to you?"

"You better sit down............it's bad news."

"He's dead...isn't he?"

"There wasn't anything they could do," sighed Roni. "In any case, the less people we have like that in the world, the better."

"Do they know who he was?"

"Paul thinks he was a professional. Definitely military."

"What?" exclaimed Liz. "Why would somebody want to employ a military assassin to kill me? I've never had anything to do with the military! My only crime is working in a small business call centre! What the hell is going on Roni?"

"Whoa calm down Liz! Everything's going to be okay! He was probably some psycho gone AWOL! I know how bad it sounds but it'll be sorted, don't worry," replied Roni as he sat her gently down on his sofa. "Look, here's some water. Take one of these tablets now and get some rest."

"What about the pub Roni?"

"Oh, it can wait for the moment. Besides, we haven't had this much excitement here in years."

"I hope it doesn't cause any problems for you!" Liz said anxiously. "I've never been in trouble in my life, Roni!

You have to believe me! I don't understand why this is happening!"

"It's okay! Don't worry about me or the pub. If anything you've probably given my trade a boost! Once the gossip mongers get going, everyone will turn up out of the woodwork wanting to know what happened."

"What are you going to tell them?" asked Liz.

"The truth! Some wacko strides into my pub, kidnaps and threatens one of my valued friends with a gun, and then tries to kill her. There was a struggle he slipped on the ice... end of story!" replied Roni. "That's more or less it isn't it?"

"I think so. I don't remember much, "Liz sighed.

"It's the shock. Don't worry about it. Anyway, you probably shouldn't try to remember it, at least not yet. Oh, whilst we're on the subject, Paul's talking to one of the officers downstairs now......They want to talk to you. Do you feel well enough to see them?"

"Not really, but I suppose it's best if I get it out the way sooner rather than later. What a nightmare!"

"Tell me about it!........We managed to clear the pub in two seconds flat last night.....There was an ambulance near the footpath. ....Police were everywhere.........well at least there was six of them........the rest were in action elsewhere........dealing with drunks.....Dennis stayed on to watch over things in the bar......whilst Paul and John dealt with the police and Paul's wife Helen looked after you..... It was like Piccadilly Circus with all those flashing lights everywhere!"

"It is New Years Day today, isn't it?" asked Liz.

"Oh hell!.....That reminds me, I've got forty people booked in for New Years Day lunch! I better get my skates on and get those joints in the oven. Don't panic!........I'll not be a minute........I've got to check the kitchen and make sure the chef's okay."

"I'm sorry about all the trouble."

"It's not your fault……..I knew that guy was trouble when I first laid eyes on him…….I said that to Dennis last night…….Anyway…..I'll be back in a tick."

Roni left Liz sitting in his living room and went downstairs to the kitchen. A plain clothed officer was writing down some notes as Roni crossed the hallway to the restaurant kitchen.

"Excuse me, sir……Roni is it? I'm Detective Sergeant Steve Alexander."

"How can I help you?"

"Liz. Is she upstairs?"

"Yes……….. but go easy on her……..She's a canny lass and she's had one hell of a shock! If you ask me, that guy got what was coming to him. It's just such a shame that it had to involve Liz. We all love her to bits! Last night, bless her, she spent the whole evening reading palms to raise money for the kids in the hospice. Who would want to hurt her? She wouldn't hurt a fly!" explained Roni.

"I understand sir. We've taken several statements from your customers agreeing whole heartedly with what you're saying. Nobody seems to know who the man was or why he targeted Liz. But don't worry, sir we'll get to the bottom of this!" he reassured him. "Can I go on up?"

"Yeh, sure…….I'm just off to the kitchen…….I've got to open up in a couple of hours and I've got forty people booked in for lunch!……….What a hell of a start to the New Year!"

"I know what you mean."

Roni disappeared into the kitchen as the officer made his way up the stairs. Steve was a detective sergeant with the local constabulary and had been investigating local murder cases for the past five years, since he graduated from university. He was tall, slim and fair and dressed in an off-the-peg suit, which he wore with an air and style that made you think that his clothes were tailor made. Being a keen athletic type, he strode up Roni's stairs without losing a breath and entered the living room where Liz sat huddled up on the sofa, pale and drawn with shock.

"Sorry to bother you miss…….Can I just confirm that you're Liz Curran, yes?"

"That's correct."

"I'm D.S. Alexander……Detective Sergeant Steve Alexander. I appreciate that you've been through a terrible ordeal so I'll try to keep this as short as I can. I need to ask you a few questions about what happened last night…. Are you okay to do that?"

Liz nodded and took a sip from a recently made hot cup of tea, whilst Steve sat down in the armchair opposite her. Placing his clip board on his lap and extracting a pen from his inside pocket, he began to fill in details at the top of the statement sheet.

"Can I just confirm, your full name is Liz Curran?"

"That's right."

"Can I just confirm your address?"

"11 Valley View Road, Faregate."

"Date of Birth?"

"11th October 1976"

"Marital status?"

"Single."

"Any boyfriends? Partner?"

"No."

"Okay, that's the preliminary questions out of the way……Now,…..I want you to tell me everything that happened from the moment you arrived at the pub last night…….What time did you arrive?"

"It was about eight o'clock."

"Did you arrive with anyone?"

"No, I was alone."

"I gather that you were part of the entertainment last night?"

"That's right. I was doing my bit as Mystical Liz, palm reading ….Last night was my first official gig.......to raise money for charity."

"You don't look like a stereotypical fortune teller to me."

"You're right, I'm not. I was only doing it as a personal favour to Roni to raise money for charity. I don't usually do this sort of thing."

"Forgive me for asking what might seem a stupid question, but if it's not something you usually do, how are you able to do it? Is it a talent you have or were you trained to do it?"

"I taught myself to read palms from studying books. It's quite easy once you know how."

Steve pondered her answer for a moment, before asking, "So it's really more of a hobby, is it?"

Liz looked at the detective and puzzled over whether she should tell him the full truth about her abilities or not. Steve evaluated her hesitancy and searched her gaze, suspicious that there was somehow a lot more to this palm reading than Liz was prepared to discuss.

"I was curious," she answered.

"You were also pretty good at it from what I've heard," said the detective as he flicked back through the pages of his notebook. "She told me exactly what my kitchen looked like and even came out with words and expressions I always use at home. It was like she could see it in every detail….." quoted Steve from a witness's statement. "That's not palm reading is it? As I understand it, you read the lines on somebody's hand which tell you about their character and events. Your palm can't give you that kind of visual detail can it?" he asked carefully.

Liz took a deep breath and gave out a heavy sigh.

"I don't really like to talk about what I can do. People can get very funny about things they don't understand. If I'm honest, I'm not sure I fully understand it myself," she explained. "I read palms, and that's pretty straight forward, but sometimes I make a connection with that person. I also read their body language."

"What sort of connection?" he asked intrigued. "Are you saying that you're also clairvoyant in some way but afraid to admit it?"

"It depends on what you mean by clairvoyance. If you mean, do I communicate with ghosts and the dead......well no, not exactly. I don't believe that I do that. If you mean, can I read minds...... perhaps I can."

"What do you believe?" asked Steve curiously.

"I believe that energy, particularly life energy, is never lost, just converted or transformed. I believe that when we die, our physical bodies are broken down into their mineral components, unless you're cremated of course. As for our spirit, our life force, I believe that it still exists somewhere, just in a different form. I don't think there's anything supernatural about it. It's just electrical energy at the end of the day. I believe that, like a radio receiver, I have the ability to tune into this electrical energy, but we all have that potential." Liz explained.

"Okay, I can understand that, but someone told me that you have seen ghosts. How do you explain that? Surely that is supernatural?" asked Steve.

"I've seen what you call 'ghosts', I've even felt their touch, their force. I think a lot of us have, but I've never considered it to be unusual. Supernatural? Again, I think that they are formed by residue energy left behind at the site of their 'sudden' death which we can all potentially see if our minds happen to be tuned into that energy frequency. Alternatively, they could simply be an energy projection from an event in the past or the future. If you think about radiation and how it can still exist in some cases for hundreds if not thousands of years after an event, dependent upon what it is. Then, why can't we?"

Steve sat pensively for a few moments, scribbling a few notes in his book and nodding to himself.

"Do you think that some people around here would object to your palm reading?" asked Steve.

"What you mean is, would anybody feel so strongly against it that they'd want to kill me? No I don't think so."

"Could you have said something to one of your customers that offended them or made them feel threatened?"

"I'm very careful what I say. I always consider people's feelings. But as to whether I've offended them, you'd need to ask them that."

"That's okay." He replied.

"Are you trying to suggest that I provoked the attack?" asked Liz alarmed.

"I'm just trying to eliminate the possibility and establish a motive for the attack," he replied defensively. "Is there anything else you can tell me about last night? What did he say to you?"

"He told me that he was carrying a gun and to act like I was reading his palm. Then he said, I was to get up and leave or he'd use the gun. So I did what I was told. I packed up my things when he asked and left. He followed behind and told me to take the footpath, "Liz explained.

"Did he say anything else?" asked Steve.

"I asked him why he was doing this and he said he was ordered to do it."

"Ordered? Do you know who by?" enquired Steve.

"He wouldn't say. Then I slipped on the ice and he threatened to shoot me there and then if I didn't get up."

"So he was trying to take you somewhere. Do you know where?"

"No."

"Then what happened?"

"Something darted out of the bushes, a fox I think. It startled him and he turned."

"What happened next?" asked Steve as he jotted down more notes in his book.

Taking a deep breath in anticipation of what she was about say, Liz looked anxiously at the detective, searching his face for signs of compassion.

"I knew it was probably my only chance to get away, so I kicked the backs of his legs to knock him down," she confessed. "Then I ran. I didn't stop to see what happened to him, I just ran, back to the pub. Are you going to arrest me?" she asked anxiously.

"I would like to take you into protective custody."

"Am I under arrest?" she asked.

"I can't say at the moment. We need to examine all the evidence including the post mortem report before a decision can be made. Let's just say, I can't rule it out at this point. But the reason I want to take you in is because I'm very concerned that this man was a professional who was hired to attack you and it may happen again. Only next time, it might be successful unless we can work out who was behind it and why," replied Steve as he closed his notebook and returned it to his inside jacket pocket.

"So you accept that it was self defence?" she probed dissatisfied with his vague answer to her original question.

"Like I said before, we need to examine all the evidence. For instance, you state that you knocked him down but you didn't see him hit the ground. It's likely that the fall caused him injury, but we don't know yet, whether it caused his death. If it did cause his death, we'd have to carry out further investigation. So until this is all sorted out, you need to be somewhere safe in case they try again!" explained Steve. Then a sudden thought crossed his mind.

"You said before, that he asked you to 'act like you were reading his palm'. Did you? Did you read his palm?" asked Steve. "It might give us a clue to who he is or who is behind all this."

Liz thought for a moment, recalling the images she'd seen the previous evening, as Steve retrieved and re-opened his notebook.

"I didn't read his palm," she began and a look of disappointment came over the detective's face. "But I did make contact," she added.

"What kind of contact?" he asked eagerly.

"I managed to get into his thoughts, his recent memories."

"What did you see?"

"He was standing on guard in what looked like a laboratory. There was electrical equipment everywhere and computer screens and monitors," Liz replied.

"Do you know where the laboratory is? Could you describe what you saw outside, through the windows?" asked Steve.

"That's just it! There weren't any windows. It was underground. It looked like it was in a cave."

Steve scribbled down a few notes.

"Was there anyone else in the laboratory?" he asked.

"There were two men."

"Can you describe them?"

"One was lying on some kind of medical chair with wires connected up to his head. He looked horrible, dirty like he was a tramp, a vagrant. He looked straight at me. He was disgusting!" answered Liz.

"What about the other man?"

"He wore a white lab coat, average build, grey white hair and looked middle aged."

"Do you know what they were doing? Did they say anything?" asked Steve.

"The man in the white lab coat was watching the monitors. I think the images were being picked up from the other man's brain."

"Could you tell what the images were?"

"That's what shocked me. They were pictures of the village, my house and then my bedroom. Somehow they could see inside my house and the man in the white coat picked up a radio and told someone that he'd found me and to send a small squad in and make sure there were no witnesses."

Steve looked deep into her blue sparkling eyes, as his mind mulled over all of the evidence in his head. Instinctively and daringly, Liz took his hand in hers and felt the soft, smooth but firm skin of his palm. This was not the hand of a practical person. With its long dexterous fingers and neatly manicured nails this was the hand of a person fixated with detail….an artist of music and paint………well educated in the sciences, literature and cultural pursuits……She closed her eyes and concentrated.

Initially shocked by her touch, Steve sat quietly watching the mysterious young woman before him, waiting to see what she would do or say.

Images flashed before her of a child ferried off to private school, with departures and returns of such polite and controlled coolness, it made Liz shiver. She could feel his loneliness, not that dissimilar to her own. A man trapped by duty and expectation, disenchanted by his family traditions craving drama and a passion that made her blush.

"Are you alright?" Steve asked.

"I'm fine," she replied. "You're a lot like me," she added smiling.

"How do you mean?"

"Strict upbringing. Family traditions. You felt stifled. You had to get away from it. That's what I did. You like to let your hair down sometimes though, just like me. You try to be unpredictable but it doesn't quite work the way you want it to, and underneath the surface you're quite a wild thing at heart!"

Steve frowned and pulled his hand away from her.

"I'm sorry. I didn't mean to embarrass you it's just refreshing to know I'm not the only one that feels like that."

His mouth went dry and he coughed lightly, quite clearly ruffled by her intuitive or, as she would put it, scientific assessment. This wasn't a trick. She certainly seemed to have a talent for reaching deep into his thoughts, memories and feelings.

"Okay, I can guess why you did that. You wanted to prove to me what you could do, right?" he asked.

"Until people experience it for themselves, they don't always believe it. Even now, without proof, you might turn around and say I was making it all up to cover myself," Liz explained.

"That's true," Steve agreed.

"But at least now, you've got personal proof that I could be telling the truth."

"This might sound stupid but I have to ask it. If you can read people's thoughts and memories, can you see their future too?" asked Steve.

"Sometimes," she replied cautiously.

"Have you seen your own future?" he asked.

"Glimpses."

"Anything you want to tell me about?"

"It is what is yet to come."

"That's a bit cryptic……mysterious."

"I'm trying to be careful."

"Why? .....Do you think if you tell me it will have some sort of impact on what's going to happen?" he asked curiously.

"Possibly."

"So you must believe that it is possible to change your future?"

"I don't know. But if it is possible, we don't know what the consequences of that change could mean," she answered.

"I have to ask, did you know that you were going to be attacked?"

"No."

"Do you know what is going to happen to me?" asked Steve.

"No. Do you want to know? Are you prepared to accept the consequences of knowing?" she asked.

"Well, when you put it like that, I'd rather not know," he said. "So you don't believe in fate then? You don't believe that our lives are already mapped out and can't be changed?"

"I never said that. I know there are some theories out there that say the past, the present and the future all exist at the same time and therefore the future has already happened. Whether or not we can change it, I don't know. Whether we're meant to change it, I don't know," she confessed.

"Then why could you see your future? What was the purpose if you weren't meant to change it?"

"To be prepared for it," Liz replied. "To lessen the blow."

"But that's change too, isn't it? Reducing the impact?"

Liz thought for a moment, balancing Steve's argument against her recent vision.

"Yes, I suppose it is," she admitted.

"So, I think you know something that's going to happen, that might help this investigation. Is that possible?" asked Steve. "If you know anything, however small, please tell me."

"And who's going to believe you? What are you going to do about it?" she asked.

"Look, based on the evidence of what's happened so far, I would say that it is highly likely that you are in some sort of danger and I'll do everything I can to protect you. But you have to help me here!"

"I had a vision the night before last. I was in some kind of mine. There were explosions and the whole place was shaking and filling with water. I was trying to escape," she declared reluctantly.

"Okay. Do you know what sort of a mine it was?" Steve asked.

"I don't think it was a coal mine. I think there was silver down there. I could see it in the walls."

"Was anybody else there with you?"

"Yes, a man." she said, remembering the handsome stranger who'd helped her to escape the rising water.

"Can you describe him?"

"Tall, slim, dark hair. He said his name was Iain," Liz replied as she recalled the puzzling things he'd said to her.

"Something's puzzling you. I can see it in your face. What is it?" asked Steve with impatient curiosity.

"He said I'd already told him it was going to happen."

Steve sat back in the chair, stunned by her unexpected response. Liz sat quietly waiting as the detective gathered his thoughts.

"Does anyone else know about your vision?" asked Steve.

"No. Do you seriously think I would mention something like that to anyone? They'd think I was nuts! You probably think I'm nuts, but you did ask!"

"Does anybody else know about your ability to read thoughts?" asked Steve.

"I'm not stupid. If people realised that, can you imagine how they'd react? No, I've only recently been able to do that and I've kept it a closely guarded secret."

"So you weren't born with it, your clairvoyance or whatever you want to call it?" he asked.

"I don't think so. I don't remember having experiences or visions as a small child," she answered.

"Do you remember when they began?"

"I think I was about thirteen, not long after the accidents," she recalled.

"Accidents? What accidents?" he asked concerned.

"It was an electrical experiment at school. We were trying to prove how electricity can travel through the body from person to person, only it went wrong. I wound up taking the full force of the electricity and was blown across the lab. Then a couple of weeks later, I volunteered to demonstrate the Van de Graff generator."

"Oh, I remember that. It's used to demonstrate static charge and makes your hair stand on end," Steve remarked.

"Well it didn't, …. make my hair stand on end I mean."

"Was it broken?"

"Apparently not."

"What happened?" asked Steve intrigued.

"I was left there for more than half an hour, charging up. Then zap! As one of my classmates came within six feet of me, a flash of white light shot out from me and zapped her. For a moment we were connected by this white flash of light and it hurt!" she remarked.

"Were the accidents ever reported?" asked Steve.

"I don't know. I know they banned the human chain experiment from our school after what happened to me. So, I guess they must have done."

Steve turned over the page in his notebook and scribbled down the details of Liz's statement. When he was finished, he looked across at Liz. She could see his brows furrowed with deep concern.

"So what happens now?" she asked.

"Until we can work out exactly what's going on, I think you'll have to come with me," answered Steve.

"What about my family, my friends? What do I say to them?" she replied anxiously.

"Nothing. The fewer people know, the better," he replied sternly. "I need to make a couple phone calls.......
Wait here."

Steve got up and taking his mobile phone out of his pocket, he ventured into the bedroom to make his phone calls. A short time later he returned.

"You need to come with me....NOW!"

Stunned and shaking, Liz got to her feet and followed Steve down the stairs to the car park at the rear of the pub. She was devastated....Her peaceful and tranquil little world had been over-turned. All her neat little plans for the future had gone up in smoke.....Her dreams of danger and adventure were now a harsh reality which she couldn't escape. Somebody wanted her dead. But why?

"What's happening Liz?" shouted Roni from the kitchen doorway. "Where are they taking you?"

"I don't know."

Steve turned around to look at Liz. She saw the urgency

in his face and knew she had to go with him. She had to trust him!

"Let's go." He said.

His car, silver and elegant, shone in the crisp winter morning sunshine of that New Year's Day. Steve opened the rear passenger door and Liz climbed inside and shivered as she sat back in the leather upholstered seat.

"I'll have the car warmed up in a moment..........You'll be okay....I promise....I've got contacts who can help."

Still stunned by her ordeal, she found it hard to believe that this was all happening to her. This sort of thing never happened to her......it happened to other people.......it happened on TV.....It didn't happen to her. Her stomach churned as Steve climbed into the driver's seat and glanced at her through the rear view mirror.

"If you pull down the central arm rest.......there's a compartment behind the seat......you'll find a car blanket to keep you warm.......Try and get some rest....We've a long journey ahead of us."

Liz did as she was bid and retrieved the blanket. It's long synthetic and cashmere fibres felt soft and silky against her skin. After fastening her seat belt, she stretched out the blanket and tucked it in around herself. She knew Steve was right......she needed to rest if she was going to muster up enough energy to face what was to come. Closing her eyes, she focused on her breathing and blocked out the flashbacks of her ordeal, until, exhausted, she slumped into a deep and haunted sleep.

CHAPTER 7

LIZ SAT AT THE BACK of the lecture room and turned over a new page in her notebook, smiling at the irony of its simplicity compared to her life. In the space of a few months she'd acquired a new life, a new identity and new challenges which she'd previously only dreamt of. The only drawback was, that she was not permitted to make contact with any of her former family or friends until the whole case had been thoroughly investigated and resolved. She was safe for now, in her artificial new life, enjoying her freedom from her monotonous old call centre job. When they'd asked her what she wanted to do during her 'exile', she had opted to develop herself and entrench her mind in stimulating studies. She'd always wanted to go to university but had neither the money nor the qualifications when it had mattered, to enrol. Now she had the opportunity, albeit by virtue of her situation rather than by money or personal merit. Still, she was making the most of it, and whatever qualification she managed to achieve, that would be purely down to her efforts. Then, once she'd graduated, she could change her career with a few new qualifications under her belt. Anything was possible.

With this positive thought in her mind, she justified her absence from her family and friends, convincing herself that the whole situation was temporary anyway and in a few months, when it was all over, she'd be able to return to visit them and enthral them with her adventures. Patiently she waited for word about the investigation but it had been months since Steve had contacted her in the agreed manner. He'd thought it best, that contact should only be made by post and in some cryptic and random fashion, to reduce the risk of anyone tracking her down. So, now and again, she would receive a postcard containing a coded message telling her that everything was okay and she should stay put. The message would read: *'Some people come and go quickly in our lives. Then there are some who stay in our lives for a while and we are never the same. S.'* The last one though, which she had just received that morning, contained a new disturbing message. It read: *'Some people come and go quickly in our lives, slipping away secretly into the night taking our thoughts and our hearts with them. S'.* Something was wrong. They must have found her, if Steve was now telling her to leave.

For months now, thanks to Steve, she had moved to York under her new identity of Liz Finlay. Steve had a cousin, Bryan, who was a caretaker at the Halls of Residence attached to the University. So, disguised as a student, Liz had moved into a flat there and fitted in well with her co-students despite being a late transferee on to the psychology course. To provide her with a moderate income, Bryan got her a job in the Students' Union Bar, that way she was able to convince people of her income whilst remaining relatively safe and secure on campus with little need to venture far, at least until the heat blew over.

Liz hated living a lie to hide from her past. She had always been brought up to be honest, to tell the truth. Yet, here she was, living like a spy under a false identity, weaving a web of fiction and deceit, to preserve her own survival. I hope I don't burn in hell for the stories and lies I've had to tell, she thought. She seldom socialised for fear of letting some vital truth trip from her tongue, and often sat alone in class to avoid any conversations that might be directed towards her.

She didn't like lying to people, but it was steadily becoming an occupational hazard of her current situation.

In order not to betray herself, when she'd first began her new life, she had sat down and written a thorough fictional profile of her fictional past life, memorising it and sticking to it like one of her well rehearsed call centre call scripts. She knew that if she had to lie to people, it was important that there were no inconsistencies. Her new life had to be quite unremarkable to ensure that she didn't attract any unwanted attention, and as for deep meaningful friendships, they were a commodity that she could ill afford at this point in time. Not only could she place her own life in more danger, she might also endanger someone else, someone she cared for. So she had, friends and acquaintances, but maintained them at a very superficial level.

The ink flowed from her pen and her right hand seemed to develop a life of its own, as she captured the essence of the lecture that morning. Since she'd read the postcard, she'd found it incredibly difficult to keep her mind on her studies, wondering what was happening and what she needed to do. As she paused for a moment to gaze pensively out of the window at the back of the lecture room, she failed to notice the replacement Professor who entered the room after the first hour long lecture. The tall, handsome stranger with the brightest of brown eyes with just a hint of golden sparkle, walked to the front of the lecture room, and addressed the students.

"Good morning everyone!" he greeted joyously. "I'm Professor Sinclair. I will be replacing Professor Greenwood who has sadly been taken ill and isn't expected to return for several weeks. I will endeavour to fill his shoes as best I can and to get to know you all over the coming weeks. So if you have any burdening issues that you think I can help you with, just pop down to my office which is on the ground floor, near the far end of this building!" He concluded in his lilting Scottish accent.

It was the voice that drew her attention to him at first. She knew she'd heard it before somewhere, but she couldn't quite place it. Gazing at him as he stood tall behind his desk dressed in semi smart trousers, shirt and tie, she recognised his face and felt instinctively like they had met before. She couldn't remember ever having seen him around the university campus, or during her infrequent outings to the local hostelries either, but his face was distinctly familiar to her. His short and glossy dark brown layered hair was styled fashionably messy, flicked slightly to one side with his fringe flopping forward, on to his pale brow. Then she noticed his eyes, a combination of dark brown and gold, like chocolate and caramel, but with a nine carat gold sparkle that glinted cheekily every time he smiled or posed a challenging question. They had met, she decided, remembering the way she'd felt when she'd first seen those eyes. They'd looked serious then, when they'd first met. Yet, she still couldn't remember where or exactly when that was. Insatiably curious, she dared once or twice to make brief eye contact with him and searched his expression for some clue of their previous meeting, but all he did was smile politely in acknowledgement of her attention. Was it her imagination or wishful thinking on her part, or was she really picking up from him a discreet feeling that he recognised her? For more than an hour, his rich, smooth and tantalising voice preyed on her mind and teased her memory as she struggled to recollect their encounter, until her thoughts were disturbed by a voice whispering to her from across the table in front of her.

"Liz," whispered Janice. "Did you get a ticket for the Summer Ball tonight?"

"Yes," she replied impatiently.

Janice lived on the same floor as Liz in the Halls of Residence and often pestered her for coffee first thing in the morning. Just turned twenty, Janice was a bit of a social butterfly, with her bleached blond hair and stunning looks, she didn't have to try very hard to attract attention. More interested in nocturnal studies than daytime lectures, Janice had a reputation for being a bit of a man-eater. Several times Liz had noticed the stealthy arrivals and departures of Janice's suitors in the middle of the night and was thankful that her accommodation wasn't right next door to hers. With her heaving cleavage and highly polished monstrously long artificial talons, Janice would swoop like a preying mantis on any naïve young male who paid her any attention. Consequently, the Summer Ball was a 'must do' event in Janice's social calendar, providing ample opportunity to sample a broader range of potential suitors under the same roof. Sometimes she even shamelessly indulged in more than one suitor during the course of an evening. Whilst her conduct was infamous and her appetite voracious, Liz couldn't help but feel sorry for her, wondering what it was she was trying to find amongst all those young men, who were quite clearly only interested in one thing. To them, Janice was like a necessary set text in their induction to student social life. You checked her out, borrowed her, used her, made a few notes, then put her back on the library shelf. Once read, never forgotten, though Liz was quite sure from the expression on several exiting ex-suitors faces that they hoped and prayed they would forget.

"You will be there won't you?" whispered Janice anxiously.

"Yes."

"I need you to be my watcha-me-call-it?"

"Chaperone," replied Liz.

"Yeh, one of them," Janice continued. "Someone slipped

something in my drink last time and the only thing I remember was having a fantastic view of the stars and the city before passing out."

"I think we all had a fantastic view that night," sniggered Philip on the next table.

"I could hardly remember a thing the next day. I still don't know what happened but I've been getting strange looks off that weasel of a campus caretaker ever since," gabbled Janice.

"I think it might have had something to do with the double D fluorescent bra he found tied to the radio antenna on top of the communications building. The caretaker had to take it down because low flying aircraft were mistaking it for the outer marker to the private airstrip nearby," whispered Philip.

"I always wondered where I'd left it," she whispered to Liz, who couldn't help but frown with disgust. "Cheer up Liz! You look like a wet weekend.........It'll be a riot.......You'll see. Just make sure no one slips anything in my drinks, okay?. We girls have to look after each other you know!"

Liz cringed. She didn't really want to go to the ball, but not going would attract more attention than she cared for at this point in time. So she had reluctantly agreed to be Janice's chaperone. By hiding in Janice's shadow, she believed that she could deflect any unwanted attention straight into Janice's lap, literally.

Disinterested by the last minute gossip of who was wearing what and who was going with who, Liz carried on drafting her lecture notes whilst still trying to figure out where she'd met Professor Sinclair before. Adding this dilemma, to the curious post card she'd received that morning, Liz felt instinctively cautious and suspicious, wondering if perhaps the Professor's arrival wasn't just a little too timely and a bit more than a coincidence. Liz wasn't sure. In any event, regardless of whether or not the Professor was involved, all Liz could do was wait and hope that nothing transpired that would thwart her discreet disappearance after the Summer Ball that night.

Softly and carefully, the Professor began to tread the well worn path around the lecture room, delivering his lecture with his inimitable charm and lilting Scottish accent, pausing only briefly, to answer questions from the students around him. He had observed Liz sitting near the back of the lecture room several times during the course of the morning, but had been quite surprised when he'd failed to locate her name on the list of students he'd been provided. Assuming this to be an administrative glitch of some kind, he resigned this particular issue to the back of his mind. There was no mistaking her, not even when she disguised herself in the typical student uniform of shabby jeans and faded t-shirt. She was a remarkable woman, he thought. From the moment they'd shared eye contact, he had recognised her unique, memorable, vivid blue sparkling eyes. Rediscovering her when he'd least expected it, had given him quite a jolt, and as he continued his leisurely promenade around the lecture room, he suddenly felt ill-prepared and unconfident to welcome her back into his life,

For years he had searched high and low for her in the hope that they could be reunited. He had found her that fateful New Years Eve, determined to be with her. Then, uncertain of the possible consequences, he had consulted his close friend Fraser Hughes, who had warned him against making contact. Disappointed and frustrated he had returned to York, impatient for events to take their course. Now, out of the blue, there she was, not quite as he remembered her, but it was her without a doubt!

Gazing at her briefly across the room, he could see her slouched over her notebook, isolated from the others, transparent in her intentional seclusion. Approaching her and reacquainting himself would need delicate handling, he concluded, or he'd most likely frighten her away. So, using every ounce of willpower at his disposal, he reined in his overwhelming and impetuous desire to rush up to her and sweep her off her feet. With an impressive air of coolness, given the circumstances, and being the gentleman that he was, he approached her table with the utmost discretion.

"So for next week, I want you to prepare arguments for discussion as to whether you think 'justice' is the only aspect of moral reasoning that we apply when we make moral choices or whether our feelings of compassion and caring for our fellow man also play an important part…."

If only he knew, thought Liz, as she scribbled down some final notes in her book. Then the Professor suddenly placed his left hand down on the table beside her and with a passion normally confined to a Shakespearian tragedy or Victorian melodrama, he delivered one of his well renowned borrowed, parting quotations.

"So until next week…think on these words from Charles Dickens: *The most important human endeavour is the striving for morality in our actions. Our inner balance and even our very existence depend on it. Only morality in our actions can give beauty and dignity to life.*"

With that, all the students took their cue to pack up their belongings and head off for lunch. Liz could feel the electricity in the air and the Professor's eyes burning deeply into her, as she slouched over her notebook. He might have been masking it well enough for the benefit of onlookers, but she could sense that something was up. If only she could remember where she had met him before, she thought, as her nerves began to tighten like guitar strings ready to be plucked. Then he spoke. Unlike his teaching voice that rose and dipped like a rollercoaster to keep his students attentive, this time he spoke with a soft, rich and smooth tone like a slow flowing river on a summer's afternoon. His charming tantalising tone caressed her ears gently, driving away all of the other louder unwanted distractions in her vicinity.

"I'm sorry, I don't know your name?" he lied convincingly." I'm Professor Sinclair. Iain Sinclair."

Suddenly Liz's head felt like it was about to explode as his name triggered the connection in her mind. At last, she screamed inside her head. She suddenly remembered who he was, where they'd met and how he'd introduced himself to her as 'Iain'.

"Liz, stay with me.......I know you're confused..........You said this would happen, "he continued." Try to remember...... You know me......I'm Iain."

He was her saviour in her vision. I must have told him and warned him of what was to come, she thought. Then a bigger realisation struck her. That hadn't been a vision she'd had. She had actually been there in the mine, with him. That's what he meant about me being confused, she thought. Slowly the pieces of the puzzle began to form a picture in her mind. Iain was in her future and he knew her well enough to have shared in her secrets and her abilities, but how and why? She asked herself. Something must bring us together, she thought. But what and more importantly, when?

"Liz? Are you okay?" asked Iain looking concerned. "You suddenly phased on me! Was it something I said?"

Liz snapped back to reality and observed Iain's puzzled expression.

"I'm sorry," she apologised. "A sudden thought crossed my mind."

"Penny for them?" he asked.

"It's nothing," she replied dismissively.

"It couldn't have been nothing," he remarked." You were gone, I mean completely! Are you sure you're alright Liz?"

Liz suddenly sat up straight and stared at him, curiously.

"You said you didn't know my name, a moment ago." she said suspiciously and began puzzling over the coincidence of their meeting that day. Perhaps her instincts were right, she thought. Perhaps something big was about to happen in her life that day and perhaps Iain was involved. Everything was certainly pointing in that direction, she concluded.

"My name's Liz… Liz Finlay, " she replied suspiciously. "But then, you appear to know that already."

Iain's eyes sparkled as he tried to think quickly of a reason and then noticed her notebook on the table.

"It's on your notebook," he replied, almost gasping with relief as Liz blushed with embarrassment at her oversight. How could he, have been so stupid to make a slip like that, he thought. Now was too soon for true confessions about their past relationship. The right time would come soon enough, and then she'd be ready to listen and understand. Thankfully, this time, he was now off the hook. But why was her name different, he asked himself. That was why he couldn't find her on the student register. She'd never mentioned to him that she'd been married. Iain tried to think back to what she'd said to him all those years ago.

"I'm sorry," she apologised again. "It's been one of those days!"

"So you're not usually this paranoid?" he asked. "I'm pleased to hear it!"

"I've got a lot on my mind at the minute," she sighed.

"Certainly seems it. Anyway, I just wanted to have a chat, to see if you need any lecture notes or help, now that Professor Greenwood is indisposed. I'm planning to have a chat with all my students and decided to start from the back of the room and work my way to the front. So I guess that places you at the top of my list," he explained. "Do you have a few minutes to spare? "

"I'm afraid I'm busy this afternoon, Professor," interrupted Janice nosily. "I've got to zip off to the hairdressers and pick up my outfit for tonight. But next week will be okay for me."

"Thanks Janice. I'll make a note of that," replied Iain trying to stifle his irritation at her rudeness. "Liz?" he asked again.

"Fire away," she replied.

"Okay then," sighed the Professor relieved as he carefully sat down beside her. "Am I right in thinking, that you only transferred to this course fairly recently?"

"That's right,"

"Is there anything I can help you with, anything you need to catch up on, or even any questions you'd like to ask me?"

Searching his eager and inviting eyes, she wondered why they had been brought together now. Iain raised his eyebrows eager to hear her response.

"I'm fine," she replied cautiously, trying to avoid eye contact.

Iain was devastated, though he did his best to mask his frustrating disappointment. She must have her reasons, he thought. Another time, another less obvious place perhaps, away from prying eyes and ears. But at least she was here, and however awkwardly, he'd succeeded in breaking the ice with her. Maybe the right time and place will present itself, and when it does I'll be ready, he consoled himself.

"Are you sure?"

"Absolutely."

There was a pause, and Liz felt sure that Iain wanted to ask her something else, judging by his oddly hesitant behaviour. Did he want to say something to her in confidence and couldn't because of present company, she thought. She wasn't sure. Then a sudden thought crossed Iain's mind.

"Was there something else, Professor?" she asked.

"The Summer Ball is on tonight, to raise money for charity …and I'm trying to encourage my students to attend, "he lied again. "It's for a worthwhile cause! Are you going?" he asked.

"I've got a ticket…..but I'm not sure if I should go…." she sighed heavily. "I don't really know anybody except Janice."

"You should go! You never know……you might enjoy it. …Go on, it'll be a blast! It's a great opportunity to meet people, especially if you're a Fresher!.....I got absolutely smashed at my first Summer Ball, " he confessed excitedly. Then he remembered something and added in a cautionary tone, "Oh, yes. That reminds me. A word to the wise…… avoid the punch…….lethal stuff….You never know what's been put in it. Some poor girl drank a bit too much of it last year and they found her underwear…"

"dangling from the antenna at the top of the communications building?" Liz interrupted.

"Yeh, that's right! It startled the hell out of some pilot apparently, who mistook for a runway marker!" continued Iain.

Philip sniggered as Janice finally blushed.

"Thanks, I'll remember that," Liz replied, flattered by his attention. "I'm still not sure though." she added carefully.

"You better be there!" demanded Janice. "Remember you're my….watcha-ma-call-it?"

"Chaperone!" chorused Liz, Iain and Philip, before bursting into laughter.

"Are you going, Professor?" Liz asked curiously.

"Of course!.....I wouldn't miss it for the world!……..Mr Dance Fantastic that's me!" he beamed immodestly. "I can tantalise in a tango, flourish in a flamenco and scintillate in a salsa, " he declared dramatically. "So if you don't go, you could miss out on the opportunity of a lifetime! Oh, and apart from me, you can meet all sorts of other interesting people too..." he replied. "In fact, last year, I had a pretty interesting conversation with Professor Fraser Hughes regarding his theories on thermodynamics." Iain began, hoping that the subject topic might trigger a reaction. "Mind blowing stuff..... and sounds incredibly exciting after a few glasses of wine!" he added enthusiastically.

Philip and Janice immediately began to lose interest in the conversation and turned their attentions elsewhere, much to Iain's satisfaction.

"I'd love to hear more, Professor, but I've got to dash remember. Hairdresser's appointment," said Janice, as she made her escape.

Iain looked at Liz, wondering if she would leave too, but she didn't.

"I don't suppose you're interested in science, are you Liz?"

"Actually, I've been fascinated with science for years," she said.

"Really!" he replied trying to act surprised. "I'm a bit of science buff myself! I've read one or two books, watched a few programmes, the usual sort of stuff" declared Iain. "What is it that attracts you to science?" he asked curiously.

"Honestly?"

"Honesty's best........"

"I just find it fascinating, learning about the universe and everything. How it's all connected going right back to the big bang itself. It just seems so impossible that an explosion of gases and chemical elements could eventually, albeit over billions of years, lead to us, probably the most sophisticated pieces of biological engineering."

"Roll up! Roll up! Sign up for your science degree courses here! Baffled about the mysteries of the universe, then look no further! Enrol now and expand your mind as you expand your knowledge!" Iain announced jokingly. "Crikey you've convinced me!" Iain smiled wryly. "You can start tomorrow as my PR person! When you put it across like that, how could anybody not resist wanting to know more!"

"You're just taking the Mickey!" replied Liz. "I knew you'd laugh."

"Hey, I'm not laughing! I'm just saying, you've got a real passion for the subject. Maybe you should be studying science instead of psychology. Which begs the question, why are you…… studying psychology, I mean?"

"Science I suppose," she answered.

"That's a new one on me!" remarked Iain. "Students usually say, it's because they want to go into social work, or they want to understand more about people. But as a science?" he questioned.

"I want to understand more about how the brain works," Liz declared.

"Hmmn," puzzled Iain. "May I ask why? I'm just curious. I like to understand what motivates my students."

"Personal reasons," She answered cautiously.

"Ohhh," sighed Iain disappointed, as he realised that the line had been drawn. "Sorry, didn't mean to dig…." sighed Iain.

"That's okay. Anyway," she replied. "I really should be going," she said as she picked up her things and made an attempt to stand up and leave, curious to know if he would stop her.

"Off to the hairdressers?" asked Iain.

"No. Off to lunch, before all the good stuff goes! I'm starving!" Liz declared.

Iain breathed a sigh of relief.

"Mmmmmn I think steak and kidney pie's on the menu today. "

Liz looked at her watch, and stood up quickly.

"Sorry Professor, must dash!" she said, before heading towards the lecture room door.

"I'll catch you at the Ball then!" He shouted after her, as Liz dashed out into the corridor and was gone. Sighing disappointedly, he gathered his thoughts and rose to his feet. A faint aroma of meat and gravy drifted in from the corridor as a student walked by, carrying a take-away carton from the refectory. "Mmmmmn Steak and kidney pie – Saved by the smell!" he laughed as he locked the classroom door and headed off for lunch.

On the way to the refectory, Liz caught up with Janice.

"Did he say he was going to the ball?" asked Janice.

"I think so."

"He's a dish. ….. What do you think?"

"I didn't notice," replied Liz.

"In fact, it sounded almost like he was asking you out on a date!" she jabbered. Janice had a reputation for always being obsessed by young handsome men. She thought every man fancied her……and with her figure and good looks….. she was probably right. Still, like most people, Liz never saw conceitedness as a personality trait to be admired, but Janice seemed to get away with it.

"No, that's not possible. I don't know him, and besides, I didn't think it was allowed, Professors fraternising with students."

"You'd be amazed what goes on!" declared Janice. Then she teased," So you do fancy him! "

"No. I'm not really into relationships at the moment…."

"Course you are!……."

With that, Janice marched Liz down to the refectory for some lunch, whilst continuing to babble on about what she would be wearing that evening and who the hottest dates were. Liz just smiled, trying to blot out the sound of Janice's excited chatter and thought back instead to her first conversation with Iain. He had seemed quite nice and sincere, too nice, in fact, to be dragged into her complicated and dangerous life. *'Leave it be,'* she thought. If Iain was to become a part of her life now or in the future, she didn't want it to be because she'd pulled him in, based on some vision or projection of her future.......Besides, she was leaving tonight. What could possibly happen tonight to bring them together, she asked herself. It seemed more likely to her that they were meant to meet each other again, perhaps under different circumstances, in a different place.

"Are you listening Liz?" asked Janice, aware that Liz seemed to be staring into space.

"Sorry?"

"I'll come round to your flat about six.....Is that ok?"

"That's fine."

Iain strolled into the refectory and took a deep breath to inhale the aroma of meat soaked in gravy and rich pastry. He hadn't eaten anything yet that morning, consequently his stomach growled like a leopard ready to pounce as he headed towards the food service counter. Then, just in the corner of his eye, he spied Liz sitting at a table opposite Janice and watched her sparkling and captivating blue eyes from a distance. Thinking back to their earlier conversation, Iain was convinced that she must be in some kind of trouble. Why else would she be so suspicious and cautious and living under a different name, he thought to himself. But more importantly, why was she here, right now? Just as Liz could sense the approach of some unknown significant event in her life, Iain too could sense that something was about to happen. His mind pondered over the likely scenarios in his imagination as he stood in the refectory queue, waiting to be served. Glancing across in Liz's direction, Iain began to contemplate their inevitable next meeting.

"Do you want chips with that?"

Iain snapped back to reality and turned to look at the middle aged portly figure of a woman who was holding up a plate containing his steak and kidney pie. He glanced quickly at the limp anaemic looking rectangular fingers of fried potato that sat in the warming tray nearby and frowned.

"I think I'll have boiled potatoes today, Maggie...... with just a few carrots."

"You gone off chips then, Professor?"

"Hmmmmmn."

"Or perhaps is has something to do with what's going on over there..." said Maggie, nodding in Liz's direction. "What happened to the last one?"

"Dull.......too dull," he sighed.

"What you want is a good, jolly bundle of fun like me to keep you company....And I know how much you like my cooking.........I'm halfway there already.......You know what they say.......The way to a man's heart....."

Iain smiled, pretending to be flattered but, cringed inside at the thought of spending even one night in the company of such an unattractive woman who wouldn't have looked out of place on an Olympic shot-putting team.

"Oh...well......Suit yourself."

Maggie handed him the plate of hot food and watched as Iain drifted away towards a nearby table to consume his lunch.

Liz felt the hairs rise on the back of her neck as she sensed that someone was watching her. Wondering if this would spell trouble, she cautiously raised her head and tentatively gazed across the refectory. Iain caught her gaze and beamed a broad smile at her. She blushed and breathed a sigh of relief. Pointing at his plate of hot food he mimed across to her *'The steak and kidney pie is fabulous.....you should try some."*

Liz nodded in acknowledgement and smiled. Janice turned to look over Liz's shoulder.

"I told you he fancied you…"

"I'm not interested."

"Oh yeh.......I can see that!" Janice remarked sarcastically.

Finishing her cup of hot dark coffee, Liz said her farewells to Janice and left. As she made her way across the refectory, Iain couldn't help but follow her with his eyes as he consumed a mouthful of pie. She might be differently dressed compared to what he had been used to seeing, and she might be living under a different name, but she was definitely and unmistakably his girl. She just needed to get to know him again he thought, as a tall dark figure appeared from a table behind a far pillar and followed Liz out of the refectory. Iain frowned. Somebody else was interested in Liz but for far different reasons. Iain could sense that something was about to happen and trouble wouldn't be far behind. Finishing his pie and washing it down with a large gulp of coffee, he set off after Liz and her stalker.

Keeping a safe distance behind the stalker, Iain followed quietly behind as Liz made her way across campus to the halls of residence. Iain watched as the stalker, indiscriminate from the other students increased his pace and was less than twenty feet away from her when a university security guard suddenly appeared in the quadrangle and halted the stalker in his tracks. Iain watched as the security guard appeared to utter some harsh words to the stalker, who then skulked away towards the car park. Looking up, the guard noticed

Iain standing on the opposite side of the quadrangle. Iain nodded an acknowledgement and the guard reciprocated before retreating back into the nearest building. By this time, Liz had reached the safety of the halls of residence, then after punching in her security code into the door lock, the door sprung open and she stepped inside and disappeared. Happy that she was safe, Iain retreated and headed back to his office.

CHAPTER 8

THE STREETS WERE BUZZING WITH evening traffic, as the city's birds headed into the trees to begin their evening cacophony of incessant twitter. In stark contrast to their stressfully, shrill voices, the balmy evening air was filled with the calming sweet perfume of honeysuckle drifting from the city's parks. When Liz arrived at the summer ball, she couldn't resist sniffing the delicate fragrance which loitered in the evening air, as she climbed out of the taxi. Looking far away across the park's lawns and blossoming floral beds towards the horizon, she noticed the beautiful dark pink and yellowy gold hues in the sky that reminded her of summer ripened peaches, freshly picked and ready to eat.

Carefully climbing the palatial stone steps as the sun began to set behind the historic 18th Century country hall, she could just make out the soft wave of scintillating string music as it floated sublimely through the air to greet her from the main ballroom. Feeling awkward and as nervous as a debutante at her first palace ball, Liz slipped discreetly through the main doors into the foyer. Wearing a deep, royal blue, full-length evening gown, dark blue satin high heels, a single solitaire pendant and earrings, she looked like a serene princess from a modern fairytale. Janice had insisted on styling her hair into a regal French pleat, held in place with, what seemed like a hundred hair pins.' *If someone comes near me with a magnet,'* Liz thought,' *it'll be more like fatal attraction than physical attraction when all those pins fly through the air at a rate of knots!'* She shivered as she visualised the scene of utter chaos and carnage left by the attack of her killer hair pins.

Stepping through the antique doors into the fairytale world of gowns and Dickie-bows that she'd often dreamed about as a child, she remembered too her favourite Grimm's fairytale from so long ago. She'd always wondered what it would be like to attend a ball, to glide gracefully down a panoramic grand staircase and waltz the night away in the arms of some gallant, handsome young man. In her life so far, the only gliding she'd ever done was on black ice....... usually followed by a pretty rough landing on her derriere.

"Could I see your ticket please?" asked the doorman.

Liz opened her small blue clutch bag and flashed the gold embossed card at him.

"Thank you. The Great Hall is just across to your right and the bar is immediately on your left.....Enjoy your evening!" he said politely.

"Thank you."

Being careful not to slide on the polished floor, and adjusting to the higher altitude of her teetering high heels, she held her chin up and exercised conscious deportment as she entered the Ball. The University Quartet sat in their prestigious corner of the Hall, with the men resplendent in their smart black tuxedos making up the brass and percussion section, whilst the women serenely elegant in their simple black evening dresses sat poised with their violins and flutes, ready to play. As she stood alone in the Hall, the quartet began to play Strauss, whilst a sea of black suited men flowed rhythmically around the dance floor with their brightly dressed partners. As she scanned the Hall, she noticed several groups of men and women gathered around the peripheral edges of the dance floor, sipping wine and chattering like gaggling geese, yet there was no sign of the one person she had been appointed to meet there. Janice had departed for the ball half an hour earlier but was nowhere in sight. Perhaps she'd already been acquired by some young stud with an obvious agenda, thought Liz as her eyes continued scanning the remainder of the Hall.

Iain entered the ball a short distance behind Liz, carrying two glasses of wine. Having been forced to wait in a queue at the bar for nearly fifteen minutes before eventually being served, he had decided to be energy efficient and time efficient, purchasing two glasses of wine, to save him the torture of a second imminent, time consuming trip. Taking a quick gulp of wine from the glass in his left hand for Dutch courage, he looked at the increased number of amply sized women thumping around the dance floor, then he gazed down at his highly polished, currently intact feet and whispered, "Here's to anaesthesia," before taking another larger gulp of wine for good measure.

He suddenly recalled how, during last year's ball, he had been almost crippled when a heavy, mis-footed high heel had pierced his toe. Screwing up his face in excruciating pain, he had yelled out a tirade of expletives culminating in, "You clumsy clod hopping hippo!", only to find that the responsible, rather rotund lady, wearing what appeared to be a mauve silk tent supported by guy ropes for straps, was none other than the Faculty Head's younger sister. Fortunately, his boss had taken pity on him, granting him clemency when Iain was forced to spend the following six weeks with his foot in plaster as a result of the injury he sustained. 'He's lucky I didn't sue her for personal damages,' Iain thought as he looked at his foot again and flexed his toes, before spying a young woman in an elegant deep blue evening gown standing just ahead of him.

Her pale neck was long and slender like a swan, flowing down to her bare shoulders, and her hair was exquisitely elevated into a distinguished aristocratic style. He watched as she gazed around the Hall, searching for someone, her soft pale shoulders rising and falling in time with her nervous breathing. Drawn towards the unfamiliar beauty before him, he quietly but quickly, strode up to her before anyone else had a chance to move in. As he drew closer, an invisible mist of enigmatic and exotic perfume filled his head and he leaned forward to whisper eloquently in her right ear. Liz sensed someone was standing behind her, as his warm breath close to her skin, made the hairs on the back of her neck prickle. 'If this was some slimy nerdy geek, she'd politely but firmly tell him to buzz off,' she thought as she began to turn around.

"You look like you could do with one of these," Iain said in his most charming and sophisticated voice, holding out the full glass of wine towards her.

Liz's heart pounded excitedly as she recognised the smooth rich voice with its unmistakable Scottish lilt. Had he been looking for her and what did he want with her, she thought as she faced him.

Iain swallowed hard, his eyes transfixed by her unforgettable, piercing blue eyes and her exquisite beauty. He smiled with embarrassed surprise, taking a step backwards to marvel at her transformation, from the former 'Miss Inconspicuous', to the mirage which now stood before him. Seeing the wide-eyed expression on his face, Liz looked quickly to her left and right, and then down at herself self-consciously, as her heart pounded nervously. His eyes twinkled and his mouth went dry, reducing his voice to almost a croak as he remarked,

"Oh it's you! I didn't recognise you in a dress."

"Professor!"

"That's right…It's me…In the flesh…Mr Dance Fantastic ready for action, "he announced in his boisterous teacher tones, as one or two faces stared at him disapprovingly. "But let's drop the formalities shall we?" He suggested. "Just call me Iain," he instructed as he studied her appearance.

"What's wrong?" She asked. "You're looking at me like I've suddenly developed two heads!"

"You look….incredible!" he said before adding softly and discreetly in her ear, "Exquisite!"

Liz blushed awkwardly. She hadn't expected to hear such flattering comments from someone she hardly knew, particularly not from her apparently eminent Professor. Iain suddenly remembered his manners and the wine in his hands. "Here…..have one of these……. You look a little nervous."

Liz nodded sheepishly.

"This'll help you to relax. It's good stuff….." He said offering her a glass. "A fine bouquet infused with pears and melon…….An ideal wine to melt away the dullness and pomposity of such grandiose occasions as these," he whispered with a wry grin.

"Thank you." She smiled shyly, taking a delicate sip from the glass, conscious of his attention.

"Go on…be daring!" said Iain. "The rush of alcohol will leave you feeling just that little bit giddy…….It'll be fun… Go on be brave……You'll forget about being nervous, I promise!….Trust me!" he implored.

"Anybody might think that you were trying to get me drunk, Professor," Liz whispered.

"Who cares what others think!" announced Iain wryly as he held out the glass to her. "It's what you think that counts," he said, as his eyes flashed mischievously.

Standing poised and confident in his black velvet tuxedo, crisp white shirt, Dickie bow and black, dress trousers, Liz couldn't help but admire the obvious effort he had made since that afternoon, to spruce up his appearance. A far cry from the flamboyant, extrovert professor she'd met for the first time earlier that day, now with his freshly washed hair, neatly groomed, apart from his renegade fringe which dared to hover defiantly over his brow. For a cleaned up university professor, Liz found him quite handsome, dashing in fact, as he presented an air of relaxed sophistication, which she found quite alluring.

Watching him as he put the glass to his lips and took a healthy gulp, she cautiously tipped her own glass into her mouth and swallowed the smooth medium dry white wine with its accurately described fruity notes.

"Good girl," praised Iain, just as she coughed swallowing the last of the wine from her glass. Immediately, her pale cheeks flushed red again, as Iain took

her empty glass delicately from her hand and placed it along with his own, on a nearby table. As she regained her composure, Iain caught her delicate hands and led her out on to the dance floor before placing his arm around her waist and pulling her close to him. Allowed no opportunity to think or object, Liz blushed and lowered her gaze to hide her shyness.

"What are you doing Professor?" she whispered nervously.

"I'm leading you on to the dance floor."

"But why?" she asked surprised by his impulsive action.

"That's a silly question to ask," he laughed. "Why do you think?"

"I thought Professors weren't allowed to fraternise with students."

"That's just out dated protocol. Don't worry about it, unless of course you'd rather not dance with me?" he asked coyly.

"But I don't know you..."

Abbygail Donaldson

"I don't know you either ......so that's something we've got in common right away!" he replied quickly. "How do you think men and women were first introduced to each other centuries ago? Men didn't always go around bashing their women on the head and dragging them back to their caves, you know. We packed that in at least ten years ago!" he teased.

"You just drag them on to dance floors instead!" retorted Liz.

"Very good. A quick return, that shows you have a sharp mind," he replied smiling back at her, as he led her through the dancing couples into the centre of the floor. "See, I'm beginning to learn something about you already," he added as they approached the centre of the dance floor. "Here we are," he said as he gently pulled her towards him.

Liz blushed shyly as Iain placed one hand around her waist and gently led her into the waltz with the other. She could feel his body pressing lightly against her, and suddenly she had the strangest recollection that she'd felt his embrace before. Mildly confused and nervous she confessed timidly,

"I don't know how to waltz."

"Well then, now's your chance to learn and you can kill two birds with one stone. You can get to know me and I can teach you to dance at the same time! Now I can't say fairer than that, can I?" He chirped. "And, it's as easy as…one two three, one two three, one two three…" he said as he led her this way and that way in time to the rhythm, with her long blue gown rippling and ebbing like soft blue waves around the dance floor.

Occasionally, when Liz wasn't looking down at her feet, trying to keep in step, she would look up into his brown and golden eyes that sparkled brightly with the reflected light from the chandelier above their heads. His gaze and his embrace were warm, relaxed and reassuring, as if he'd held her that way many times before, endorsing her vague recollection of a previous encounter.

"I tell you what, how about, you ask me a question, then I ask you one. That's fair," he suggested.

"I guess so," she replied nervously.

Gazing down into her deep blue frightened eyes, Iain smiled.

"Right then," he began. "What do you want to know?"

"Your voice, it sounds Scottish. Whereabouts do you come from?" she asked curiously.

"I was born about a mile from Libran's Loch in the West of Scotland," Iain answered. "How about you? Which part of this beautiful green isle do you come from? I would hazard a guess at the North East? Newcastle perhaps?"

"Close enough," Liz replied as Iain turned her carefully beneath his arm.

As her face passed close to his, she noticed him smiling softly and contentedly at her.

"Your turn," he whispered to her.

"I don't know what to ask?" she replied.

"You can ask me a personal question if you like. I won't bite," he said coyly.

"Do you have a family?" she asked carefully.

"You mean, am I married?......No. Bit of a free spirit, that's me, and I have my reputation to think of! Don't get me wrong, I love women! I adore them, with all their unique idiosyncrasies. I just haven't met anyone I'd want to commit to, yet!" he declared. "My turn."

Whisking her around the corner of the dance floor, the skirt of her dress sailed outwards and then inwards again, its weight pushing her closer and closer into his arms. With her face close to his he asked discreetly,

"Are you married? Divorced?"

"Single," she replied lowering her eyes slightly to avoid his gaze. "Where did you learn to dance, Professor?" she asked changing the subject. "You waltz like a pro. I can't imagine you attending any dance classes."

"I'll take that as a compliment," he replied beaming. "It was a few years back. I knew someone," he hesitated.

"A woman?"

"Yes," he replied. "She taught me."

"She must have been very good," remarked Liz.

"She was," he said looking straight at Liz, like he was looking deep into her soul. "She was the best!"

A sudden shiver ran down Liz's back and for just that moment, like the vague recollection she had of a previous encounter with him, she got the distinct impression from the intense look in his eyes and the inflection in his voice, that she might be the woman he was referring to. But that was impossible, she thought dismissively. If she'd ever met Iain before and especially if she'd taught him to dance, she would have remembered.

"Did you like her?" Liz asked.

Iain stared into her eyes but said nothing. Sensing it was a highly personal and sensitive subject, Liz added quickly,

"Your turn."

"What's your name?" Iain asked as the wine and the energetic dancing began to make her feel slightly dizzy.

"You know my name Professor, it's Liz. Liz Finlay," she answered curiously.

"Is it?" he asked.

"What do you mean?" she replied nervously.

"There's no personal file for you in the office," Iain replied. "Other than on the enrolment register, there is no record of you anywhere," Iain replied seriously. "Either, you don't exist or you're using a false name. Furthermore, I saw someone follow you from the refectory at lunch time. What's going on Liz?" he asked discreetly.

"Someone was following me?" she asked worriedly. Maybe that's who Steve was trying to warn her about, she thought.

"Yes. He followed you to the halls of residence, but he was intercepted by the campus security guard," stated Iain. "And he didn't look like a love-struck student either!"

"So, you did some digging and found some discrepancies?" she asked.

"Yup. That's about the size of it!" Iain replied.

"You haven't told anyone have you?" she asked anxiously.

"Why? Who are you hiding from?" he asked. "What kind of trouble are you in? Not drugs I hope?"

"Good God, no! I never touch the stuff!" Liz exclaimed.

"Well at least that's something I suppose," Iain sighed. "So, tell me, who are you hiding from? What have you done?"

"I haven't done anything! Why are you automatically assuming that I might be guilty of something?" she asked. "If you must know, I was worried in case you'd blown my cover, but I don't suppose it matters now anyway."

"Blown your cover? What are you, MI6 or something?"

"No. I'm in witness protection."

"Ahhh," Iain responded. "I must admit, I didn't think you looked like the spying type although, in that outfit, you'd probably make a good Mata Hari," Iain smiled. "Okay then, tell me what's going on?"

"I'll tell you, but not here."

"Fair enough," he replied. "Why don't we go into the bar? It's pretty quiet in there, so we can talk," he suggested.

Liz nodded. "Right then, follow me," he said reassuringly as he took hold of her hand and led her across the foyer to the adjacent bar.

Since she had disappeared from the pub that New Year's Day, Iain had been wondering what had happened to her. She had just vanished without a trace, until she turned up, months later, in his lecture room. Had she been at the university all this time without him knowing, he thought. He knew the campus was big, but he found it odd, that they hadn't bumped into each other earlier. Maybe it just hadn't been the right time. But why, now? He asked himself.

"This way.......the bar's in here. Watch out for the lively ones," he remarked as he nodded towards a group of bored and miserable senior university professors. "Any minute now they'll start break-dancing in the middle of the floor. They might even break-face and smile," whispered Iain jokingly into Liz's ear, trying to break the tension.

Liz smiled.

"Don't worry," he said softly. "I'm sure everything will work out."

Liz looked down at her feet, as she suddenly felt all the emotion that she'd held bottled up inside her, welling up in her mind. An overwhelming anxiety took hold of her and she began to find it hard to breathe. Iain noticed the colour drain from her cheeks and placed his arms around her waist to steady her.

"Here," he whispered. "Lean on me. Are you okay?"

"I think so," she muttered. "I'm just feeling a little bit dizzy."

"I'm sorry," said Iain. "I shouldn't have pressured you like that. It's serious, isn't it?" Liz nodded.

Walking through the two large wooden Georgian doors into the large room, Iain spied a vacant sofa near the palatial

French windows leading out on to a veranda and guided Liz towards it.

"Wait here.........I'll be back shortly. And don't do anything I wouldn't do!" Iain teased as he strode over to the bar under the scornful observation of the vintage academic gentry.

The bar stood just to the right of the large regal fireplace and Iain pulled at the tight collar of his shirt as he approached it and placed a twenty pound note on the marble counter.

"Two glasses of your finest Chardonnay, young man and don't spare the grapes!"

The bar man raised his eyebrows, as he removed two large wine glasses from the cabinet behind him. Waiting for their drinks, Iain turned to glance across the bar at Liz, who sat nervously waiting for his return. Iain couldn't help but notice the starlight sparkle in her hair as the chandelier light bounced off the tiny metal hairpins subtly embedded beneath her tresses. Her eyes too drew his attention, like deep blue flawless sapphires, reminding him of the deep blue waters of the loch back home.

Over the years, he'd rehearsed this scene so many times, imagining how, where and when they would meet, but he'd never thought of this. Strangely too, now that she was here, with him, he was almost completely lost for words, feeling like an awkward, excited teenager on his first date. Part of him wanted to wrap his arms around her and tell her everything about their past together, but knowing that this might have disastrous consequences, he kept his true feelings under lock and key, for now. Only when she had discovered his past for herself, could he be sure that his actions wouldn't disturb the delicate balance of their relationship in the present. Distracted by his thoughts of her, Iain failed to notice the bar man sliding the full glasses towards him on the counter.

"Your drinks sir." Announced the bar man.

"Oh, right! Cheers!" acknowledged Iain as he turned towards the bar and pocketed his change before picking up the glasses and heading back towards Liz. As he approached, he could see from the distant look in her eyes that her mind was miles away, elsewhere.

"Penny for them?" he asked.

Liz looked up.

"I can tell this is really worrying you," he said. "I'm a good listener you know…. It comes with the territory……." He said encouragingly, as he sat down beside her and handed her a glass. "I won't bite either."

"Thanks," she sighed gratefully.

Taking a good sip of wine from his glass, Iain leaned against the back of the sofa and stretched his other arm along its top, behind Liz.

"Okay then, why don't you try starting at the beginning."

Liz turned to face him, then taking a good gulp of wine and a deep breath, she began.

"My name's not Liz Finlay."

"Yeh, I think I worked that one out for myself."

"It's Liz…..Liz Curran."

"Pleased to meet you Liz," he said, feigning surprise at her real name. "You're doing great so far…Carry on," Iain encouraged.

Liz looked Iain straight in the eye, and with a heavy sigh she continued.

"I'm 29 years old, and as you rightly worked out from my accent, I'm from the North East."

"Nice bunch of people, most of them! Warm and generous! Spent some time there way, way back," commented Iain. "Sorry. I interrupted," he apologised.

"Last New Year's Eve, someone tried to abduct me," she declared.

"Do you know why?" Iain asked.

"I haven't the foggiest idea," she replied. "He just said he was following orders."

"From whom?"

"That's what I asked, but he wouldn't tell me," she said.

"What happened?"

"I was at the New Year's Eve party held at our village pub. I'd been asked to put on my palm reading act to raise money for charity. I hadn't done a proper gig before. It had always just been my party piece, if you know what I mean."

"I understand."

"I'd been reading palms all night, then this young man, in his thirties staggered over to my table, asked if I was legit and gave me his palm. "

"So you read this chap's hand…….and presumably you saw something interesting?"

"He was some kind of military guard for some top secret project."

"How did he know you?"

"He didn't…..At least I thought he didn't," replied Liz.

"What do you mean?" asked Iain curiously.

"The palm reading was just a decoy," she said. "He used it to get close to me. Then, he showed me his gun and forced me to leave with him."

"Where did he take you?"

"He forced me along the dark country footpath near the pub, but he wouldn't tell me where he was taking me."

"So what happened?" asked Iain, concerned.

"I slipped on the ice and fell. When, I didn't get up

straight away, he threatened to shoot me on the spot. Then, something, a fox I think, dashed out of the bushes and startled him. I made the most of it and kicked his legs out from under him. As he hit the ground, I scrambled to my feet and ran like hell back to the pub!" Liz explained noticing the shocked expression on Iain's face as he sat in silence taking in all the information.

"What happened then?"

"My friends from the pub went back to find him but, he was dead."

"Have they told you how he died?"

"They said that there were contusions consistent with a serious fall."

"So it was an accident, or at least, made to look like an accident," replied Iain as he placed his arm around her shoulders to comfort her

"You're just saying that to make me feel better."

"Listen! It was an accident! You were defending yourself against a hired assassin! You were lucky to have escaped in one piece! What we need to do now, is to figure out who wanted you abducted and why," Iain concluded.

"Whoever they are, they're still out there, somewhere. That's why I'm here, hiding, at least until tomorrow."

"Why? What happens tomorrow?"

"I'm leaving. I'm going into hiding again, but at least you'll know the reason why. "

"Why tomorrow? I've only just told you about the stalker. "

"I got a postcard this morning, warning me to move on. As for that stalker you saw earlier, I know he'll be back!" said Liz anxiously.

Iain thought for a moment, as he tried to work out a solution in his head.

"Are you sure that running away again is the best thing

to do? Obviously, I appreciate you don't want to be a sitting duck, but there must be a better way of sorting this out, or else you'll spend the rest of your life permanently looking over your shoulder," said Iain deeply concerned.

"I know, but other than playing for time, and hoping that they figure out who's behind this, I don't know what else to do."

"So until they catch him, you're going to let them leave you out in the cold, dangling like bait? Well, I'm sorry, I just can't allow that to happen! It's no good trying to dress it up any other way. You've got to let me help you sort this out!"

"It's not your problem."

"I'm not going to leave you to face this alone, that would be complete and utter madness!"

"But I'm nothing to you!" she replied. "Why would you want to risk your job and your life for me? I'm nobody."

You're not nobody," Iain said softly. "And somebody else agrees with me. The person who thinks you're important enough to abduct. We need to get you somewhere safe until we can come up with a plan to figure out who's responsible, why they're doing this, and how we're going to stop them!"

Liz knew Iain was right. She did need help and there was something about him that made her feel that she could trust him. It was more than just his genuine concern, he made her feel 'safe'.

"How did you know he was involved in some top secret project?" asked Iain, curiously. "Don't tell me, you saw that in his palm?" he asked, as he scrutinised his own hands.

"Not exactly," she replied.

Iain looked at her puzzled.

"I'm not sure quite how to explain this?" she said hesitantly.

"Try me."

"I saw it in his thoughts," she replied cautiously.

Iain feigned surprise.

"So you're a clairvoyant as well as a palm reader," he said.

"No. It's a long story and far more complicated than that, "Liz replied.

"Well, unless you're in a desperate hurry, I'm all ears."

Taking another deep breath she turned her mind back to her school days.

"When I was about twelve years old, I had a couple of accidents at school, involving electricity. I didn't think that they'd caused me any real harm at the time, but from that point on, strange things began to happen."

"What sort of things?" he asked intrigued.

"They were just little things at first. "

Iain took another gulp of his wine and listened avidly to everything she said.

"I discovered that I could sense things about people and places as well as seeing auras…So, thinking it might help to draw out what I was picking up from people, I taught myself to read palms. The palm reading bit was easy. Anyone can do it… You can learn to read the lines on a hand just like some people can read shorthand….What was important about it though, was it allowed me physical contact with them, to actually touch the energy they were transmitting," Liz explained. "The physical contact I had with the other person opened up a connection to their thoughts, their memories and their future. I began to see snapshots of their life, I saw what they saw, felt what they felt and I realised that I had become some kind of conductor of thought and emotional energy."

"Aaah…So you used the palmistry to disguise your true 'gift'."

"It certainly saved me from a lot of awkward questions."

"But there must have been some people who questioned how you got so much information from just a few lines, just as I've done?"

"You're right. From time to time, there were one or two critics and sceptics who thought that it was some kind of trick, and there were some people who never came back."

"You probably got too close....made them feel uncomfortable or threatened even," suggested Iain.

"In the main though, people seemed to accept the mysticism as part of the fortune teller package ..."

"So how did you handle the sceptics?...I know, let me guess, you scanned their thoughts for something unique and highly personal that only they knew, to embarrass them a little perhaps?" guessed Iain.

"Yeh, and it works.....The only problem then is, ...the real truth behind their scepticism comes out.....Some became frightened or angry about my ability....like I'm some kind of demon or freak to be feared..... They don't understand what they can't see.....Others thought that because I could see their situation in every minute detail.... that I could solve all their problems too...That's when I became more of a counsellor than a fortune teller."

"And of course, because you were soaking up all their negative emotional energy at the same time, they went away feeling physically better and more positive?"

"Yeh, that's right."

"So you're really a thought healer, an empath, not just a thought reader."

"I guess you could say that," she agreed, then looked at Iain curiously.

"What's wrong?" he asked.

"You don't really seem surprised by any of this," she replied.

"Should I be?" he said. "You forget. I'm a psychologist. I've studied how the brain works and how people think and behave. In my doctorate days I studied many patients with medical and psychological disorders, some of which gave these people unusual skills."

"Hang on. Are you trying to say that I'm ill or nuts?" she asked defensively.

"Not at all! You said yourself, you had an accident that seems to have been the root cause for these gifts of yours and what I'm saying is, that the brain is a marvellous complicated organic electrochemical engine which is capable of many things. Whatever happened when you had your accident, your brain found a way, not only to survive but to make the best of the new circumstances of its existence. It adapted. It found new neural pathways to bypass any damage and may have reactivated or discovered previously inert abilities in the process," Iain explained. "You said before that, you feel what people feel."

"Yes.......I feel their pain........their joy.......their worries.......everything....The whole emotional suite!"

"How on earth do you carry all that emotional baggage around with you? I find it hard enough to carry around just my own, never mind somebody else's."

Iain had a pretty good idea how she did it, but he wanted to see if she'd figured it out yet, for herself.

"Once I break the connection or leave the situation, the memory of what I've seen and felt from them, disappears very quickly, like it's a once only live broadcast never to be played back. Just like when you run a computer program directly from its setup disc instead of loading it onto the hard drive. All the memories of the events stay with the other person. I only see them and experience them for as long as the disc is running, when I'm in direct contact with that person. I still suffer the consequences of that knowledge or empathy. Afterwards I'm emotionally drained."

"I'm not surprised," Iain remarked. "So somehow, you're able to upload a transfer of electrical brainwave information directly through physical contact! Now that is amazing!" Iain smiled excitedly.

"Do you think so?" she asked.

"It's brilliant! Like I said, the brain is a marvellous thing and we're only just beginning to scrape the surface of its true potential," he said delicately placing his hands on hers.

Suddenly, without either of them consciously wishing it to happen, Liz felt the jolt and the timeline rippled. As Iain's adrenaline increased with his natural and suppressed excitement, the surplus brain energy that was generated, found a way to discharge into Liz. Suddenly, her eyes lit up as she made the connection in her mind. Strange images of Iain and his past life flooded her conscious mind. There were so many images, far in excess of those from other people. She saw him in all kinds of situations, split second snap shots of events in his life spanning nearly three centuries. She saw someone older. Not his father. Then he seemed younger again and for just the briefest moment, she was there, in his head, not as herself but like the mirage she'd experienced when she'd found herself on that beach. He knew her! He knew her magic! That's why he'd paid particular attention to her! But strangely, she had no recollection of ever meeting him before, except …..Then , the details of her projection, came back to haunt her. That was where she'd met him. He was the stranger who had kept her safe and helped her to escape from the mine! But why was she in his past too? She didn't understand.

The sudden revelation left Liz completely stunned. What did it all mean? First of all that morning, she'd received the postcard telling her to move on. Then, according to Iain, someone had been following her from the refectory, and now this. Something big was about to happen, and Liz could feel all the pieces of the puzzle starting to come together.

"Liz?" he asked, concerned by the sudden strange expression on her face. "Liz? What's wrong? Hello, Earth calling Liz?"

Liz's eyes were wide open as she gazed at Iain.

"You!" she exclaimed with surprise.

"Yes, the last time I looked in the mirror, it was definitely me! A bit smarter than usual admittedly, but 100% unadulterated me!" he replied flippantly. "What is it?"

"I'm not quite sure how you're going to take this. I'm not sure I understand this myself! It doesn't make any sense!" she said confused.

"Okay, …go ahead.." he replied, waiting with trepidation for the punch-line.

"We've met before…"

"Have we?" Iain asked, curious to know what she remembered. "And how does that all fit into this?"

"We've met…..but not in the conventional sense." Liz hinted cryptically.

Iain feigned puzzlement, sensing she was about to say something he probably already knew.

"Have we or have we not met before?" asked Iain impatiently, trying to draw the answer from her. "You've got me on tender hooks!"

"As well as sensing things about other people, I experience 'snapshots' of past and future events in their lives and sometimes my own," she began cautiously.

"Go on."

"I had a snap shot about you. Only, it wasn't like any other snap shot I've ever had before, "she paused. "It was a snap shot of a future event but with one huge difference. I was actually there!" Liz declared.

Iain sat up straight with surprise. He hadn't expected that answer at all!

"Let me get this straight. You were there, in the future, with me?" he asked.

"Yes."

"How do you know you were actually there and that it wasn't some kind of dream or vision?"

"Because of what you said," Liz replied.

"What I said? How can that be proof?"

"I was confused, as you can imagine. I didn't know where I was and I didn't know who you were. Then you said, it was okay.....I'd told you that this would happen.......You somehow knew, that I wasn't my usual self and you told me your name," Liz explained.

"You weren't your usual self?" asked Iain puzzled.

"I'd projected into my future self."

"But how did you work that one out?" asked Iain.

"When I found myself back in my own bed, back home, I was covered in bruises and the sheets were all dirty from where I'd been."

Iain sat quietly for a moment, gently turning the wine glass in his hands.

"You know me from your past too, but the images were too many and too fast for me to decipher. Why didn't you say that you knew me? How do you know me?" she asked with almost a desperate tone in her voice. "Who are you?"

Iain sat quietly perplexed. How much had she seen? Had the damage already been done? Should he tell her the truth? Was she ready for the truth? And how did this all fit in with what was happening to her now?

"Past life regression," he said sighing deeply, commending himself at his quick thinking.

131

"Past life regression?" she asked.

"Yeh. It usually happens during controlled hypnosis. A person in deep hypnosis can access parts of their subconscious, sometimes believing what they see to be their past life."

"I know what it is," she replied. "But that doesn't explain my presence in the future with you."

"Well, I can't explain it either, especially if you don't tell me what happened."

"I don't know whether I should tell you or not, " she confessed. "It's bad enough that I know about those events….and the impact that just knowing could have on the situation…But if I tell you, it could change your whole perspective of the future. It could change the way your life goes."

"Aaah," he responded. "It's a bit late for that, I think." Then making another quick recovery he said, "But if the theorists are right and the future has already happened… and we can't change it, ……..don't you think I'd rather be prepared for what's going to happen?"

Liz thought for a moment.

"You're right……To be fore warned is to be fore armed, as the saying goes."

"Exactly!" said Iain.

"So you believe me then…..about the snapshots, about projecting forward to the future?" asked Liz. "And you don't think I'm crazy?"

"Nah, you're not crazy! I believe you! But you're going to have to tell me everything now! I want to know everything that's going to happen!"

"You better get us some more wine then……" suggested Liz.

"Ohh. That bad is it?" frowned Iain.

"You asked…………Do you still want to know?"

"Well, I think we've passed the point of no return!

You're going to have to tell me…now! Maybe your past life regression, or whatever it was, was trying to give us a clue. Maybe we're meant to be brought together for a reason and maybe this is it…." He said, as he got up from the sofa to wander off to the bar. "We still have to figure out who is trying to get to you and why! Maybe your 'projection ' into the future and what we do together will give us a clue as to why this is all happening," suggested Iain. Then, changing the subject slightly, to lighten the tension, he said, "Could you imagine it though, if everyone could do that? Projecting into the future, to see exactly who you were going to be with! You'd put all of those dating agencies out of business!"

"You might change your mind," Liz suggested. "And change your whole life as a result."

"True."

Liz shook her head and smiled at Iain as he got up to go to the bar. Meanwhile, Liz relaxed back against the sofa, relieved that she'd got that one off her chest. It made such a difference being able to share her complicated situation with someone, but not just anyone. She knew from her projection that Iain would protect her, she could trust him and he had the skills to work out and understand what was happening to her. She still didn't quite understand their past connection, if there really was one. Maybe they'd find out the reason for that too, in time. What was important now was, how she was going to tell him what lay in store for them.

Suddenly she felt the hairs prickle on the back of her neck and the coldness of sharp steel against her back……Her muscles tensed and she felt the knife blade slide over her tender soft skin. Then, as the knife stopped moving and she felt the pain of its sharp point dig into her, she held her breath wondering if it was already too late. Would this be where it would all end for her? Had her vision or projection of the future been that wrong, she thought as the gloved right hand came over her right shoulder, and grasped her throat.

"Don't say a word." The voice was deep and rough with a distinct west country accent. "One word from you, …and it'll be your last!….Now get up slowly and move towards the door.…..No sudden moves."

Carefully, Liz rose to her feet and inched her way towards the open French windows leading out into the garden. With his gloved hand still clasped around her throat, she struggled to swallow. Across the bar, she could see Iain standing, waiting to be served. He was so near and yet, so far away, she thought as she tried to stay calm and controlled. Maybe she could get inside his head and find out who he was working for. With this in mind, she began to concentrate on her abductor, focussing her thoughts on his. Through his hand around her throat, she could make the connection and with her fear and her excitement heightened, the stream of energy began to flow between them, leaping from her nerve cells to his. Suddenly, and with surprisingly little effort, like accidently typing in the right password into a computer, she was in. Images of his violent childhood emerged, showing Liz years of the abuse he suffered as a child. But she wasn't interested in that. She needed to find out who he was working for. Fighting to stay conscious as her abductor pulled her backwards towards the French windows, Liz frantically searched his mind for clues.

A second hand wrapped itself around her slender waist and lifted her slightly off the ground, just enough so that her feet didn't make a sound on the beautiful highly polished wooden floor. In a second the gloved hand moved up her neck to cover her mouth. The cool evening air made her shiver as she struggled in his firm grasp, whilst her abductor proceeded to drag her out of the French windows, across the veranda and down the stairs to the garden below. The ball carried on, its golden halcyon light cascading out into the night, indifferent of the drama being played out in the garden. Reaching the bottom of the stone stairs, the abductor threw her down onto the ground in the shadows and she felt the icy cold wetness of the well tendered lawn, slimy against her skin. The abductor grabbed her body and flipped her over on to her back before kneeling astride her, and pinning her arms and legs to the ground. After tying a gag around her mouth, he pulled out a small radio from his back trouser pocket and spoke into it.

"Central…this is Alpha 5,"

There was a short crackle on the radio then a voice came back.

"Alpha 5, is target acquired?"

"Yes."

"Evacuation Team e.t.a. at pick up point, three minutes."

"Understood."

The abductor placed the radio back into his pocket whilst Liz lay pinned down on her back, wet and very cold, pondering her fate. She had three minutes to escape before reinforcements arrived. But what could she do? The abductor looked down at her, revelling in his power and pointing his sharp knife at her already enflamed throat. She felt the cold steel against her skin once more, as he slid the blade down from her neck towards the top of her strapless bodice.

Iain returned from the bar to find Liz had gone. He placed the glasses of wine on the table and noticed that her small clutch bag was still on the sofa. Then, he noticed that the French windows were open and ventured outside on to the steps, thinking that she might have popped outside for some fresh air, but, there was no sign of Liz anywhere. Why had she left, he asked himself. Had she had second thoughts about telling him what was going to happen? Iain's first instinct told him that something was wrong. Liz was in danger. Maybe the stalker had returned as Liz had predicted. Worried that something terrible could have happened to her Iain walked over to the majestically carved stone balustrade at the top of the steps which led into the garden. Peering into the darkness for any signs of her departure, he thought he heard something rustle beneath him.

"Liz!.......Liz!" Iain shouted out into the darkness.

Liz flinched and tried to force a scream, as she heard the sound of his voice calling to her, but her abductor gripped her mouth so tightly, she felt the pain of her soft tender cheeks being crushed against her teeth.

"Don't move or make a sound.......I never miss with a knife......you squeak ... he's dead."

Liz lay helpless, wondering what to do. Having tried unsuccessfully to find any meaningful clues from her abductor's thoughts, she focussed instead, on Iain. She wasn't in physical contact with him, so the connection would be weak....but it might just work. If she concentrated hard enough and deep enough she might just be able to project, she thought to herself. But doing that would leave her vulnerable in the clutches of her violent abductor, she thought. Still, she had to try something. She had to warn Iain. Slowing her breathing and closing her mind to all other distractions, she sank into a semi trance like state. The guard looked down at her as he felt her stop struggling, and noticed that her body had gone limp. Thinking she had fainted, the guard sat up and kept watch for the rest of his team.

"Professor," her sweet soft voice called to him. "Professor," she called again. "Don't be afraid......I won't hurt you." Iain felt her voice inside his head, a familiar voice calming him....filling him with a warm glow, the way she always did when she arrived in his life. In the darkness he closed his eyes and searched in vain for her image in his head, but only her voice was there.

"Open your eyes, Professor. I'm here." She whispered.

Just beside him at the top of the steps, on the edge of the shadows, there she stood, the gentle balmy night breeze blowing softly through her hair and rippling her long blue gown. Golden stars glittered all over her and her eyes sparkled like the purest sapphires he'd ever seen. The sight of her pure form brought memories of his past flooding back to him and he swallowed hard to fight back the pain of his heart ache that he'd carried for so long. He remembered how he'd gazed in wonder, the first time she'd revealed herself to him all those years ago, as he reached out to her. Once more, he stood before her, entranced by her unworldly beauty, as he listened to the serene bewitching music of her voice inside his head. God I've missed you so much, he sighed to himself.

Liz heard his thoughts and blushed. This stranger whom she'd only met that day, not only knew her, she realised, he was in love with her too and had been for a while. Her heart began pounding hard. She hadn't expected that. Iain quite clearly knew a lot more than he was letting on, she thought, but what was he hiding and why? They must have met before somewhere, but how? That was the mystery she intended to solve more than any other.

His fingers tingled on contact with the projection, as he connected with the trillions of invisible charged particles that formed her image. She was like lightening itself, powered by her thoughts and the energy she harnessed from a yet unknown source. She was quintessentially beautiful and no less magical than the surrounding starlight which had travelled trillions of miles across space to sparkle in the sky above them.

Suddenly, a strange luminous green mist began to engulf them both and he felt his spirit elated once more. Liz looked anxious at the mist around them, wary that it might be some kind of toxic cloud, but when she looked at Iain he appeared to look strangely unperturbed by it. In fact, he seemed to respond to it like it was a warm protective blanket. His face glowed with contentment as the familiar wonderful feeling of intoxication overwhelmed him.

"Professor? Try not to breath it in… it could be poisonous!" Liz warned.

"It's okay, really! I feel wonderful! Energized! I don't think it's anything to worry about," Iain reassured her.

Concerned and puzzled by Iain's bizarre, familiarity with the mist, Liz's projection reached out into the green haze to softly touch him and reassure herself that he was okay. Shaking her head, she tried to understand why Iain hadn't been dumbstruck with shock at her presence. He wasn't even in awe of everything that was happening around him now. Was it her imagination, she thought to herself, or did he really appear like he was welcoming an old friend. But how could he feel like that? She asked herself. It just didn't make sense at all. Question after question ran through her mind in her attempt to settle on a satisfactory answer, until a familiar voice from her past suddenly presented her with a suggestion.

"Always remember, when you're trying to work out a problem, step back from it for a moment, and think carefully and objectively about it. Once you discard the factors that are incidental and not relevant to the problem, you can then begin to see the basic situation and rationalise logical, plausible conclusions. The simplest solution will present itself and invariably this will be the answer..." said her physics teacher.

Looking directly at Iain she began to balance the evidence in her head. Firstly, he had approached her. Secondly, he hadn't been surprised by the fact that she was using a false name or the fact that she could read thoughts and had visions. Furthermore, he wasn't at all surprised by what was happening now. Why? Because somehow he already knew, she concluded. Maybe, he had visions too. Maybe she wasn't alone in her abilities and maybe that was why she'd had a vision about him. Perhaps through their abilities they were connected in some way?

With the light from her sparkling translucent hand, Iain's face lit up before her in the darkness as she lightly stroked his cheek. From the instant that her electrical whisper of a touch connected with him, his face began to change. As the gentle pulse of electromagnetic energy radiated out from her fingertips across his face, she watched in wonderment as the early signs of wrinkles around his eyes and the frown lines on his brow began to fade. He had aged only a decade since their last meeting, but the years of frantic searching in between and his efforts to investigate and research the science to explain their connection, had taken their toll. But now, miraculously within seconds, those ten years of wear and tear had vanished. The molecular structure of every single cell in his entire body, was restored to their optimum appearance and functionality. Looking up at the sky almost expectantly he watched as the un-forecast storm clouds began to gather in the previously cloudless and starlit summer night sky.

Bewildered by the mist's effects and surprised by his welcoming approach to her ghostly projection, Liz sighed with relief as the mist receded and the renewed Professor stood smiling before her. Still puzzled by his unexpected ease and calmness, Liz focussed her thoughts back on to the emergency at hand. Her conclusions about Iain's behaviour would have to wait, she said to herself, as she began to whisper her instructions to him.

"Professor!" she called to him. " I don't know how long this image of me will last, so you must listen carefully......
In less than three minutes a team are arriving to take me away somewhere.......I'm being held at knife point just below the steps, in the shadows..."

Iain turned to head towards the stairs leading down to the garden.

"Wait......He's threatened to kill you if you get close..." Liz warned.

"What can I do?" he asked.

"Take the far staircase and come round behind him.......I will try to keep his attention..."

"Are you okay? Has he hurt you?" asked Iain as his recent look of contentment turned to consternation.

"I'm okay for now, but you must hurry!" she replied.

She had barely finished her answer when, just as quickly as it appeared, her mirage was gone and Iain stood alone on the steps once more. Quietly, and quickly he retreated back into the bar, to look for an alternative entrance into the garden. Finding another set of open French windows further along the garden facing the side of the grand hall, he discreetly crept out into the garden, several metres behind the abductor. As the moonlight shone down on the well manicured lawn almost spotlighting the grandiose stone steps further ahead, Iain could just make out a silhouette crouched on the ground in the shadows. Holding his breath, lest his warm vapour betray his presence in the chilled night air, he clung to the edge of the deepest shadows from the balustrade, and crawled quietly towards Liz and her abductor. The cold wet soil beneath him, soaked through his crisply pressed black dress trousers, striking coldness into his knees like the sharpest of knives. As he reached forward with his hands on the ground, pulling the fabric of his jacket tight across his back, he heard the inevitable rip of stitching as one of his sleeves pulled apart from the main jacket.

Having returned to her body physically weakened by her first controlled projection, Liz struggled but failed to free herself from her burly tormentor.

"I said, don't move.......Maybe you need to learn not to disobey me," he threatened, dropping forward over her, and pressing the knife against her chest. His face was close to hers, smelling her as he ran his hands over her trembling pale soft skin. Then taking a firm grasp of her bodice near the concealed zip that ran down the side of her dress, he yanked it towards him. Liz tried to cry out as she felt the zip and the fabric being ripped apart and screwed her eyes tightly shut as his coarse hands searched sadistically beneath the torn cloth to settle on the soft mound of her breast.

"Not a word," he growled in her ear, as he squeezed her flesh. "You fell, got it!" he instructed.

Liz's eyes filled with tears of fear, as she prayed for a miracle to release her from her torture. With only a few minutes until the rest of them arrived, she knew he wouldn't dare try anything else. All she had to do was hang on. With eyes staring wildly at him, Liz fought against him, twisting and turning beneath his weight as he pawed her soft skin.

"Your punishment is my pleasure!" he snarled as streams of tears ran down her cheeks.

Incensed by what he could see, Iain's rage erupted incontrollably, and he launched himself at Liz's attacker roaring,

"Get off her NOW!"

Diving through the darkness at the startled silhouette before him, Iain caught the abductor by surprise and toppled him backwards on to the grass. The moonlight caught the blade of the knife, as the abductor frantically tried to reach it through the short blades of grass, just a foot away from him, but Iain stretched his foot across to it and flicked it further into the blackness of the rose bed. Tearful and shaking, Liz struggled to her feet, a sad, bedraggled and pitiful version of her former self. Cowering against the baluster at the base of the steps, she watched helplessly as the two men grappled in the dark, rolling over on to the edge of the flower bed and then back on to the wet lawn again. As their fists flew at each other, Liz could hear the sickening sound of their impact against flesh and bone, and she cringed hoping that Iain was okay. Although Iain was the weaker of the two, he fought back courageously with his new found youthful verve, fending off blow after blow. Successfully, he managed to block some of the punches with his forearm until suddenly, the abductor lashed out with a powerful right jab which caught Iain on his jaw. As its force sent him reeling backwards towards Liz, the ferocious abductor retrieved a second knife from his ankle and leapt towards Iain with the blade poised at his chest. Raising his arms up to block the attack, Iain watched in horror as his attacker suddenly froze in his tracks and dropped to the ground like a stone......He was dead. Caught across the boundary between the shadows and the pool of moonlight cast down on the lawn, Iain and Liz gazed in terror at the illuminated and bloody exit wound which had instantly and grotesquely obliterated most of his upper face. He had been shot cleanly through the back of the head by a sniper. Liz stifled a scream as Iain crawled over to her and placed his soiled torn tuxedo around her shoulders.

"We need to stay down in the shadows..." he whispered. "There's someone out there somewhere...If we move from here...we're sitting ducks."

Trembling with shock, Liz felt comforted by the warmth of Iain's jacket, and even more comforted when he hugged her close to him. Through the soft warmth of his shirt, Liz could feel his heart racing against her cheek. Anxious that the team would arrive soon, Iain knew they needed to get out of there quickly.

"Follow me, "he whispered. "But remember, keep close and keep low to the ground."

With that, he crept back slowly towards the far French windows, whilst checking that Liz was managing to keep up, behind him. Reaching the open doors and keeping close to the walls of the building, well into the shadows, Iain slipped quietly back into the bar.

"We can't go into the bar dressed like this...What will people think?" whispered Liz behind him.

"Never mind what people might think! You can't stay out there Liz....Not if you don't want to wind up in a box!" replied Iain firmly. "Come on! They'll probably think we've been...you know......in the garden..." suggested Iain.

Trembling, Liz reached out towards him and Iain clasped his hand around hers, pulling her gently closer to him.

"I don't think we have a choice...If we don't go back in, we have to deal with his team as well as that marksman out there," he whispered softly. "Just look straight ahead, don't make eye contact with anybody and leave all the talking to me. Trust me."

"What about the body?" she asked." They'll know we've been involved. They'll think we did it!"

"That shot was probably made by a high calibre rifle, which even if I had one, I couldn't very well hide it in my back pocket, could I?" Iain replied as he tried to brush off the worst of the dirt and blood splatters from his once white dinner shirt with its now battered and twisted Dickie bow tie. Wearing his jacket to preserve her modesty and cover up the tear in her dress, Liz clung closely to Iain as they walked back into the bar. Walking back towards the sofa where they had been previously sitting, and trying to act as if nothing had happened, Iain picked up his wine glass and swallowed its contents. Liz appeared behind him, picked up her bag and drank her wine.

Several heads turned and glanced at them as they made their way across the bar to the hallway. Iain's suit was ruined from the tussle in the garden, his knees covered in soil and mud as he squelched in his now dulled black and muddy shoes across the finely polished floor. As for poor Liz......her once beautiful hair was now matted, wet and dirty, whilst her dress, caked with mud on the back and wet, stuck to her legs making it difficult for her to walk. Faces stared aghast as the young woman who had only minutes before, turned heads with her serene, elegant beauty, now turned heads in horror to look at her present sorry state. Silence echoed from the guests standing around the room and the barman put down the glass in his hand and stared in disbelief as Iain and Liz headed for the door into the hallway.

"A word to the wise, ...don't go out there,...you'll get far more than you bargained for!" announced Iain smiling with his inimitable charm as he coyly adjusted his tie and winked cheekily at his horrified and bewildered audience. Mortified, Liz skulked out of the door into the hallway. Together, they passed a rather puzzled looking doorman who watched them leave and flag down a taxi.

In the back seat of the taxi, Iain reached across to Liz, beckoning to her to sit closer to him for comfort. Sliding across the shiny black seat, Liz looked up into his face with uncertainty in her eyes as he carefully laid his arm around her. His eyes sparkled as he smiled reassuringly.

"Are you okay, Liz?" he asked softly.

"I don't know….Stunned I guess," she replied nervously.

"I'm not surprised!" Iain remarked. "I'm pretty shocked myself! I'm not accustomed to having moonlight brawls in my best dinner suit…….I find the dickie bow and the fitted tux makes movement quite restrictive, don't you think?" he asked rhetorically, trying to lighten the mood of that moment and flashing her a big broad grin.

Liz smiled weakly.

"Come on! You can do better than that!" he encouraged teasingly. Then seeing the pools of tears brimming in her frightened and helpless eyes, whilst her body trembled under his arm, his patient self control dissolved and impulsively he kissed her smudged and tearstained lips. Liz stiffened momentarily completely surprised by his unexpected advance, but as his warm soft mouth brushed hers and his warm breath heated her cold cheeks, his kiss melted her fears and she knew she was safe in his arms.

"Professor…" she said eventually after he released her.

"Iain …call me Iain," he corrected, softly.

"Iain …… We're not strangers are we?" she asked cautiously.

"Well, you did say back at the hall, that we had met before in one of your visions, " he replied.

"Strangers don't kiss like that," she remarked.

"Don't they?" he answered coyly. Then, tactically changing the subject, Iain suddenly said, "Ah, thank you, that's just reminded me……you didn't tell me what you saw in your vision. "

Liz ignored his diversionary tactic.

"It felt like you'd kissed me before…but that's not possible, and you've accepted me and everything that's happened as if it were expected, "she probed carefully. "I don't know anything about you, other than you've just saved my life and that you will again in the future, but you seem to know an awful lot about me," she quizzed. "That back there, was the very first time I've projected like that and not even I knew how that was going to turn out and yet you knew. You even smiled like I was some long lost friend, and as for that green mist stuff, I certainly didn't have a clue about it! But you did? So how the hell do you explain that?" she asked nervously. "Who are you, who are you working for and what exactly do you know about me?"

"Gosh, you're good! Has anyone ever told you that! You'd make a great detective or analyst…" he replied.

"Please!" she pleaded shakily. "I know people are after me….to kill me. Why? I don't know! I need to trust someone! I want to trust you! But you've got to tell me the truth! I know you're hiding something from me and unless you tell me what's going on, I'm getting out of this taxi right now!"

"I'm sorry," he sighed heavily. "It's just the truth …… Firstly it's a little tricky to explain. Secondly, there might be consequences and thirdly, I'm not sure you'd be able to handle it, at least not right now," Iain replied. "Oh and this is not the best place to discuss this. Please trust me. You will have your answers soon…..just not here."

"Then at least tell me who you are?" she asked.

"That too, will be a little hard to swallow, I'm afraid. I think it's best that we wait until we get back to my house and after we've had a chance to get cleaned up and have some hot food, I'll tell you what I know."

Liz could see that Iain was being sincere and that he honestly wanted to help her. He had risked his life to protect her from their pursuers. The least she could do was to give him a chance and hear him out. Then she'd decide whether or not she could totally trust him.

"Okay. Take me home with you, Iain," she replied.

Iain smiled broadly as Liz sat back and rested silently in the back seat, going over the events of that evening so far in her mind. The taxi continued on its journey out of the city and along the winding country roads to Iain's cottage. Their journey together was only just beginning.

CHAPTER 9

IAIN LIVED IN A SMALL isolated two bedroom cottage that overlooked wide expanses of farm land and a nearby forest about ten miles outside of York. The cottage had been a little run-down after its previous occupant of over fifty years, had passed-away, but Iain had spent many of his weekends lovingly restoring it to its former glory. A short gravelled driveway led right up to the front door of the cottage, whilst a reasonably sized garden, enclosed by a thick hedge, lay at the rear. Beyond the hedge were, acre after acre of farmland regularly cultivated with cereal crops. The ground floor of the cottage consisted of a small farmhouse kitchen and adjacent living room, whilst the upper floor consisted of a master bedroom, a small second bedroom at the back of the cottage, a study and a bathroom. Having taken some advice from a colleague in the fine art and design faculty, Iain had sought out the appropriate furniture for the cottage from antique showrooms and auctions in Harrogate and further afield. With his knowledge and experience of history, he had a keen eye for spotting the genuine antiques from the fakes and had succeeded in securing some beautiful period pieces for his living room as well as his favourite piece, a captain's writing desk, which he kept in his study. Fine lace curtains framed by subtle summer floral print drapes, adorned each of the quaint small square paned windows in the cottage, adding the finishing touches to its authentic and all together picturesque appearance. In fact the only items of fixtures and fittings in his cottage that reflected modern life, disturbing the otherwise perfect period tableau, where his gas range, fridge and washing machine in the kitchen, a small TV in the living room and his computer equipment in his study, which functioned as his own private office. He even had an old antique, squeaky, wooden swivel chair to sit at his captain's desk and view the panoramic landscape from his window, which stretched for miles and miles. He had never brought guests back to his cottage before, except for his closest friend Professor Fraser Hughes, who would occasionally burn the midnight oil with him and share his indulgence of fine aged single malt Scottish whisky. They would while a way the hours in front of his roaring log fire, sharing memories and stories of their homeland in western Scotland until the soporific effect of the flickering flames in the fireplace sent them drifting off to sleep.

"How long til we get there?" asked Liz.

"About thirty minutes. Don't worry, you'll be fine......I promise." Iain replied reassuringly.

Liz sat nervously beside him in the backseat, unsure of where she was going and uncertain of what was immediately in store for them. As she looked out of the window of the taxi and watched the stars sparkle in the night sky, she recollected the events of that day which had begun so mundanely, but which had now escalated into something extraordinary. She could sense that there was more trouble to come and that perhaps that night would be the longest one of her life. Looking down at herself, covered with dirt and her dress badly ripped, with her shaking pale white fingers, she tried to pull the pieces of her torn bodice back together in a sorry and futile attempt to undo the damage that had been done. As the full impact of the evening's events revisited her, and she saw the image of her attacker's obliterated face, her whole body began to shiver and the river of silent tears cascaded down her pallid and drawn cheeks.

Iain looked across at Liz sitting next to him, her formerly serene and majestic appearance reduced to rags and his face suddenly changed from a calm thoughtful look to one of deeply serious concern. Feeling her limp clammy palms and her racing pulse, he realised that she was going into shock.

"Driver! Put your foot down! It's an emergency! I'm a doctor and I need to get this lady back to my house quickly!"

"Yes, sir," drawled the taxi driver as he glanced into his rear view mirror with a smirk, until he saw Iain's angry face leering back at him.

"I meant what I said! Now move it!" yelled Iain.

Immediately, the taxi driver floored the accelerator pedal and sped off along the winding country roads towards the cottage. Iain pulled Liz gently towards him, wrapping himself around her to warm her and comfort her.

It wasn't long before the taxi slowed down and took the right hand turn to drive up to Meadow Cottage, Iain's home. Just ahead of them, further up the lane on the left, they could just make out the entrance to the cottage. A large opening in the dry stone wall marked the beginning of the driveway leading into the small enclosed gravel parking bay in front of his home. A small winding river bubbled gently along the boundary of the property and four majestic ducks huddled together along the bank side next to the small stone foot bridge that crossed the river. Another two ducks sat quietly sleeping on the opposite bank, as they arrived.

Climbing out of the car, Iain paid the driver before carefully lifting Liz out of the backseat and into his arms. Within seconds, the taxi had disappeared down the lane on its return trip back to York, leaving Iain standing in the gravel driveway with Liz unconscious in his arms. Looking like refugees from a major battle, Iain carried Liz up the garden path to the front door, and after a little precarious manoeuvring, managed to retrieve his key from his pocket and unlock the front door. The solid oak door creaked, as Iain pushed it open to reveal a low narrow hallway. Stepping carefully inside, he pushed the door closed behind them, with his back and carried Liz up the hall way and into the living room.

Placing her gently on the sofa in front of the fireplace, he set to, to light the fire then fetched a warm blanket to cover Liz. Lifting her carefully and swaddling her in the blanket, Iain ran off to the kitchen to fetch a glass of water. Then sitting on the edge of the sofa with Liz resting in his arms, he dripped the water gradually into her mouth and swept the matted dirty hair from her face. It didn't matter to him what she looked like, she was there, in his arms at last and nothing and no one would ever take her away from him again.

After a few minutes, Iain felt her pulse, and satisfied himself that the worst had passed and she would be okay. Then resting back against the arm of the sofa and gently stroking her brow with his fingers, he watched the flames flickering in the fireplace until his eyelids, heavy with fatigue, closed softly and he drifted off to sleep.

A couple of hours passed before Liz's eyes flickered open to see the dying red glow of the embers in the fireplace. With a vague recollection of having been seated in a taxi, she deduced that she must be in Iain's cottage. Gazing slowly around her before carefully sitting up, in the pale moonlight that streamed through the living room window, she could just make out the general quaint features of the room. Then, she realised she had been resting against Iain who was just beginning to open his eyes, stirring from his sleep.

"Hey," he sighed softly. "How are you feeling? You had me worried for a minute there."

"Is this your house?" she asked.

"Yes. I carried you here from the taxi," he replied. "You were out cold, so I brought you in here to warm you up, "he added. "Feeling better?"

"Stunned, wiped out…"

"That's only to be expected. You've had a hell of a shock! Just take it easy and try to rest." Iain suggested sympathetically.

"I know it's late but is there any chance I can get cleaned up?" she asked. "I feel dirty and uncomfortable."

"Yeh, sure. The bathroom is just along the end of the hall and up the stairs…You can't miss it." He informed her. "Are you sure you can manage okay?" Iain asked concerned.

"I think so."

"If you need a hand, just give me a shout. In the meantime, I'll find some clothes for you to change into…." He said. "And how would you like a nice warm glass of mulled wine to warm you through," he asked.

"Sounds lovely……..I've only ever drank mulled wine at Christmas."

"That's what most people usually do……..But I'm not most people, as you can probably gather …I love spontaneity …..and I love challenges and adventure ……I'm that sort of man," reaching out to touch her hand as she carefully rose to her feet.

"I think I guessed that," she replied, watching him as he stood up in front of her. Then, carefully brushing her tousled dirty hair aside, Iain lifted her chin gently, and this time Liz was ready. Whoever he was, Liz was deeply intrigued and she wanted to know more about him. As he pressed his mouth to hers, she looped her arms around his neck and felt his excitement.

"Thank you," she whispered as their lips parted.

"What for?" he asked softly.

"For saving my life," Liz smiled.

"You're welcome," he replied. "A friend in need is a friend indeed."

"But we're more than friends, aren't we?" Liz asked. "I can feel a bond between us. What is it Iain? I don't know you and yet I can feel your closeness, like we share a secret. It's not just what will happen in our future, is it? We've shared a past together too, haven't we?"

Iain dropped his gaze.

"Perhaps there is something in what you say, but I cannot tell you. There are some things you need to find the answers to yourself. All I can say is this. Be patient. I don't know exactly when it will happen, but you'll find your answer soon."

Puzzled by his statement, Liz smiled and made her way up the bathroom, which stood just at the top of the stairs. It was quite a small room, just large enough to accommodate a bath with a shower, a toilet, a sink and a small cupboard for storing towels and toiletries. Standing on the soft deeply piled rug next to the bath, she peeled off her still sodden and muddy dress and let it fall to the floor in a tattered heap around her ankles. Stepping out from the centre of the heap, she looked at her reflection in the bathroom mirror briefly and gently stroked the cuts in her skin caused by the knife blade, before proceeding to patiently remove the plethora of hairpins that remained beneath her tousled curls. Then pulling the cord to switch on the shower above the bath, she stepped into the cold tub and allowed the powerful warm jets of water to clean and massage her body. Taking a drop or two from the shampoo bottle that stood on the edge of the bath, she carefully massaged it into her dirty matted hair, sending a scurry of soil particles and tiny twigs plummeting to the bottom of the bath. The dirty water pooled at her feet as she frantically scrubbed at the dirt under her nails and rinsed the shampoo from her hair. Even when she was satisfied that she was thoroughly clean, flashbacks of her attackers hands on her body set her scrubbing again.

A short time later, she heard a light tap on the bathroom door which made her jump.

"Liz?....Are you okay in there?"

"I'm fine, thanks," she replied.

"I've got some clean clothes for you…I'll leave them just outside the door."

"Thank you…"

"Don't mention it."

As she heard Iain's soft footfalls descending the stairs again, Liz stepped out of the bath and relished the softness of the large white bath sheet she placed around herself. Opening the bathroom door, she looked down to see a neatly stacked pile of clothes consisting of a soft white cotton shirt; a pair of jeans; a white t-shirt and a pair of white sports socks. Selecting the long white t-shirt, she put on her underwear and donned the shirt, before gathering the remaining items in her arms and depositing them in the guest bedroom which was next to the bathroom. Then spying a bathrobe that hung on the back of the bedroom door, she put it on and made her way back downstairs.

"The living room is just to your left…"announced Iain from the kitchen as he heard Liz stepping carefully down the stairs. "Make yourself at home."

Liz did as she was bid and re-entered the living room which ran the full length of the house. Now that Iain had switched on the small ornate wall lamps, Liz could see clearly that a small bay window overlooked the front of the cottage and the driveway, whilst another square bay window at the rear, incorporating a cushioned window seat, overlooked

154

the small hedged garden at the back and the fields beyond that. The cottage had all the trade marks of a quaint country dwelling. There was an open fireplace with a stone hearth for burning logs. Small plump cushioned sofas stood centrally in the room facing the fireplace and chintzy summer print curtains hung at the small paned windows. Liz sat down on one of the sofas and waited patiently for Iain to return. Two or three minutes later, he materialised, significantly cleaner too and wearing fresh casual clothes. In his right hand he carried a warm earthenware jug containing the sweet warm mulled wine and in the other hand he carried two large wine goblets.

"Here you go…..This'll soon warm you up," he said as he filled a goblet with the wine and handed it to Liz, before filling one for himself. "I'll just set the fire going again… and we'll soon be as warm as toast."

Liz cupped the goblet with both hands and carefully sipped the warmed spiced wine. Fruit and cinnamon flavours drifted across her palate, comforting her with happy memories of childhood Christmases back at home, whilst Iain placed the logs and tinder in the grate and lit the fire. Sitting on the floor, back from the hearth, Iain scrutinised the fire carefully watching the flames engulf the tinder before they began to ignite the logs. Placing a fine mesh guard in front of the fire, Iain sat upright with his goblet of wine and took a sip. Leaning against the front of the sofa and looking up at Liz, he said:

"Why don't you sit down here next to me….nearer the fire?"

Liz smiled in response, and glided gracefully from the sofa down on to the rug in front of the hearth. It wasn't long until the fire became well established, and they sat in silence, mesmerised by its display, as they sipped their wine. Occasionally, Liz glanced up at Iain, but he was lost,

lost deep in the flames as his eyes reflected their glow. He seemed a million miles away though she was right there by his side.

Finishing the last soothing drops in the bottom of her goblet, Liz pulled her knees up to her chest and rested her chin on her knees.

"Do you think anybody followed us here from the ball?" She asked.

"Good question."

Iain stood up and went across to the window overlooking the front of the house. The moon shone down on the enclosed driveway, it's light bouncing off the slightly wet gravel, causing it to glisten like a myriad of scattered coins. Not a soul stirred, and even the gentle cooing of the roosting ring doves had long since fallen silent in the darkness. Satisfied that they were alone, Iain turned away from the window and watched for a moment, the tantalising shadows from the flames as they danced over Liz. Her wet hair hung straight down her back, and as she turned to look across the room towards him, the moonlight through the window caught the crisp blueness of her eyes. Even though she sat huddled in his oversized bathrobe, to Iain she looked exquisite in the firelight.

"Is there something wrong?" she asked.

"No.....there's nothing wrong at all." He answered and strolled over towards her.

Re-seating himself beside her, they each tried to say something but couldn't. There were so many questions and so many more answers they wanted to exchange. Then looking at Liz, Iain looked deeply into her eyes and asked,

"Are you sure you're ready for this?"

Liz nodded.

"Okay. I'll take it one step at a time. I'll tell you what I can, then you can tell me about your projection to the future, "he began. "I am Iain Sinclair, psychology Professor. I'm also a lot of other things too! I'm a doctor, a teacher, a writer…… in fact I have a whole string of different qualifications."

"But how's that possible? It takes years to become a doctor… a teacher and you only look…." Liz stopped mid sentence as she looked at him in the glow from the fire. "You did look as though you were in your mid to late thirties …..but now, unless I need glasses, you look younger," Liz concluded. "None of this makes sense."

"How old do you think I am?" he asked.

"Now, I would say…late twenties?" she suggested.

"And you'd be way off!" he answered.

"You're not going to tell me that you've found some secret to eternal youth and your three hundred years old," she said.

"292 actually," he whispered.

"What is?" she asked.

"My age."

Liz looked at him sharply.

"That's not funny. Tell me the truth!" she frowned.

"I'm serious."

Liz's mouth dropped open and she quickly began to work out the mathematics in her head.

"You're not really trying to tell me that you were born in 1718? That's not humanly possible! How can it be possible?" she asked disbelievingly.

"With your help," he whispered in her ear.

Liz's eyes widened with shock and surprise.

"You've already witnessed it for yourself, this evening," Iain added.

Liz shook her head, "I don't know what you mean?"

"Yes you do. When you touched my face in that green mist, you saw my face change didn't you? You saw the years magically drop away?"

Gasping with surprise she exclaimed,
"How the hell did you know that?"

"I'll get to that in a minute," Iain replied. "Your projection is pure electromagnetic energy which is only visible at a certain frequency. You can generate that frequency through your thoughts and when you project, you usually project into another person's thoughts but sometimes you project externally, like you did earlier on. When you project externally, you focus on your target so that their subconscious thoughts are tuned into that frequency too, so that only they can see your image and hear your voice. As for the green mist, it's an electrical aura that only appears to occur when you and I meet, and you externally project. It's a kind of electromagnetic anomaly resulting from our two bodily fields coming into contact with each other. At least, that's what my friend Fraser has concluded."

"Your friend?"

"Yes. Professor Fraser Hughes is an eminent scientist who works at the university. He and I studied together and we've known each other for years. It's with his help, we managed to work out how you do what you do," explained Iain. "Anyway, as I was saying, when the mist occurs and our fields converge, if you make direct contact with me, the highly charged electrons from your projection zap my cells and restore their programming, effectively rejuvenating my entire body!"

Iain paused. He could see the look of utter perplexity on Liz's face as she sat staring at him.

"I did warn you it would be a little tricky to explain, and I know it's a lot to take in," he added defensively.

"So," Liz eventually began. "If I understand you correctly, you're 292 years old and I'm responsible for the rejuvenation that has kept you alive this long."

"Good girl! That's right, you've got it!" Iain smiled.

"Hang on! To do that, I would have to travel back in time to rejuvenate you!" Liz concluded.

"And your point is?"

"You're not serious! Time travel's not possible, is it?" she exclaimed shaking her head.

"I'm afraid it is! I'm living proof of that, ask Professor Hughes! He's compared my DNA to those of his students and I'm more or less eight generations short of a full tree, if you pardon my expression," he explained. "With every generation, more information is added and carried by your genetic DNA. It's like an autobiographical personal genetic history book going back to the origin of man himself."

"I'm still not convinced," she said.

"Then how would we know all this about you?" asked Iain. "What other explanation is there?"

"I don't know. What I do know is I haven't ever visited the past!"

"You've visited the future though, you said so," remarked Iain. "You said that you were there in the future when you met me. So, you should be able to accept that the opposite is also possible, for you at least. Why don't you tell me, what happened?"

"We were trapped in a mine somewhere. There was water flooding the mine and explosions going off deeper down the shafts. You rescued me and brought me back to the surface. There were guards chasing us and then they just vanished. That's all I remember."

As a few more pieces of the puzzle began to slot into place, the timeline quivered excitedly.

"Interesting," remarked Iain. "I can't figure out why we would be at the bottom of a mine, but I'm sure we'll find out why soon!"

"So if I don't remember meeting you before, that means

that these trips into the past haven't happened yet, doesn't it?" asked Liz.

Iain nodded.

"And are you saying that I always travel back to you?" she asked curiously.

"I believe so. You've certainly never mentioned any trips to meet anyone else, except my mother."

"Your mother?"

"Maybe I shouldn't be saying these things to you….. it might change things. But yes, on the day I was born, I know now that it was you who came to visit her to save her and my father from some evil man. If you hadn't been there to stop him, we'd have all been killed," said Iain.

"How do you know all this?" Liz asked.

"My mother would often tell me the tale as a child, to warn me of the dangers lurking out there on the hillside. She spoke of a beautiful blue eyed angel like spirit who saved my father from the brink of death and my mother too. My mother called her my guardian angel and she was right. Whenever I've been about to face evil or danger, you've arrived with the storm clouds, just like the ones that appeared earlier this evening when you warned me on the veranda. The storm clouds seem to be linked to your projection," Iain explained. "They're like your trademark or signature. Oh, yes. I meant to mention. You've never physically travelled to the past. It's your thought projection that travels, whilst you stay here in the present."

"Has Fraser worked out why I'm drawn to you like that?" she asked.

"Not yet. He thinks that there's probably a major piece to this puzzle which we haven't come across yet, that might help us find that answer."

Then, as Liz stared into his dark brown and honey golden eyes she asked.

"Why are you helping me?"

"Because I want to and I think I was meant to," Iain replied.

Liz leaned back against the edge of the sofa mulling over everything he said.

"You sound so convincing," Liz said at length.

"That's because every single word I've told you, is the truth, even if it is, I admit, one hell of a hard pill to swallow!"

"Do you think it has anything to do with why somebody wants me killed?" Liz asked curiously.

"It might be, but I can't see any links to it at the moment. There's only you, me and Fraser who know about it. That policeman who you said, brought you down here, he doesn't know that you can project does he?"

"I don't think I mentioned it. I only mentioned that I had the accidents as a kid and that I can read thoughts, "recalled Liz.

"Hmmn. We'll need to draw up a plan to get you somewhere safe until we can figure this all out," said Iain thoughtfully.

"Is there anything else I need to know?" she asked.

"I would have thought that was more than enough for now!" replied Iain. "I daren't give you any more details about each of your visits to me in case you change what happened and it causes some kind of paradox. We have to be really careful. That's why I couldn't say anything before, until you'd been able to draw some natural conclusions for yourself."

Gently pushing himself up from the floor, Iain stood up and made his way towards the door of the living room.

"Hungry?" he asked as he turned for a moment to look back at her.

"A little."

"I'll be back in a couple of minutes." He replied.

Liz sat alone in front of the fire trying to understand the conundrum of their situation. She had so many pieces of the puzzle bouncing around inside her head yet very few of them seemed to fit together, or make sense. Could this have really all stemmed from a silly little electrical accident at school? How had she connected with Iain? Were her future visits back into his past controlled or was there some other factor they hadn't come across yet that was the key to her whole situation?

Quickly and quietly she got to her feet and looked around the room. There had to be something here that might give her a clue, she thought. Slowly walking around, she gazed at the paintings on the wall and the ornaments above the fireplace and on the shelves, but nothing remarkable jumped out at her. Suddenly she had an idea. Walking over to the wall mounted bookcases she began to browse along the titles. There were no paperbacks or magazines only hardback novels. He possessed quite a significant collection of classic literature and poetry but nothing less than sixty years old. The music on the other hand contained quite a mixture of classical through to modern, rhapsodies through to rock, Albinoni through to ZZ Top. The room itself was cosy and comfortable, a tranquil sanctuary away from the rat race of the city. But something was gnawing at her, something so obvious. She tried to think what could be missing. Finding a small picture frame tucked away towards the back of a dresser, she spotted a fairly recent photograph of Iain standing next to Professor Hughes, whom she recognised from the 'wall of fame' in her faculty reception area. That was it! She thought to herself as the penny dropped. There were no family photographs anywhere in that room. He had no evidence of having a family history. He could have been an orphan, she considered then dismissed, shaking her head.

She couldn't imagine Iain as an orphan. He seemed pretty strong spirited and stable.

"I'm not a bad person, you know…" Liz jumped and turned to see Iain standing in the doorway, carrying a tray of sandwiches and hot coffee. Liz flushed red with embarrassment.

"I know you're not, it's just I have so many unanswered questions and I need to understand what connects us and why we've been brought together like this. I know this sounds crazy, especially when I read palms, but I don't believe in all that mystic stuff. I've always believed that there's a rational explanation for most things," Liz replied. "I just had a sudden thought that maybe there was a clue here. Perhaps something that provides that tangible connection between us. I have to find that connection! I really can't accept that all of this is about me! I've never been important in my life! So how come this happened to me?" Liz asked desperately, as she stood in the centre of the room gazing anxiously at Iain. "I'm scared Iain! Really scared! What's happening to me?"

Iain placed the tray down on the coffee table and dashed over to where Liz was standing. Wrapping his arms around her, he pressed her head gently against his chest and kissed her hair as he rocked her softly like a mother soothing her infant.

"I'm sorry," he whispered gently. "I shouldn't have told you."

"That would have just made me more suspicious of you, and you're right I do need to trust someone and I don't want to be alone right now!" she said as she looked up into his concerned eyes. As she gazed at him despairingly, comforted by his protective embrace, Iain smiled softly. Having waited centuries for this moment, Iain savoured every precious second of their time together, like they were rare priceless diamonds, and just like diamonds, she needed protection from everyone, including himself, who sought to exploit her abilities or vulnerabilities.

As he calmly released her from his embrace, he could see a look of hurt and confusion on her pretty tear stained face.

"Come and have something to eat," he said softly.

The smell of richly roasted coffee teased her nose as Iain led her gently back to the fireplace. Sitting down on the rug in front of the fire, Iain beckoned to her to join him. Like an embarrassed school girl, she sat next to him quietly, munching on the chicken sandwiches he'd freshly made for them whilst pondering his self restraint.

"Are they okay for you?" he asked.

"Mmmmn," she nodded, with her mouth full.

"Are you okay?" Iain whispered softly.

"I'm sorry….I.."

"Look! No more apologies. I think we've both said plenty for one evening. We've both been through the mill, so let's not be too hard on ourselves, okay?" replied Iain.

For a few minutes, they sat eating sandwiches and drinking coffee before Liz asked,

"So you know Professor Hughes?"

"Yes. He's a very good friend of mine. He's a very clever man," Iain replied. "That's him in the photograph you were looking at."

"Yeh, I recognised him. I've seen his photo before in the faculty building," Liz replied.

"He lacks one or two social skills, but that's due to his research and many years of academic study. Like most scientists, it's made him a bit eccentric but, once you get past that, he's really a great guy."

"What does he specialise in?" Liz asked curiously.

"He's currently working on experiments to prove

whether the theory that the past, present and future exist together is correct," Iain replied. "It's still very much a paper theory at the moment but, you might be able to shed some light on one or two things. At the very least, you could point him in the right direction. I know he'll have lots of questions himself."

"This is a lovely cottage," she remarked. "Have you lived here long?"

"Since I graduated." He replied.

"Have you thought about moving back up to Scotland, back home?"

"Too many memories."

Liz sensed the tension in his voice and dropped the subject.

"Can you tell me anything about your past? Your childhood? Your life before all this?" she asked. "I'd really love to know, especially if you are 292 years old. You've been alive since before the start of the industrial revolution. You've experienced the impact of every technological change up to now!"

Iain lifted his head and looked at Liz. The reflection of the flames from the fire, danced playfully across his face.

"I'm sorry. Fraser's given me strict instructions not to tell you anything significant about my past. It's too risky."

"Can't you even tell me normal everyday things about yourself? Like what's your favourite colour? What food do you like?"

She reached out and gently stroked the side of his face. His skin was soft and smooth like velvet. He wrapped his hand around hers and coveted her touch for a moment before shaking off his worry and frustration and breaking into a broad smile.

"Green. I like green, especially dark green. It reminds me of the trees back home. As for food, it has to be French with plenty of garlic and wine and of course good company. What else would you like to know?"

"Can I ask a personal question?"

"Aahh! Now we're getting to it." Iain remarked.

"Relationships? I'd expect during the past three centuries you've had quite a few."

"Of course I have.........I wouldn't be a true passionate Scotsman if I didn't!" he proclaimed. "Like I said before, I'm no monk but I'm no gigolo either."

"I know you said before that you haven't been married. But have you ever loved someone?" Liz asked curiously.

Iain thought for a moment, reflecting on the few occasions he succumbed to female affection.

"Like I said, I've met one or two women in my time but never anyone special enough that I wanted to marry. There were one or two who even proposed to me, but I said no," Iain replied.

"Do you mind me asking why?"

"I had my reasons."

"Didn't you love any of them?" asked Liz.

Iain looked straight into her eyes with a seriousness that surprised her.

"What do you think?" he answered with eyes sparkling impishly back at her.

"I know you said you can't tell me about anything that happened when I visited you, but can you at least tell me about our relationship? Were we friends …. or lovers perhaps?"

Iain dropped his gaze.

"Don't. You know I can't tell you anything."

"You don't have to. I can read it in your face," she replied. "We did have a relationship didn't we?" she asked, determined to understand his side of the relationship.

"I can't…."

"Why can't you tell me? It's in your past, and you can't affect it." she asked insistently.

"But you can!"

Liz searched the depths of his eyes for clues. She knew there was a lot more to all this, and she could sense it too, a deep, deep wound of enduring pain. "You must be able to tell me at least, how you've been able to survive all these years without a wife or family. Something must have motivated you to keep going this long. If we're going to face the future together, in some capacity, I just want to be able to understand who you are. You seem to know quite a lot about me. Can you blame me for wanting to know about you too?"

"Yes, I'd agree with you normally, but ours is not a normal relationship as such. I've probably told you too much already and we may yet suffer the consequences for that," he replied carefully. "In this relationship, there have to be rules not just to protect us but anyone and anything connected to us. Time is a fragile thing."

"But you're the living hypocrisy of that. You shouldn't exist outside of your normal life span. Any serious damage to 'time' has already been done. What difference is it going to make if you do tell me about our past?"

"It's complicated."

"How complicated can it be? Or are you worried that I might not accept what's happening. Are you worried that it might change the way I feel about you?" she asked. Then looking deep into his eyes and sensing his inner grief and fear, she sighed deeply. "That's it isn't it? You're afraid you might lose me, that I might reject you, even when everything you know about me tells you otherwise."

"Free will," said Iain. "We should always have the freedom to make our own choices whatever they are. I won't take away your right to make up your own mind, by saying something that you might feel obliged to live up to or to change, "said Iain nobly.

"How do you know that my choice hasn't already been made?"

"People ask questions to help them make decisions and choices. Whilst you're still asking questions, whilst you're still finding answers, the jury is still out. "

"Then help me. Tell me what I need to know so I can make my choice."

"I can't. At least not yet anyway," Iain replied. "You're just going to have to trust me on that."

"Okay," she sighed. "I take your point. I just hope I find out soon."

Liz nodded respectfully.

"Anyway, on a lighter note, how are you feeling now?" asked Iain. "A bit calmer perhaps? Is my Scottish charm working on you yet?" he grinned broadly.

"Mmmmmn."

"Is that the best you can do?"

Liz stifled a laugh.

"What's so funny?"

"I'm sorry.......I just had the funniest vision of you wearing a kilt!.......Although, …..if you don't mind me saying…..I imagine you'd carry a kilt off quite well!"

"I look absolutely fantastic in a kilt, I'll have you know!......If it's good enough for Mel Gibson…. it's good enough for me!" He declared, then added, "Wait here……..I won't be a minute."

With that, Iain dashed out of the living room and Liz heard the padding of his feet on the stairs, as he dashed up to his bedroom. There were sounds of wardrobe doors being opened and boxes being moved, a few moments of relative quiet, then Liz heard the padding of his feet again, as he came back down the stairs.

"So,….what do you think?"

Iain stood in the doorway of the living room wearing his Sinclair tartan kilt accompanied with a plain white open-necked Ghillie shirt.

"I wear this on special occasions…..It's the Sinclair tartan……well, one of them anyway…there are several… but I always prefer this one.."

With his rich brown hair, trim tall figure and shapely legs, he cut quite a dashing image dressed in his kilt.

"Come on now…don't be shy! What do you think?"

"I have to admit…..you look…. very smart, sexy even."

Iain grinned broadly.

"I'm sorry….I have to ask…"

"They always do…….."

"And…"

"Officially….yes….I do wear it in the traditional way……sometimes." He admitted. "It can be ….quite a liberating experience……It can also be damned draughty and itchy too!"

They both burst out laughing as Iain sat down beside her carefully, to avoid embarrassment. Then wrapping her arm around his, they sat and watched the fire together exchanging funny inconsequential stories from their past. Liz couldn't help but smile. Iain was really trying hard to distract her from recent events, and he was succeeding rather well, too. The trauma of that evening seemed only a distant memory now, as she focussed her attentions on Iain. She had woken that morning, alone and uncertain. Now, here she was, comfortable and at home with a man that she felt truly comfortable with for the first time in her life. He seemed to know just the right things to say to her, and he had so many wonderful and funny stories, tales of everyday life which he knew posed no paradoxical threat. In some ways, she didn't mind that he couldn't tell her about the important moments in his life. Those events he had to keep secret added an air of mystery to him which Liz found quite intriguing and captivating.

Suddenly the antique wall clock struck two.

"Is that the time?" he asked surprised. "You need some rest! Your bedchamber awaits m'lady!" he announced.

"Thank you kind sir," she chirped as she stood up and followed him out of the room and up the stairs.

Taking her to the door next to the bathroom, Iain pushed it open and announced, "This is the guest room. You should be okay in here, but if there's anything you need at all, I'm just across the landing."

For a moment they stood in the doorway of the bedroom looking at each other, unsure how to part company. Then, smiling softly she jumped up on to the tips of her toes and kissed him softly, before whispering, 'goodnight' and 'thank you.'

Iain watched silently as she stepped into the bedroom and slowly closed the door behind her. Then leaning backwards against it, she closed her eyes, sensing his presence on the other side of the door. She knew, from his thoughts and the way he kissed her that he wanted her, and, in all honesty to herself, she felt strangely fascinated by him. Something about him made her heart race whenever he was there, and it was racing now, certain that he would knock on the door and invite himself in. Iain stood on the other side of the door, certain that she would open it again and that his gentlemanly resolve would falter. Climbing into the guest bed, no sooner had her head touched the pillow, than Liz was asleep. Iain placed his hand softly on her door, cursing the overwhelming sense of duty and honour that prevented him from walking into her room and seducing her. But, knowing their current situation and the infancy of their relationship from her perspective, Iain, turned away from the door and left Liz to rest peacefully, heading across the landing to his own room.

CHAPTER 10

THE BEDROOM WAS DARK AND quiet, with only the light rustling of the trees outside breaking the silence of that balmy summer's night. Dreaming wishfully that Iain was there beside her, Liz hugged the spare pillow tightly, as she drifted into a deep sleep. Meanwhile, Iain lay awake, staring at the ceiling, consoling himself that he had done the right thing but praying for the time when he could reveal all his secrets to Liz. Slowly, the resultant fatigue of the evening's events closed his tired eyes, and he fell into a tormented sleep.

"Liz." From the depths of her tranquil slumber she heard the faint whisper of her name being called. "Liz." The whisper was a little louder and the voice seemed familiar to her. Was she dreaming the voice, she thought or was it real? Her eyes flickered open. The room around her was still dark and undisturbed. But then, as her eyes adjusted to the darkness, she could just make out a tall dark silhouette standing in the shadows. Her eyes opened wide, and she tried to remember quickly where she was. The silhouette came closer, until the moonlight caught the profile of his face.

"Steve?" she asked disbelievingly. "What are you doing here?"

"I came to warn you."

"What's happened? …..How did you find me?" asked Liz.

"Someone broke into my office two days ago, and stole

172

my laptop which I kept locked away in my filing cabinet.....
The laptop held encrypted files containing emails and
transcribed statements from everyone who was interviewed
in connection with your attacker......including emails
backwards and forwards to Grant Sloane who works for
university security."

"So that's who was keeping an eye on things?" she
answered.

"He retired from the force a couple of years back, when
he moved down to York.....He's a good friend... and a good
man to have as back up in tricky situations.......So I got in
touch with him and asked him to be discreet....... He's also
licensed to carry a gun."

"So what happened after you'd discovered the laptop
had gone?"

"I got straight on to Grant and asked him to step up
the surveillance until I could get here........He was at the
Ball.......He saw what happened."

"Then why the hell didn't he make himself known to
us?" she asked crossly. "We could have done with some
help......especially when we were pinned down by some
assassin who happened to shoot the guy Iain fought off."

"Grant was better off where he was.........He wouldn't
be able to protect you if they knew he was there and they
knew who he was..."

"Hold on......... Are you trying to say that this Grant
shot the guy who grabbed me.......Shot him clean through
the back of the head?"

"Yes."

Liz shivered.

"In fact, he's patrolling the perimeter as we speak.........
They'll be here soon...That's why we need to leave right
now!"

Suddenly, the bedroom door flew open to reveal Iain

standing in the doorway, wearing only a pair of black boxer shorts and brandishing a cricket bat.

"Leave her alone!" he bellowed. "I warn you, I'm lethal with this thing!"

"I've got no doubts about that!" replied Steve. "You might want to keep it handy."

"It's okay Iain! Iain meet Detective Inspector Steve Alexander. Steve meet…."

"Professor Iain Sinclair, if I'm not mistaken."

"Do police inspectors normally make house calls in the middle of the night? Do I know you?" asked Iain, still half asleep.

"No we've never met and I'm sorry for barging in like this, but Grant has kept me up to speed with all of Liz's contacts. You did a good job at the ball. Anyone would think you'd had some training in urban combat."

"Hmmn. So why are you here?" asked Iain.

"As I've just explained to Liz, trouble is on the way and we need to evacuate now! Get your clothes on and grab what you need quickly!"

"Where are we going?" asked Iain suspiciously.

"There's no time to explain now. I'll tell you later. We must get going now!"

Iain and Liz looked at each other, stunned by the harsh reality of their situation and the sudden escalation of events. As Liz looked to Iain for guidance, he spotted the small pile of clothes he'd fished out for Liz and tossed them to her, on the bed.

"Get dressed."

Liz looked momentarily at Steve, who coughed politely and turned his back to allow her to slip into her clothes. Iain dashed to his room and grabbed some jeans, a shirt, a jacket and his trainers and proceeded to put them on. As he waited, Steve looked out of the bedroom window carefully and caught a quick flash of a mirror near the entrance to the driveway.

"We need to move now! There's no time!....Follow me!"

With that, Steve vaulted across the room, closely followed by Liz. Iain met them on the landing, whilst still trying to fasten his shirt.

"How'd you get in?"

"Bathroom window......That's the way we're leaving!"

Rushing into the bathroom, Steve indicated to them to keep low and keep quiet. The bathroom window was open and they could see a narrow rope suspended from the top of the drainpipe above the window, down to the ground. Pointing to Iain, Steve indicated for him to climb out of the window first, followed by Liz. Iain nodded in acknowledgement and proceeded to climb on to the windowsill before leaning out of the window to grab the rope.

Holding the rope tightly, he turned to look at both of them before abseiling slowly down to the ground. Once he was on the grass, Iain looked back up towards the bathroom window and gave the thumbs up to Liz, who was peering down at him. Liz climbed up on to the sill, and copying Iain's actions, trying not to look down, she carefully lowered herself to the ground. As she neared the ground, Iain reached up to support her.

Suddenly, they heard an almighty crash as the front door burst open, and several armed men stormed into the cottage. Steve quickly climbed out of the window and dropped to the ground. As the three of them huddled in the darkness against the back of the cottage, a dark shadow emerged from the hedge and beckoned towards them. Keeping low and quiet, Liz, Steve and Iain dived into the hedge after Grant and followed him through the tight mesh of branches and through into the field on the far side.

Sticking close to the hedge, Grant led the small group along the edge of the field and into the woods. Once they had ventured past the third row of trees and were unobservable from the cottage, Grant stopped.

"About two miles from here, there's a small lake......"

"Yes, "acknowledged Iain. "I know it well......."

"On the far side of the lake is a small wooden jetty.....Behind the trees near the jetty, I've stashed a four by four.......It's loaded with gear.....Here's a map of the area, " he announced, pulling a small rectangular sheet of folded paper from his pocket along with a small torch. Shining the torch on to the map, he pointed out the direction they needed to take. "Once we get to the car, we'll need to keep off the main road til we reach Stamford Bridge.....Then we can merge with the commuter and tourist traffic heading west bound into York..... If we follow the route I've marked out on the map, this will take us directly into the heart of York."

"Isn't that just a bit too public?" asked Iain.

"Not if you use the route I've worked out for you.... using the old Snickelways and ginnels..."

"Oh, you mean the secret passageways that run through the centre of York itself...." said Liz.

"Do you know something about them?...." asked Iain.

"Every summer, when I was a kid, my parents used to bring us into York and we'd explore the old Medieval streets and city walls."

"Once you've entered the Snickelways.....make your way down to the river at Bridge Street.....There's a boat waiting.....'The Blue Rose'.." instructed Grant.

"Unusual name for a boat," commented Liz curiously.

"It's a statement of improbability" answered Steve.

"Nice," remarked Iain. "Is that an indication of our likelihood of escape perhaps?"

Grant scowled at them impatiently.

"We need to move….." suggested Steve. "Grant…..You go on ahead…"

Grant nodded and trotted off stealthily through the trees.

Steve took the lead, with Liz and Iain immediately behind him. Creeping quickly through the woods, wary of straggling tree roots and all manner of treacherous obstacles in their path, they could just make out the first strains of daylight poking its way through the trees. The first rays of sunlight pierced the darkness like searchlights, casting an eerie misty glow through the heart of the woods. Liz noticed the beauty of the spiders' webs suspended from the trees and bushes, now made visible by the morning dew that had settled on their delicate strands. Tired but surprisingly undaunted by this new adventure, she placed her life and her implicit trust in the three men who now accompanied her.

The floor of the woods was damp and soft under foot as they beat their way through tall ferns and bracken towards the distant lake. Small animals, startled by the moderate disturbance of tramping feet, darted away from them in every direction. Liz jumped as she suddenly heard the gentle rapid knocking of a distant woodpecker attacking the bark of a tree. Though the lake was just less than two miles away, their journey seemed to last forever and was fraught with obstacle after obstacle. Eventually, in the distance, they could just make out a broad band of light stretching out ahead of them, as they neared the clearing and the lake.

Entering the clearing, Liz, Iain and Steve marvelled at the almost heavenly shaft of sunshine that shone down on to the lake, creating a gold and white misty mirage above the surface of the water. Flying insects of various sizes and shapes, including beautiful neon blue dragonflies, filled the air in the centre of the clearing. Fragrant flowering bushes around the edges of the lake, cast their flowery boughs upon the rich dark water, as if offering their blooms to the mystical water nymphs occupying the murky depths. Only now, standing near the edge of the lake, could they hear the chirpy dawn chorus of the early rising birds, previously deadened by the surrounding trees.

Grant signalled to them from across the lake to keep low, as they began to hear the rhythmic whirring and chugging of helicopter blades turning above the tree tops. Instinctively, they all dropped to the ground near the waters edge. In the distance, further back down the trail, they could see the movement of ferns and torches, in addition to hearing the sound of heavy feet tramping through the undergrowth towards them.

"They've found our trail…" said Steve. "We need to split up…..to confuse them…..I'll go eastwards and meet you near the jetty…… Iain, you take Liz and head west around the far side of the lake."

Nodding in agreement, they headed off around each side of the lake. The sound of the helicopter grew even louder, as it hovered over the clearing, sending animals and birds scurrying into the safer darkness of the woods.

Taking Liz's hand, Iain led her through the trees and bushes, unaware of their proximity to the water's edge. A small inlet lay just ahead of them, obscured by the long grass, bushes and reeds. Suddenly the ground gave way beneath their feet, sending them plummeting into the cold murky water.

The water felt heavy and oily around them, tainted with tree tannin and various algae. The water was about four feet deep where they were, but the slippery mud and the complex matrix of tree roots and weeds coming up from the lake bed, made it almost impossible for them to keep their balance. Liz looked at Iain, wondering what to do.

"We'll hide in the centre of those reeds over there,..... right near the bank side.....and I know that this probably comes straight out of some old Hollywood film but,........ if we snap off a couple of the reeds....if they get too close, we can use them to breathe under the water..." suggested Iain. "But remember to keep your eyes tightly closed and don't swallow any of the water," warned Iain. "These lakes can contain poisonous algae. So be careful."

Shivering from the coldness of the water, she nodded, and together they made their way carefully into the reeds, nestling up to their chins in the water.

Suddenly they could feel and hear the dull thud of heavy boots running along the bank side above their heads. Iain held Liz close and placed the snapped reed in his mouth. Liz followed suit, and descended below the water. Even though the water deadened the sounds above their heads, they could still feel the dull thuds of the military boots pounding along the bank side. Keeping her eyes tightly closed as instructed, they waited for the danger to pass. The acrid bitter taste of the water and the reed made her want to gag, until finally she couldn't bear it any longer and raised her face out of the water. She carefully wiped the water and mud from her face and eyes, and as she began to regain her visual focus, she looked through the reeds down to the far end of the lake where the jetty stood. She could just make out several dark figures grouped near the jetty. One was talking on a radio to someone whilst gesturing to the others to fan out through the woods. Iain surfaced beside her, and watched for a moment.

"Are you okay?" he whispered.

"Fine.......Nothing that a hot bath and a good scrub down couldn't fix..."

"They seem pretty desperate to find you," said Iain. "They must have found out something about you from the laptop.......something they're very interested in.......How much does Steve know?"

"Quite a bit......He knows about my mind reading but he doesn't know everything....."

"He doesn't know about your projections?"

"No..."

"Good......That means that they don't know either........ So we've still got an ace up our sleeve...."

"Do you think we can climb out yet?"

"No.......I think we should carefully make our way around to the jetty, keeping close to the bank side and the reeds...for cover.......We can't afford to take any chances."

"Okay...."

Seeing the last of the men disappear through the woods, Iain and Liz emerged from their hiding place in the reeds and waded slowly down towards the jetty. Grasping a thick dead tree branch, Iain pushed it just ahead of them, in case they needed to hide quickly. Holding on to his shoulder, Liz waded behind him, turning her head occasionally to look back, in case there were other armed men in the woods. As they drew near to the jetty, they heard the thud of feet on the bank side just above them. Grabbing Liz's hand, Iain dragged her quickly under the old wooden jetty, to hide.

Huddled in the cold darkness, Liz and Iain peered up through the split and rotten timbers of the jetty, to see who was there. Presently, two figures crouched on the bank side at the start of the jetty.

"Liz.... Iain .....Where are you?"

It was Steve.

"We're down here........Help us out..."

With that, Liz and Iain pulled themselves out from under the jetty and Steve grabbed Liz's hands to pull her up and out from her watery sanctuary. Grant moved alongside and helped Steve as they lifted her clear of the water. Then grabbing Iain's hands, they pulled him up on to the jetty.

"I hope you've got some spare dry clothes in that vehicle of yours?" enquired Iain.

"Yeh….there's some t-shirts and combats in the boot…….they'll do til we get you down to the boat."

Steve tried hard not to laugh as Liz and Iain stumbled off the jetty on to dry land, looking like rejects from a swamp monster movie. Liz looked down at her sorry state and sighed.

"Why is it, that since I've met you, we've been dragged through the mud, had our clothes torn and now we've been submerged in a quagmire. A roll in the hay would have done just fine for me!" grinned Iain wryly, as he looked at Liz.

"They say mud is good for your skin," he added. "But I'm not so sure about the twigs as hair accessories." They both chuckled.

"When we get out of this," began Liz. "You can treat me to a nice spa."

"Where did you go, Steve?" asked Iain.

"I hid underneath the bushes about a hundred yards away from here………It was a bit prickly…….my neck's ripped to pieces…but I'm okay." He replied. "I heard something splash in the water…"

"We fell in," said Liz.

"So I gather….."

Liz noticed the blood stains on Steve's shirt and examined his neck.

"We better get those cuts seen to…..or they could get nasty…..Is there a first aid kit in the boot as well?"

"There's some plasters and disinfectant in a tin in the glove compartment…….They've been there quite a while…"

"Anything's better than nothing…" she replied.

Just beyond the trees, surrounded by carefully placed leafy branches, the four by four stood camouflaged against unwanted prying eyes. Each of them helped to pull away the branches, then Grant opened up the boot. Pulling out a black duffle bag from the back of the boot, he undid the cord and rummaged around inside it.

"Here…..catch!"

With that he pulled out a couple of large plain black t-shirts, combat pants, and socks, and tossed them to Liz and Iain. Slowly Liz began to strip off her smelly, dirty and sodden shirt, exposing her naked wet skin from waist upwards, not caring about the attention she was drawing. Quickly, all three men turned away politely. After pulling on one of the t-shirts, she proceeded to remove the soaked trainers and socks from her feet, followed by the heavy water laden jeans. Pulling on the large pair of combat pants, she pulled the belt in tight.

Meanwhile, Iain had succeeded in stripping off his own wet and muddy clothes, before tossing them in the boot adjacent to Liz's cast offs. Pulling on the combat pants and t-shirt, Liz and Iain stood together like a pair of raw army recruits. Looking at each other for a second Iain broke into a wry smile.

"Looks good….Hey we could start a new trend….."

"You'll be less of a target in that gear…." remarked Grant. "…and with the way you two smell after being in that water…..if they send out any dogs after you…..they'll not be able to pick out your scent."

"Serendipity……" said Iain.

"More like 'bit wiffy'…." sniffed Steve.

"Look on the bright side, if it increases our chances of survival, I'm all for it!" acknowledged Iain. "I just wouldn't endorse it as my favourite cologne, if you catch my drift!"

"Oh we catch your drift alright…..Hand out the nose pegs Grant!" said Steve.

Locking up the boot, Grant made his way around to the driver's side door and climbed in.

"I think you two better climb in the back……They won't recognise us, if the vehicle is spotted…." directed Steve.

With that, Steve went around the far side of the four by four and climbed in the front passenger seat. Liz and Iain climbed in the back seat, and strapped themselves in, then, gripping the ceiling handles above each back seat door, they braced themselves for a bumpy ride.

"Hang on……this could be a rough …" announced Grant, as he turned the key in the ignition.

At the first turn of the key, nothing happened. Grant turned the key again. This time they all heard the faint sound of the engine clicking into action.

"Don't worry," said Grant. "The car's been standing for a couple of hours in the damp…..it should fire up in a second…"

As the key turned for a third time, they heard the clicking noise again……but this time, it wasn't the car…… Outside, standing by the driver's door, was one of the armed men…..cocking his weapon, ready to fire.

"Get out!"

They all looked at each for a moment, wondering what to do.

"Get out! Now!"

Liz leaned forward and whispered, "What are we going to do?"

"I don't think we've got a choice," said Iain quietly.

"Liz, try and distract him," directed Steve.

"You're kidding, right? What with?" she asked naively.

"Give a guess? It might be our only chance," replied Steve.

"Ohhh."

"You can't ask her to……." protested Iain.

"Shut up!....She's our only hope," whispered Steve. "Give it all you've got."

The armed man struck the driver's window with his gun and yelled, "Now! Or I'll shoot!"

Carefully, they all got out of the car and gathered just in front of the vehicle. The armed man, who looked to be in his mid thirties and had dark hair and rugged features, stood to attention.

"Hands above your head!" he yelled, as he released the safety catch and aimed the gun at them.

Taking a deep breath and imagining she was some great femme fatale, Liz mustered up as much courage as she could and slowly took a step forward towards the man.

"It's okay! It's me you want! You can let them go!" she said seductively as she took another step towards the man.

"What's she doing?" whispered Iain to Grant.

"What women do best, tease." replied Grant.

"Hold it right there or I'll shoot!" yelled the soldier.

With her heart pounding hard in her chest, Liz hid her fear behind pouted lips and stepped closer towards the gun, keeping eye to eye contact with the soldier. Then, concentrating hard on his thoughts, she closed her eyes.

"What's she doing?" asked Grant.

"I think she's trying to get through to him…." suggested Iain.

Reaching out with her thoughts into his mind, she sent erotic images of herself, deep inside his head. His thoughts were filled with her…..He could smell her sweetness instead of the marshy stench. He could see and feel the softness of her body posing provocatively before him, as her softly whispered suggestions echoed in his head.

"You want me don't you!"

The soldier, confused by the images in his head and the real figure standing before him, froze as Liz stepped sassily closer and closer to him. Then, as she stood right in front of the gun barrel, she slowly pressed her chest against it. The soldier's eyes widened, as the real life figure became overlaid by the naked images inside his head. In his mind she stood naked before him, and he admired her voluptuous form. His palms began to sweat as she gently placed her fingers on the gun, carefully sliding her fingers along the side of the barrel, pushing it gently to one side as she moved closer to him. Iain and Steve looked curiously at each other, unable to understand why the guard was so mesmerised by a fully clothed, badly dressed woman who stank of pond scum.

"He can't possibly feel attracted to someone who smells as bad as you two do, surely?" whispered Steve. "She must be casting one hell of a spell in his head."

"You haven't seen how beautiful she is when she appears in your mind, have you?" asked Iain.

"I'm not sure you'd want me to, if you two are an item," Steve remarked. "How does she do it?"

"We think she can tune her thoughts into a unique frequency which is common to all living things, like tuning in a radio. Once she's tuned into you, she can read your thoughts, your past, and your future. She could be convincing his mind that he is seeing something other than what we can see, and from the look on his face, whatever it is it's got his full attention," whispered Iain. "So be ready to move."

The images became so intense inside the soldier's head, magnified by his desires for the real body that stood close to him, connecting with him, he failed to notice Grant's disappearance. As he dropped his gun limply to the ground and pulled Liz hard towards him, her sparkling and mesmerising blue eyes were the last things he saw. The knockout was instant, as the full force of the thick sodden branch hit the back of his head, forcing Liz to jump back to avoid it's impact. Caught completely by surprise, the soldier's knees buckled and he collapsed in a heap at Liz's feet. Liz looked down at the limp body, whose head was resting against her thighs. Using both hands, she pushed the soldier backwards til he fell flat on the ground. Standing over him, she shivered and cringed at the memory of her experience inside his head and the lustful thoughts he had for her.

"Have you killed him?" she asked Grant.

Grant knelt down and placed his hand on the man's neck to feel for a pulse.

"No….He'll just have a king size lump on the back of his head and one hell of headache." He replied. "Never mind him……..What did you do?.....That guy looked freaked out?"

"That's a man's imagination for you!" she replied. "At least he'll have sweet dreams."

Liz turned back to look at Steve and Iain, who stood behind her, stunned by the scenario played out before them. Looking at the tired, dirty but still beautiful face before him, Iain grinned broadly with warm golden brown eyes gleaming like melting honey in the morning sunshine.

"There you are! What did I tell you? She's a knock out!"

"Very funny Professor," remarked Steve.

Still tired from the previous evening's escapades and further drained by her thought projection, Liz felt a little light headed and stumbled as she walked back to the vehicle. Iain leapt forward to catch her before she fell. "Whoa…. take it easy!" said Iain, as he wrapped his arms around her to steady her. "Give her a minute!………She's tired….She needs to rest."

"I would, but those others could return any minute. We need to move now!" demanded Grant.

"He's right……there could be more of them coming back……He may have radioed for back-up." said Steve.

"What about taking him with us?" suggested Liz. "I could find out who he's working for……and what's going on."

"Too risky…" muttered Grant.

"He'd slow us down…….He'd be a liability…..prepared to turn on us at any time," added Steve.

"Let's move!" commanded Grant.

With that, they climbed back into the car, leaving the unconscious soldier behind. Turning the key in the ignition once more, the engine revved, Grant engaged the gears and pressed gently on the accelerator. Mud and dead leaves flew out from under the back wheels as they bit into the soft ground, before the car juddered forward.

"Hang on!" shouted Grant above the noise of the engine.

With that, Grant stepped on the accelerator and the four by four advanced forward, snapping branches and churning out mud in all directions. There was no road through the woods at this point, so they ploughed through the undergrowth with Grant concentrating on the terrain ahead, whilst steering the vehicle away from the lake. Iain and Liz hung on to the handles above their heads and wedged their feet under the seats in front, as the vehicle bounced over the obstacles in its path, throwing them this way and that way inside the car like dice in a shaker. Steve pressed his feet firmly into the passenger foot-well, and braced his arms against the dashboard. A sudden wave of mud splattered across the windscreen, as the right front tyre hit soft marshy ground. Grant quickly flicked on the wipers to clear the screen.

"How long til we're out of the woods?" asked Steve.

"It's about a mile til we hit the next field…."

"What then?"

"We'll follow the tree line south bound til we hit a minor road….heading into Stamford Bridge…..That way, … if the helicopter is still hanging around…..the trees should still provide us with cover…….The going should get easier too."

"Where do we go after Stamford Bridge?"

"We head west into York ……"

Though it felt like a lifetime, it took about ten minutes for the vehicle to plough its way through the rough terrain to the edge of the woods. Liz and Iain were beginning to look almost as green as the undergrowth around them by the time they reached the tree line.

"Crikey, that was worse than a North Sea ferry crossing in the middle of winter!" remarked Iain. "You look like I feel!" he said as he looked at Liz.

"Cheers!" Liz replied frowning. "Thanks for reminding me. Stop the car!" she yelled. "I'm going to be sick!"

"That's just great!" fumed Grant.

"Come on…" said Iain. "Give her a break!"

Grant stopped the car. Quickly, Liz jumped out of the back seat and dashed behind the car. With the engine ticking over gently, they could hear the faint sound of the helicopter rotor blades in the distance. Iain got out of the car and went to comfort Liz.

"Where do you reckon they are?" asked Steve looking up towards the top of the trees.

"Far side of the woods…….that's the quickest route to the nearest village." replied Grant. "That's why I didn't head in that direction. I knew it would be the most likely place they'd look!"

Iain approached Liz, just as she stood upright to take a deep breath of fresh country air.

"Are you okay?"

"Yeh,… I'm fine. I don't think that lake water or the car journey went down too well with my stomach."

"You'll feel better when you've had some good solid food and a good old cup of tea…" said Iain comfortingly. "You know……you were incredibly brave back there…….and I appreciate, it couldn't have been easy for you…."

"I feel awful…….I've never used my gift to manipulate anyone before……I just don't do that…It's so wrong!" she said regretfully as Iain placed his arm around her.

"It's okay…..really….You did what you had to do to save us," replied Iain reassuringly.

"I wish I didn't have this damned gift!………..It's a curse!…….It's brought me nothing but trouble and I've no doubt it's the reason they're after me!…"

"It brought you to me….." he said softly.

Liz looked up into his face. There was no wry smile awaiting her gaze. No humorous tone in his voice, only a look of deep concern which betrayed his innermost feelings for her. She said nothing, but she sensed a lot.

"Hoy!" yelled Grant, from the car. "Get a move on!"

"We'll be right there!" shouted Iain. "Look Liz, ….you're not alone in all this……I'm with you every step of the way…" he said staring seriously into her eyes, then added," …..and I won't leave you…..ever!"

For a brief moment they looked at each other, before Iain took her hand and led her back into the car.

Grant stepped on the accelerator again, and the four by four cut its way through the edge of the field adjacent to the woods. Reaching the corner of the field, Steve jumped out of the car straight into the deep water filled tractor tracks that led up the old gate. Plodging quickly through the muddy water, Steve pushed in the long metal gate lever and pulled the gate open in front of them.

"Check the road!" shouted Grant.

Steve nodded and walked up towards the edge of the country road to check for traffic in both directions. Identifying that the coast was clear, he signalled back to Grant to proceed as he stepped aside to allow them through the gateway. Checking the time on his watch, Steve noticed that the face of the glass was slightly scratched from his close encounter with the bushes in the woods, but he was still able to make out the time. It was, a little after 6 am.

"Road's clear in both directions!" he shouted to Grant as the car passed through the gate.

"Cheers!"

"Hang on while I shut the gate!"

Grant nodded and drove the car out on to the road, heading south east. Steve closed the gate quickly and ran round to the passenger door and climbed in.

As Grant pulled away and headed towards Stamford Bridge, Steve, Iain and Liz looked back over their shoulders at the woods they were leaving behind. They could just make out the black speck of the helicopter hovering over the trees at the far end. Now they needed to put as much distance between themselves and their pursuers as possible, before they discovered where they had gone. Grant put his foot to the floor and the four by four took off like the wind down the road.

CHAPTER 11

LIZ WAS GRATEFUL THAT THEY were, at least, driving on a relatively smooth road now, though some of the bends were still proving a challenge to her delicate stomach. After two miles, they drew up to the junction of the A166 motorway and turned right to head towards York. The traffic was very light at that time of the morning, mainly consisting of delivery vans heading into the city.

"Keep your eyes peeled for that helicopter," asked Grant. "Chances are they'll start heading in this direction, once they realise we've got wheels."

"Isn't it risky taking this main route?" asked Iain. "We're a bit exposed here, don't you think?"

"It's a busy commuter and business route with regular police patrols......I wouldn't have thought they'd want to risk being identified. ......Somebody somewhere would have a lot of embarrassing questions to answer," explained Steve. "It's also probably the last place they'd think to look."

"Once we get inside the city walls, we'll need to ditch this car." said Grant. "With the one way system, it'll be a lot quicker on foot.."

Liz kept a vigil from her window, scanning the horizon for any signs of the helicopter as the car sped along towards the city. Steve watched through his passenger side mirror, monitoring the traffic approaching from behind, whilst Iain kept watch directly through the rear windscreen.

In the distance, Iain could just make out a black

van approximately half a mile back, but it seemed to be accelerating fast towards them.

"I think we've got company.." said Iain. "What do think Steve?"

Steve could just make out the black van overtaking a haulage truck.

"I think he's right Grant.......and he's gaining on us all the time..."

"We're approaching a major roundabout.......hang on......I'll try and get us straight through..."

The three passengers braced themselves as Grant floored the accelerator causing the car to rev loudly as it lurched forward. Liz could see the oncoming vehicles negotiating their way around the roundabout and shut her eyes whilst gripping tightly on to the handle above her head and the back of the seat in anticipation of a collision. Fortunately, there was only one or two cars ahead of them on the roundabout as Grant pulled away hard to overtake them, narrowly missing an engineer's van that was driving on the inside lane. The driver blasted his horn and swore loudly as Grant swerved past and took the exit for Hull Road. As he checked his rear view mirror quickly, he could see the annoyed driver waving gestures and mouthing vulgar profanities at him.

Iain watched, as the black van, hot on their tail, bumped the corner of the engineer's van in order to plough through the narrowing gap between the van and the two small cars in the outside lane. Already shaken by the first incident, and concentrating more on his sign language than driving, ...he didn't see the black van until it was too late.....Trying desperately to replace his hand firmly on the steering wheel, he turned hard, but too hard. There was a screech and a scream of the brakes and the smell of hot burning rubber as the engineer's van skidded and veered off the road, before smashing through a low barrier on the inside of the roundabout, throwing the driver forwards.

"Wow did you see that?" exclaimed Iain.

"I hope he's alright?" said Liz.

"Never mind that...........How close are they Steve?" asked Grant.

"Just a few feet........"

"Hang on........" shouted Grant as he checked his rear view mirror for approaching vehicles before slamming his feet on to the clutch and the brakes. Smoke spewed from beneath the back of the van as the wheels locked and long black strips of melted rubber were left on the tarmac. Everyone inside the van was thrown forward violently, snapped back by their inertia seatbelts that pulled in tightly across their chests. The black van shot past. Then changing lanes, Grant picked up his speed and accelerated towards the rear of the black van.

"Brace yourselves! I'm going to ram them!" shouted Grant.

Suddenly, one of the rear doors of the van flew open and an armed man took aim at Grant's windscreen. Stamping hard on the accelerator, Grant prised the last ounces of remaining energy out of his engine and charged at the edge of the open van door. Hitting the door, the armed man lost his balance and fell backwards. They all lurched forward with the impact, before Grant pulled back and rammed again. The back doors of the black van took the full impact and buckled under the force. Then, spying a slip road heading off to the left, Grant dropped his speed and braked before turning sharp to the left to leave the Hull Road. As they disappeared down the slip road, Grant could just make out the black van speeding away from them.

"Keep your eyes peeled........He'll try and find a way to head us off!" Grant instructed.

Liz's heart was pounding hard, she'd seldom driven over the speed limit on any road and had never been involved in a car chase before. She'd always found them thrilling to watch on TV, but actually being involved in one......well that was something else entirely. She was terrified and looked desperately at Iain for reassurance. Finding it hard to hide his own concern, Iain gripped her hand tightly.

"We'll be okay......" he whispered.

Suddenly they heard a familiar sound not far above their heads......the sound of whirring rotor blades. The helicopter had found them. Gunshots rained down on the roof of the car as Iain released his seat belt and dragged Liz down behind the front seats, covering her with his own body to shield her. The car swerved as Grant tried to dodge the waves of gun fire, but not quick enough to prevent the rear and side windows being shot to pieces, showering Liz and Iain with glass. Liz screamed as a bullet hit the side of her arm, just above her elbow, splattering blood on to the back seat of the car.

"She's been shot!!" screamed Iain at Grant.

Grant didn't respond. Steve looked sharply across at him. His head was slumped forward onto his chest and his arms hung limply. In an instant, Steve unclipped his seatbelt, and grabbed the steering wheel.

"Iain .....get Liz on to the backseat NOW!!" he yelled.

As he did so, Steve reached over Grant's body and pulled the seat lever right back, and pushed his friend's corpse away from the steering wheel. Then stretching quickly over the gear stick and across on to the edge of the driver's seat, Steve pushed the seat backwards and fumbled for the pedals with his feet as the car started to wobble.

Iain unclipped Grant's seat belt and hooking his hands under Grants arms, pulled his body into the rear passenger seat away from Steve, to give him room to drive. With her right arm unharmed, Liz gripped the belt on Grant's trousers and pulled as hard as she could, to help Iain move the heavy lifeless body.

"Liz......on three, we'll pull together.......one, two, THREE!.......Pull!"

Suddenly, more bullets peppered the car.

"So much for them not wanting to draw attention to themselves! shouted Iain above the gunfire.

Pushing Grant's body up against the back seat in between them, Iain had an idea.

"Liz.....I know this sounds macabre.....but if we're going to stay alive, ...we're going to have to use Grant's body as a shield.......We'll have to lift him up on to the back shelf...."

More bullets struck the car, shattering the rear window.

"Now!" shouted Iain.

Together, they pushed the corpse up on to the deep back shelf, a job made easier by the smashing of the window. The helicopter hung back for a moment, waiting to see what they would do.

"What are they doing?" shouted the pilot to his armed passenger.

"It's their driver. He's dead!"

"You idiot! You could have shot the girl! They want her alive!" shouted the pilot. "You were only supposed to slow them down!"

Both of them watched the car closely, as Steve managed to gain control.

Steve looked in his rear view mirror at Iain and Liz.

"You two okay?" he asked.

They both turned briefly to look at Steve.

"Liz's been shot........in the arm, " replied Iain as he ripped off his t-shirt and tore it apart to make bandages.

"Can you stop the bleeding? "

"I think so…….I studied medicine years ago…" said Iain, "But we need to get her to a doctor.."

"We can't take Liz to a hospital……They'll ask too many questions…..Do you know anybody Iain?" asked Steve.

"Yes!……..Professor Hughes…..he's a scientist, but he keeps a good stock of medical supplies at his house in case his research students have any accidents," suggested Iain.

"Accidents?" questioned Steve. "What kind of research is he conducting?"

"Hypnosis…mind expansion, but the health and safety department insisted he had fully equipped medical facilities just in case," explained Iain.

"Right!"

"He lives not far from the Minster," advised Iain shaking his head.

"What's wrong?" asked Liz.

"I was just thinking how ironic it is…His research into the universe and his scientific theories has often brought him into conflict with the church, yet, he lives right next door to them, next to the Minster…….He says it's because he continues to marvel at the mathematical and architectural genius that went into building it……."

"What's his address?"

"I can't remember the house number…but it's right on the corner……where Lord Mayor's Walk meets St. John Street…."

"Right………we'll head there, then." replied Steve. "Where's the helicopter right now?"

"Not far behind us…."said Iain. "Why don't we head for the shopping centre in Coppergate and ditch the car in the multi-storey car park…….Then we can cut through the Shambles to Petergate …..and onwards up to the

Minster?......It's a nightmare of alleys and narrow lanes in there......They'll never find us in a million years!.."

"What makes you so sure?"

"It's a Saturday.....in the Shambles.....Have you any idea how many tourists will be passing through that place today?...........You'd think it was Cup Final Day and someone was dishing out free tickets!......When I said 'nightmare'....I was talking from personal experience."

"We could lose each other in the crowds......"

"That's a distinct possibility......but we all know where we're heading....."

"What about you Liz?...." asked Steve. "Will you be able to make it through the streets?"

"I know York quite well.........I'll manage," she replied.

"Besides,......I'll be with her......She'll be safe with me!" declared Iain, smiling at Liz beside him.

Noticing how pale Liz appeared, Iain checked her wound.

"It looks like the bullet passed straight through!" yelled Iain above the noise of the rotors. "We need to stop the bleeding!"

Picking up the strips of his torn t-shirt, Iain carefully took Liz's arm and applied the strips of cotton fabric around it. Liz winced with the pain, as Iain tied the makeshift bandage.

"I'm sorry.....it has to be tight," he apologised.

"I understand," she said softly.

"Step on it, Steve!" roared Iain. "Let's lose them!"

Steve pushed the accelerator to the floor and shot along the road with the helicopter in hot pursuit. As they left Hull Road and Fraser Street behind them, the streets became narrower and more dangerous to navigate at speed, owing to the frequent delivery vehicles unloading their goods, around every corner. Thankfully, as it was still early, the streets had yet to become congested with commuter and tourist traffic, enabling Steve to nip this way and that way along the roads adjacent to the shopping centre. Finally, as Iain watched the helicopter hovering behind them, Steve drove the car through the barrier leading into the multi-storey car park.

"Ha!!" Iain laughed defiantly at the enemy. "Let's see how clever you think you are, now!........Bye bye!!!"

"We've lost them!" yelled the armed passenger in the helicopter. "Fly over the building. They've got to come out somewhere!"

Steve drove the car up the winding ramp to the second floor and reversed the vehicle into a central parking bay, away from prying eyes. Climbing out of the car, the three tired and battle weary fugitives looked at each other. Iain stood bare chested, with matted hair, combat pants and mud caked trainers. "You look like Rambo!...." remarked Liz.

"Hmmn," sighed Iain. "You've got a point........We're hardly going to blend in with the tourists looking like army camp rejects, are we?...."

"I'll check the boot..." said Steve. "Grant was always good for contingencies......He might have something else we can wear..."

Turning the key in the boot lock, Steve lifted up the hatchback door, causing Grant's body to roll off the shelf on to the back seat. He swallowed hard and lowered his head.

"I'm really sorry Steve," said Liz apologetically as she placed her good arm around him, to comfort him.

"It's not your fault.......none of this!" replied Steve. "He was a good friend....A bit belt and braces I suppose...but very loyal.." he sighed.

"We owe him a lot and we should never forget that." asserted Iain.

Steve reached into the boot. Beside the duffle bag that

had contained the combat trousers and t-shirts, there was a long travel bag. Pulling open the zip, Steve rummaged around inside it. There was a thick checked shirt, jeans, boots and a reflective waist coat. Beside the bag was a pale yellow workman's helmet.

"Must have been one of his disguises for surveillance." said Steve.

"Handy!" said Iain. "There's always some road works or construction work going on around the Minster.......No one will suspect a thing."

Steve pulled out black trousers and a black ribbed sweater with the words 'Greenway Security' embroidered in white near the left shoulder.

"That's who he worked for at the University." said Steve. "How do you fancy playing a security guard, Iain?....."

Iain pulled on the sweater and trousers and looked down at himself.

"Mmmmn, not bad....but the trainers will have to go..."

"There's some black boots here...try them on." suggested Steve.

Iain peeled off and discarded the squelching trainers, undid the boot laces and pulled them on.

"They're okay.....a little floppy...but they'll do.......So, I'm security and you're construction." confirmed Iain.

"What about me?"

The two young men looked at Liz in her black t-shirt, combat pants and muddy trainers, with blood stains dried on her arm and splattered here and there across her clothes. Iain looked at Steve and Steve looked at Iain.

Steve looked in the bag again...Nothing. Then taking off his casual suit jacket, he folded up each sleeve to the elbow.

"There you go.......put that on to cover your arm.....

and you look just like a trendy student..........a little rough around the edges, admittedly.....but people will just think that you've got that morning after look...But we need to do something about the smell," Steve remarked. "They mightn't be able to see you from the air, but your fragrance 'eau de smelly pond' will drive the crowds away from you."

"Is there anything in the boot we can use?" asked Iain.

"Nothing," replied Steve.

"What about the car freshener?" suggested Liz. "I noticed he had something clipped to the air vents."

"Good girl!" praised Iain as he dashed around the side of the van and retrieved the small plastic container containing a strong citronella gel. Breaking open the plastic cover, Iain rubbed the gel on to his clothes.

"Just rub the gel on your clothes, but don't rub it on your skin or you'll end up with a hell of a rash," advised Iain.

With that, Steve put on the workman's clothes and the three fugitives made their way across the car park to the stairs. They could hear the helicopter still hovering overhead, as they trotted down the stairs to the ground level. Unfortunately, it was too early for the shopping centre to be open, and the entrance was sealed off with black wrought iron gates.

"Damn! "shouted Iain. "If we can't get into the shopping centre, they're going to realise it's us if we leave by any of the other exits."

"I've got an idea, guys...." announced Liz. "Steve,.... you're dressed as a workman right?"

"Right."

"They always start work pretty early yes?"

"The Market Place is about five minutes walk from here......A couple of days ago, when I was shopping,.....I noticed that there was some building repair work going on outside one of the big shop fronts there. You might be able to lead them away from here ....Then we'll make a run for it into the Shambles," suggested Liz. "We'll meet up again round the back of the Minster."

"Sounds feasible," agreed Iain. "What do you think, Steve?"

"It has its risks."

"I don't see that we have much choice. Just make sure you've got your helmet on. Then they might think you're legit!" Iain suggested.

"Okay. Let's give it a try," replied Steve.

Walking to end of the archway leading out of the car park on to Coppergate, Steve peered up at the sky. There was no sign of the helicopter but the sound of its rotors told him that it must be hovering nearby.

"I think it's over the other side of the building."

"Go for it!" cheered Iain. "Don't look back. Just give them a chance to spot you....We'll give you a two minute head start."

"Be careful, Steve!" shouted Liz.

Then, looking up at the sky once more, to make a final check, Steve put on his helmet and marched away from the shopping centre, heading up the street towards the traffic lights. Stopping at the crossroads and looking carefully up towards the helicopter, he crossed the road and strode towards the Shambles.

"Who's that down there?" asked the passenger in the helicopter, as he spotted the figure walking across the road.

"It looks like it's just a workman. See, he's heading towards the others," replied the pilot.

"Follow him."

The helicopter turned slowly away from the shopping

centre and hovered just high enough behind Steve to see some of the activities going on in the surrounding area.

"Brilliant!" exclaimed Iain. "They're falling for it! Now to get you away from here........Keep close to the walls so that the shop canopies hide you from them and follow me, " he beckoned to Liz. "Come on!"

Taking his own advice, Iain kept close to the buildings as he ran up the street towards the lights. With his long legs and agile figure, he reached the junction without losing a breath. Looking back towards the car park, Liz wasn't far behind.

"Come on!" he shouted to her.

As she caught up to him, Iain checked for the position of the helicopter, which was hovering a few hundred yards ahead of them. Then taking Liz's good hand, they ran across the road and onwards, up towards the Shambles.

At the entrance, they paused on the corner for a moment to catch their breath. Looking down the quaint old narrow street, they marvelled at the odd shapes of each of the centuries old buildings which due to their age and subsidence, appeared to defy gravity with their upper floors leaning towards each other so closely and acutely, that it seemed almost possible to climb from one of the upper windows suspended above the street, to another window on the opposite side.

"Look at that! An architect's nightmare! Could you imagine trying to get building inspectors to pass that lot, if they were modern buildings? They look like they could topple over at any moment!" remarked Iain.

"I know........this is my most favourite street in the whole of York.......If you go into any of the shops here..... it feels really strange.......walls leaning this way...doorways bent at an angle......it's quite eerie!" replied Liz.

"Okay.....now you know the drill......With these

buildings blocking their view, we should be able to make it without being seen."

Dashing along the right hand side of the street, they found it hard to keep their balance on the uneven pavement and irregular cobbles whilst trying to dodge crashing into the odd shaped shop fronts. Just at the end of the street, the lane veered around to the right, just before it opened out into a small paved square. About three hundred feet away at the far side of the square, the helicopter was hovering like a huge noisy metal dragonfly.

"Can you see Steve?" asked Liz.

Iain peered carefully around the corner to the left. At the far end of the small square, there were a small number of workmen gathered at the corner of one of the lanes, adjacent to a shop. Scaffolding encased the outer walls of the building, with some men working on the upper floor levels, starting the process for removing an old window frame. Steve stood in the centre of the group, with his back to Iain and Liz.

"What's he doing?" asked Liz curiously.

"I think he's chatting to the workmen…"

"Morning fellas," said Steve to the workmen as they unloaded some tools from the back of their van.

"Aye, what do you want?" asked the short burly foreman as he got out of the driver's cab. "You here to inspect the job?"

"No…"

"If you're looking for a job, you'll have to see the boss back at the office…"

"Sorry…..I should explain…..I'm from Lane Production company and that helicopter up there is filming some long shots of this area for an action drama…….Any minute now….two of the cast are going to come running through this square and up Petergate……"

"Will we be on camera?" asked one of the apprentices.

"Most definitely…."

"Do you want us to just carry on working as usual?"

"I want you to pretend that the helicopter crew are the bad guys and you're going to try and distract them….."

"And how will we do that?…."

"Use your imagination………."

As Steve turned slightly to look back across the square, he spotted Liz and Iain peering at him from around the corner.

"Right lads!………They're here…….When I say 'action', I want you to give it all you've got!" encouraged Steve.

Sitting in the helicopter, the pilot and the armed man could see the workman talking to the other men.

"There! Told you! This was a complete waste of time! They're probably miles away!" complained the pilot.

"Action!" shouted Steve at the top of his voice.

Liz and Iain looked at each other puzzled, then observed the workmen running about waving their arms and throwing things at the helicopter.

"Come on!" shouted Steve to them. "Run!"

"What the hell is going on here?" shouted the armed passenger.

Iain and Liz ran across the square to join up with Steve, and together they sprinted as hard as they could up Petergate towards the Minster.

"Look it's them! They're getting away!" yelled the pilot, as he pointed to the three figures disappearing up the street.

Running for all they were worth, the three fugitives pounded the pavements towards High Petergate, taking a sharp right and cutting along the short narrow paved lane leading across to the South Transept entrance to the Minster. One of the solid wooden doors was slightly ajar.

"Quick!" gasped Iain. "The door's open….."

Then, together, Iain, Steve and Liz shot across the main road and headed into the Minster.

CHAPTER 12

ONCE INSIDE, THE THREE FUGITIVES stood away from the door and leaned against the wall to rest.

"What do we do now?" whispered Liz softly, conscious that her voice might echo throughout the building.

"We need to sneak across to the West doors and go around the back of the Minster." replied Iain.

"What if we're caught by the clergy here?" she asked concerned.

"We could try requesting sanctuary." suggested Iain.

"I think that went out centuries ago," remarked Steve cynically.

"Ooohh, I think you might be wrong their," disputed Iain.

"And in any case, do you really think that that lot are going to play by the rules?" asked Steve.

"I must admit, you do have a point there. It was worth a thought though," replied Iain.

"Let's just see how far we get..." added Steve.

Keeping close to the wall with Iain in the lead, they quietly made their way around the back of the information desk in the South Transept, and towards the central point of the Minster, known as the Crossing. Just ahead of them on the left, a large broad archway was sealed off by a high very ornate gateway. Checking briefly that there was no one there, they dashed quietly past the gateway to the adjacent archway and the first of the two colossal central main pillars which helped to support the Central Tower. The air in the Minster was still and intense. Centuries of religious devotion, silent prayer and praise to the Holy Trinity filled the air with powerful and emotional thought energy. Liz could sense the presence of millions of thoughts all around her, packed so tightly she felt as though she was suffocating in the midst of a packed crowd of invisible people. The words of their prayers and their desperate pleas for redemption and forgiveness invaded her mind, as if desperately seeking divine answers and absolution. Voice after voice echoed through her mind, so many and so quickly, it made her head spin. Then with the voices came the faces, some ailing or women despairing, praying heart wrenching pleas for the safe return of their husbands or sons from the battlefields of bygone wars. Then there were the grief stricken, carrying the heart crushing pain of their tragic and sudden emotional and spiritual severance from their loved ones. Liz could feel the deep cold blackness within the deepest vaults of their exposed souls, the painful void left behind like an all consuming black hole, unrelenting in its extraction of hope, love and faith, leaving only the empty human shell behind. The hopelessness cut her like an icy dagger, slashing away at her own hope and replacing it with doubt like a rapidly spreading contagion infecting and corrupting her thoughts and feelings. The once bright blue sparkling eyes, the passionate and fiery beacon of hope in Iain's heart and memories, now appeared dull and grey. As she continued to absorb the negative energy that surrounded her, Iain watched her rapid deterioration with alarm.

"Steve wait," whispered Iain as loud as he dared, whilst watching Liz's fixed expression. "Wait!"

"What's wrong?" Steve replied just as his eyes settled on Liz.

Together, in the shadow of the huge pillar, Iain and Steve

stood before Liz who remained oblivious to their presence. Feeling her wrist, then scrutinising her eyes and gently stroking her cheek, Iain shook his head in puzzlement.

"What's happened to her?" asked Steve concerned.

"I'm not exactly sure. She's cold, but that could be normal due to the coldness in here. Her pulse seems to be slowing and the colour is gradually fading from her eyes."

"So what is it?" asked Steve impatiently.

"She's not clammy to the touch, so I don't think it's shock. It's almost as if her very life, her spirit is fading, being sucked out of her.

"You're kidding right?" remarked Steve in disbelief.

"I'm serious."

"But how is that possible?"

"I don't know, but I might be able to hazard a guess," answered Iain hopefully. "based on what I know about her," he added.

"Go for it!"

"Liz can sense thoughts, feelings, atmospheres, yes?"

"Mmmmn?"

"What if thought energies find their own natural balance or level?"

"I don't follow."

"Churches and cathedrals can sometimes be very sombre places filled with sadness as well as joy. What if the energy here has been tipped out of balance in favour of negativity and sadness? If Liz is an open vessel who can reach out and touch our thoughts and feelings, what if it works the other way too? Liz told me how she always feels drained and exhausted after she's read somebody's thoughts. May be when she's receiving their thought energy, she's giving them some of her own positive energy in exchange. She's said that people often leave her feeling more energised and positive. What if the energy here is using that gateway into her mind to pull the positive life and emotional energy from her, in an attempt to balance the energies already here? If it's not stopped she could be drained of energy completely."

"That's ridiculous! That can't possibly be happening!" dismissed Steve.

"How well do you know Liz?" asked Iain.

"Well enough," replied Steve.

"Based on what exactly? A witness statement? Surveillance reports?"

"Okay I take your point," sighed Steve. "But what's that got to do with it?"

"I've known Liz a long time," confessed Iain. "We've been through a lot together, but more importantly, I know and I understand what's going on inside her head. So you're just going to have to trust me when I say, it is possible. Liz has abilities she hasn't told you about. Abilities that make this and a lot more, entirely possible."

"How do you know all this?"

"Direct experience, and based on what she's told me," replied Iain.

"Oh, come off it! I know you only met her yesterday," said Steve sharply.

"According to the surveillance report?" asked Iain.

Steve dropped his head.

"Figures. Look Steve, there's a lot you don't know, but now's not the right time to have a heart-to-heart. Just take it as read, that I know what I'm talking about," added Iain.

"Okay, say you're right, what do we do about it?"

"Get her out of here before the balancing process drains her completely. If we get her out of here and she's still in this catatonic state, then we might have a bigger problem on our hands," explained Iain.

"Understood," replied Steve reluctantly.

The early morning sunshine gleamed through the huge

stained glass windows above and behind them, casting a vivid colourful mosaic of light across the medieval stone floor between the North and South Transepts. Shafts of golden light shone down on the line of fifteen kingly stone figures that guarded the fifteenth Century Quire screen.

As Iain and Steve thought for a moment about how best to carry Liz to the far end of the Cathedral, a small trickle of blood ran down the top of her hand and dripped on to the stone floor. The voices and prayers inside her head grew deafening, drowning out the whispered concerns of her fellow fugitives. The world that was her reality was slipping away from her, drop by drop.

Suddenly, the wooden doors to the South Transept creaked open and the mercenaries who had stalked them through the woods, stepped through the Minster doors.

"Behind the pillar…now" whispered Steve.

Quickly, Iain picked up Liz in his arms and dashed across to the first large central pillar that stood parallel to the south wall near the start of the Nave. Then, lowering Liz carefully on to the cold stone floor behind the pillar, Iain held her in his arms and stood as close to the pillar as possible.

"We need to get Liz to Professor Hughes" Iain whispered to Steve. "If you can check if the coast is clear…….I'll try to get to the West Doors with her."

"You'll have to make your move right now, before they disperse," replied Steve.

Pulling Liz up and over his shoulder, Iain waited for the green light. Steve looked at them both for a moment, then spying around the side of the pillar he could just make out the leading figure issuing commands to his men on the far side of the wooden display cabinets and information desk that stood inside the South Transept entrance. He watched as the leader gestured his instructions to split up the group.

"Right...Go!" whispered Steve.

Keeping out of their line of sight, Iain ran as quietly and as fast as he could down the south side of the Nave, carrying Liz. Reaching the last pillar diagonally across from the West Doors, he turned briefly to check that Steve was okay. Having waited until he could see Iain reach the last pillar safely, Steve set off in their direction.

Suddenly, Iain became aware of a dark shadow descending on Liz and himself as he caught his breath behind the pillar. Slowly he turned around to see a tall slim elderly white haired man in clerical vestments standing over them. One of the Minster's Bishops had entered via the West Doors, as Iain made his dash down the side of the Nave. Observing the odd spectacle, the Bishop wondered if his timely arrival wasn't one of God's 'mysterious ways' of providing him with an opportunity to serve and assist in some capacity.

"What's wrong, my son?........Why are you here?......The Minster doesn't open to the public until 9:00 am......unless you are attending the early morning service which starts at 7:00am." He said.

Then, noticing the blood trickling down Liz's hand, he asked softly, "What's happened?"

"My apologies for the intrusion, Bishop.....She's been shot, by those men entering the building now!" Iain replied. "She needs medical attention."

"Shall I phone for an ambulance?"

"There's no time, Bishop! ....They're here and they've got guns!.....They've already killed one of our colleagues, so they probably won't hesitate to shoot again.......You need to get somewhere safe, Bishop!"

"Good gracious!...But I've got the congregation arriving shortly for the morning service......."

"We must leave now and you need to lock the West Doors behind us…"

"But they'll still be inside……."

"When they realise that the West Doors are locked…… They'll be forced to back track to the South Transept entrance…..Once they've left the Minster, it'll be safe for you to return….hopefully."

Just as Iain finished speaking to the Bishop, Steve caught up with them.

"Forgive me Bishop……but we all need to leave right now!" gasped Steve.

Looking over Steve's shoulders, Iain and the Bishop could just see the black clothed figures turning the corner towards the Nave.

"There they are!" yelled one of the soldiers.

"Run Bishop!" instructed Iain, as he turned to head towards the doors with Steve close behind him.

"Oh my……" sighed the Bishop, as he lifted the hem of his vestment clear of the stone floor and did his best to sprint after them.

Steve arrived at the West Doors first and pushed one of them open to allow Iain, still carrying Liz, to run straight through. As he stood holding the door, the Bishop approached.

"Come on Bishop!" shouted Steve.

Just as he shouted, there was a faint whistling sound as a high velocity bullet came whizzing past the Bishop's right shoulder and struck the door beside Steve. Steve grabbed hold of the Bishop and pulled him into the open doorway before closing the door.

"The keys please Bishop!"

Shaking from his near death ordeal, the Bishop handed the large metal key to Steve. Turning the key, Steve and the

Bishop heard the clunking of the old mechanism as the lock slid into place.

"You'll be safe here, Bishop!" he instructed. "We have to go!........Sorry!"

With that, Steve headed off into the distance to catch up with Iain and Liz, whilst the Bishop regained his composure standing at the door of the Minster. As he rested, he could hear the sound of angry voices echoing around the building followed by the sound of heavy boots running away from the doors. A few moments later, a small group of the soldiers sprinted around the outside corner of the building, heading towards the Bishop. Praying for divine guidance, the Bishop stepped back against the closed doors, as the soldiers ran past almost oblivious to his presence. It was too late. Steve, Iain and Liz had made it beyond the first row of buildings and were heading towards Professor Hughes' house.

Lord Mayor's Walk was virtually deserted, except for a solitary feral cat prowling close to the buildings. Iain was exhausted by the time he reached the corner.

"It's just over there..." he gasped pointing to his friend's house, before dashing the last hundred feet or so towards the back lane behind the property. "We should be able to get through the gate into his back yard..." he continued.

Steve tried the lever on the handle of the solid six foot high wooden gate, but it was stiff. Gently forcing the lever upwards, he managed to open the gate and help Iain into the back yard with Liz. As he closed the gate quietly behind them, they could make out the sound of heavy clomping army boots getting louder and heading in their direction. After carefully sliding the large metal bolt into place on the back of the gate, Iain and Steve stood on either side, holding their breath waiting for the soldiers to pass.

Immediately outside of the gate, one of the soldiers stopped.

"Which direction did they go in?" asked one soldier.

"I'm sure they headed left!" answered a second soldier.

Then, Steve and Iain listened quietly as they heard the two soldiers sprint away into the distance.

"That was close…" remarked Steve.

"Nothing like the thrill of the chase to get the old adrenaline pumping!" replied Iain. "Next stop……my old friend Fraser Hughes."

"Are you sure he'll be at home?" asked Steve.

"Professor Hughes is semi retired from the University and spends most of his time at home conducting his research with student subjects…….I'm pretty sure he'll be home, especially at this early hour."

Whilst Iain carried Liz the last few feet, Steve dashed ahead and knocked firmly on the back door. There was no reply. Steve knocked again, slightly louder.

"I'm coming…I'm coming!" answered an aged voice from within the house. "Who is it?...What do you want?"

"It's Iain, Fraser…"

"Iain?........Oh, Iain Sinclair,"

"Yes."

"Hold on a second while I unlock the door…….. damned nuisance these keys….but these days you can't be too careful…."

Iain and Steve could see the white haired figure of a man fumbling with a key chain behind the frosted windows of the back door. Then slowly, the door creaked open to reveal a middle aged man wearing pyjamas and a dressing gown.

"Good God!" he exclaimed when he saw Iain carrying Liz in his arms. "What on earth's happened?"

"Can we come in quickly?"

"Yes of course……Bring her through to the living room…"

Iain followed his friend Fraser along the narrow hallway,

whilst Steve closed and locked the back door. The hallway was very long, running the full length of the building, with doors leading off it to various rooms on the ground floor. As they approached the front of the house, the hallway opened out to reveal an original oak staircase leading up to the first floor. On either side of them, hanging at intervals on the wall, were photographs of Professor Hughes standing with different eminent scientists and celebrities who he had been introduced to over the years. Just across from the bottom of the staircase was the living room door. Opening it, Iain stepped through the doorway into the living room beyond, which looked as though it had not changed in over a century. With its original plaster mouldings on the upper walls and ceiling, the grand ornate fireplace and the antique furniture, Iain smiled nostalgically. It may not have been his home, or the era in time that he originally came from, but it comforted him and revived his own memories from that period which he had long since packaged away into the recesses of his mind like a distant dream.

There was no television, no radio, no phone, not a electrical gadget in the entire room. Above the fireplace, on each side of a large painting, were two delicate round glass lamps, each one containing a candle holder.

"What year is this?" asked Steve curiously as he entered the room behind Iain.

Professor Hughes smiled.

"This room contains nothing electrical or magnetic. All of the wiring has been stripped from the walls of this room to minimise the electrical influences on the brain." Iain informed Steve, as he lay Liz carefully on the sofa.

"It is essential........to my research," added Professor Hughes. "I wanted a room that was completely clear of all electrical devices to help my research subjects focus better. If you like, I'll explain it all to you later, but for the moment, other matters are quite clearly more pressing. Let's see how this young lady is doing…hmmn? Iain, I want you to sit her up for me and carefully remove her jacket, so that I can get a better look…."

Iain held Liz gently in his arms and carefully peeled off the jacket. Underneath the jacket, most of the blood had dried and congealed around the wound, whilst a small persistent trickle ran down her fore arm to her fingers. Inspecting the wound, Fraser began nodding his head.

"She's a very lucky lady. The wound looks bad but there's no bullet…..It appears to have passed straight through the skin thankfully without hitting any major arteries or bones….." he announced. "Now, fetch me a bowl of hot water and some clean towels from the kitchen. We'll soon have this cleaned up…" declared Fraser.

Iain returned a minute or so later carrying the bowl of hot water and towels, placing them carefully on the small table beside the sofa. Opening up his medical bag, Fraser fumbled through the contents to locate bandages, anaesthetics, antiseptics and cotton wool, then gently he began to clean Liz's arm. Once he'd treated and dressed the wound, Professor Hughes gently took hold of her wrist and checked for her pulse. Then taking out the stethoscope from his bag, he placed it against her chest, the side of her ribs and lifting her gently, he placed it against her back.

"She's breathing okay. Her heart rate is elevated but within tolerance. She'll be okay…….What happened?"

"This is Detective Steve Alexander, "said Iain gesturing towards Steve. "….and this is Liz."

Fraser raised his eyebrows and stared directly at Iain, quizzically.

"Liz, you say?" asked Fraser questioning the name he'd just heard.

Iain nodded.

"So you found her, after all this time! Well done!" Fraser congratulated him. "She doesn't know does she? You haven't told her?" he asked Iain.

"She's very bright, Fraser. I didn't tell her anything at first, but she began drawing her own conclusions."

"So you told her," replied Fraser sternly. "Do you realise, what that could do?"

"I remembered what you said, and I deliberately left out the detail, for that reason! But, I couldn't just stand there and say nothing, not after what happened. She was getting suspicious and I didn't want to lose her again!" replied Iain defensively.

"If she changes anything…." warned Fraser.

"Well, if I had said anything I shouldn't, I wouldn't be here now would I? The affect would have been instantaneous. May be I was supposed to tell her."

"It's possible," agreed Fraser. "How did she react when you told her?"

"As you can imagine it all came as quite a big shock!"

"Indeed!" Fraser replied.

"I don't think she would have believed me at all, if she hadn't witnessed the effect for herself!" added Iain.

"What happened, briefly?" asked Fraser curiously.

"We were at the ball. Someone abducted her. I went to find her and it happened. I'm guessing, she amplified her electrical signal beyond the cellular boundaries and used my thought waves to anchor the three dimensional representation," replied Iain.

Steve watched them both as their odd conversation and expressions seemed to be conveying a cryptic scientific code which only they knew how to decipher.

"I'm sorry, what did you say?" asked Steve.

"She projected an electrically based three dimensional image of herself to Iain. I suppose you might think of it like a hologram," explained Fraser. "Was she conscious of what she'd done?"

"Yes. She used it to warn me and to tell me where she was," replied Iain.

"Aahhhh. So she has realised that she can control and focus her energy on a target. She must have been tapping into her elevated adrenaline levels to amplify the signal. Hmmn," concluded Fraser. "I didn't realise that fear could be that powerful. Interesting!"

"Then she made contact," added Iain.

"Aahhhh. I understand now," said Fraser nodding. "You didn't have much of a choice, then."

"No."

"What do you mean you understand? I wish I did!" exclaimed Steve frustratedly.

"Who is he?" asked Fraser irritated by the interruption.

"I'm Detective Steve Alexander from Northern Command and I've been assigned to protect Miss Curran whilst she is under witness protection! Now unless you want to be charged with obstructing the police in the course of their duty, I suggest you explain exactly what's going on here!" demanded Steve authoritatively.

"For Christ's sake, Steve, will you give it a rest with the rule book! You and I both know that this is way out of your league! How do you think they'd take your reports anyway? If you're having trouble understanding and accepting what's going on and you've witnessed some of it first hand, do you think they'll be able to understand it any better?" asked Iain rhetorically.

"I'm sorry! It's just that I'm out on a limb here, cut me some slack will you? I just want to understand what's going on!" replied Steve.

"You better sit down then," suggested Iain.

Steve took his advice and sat down on one of the chairs opposite the sofa where Liz was now lying peacefully.

"You better leave it to me to explain," instructed Iain. "I can put it in less scientific terms."

"Be my guest," replied Fraser.

Poised attentively, Steve leaned forward from his seat to listen carefully to everything Iain had to say.

"It might be better if you tell us what you know about Liz and then we can fill in the gaps. How does that sound?" asked Iain.

"Yeh, that's fine by me," replied Steve. "Well, I know that she can read palms and thoughts. I've seen how she can project her thoughts into other people to influence what they see and what they do. I'm not sure I understand how she does it, I just know that she can. I know that some people with very high level connections and access to a lot of high tech equipment and surveillance are trying to abduct her or kill her. Why? Your guess is as good as mine, but I'd have to say that it may have something to do with her abilities. How they know about those abilities, I haven't a clue!"

"Okay. Liz has an ability that goes far beyond just reading thoughts. She puts it down to an electrical accident she had as a child, which firstly, destroyed her internal electrical inhibiter allowing her to accumulate and store very high levels of electrical current without discharging it. Secondly, the accident she had disrupted her brain wave patterns, altering their frequency minutely but enough to enable her to tune into, what we call, the universal wavelength. This is a wavelength of electrical energy which is as old as the universe itself and which is common to all living things. Having this reservoir of energy 'on tap' so to speak, and having the ability to tune into this frequency, which is how she is able to read our thoughts and connect with us, she has now learnt to use this reservoir of energy to project her thoughts or her image along the wavelength's pathways to any location backwards or forwards in time. She can also receive electrical signals transmitted on this wavelength whatever their point of origin. Hence she can pick up on past or future events that leave an energy residue in a particular place," explained Iain.

"Are you saying that she can detect ghosts and situations, just like a clairvoyant or a ghost hunter?"

"She has the predisposition to detect their signals audibly and visually along that frequency," replied Fraser.

"She can see them and hear them," translated Iain. "And finally, as far as we currently know, if her projection makes contact with another living person, she has the ability to recharge their cells, effectively rejuvenating them. But she can only do this when she is outputting or discharging energy through her projection. We think this is due to the exposure of some electrons within her projection which then impact with the air molecules around her, creating a green haze of aurora, like the aurora borealis. When she touches you in that exposed raw electrical state, we believe that the collision of these electrons with living matter recharges the body's cells at a molecular level. She is able to restore cells to their optimum peak of development. In other words, you become young again. As far as we know, whilst she is within her own body, this electrical energy supply is inert, inactive," concluded Iain. "Now, did you get all of that, Steve?"

Steve's face was a picture of wide eyed bewilderment. Stunned into speechlessness Steve sat open mouthed as Iain twiddled his thumbs waiting for some kind of verbal response.

"Hello, earth calling Steve! Is anyone in there?" asked Iain. "Any questions you'd like to ask?"

Steve blinked and closed his mouth.

"Yes! I can see signs of life!" teased Iain.

"How do you know all this? What proof do you have to support this theory of yours?" asked Steve nervously.

"Iain is the proof, Detective," added Fraser. "How old do you think he is?"

"I would say, late twenties," guessed Steve.

"What would you say if I told you that Iain is 292 years old," declared Fraser.

"And the reason I have survived this long," added Iain. "is because Liz has visited me many times in my past and during each visit, she projected herself and made contact with me, rejuvenating me each time. Last night, Liz witnessed for the first time, the effect of her projected contact with me. She now knows that she can effectively cancel out the effects of the natural aging process. She effectively watched as the aging clock was wound backwards and reset to the point in my life when I was physically and biologically at my peak."

Steve looked at the grey haired scientist in disbelief, until he noticed the sincerity and seriousness in his face.

"So let me get this straight. You know all this because of Liz's visits to Iain in his past."

"Correct," replied Fraser.

"Liz has managed to keep Iain alive through this rejuvenation thing for the last two hundred and odd years."

"292 years to be precise," replied Iain.

"She's only just finding out that she can do these things, so presumably that means that she hasn't made any trips to the past yet, am I right?" asked Steve.

"That's right, and that's why it's important that Liz, particularly, mustn't learn any of the details of those visits in case she does or says something differently and causes a paradox that stops Iain from being here. If that happens, every single event involving Iain over the past 292 years, will undo, like unravelling the yarn in a complicated sweater. The impact of the paradox could cause massive holes in the space time continuum."

"You're right Iain," sighed Steve. "This is way out of my league! You need somebody with a bit of science fiction savvy to help you."

"And that young man, is where I come in!" smiled Fraser.

"Fraser's been a very good friend of mine since we studied in Edinburgh together nearly forty years ago, now."

"I was studying advanced physics and astrophysics whilst Iain was studying medicine," added Fraser.

"Fraser has been helping me to research this conundrum and Liz's abilities ever since. He's also helped me to preserve my identity, for which I owe him a great debt of gratitude!" declared Iain.

"I'm not sure I want to know how you've managed to do that, or else I might have to arrest you for faking your ID," replied Steve. "And shame on you Iain for encouraging Fraser's delusional fantasies!" added Steve accusatorily.

"He's not delusional! We're telling you the truth, damn you!" yelled Iain angrily.

"Calm down Iain! It's an awful lot to expect anyone to swallow, never mind a narrow minded policeman," jibed Fraser. "You forget that policemen like to have evidence, proof. Come with me, Detective, and I'll show you some proof," directed Fraser as he beckoned to Steve to follow him into another room across the hallway which had been converted into a small laboratory.

Opening a cupboard at the back of the laboratory, the Professor extracted what looked like a small shoe box sized rectangular glass tank partially filled with a slightly cloudy gelatinous substance. Removing it from the cupboard and placing it on the bench, Steve noticed a strange pattern of short parallel lines, like the bar code on a tin of food, resting at the surface of the gel.

"This is my DNA extracted using a process called, Electrophoresis. This is my genetic life history going back through the generations. Now let's look at Iain's," instructed the Professor as he removed a second tank and placed it next to the first tank. "As you can see, Iain's DNA strand is a little shorter. If I took a sample from you detective and obtained your DNA in the same way, it would be more or less the same length as mine. With each generation we add new genetic information to our DNA, marrying the information from our mother's DNA with that from our father's DNA. Iain's DNA is shorter and less complicated by approximately eight generations, making it possible to confirm that he was born more than eight generations ago," explained Fraser.

Stunned, Steve collapsed on to a nearby stool.

"How the hell does anybody survive for 292 years?" asked Steve dumbfounded.

"You'd have to ask Iain that. But I suspect that it is entirely due to his dedication to Liz and his relentless quest to find her and solve the mystery of her special gifts. He hasn't ever confided his feelings for her to me, and I must insist that what I say never leaves this room. Having come to know Iain exceptionally well over the past forty years, and having seen him suffer tremendous heart ache and grief after her visits to him, I can reasonably conclude that he is very much in love with her," whispered Fraser softly.

"He must be!" replied Steve.

"But remember, it is vitally important that Liz does not learn of the details of her visits to Iain's past life, and she must not know of Iain's love for her, unless she discovers it naturally for herself. There must be no interference, do you understand?" instructed Fraser.

"I understand Professor."

"Good! Now I can go and put the kettle on for a nice pot of tea!"

Iain was sitting on the edge of the sofa holding Liz's hand gently in his, when Steve and Fraser re-entered the room. Steve, still visibly reeling from the information overload he'd received, quietly sat down in the chair on the other side of the fireplace. Fraser carried a small tray containing a pot of steaming tea, a small jug of milk and three mugs, which he placed on a small table next to the fireplace.

"So where did you find her, Iain?" asked Fraser.

"She's a student in the psychology class I took over for the first time yesterday. I recognised her despite her false name and non-usual apparel. Then, we met again last night at the ball. We got talking."

"Who shot her?" asked Fraser.

"We don't know. They were in a helicopter," replied Steve.

Fraser's eyebrows rose in surprise.

"I better explain," said Iain.

"I think you better," agreed Fraser intrigued.

"After the failed attempt to abduct her from the ball, Liz and I took off back to my place. We got cleaned up had something to eat and then retired to bed.

Liz was in the spare room and I slept in my room. The next thing I knew, I could hear voices talking in her room. That's when I met Steve here, who'd come to warn us that trouble was on the way. No sooner had he done that, than they arrived. So we climbed out of the bathroom window and took off into the woods. Steve had a mate, Grant who tagged along and helped plan our escape. He had a four-by-four stashed in the woods, so we headed off to find it. Once we got there, after a couple of mishaps, we set off in the four-by-four and got out of the woods and headed towards the city. Then they came after us in a van and a helicopter.

We managed to lose the van but the helicopter tailed us and began using us for target practice. Grant was killed and Liz was shot. We lost the helicopter in the city when we ditched the four-by-four in the multi-storey car park. Steve acted as decoy so that Liz and I could escape through the Shambles. We met up near the Minster and tried to lose them in the Cathedral, but they found us. Then we arrived here. That's about it, really," explained Iain massaging his head nervously.

"I'm surprised that you contemplated taking her into the Minster," remarked Fraser." "Especially knowing how sensitive she is."

"Why do you say that?" asked Steve.

"It's obvious really. That place is filled with latent thought energy accumulated over hundreds of years," explained Fraser.

"Latent thought energy?" asked Steve.

"Prayers!" translated Iain.

"To Liz it would feel like sitting in Wembley Stadium on Cup Final day. No wonder she was overcome, which is what I presume happened?"

"Yeh, that's right!" replied Steve, amazed at Fraser's accurate conclusion. "She just suddenly froze," added Steve.

"That's why," said Fraser. "She needs plenty of rest and plenty of fluids…." recommended Fraser.

"That's easier said than done…..when you've got a squad of hired killers hot on your trail!" said Steve. "We've also got a rendezvous to keep."

Iain thought for a moment as he looked at Liz, lying on the sofa.

"With those goons out there, I don't think it would be wise to cross the city in daylight…..and we could all do with some rest.......Are you sure she'll be alright?" Iain asked Fraser.

"She's been through a lot.....but, the brain is a marvellous thing. Once she's had a chance to rest and restore some balance in her mind, she should be okay."

"Right, that's settled then......We rest while Liz is recovering. Then we plan how we're going to leave here after night fall.....if that's okay with you, Fraser?" asked Iain.

"There's a spare room in the attic...with a good view of the city....You're welcome to stay there til you're ready to leave...."

"Thanks Fraser.......Ohhh, and it goes without saying.......we were never here...for your own safety," advised Iain.

"I understand......You do realise, don't you, that if somebody else has found out about her abilities, we'll have every agency in the world trying to get their hands on her," remarked Fraser. Iain and Steve both nodded. "Two questions," added Fraser.

"Yes?" asked Iain.

"Do we know who they are, and how did they find out?" asked Fraser.

"That's it! We don't know!" replied Iain shrugging his shoulders.

"Do you remember anything about Liz's visits to you that might shed some light on this?" asked Fraser.

"There were so many visits, and so many challenges and dangers we faced together. But I don't see how any of those events could impact on us here, in the present!" replied Iain.

"For someone to only come after her now, suggests that she's only recently attracted their attention, whoever they are," suggested Fraser. "To want to kill her.......they obviously see her as a serious threat!"

"I don't think they know yet about her full potential....." "remarked Iain.

"I wouldn't be so sure about that," remarked Steve. "What gives you that idea?" he asked.

"That guard in the woods wasn't prepared for her. If I'd been responsible for sending those men in, knowing what she was capable of, don't you think I would have warned them, prepared them with some kind of brain wave inhibitor or something!" Iain replied.

"What happened in the woods?" asked Fraser. "It's important."

"We were held up by one of their men carrying a gun. I don't know what she did exactly. She seemed to get inside the guy's head and kept him distracted until Grant was able to knock him out from behind," said Steve.

"I think from that, we can assume that they're now aware of her thought manipulation skills, but it still doesn't explain how they found about her and why they see her as a threat, unless they think her abilities can stop them doing whatever they are planning to do!" concluded Fraser. "Iain, you mentioned something before about Liz being able to project forwards as well as backwards in time."

"That's right."

"What exactly did she say about her visits into the future?" Fraser asked intrigued.

"Only that she's made one to some kind of mine. I was in the process of rescuing her apparently, and there were explosions going on and water flooding the mine. Do you think that they're responsible for what happens in that mine?"

"They could be. We would need to work out what sort of mine it was, where it was and why they would want to destroy it," replied Fraser.

"I can only think of one reason," said Steve.

"Go on," encouraged Fraser.

"Money! Depending on what they're mining for, it could be anything from pulling off a major insurance scam, to increasing the value of that mined ore on the world market."

"Good suggestion. Just one problem," replied Fraser.

"And what's that?" asked Iain.

"How does Liz fit into the equation? She doesn't work for a mining company or for a stock broker does she?" asked Fraser.

"No she doesn't," replied Steve. "Her records showed that she was just your average telephone clerk in a city call centre.

Fraser shook his head.

"I think we need to talk to Liz once she's had a chance to rest. She may know something that can point us in the right direction. In the meantime, we do have one very important clue," announced Fraser.

"And what's that Professor?" asked Steve.

"The mine is in very close proximity to a large area of water. So it's either a coastal mine or it's situated near to or beneath a large lake."

"Do you have access to the internet Professor?" asked Steve eagerly.

"Yes of course. You can use the computer in the lab. Do you know anything about geology, Detective?" asked Fraser.

"In case you are right about the money angle to this, focus your searches on mines very rich in mineral deposits like copper, silver, gold…"

"I get the idea, Professor," replied Steve getting to his feet.

"Iain? Can I suggest that you carry this young lady up to the attic room where she can rest."

"Show me the way Fraser," said Iain as he carefully picked up Liz in his arms.

"Okay. Follow me."

With that, Fraser led the way out of the living room and headed towards the staircase. Steve disappeared across the hall way and into the lab while Iain trailed behind Fraser making his ascent up the stairs to the attic room which stood on the second floor. As they made their way up the steep flight of wooden stairs, the banisters and steps creaked noisily under their weight. Iain gazed down at Liz, who appeared undisturbed by any of the noises around her.

"Don't worry......These stairs may be old, but they're as solid as a rock.......They just creak a bit .... like my joints." said Fraser as he turned the key in the lock of the antique and well worn oak door.

Pushing the door slowly open, they were suddenly bombarded with bright sunshine beaming through the window. The dust hung like clouds in the sunlight, the tiny particles dancing and swirling around like glitter in a glass snow globe. There was an old settee pushed into the shadows in the far corner of the room, to the left of the window, with a matching armchair beside it. A chest of drawers, which had two or three missing handles stood against the wall to their right, and beside that was a single bed which looked like it hadn't been slept in since the Second World War.

Iain walked over to the bed and laid Liz gently on top of the covers whilst Fraser opened the window to let out the stale air. The window sash was quite stiff, and Iain offered his assistance to give the archaic window frame a firm shove from the bottom, to open it. As they did so, the deadened silence of this long forgotten room was replaced with the sounds of birds singing in competition with the traffic from the streets below. The fragrant scent of flowering honeysuckle drifted in through the window, sweetening the heavy odour of old wood and rusty springs that had welcomed them on their entry into the room.

"There's a good view of York Minster from here…….. but under the circumstances, you're probably better off staying out of sight…"

"I think that's the general plan." confirmed Iain.

"You stay here with Liz. …I'll fetch you some blankets and pillows…and then I'll bring you some food and tea…"

"Please don't go to a lot of effort on our part." said Iain. "You've done quite enough as it is.."

"Nonsense…….All I ask, is that you introduce me to Liz when she's awake…..We need to know more about her visit to that mine….But see how she feels when she comes round…"

"Will do," replied Iain, as he sat down carefully on the edge of the bed beside Liz.

Fraser paused for a moment to look at Liz as she lay on the bed resting peacefully.

"She'll be fine, Iain," smiled Fraser. "It must seem very strange to you, to meet her now, in the flesh for the very first time after all of those previous encounters."

"I've spent so long searching and waiting, I guess it hasn't sunk in yet."

"You'll have to find something else to occupy your mind. What will you do now, once this problem is sorted out?" asked Fraser.

"I think that depends on Liz."

"She doesn't know how you feel, does she?"

"No….I want to tell her Fraser! I want to tell her so much, but I'm afraid, if I do, I'll drive her away!"

"She appears to have trusted you and followed you so far. Give her some time to adjust to everything else that's going on in her life at the moment. She might just surprise you, "encouraged Fraser as he left the room.

Iain listened, as the sound of creaking steps faded away into the distance. Then, reaching across the bed to Liz, he gently swept her hair away from her face and watched as the bright sunshine haloed her entire body. Gazing lovingly at her, he gently lifted her hand and kissed her soft delicate skin, whilst reminiscing of their far flung adventures together. Stretching across the foot of the bed, he lay curled around her, holding her hand gently, guarding her from the world. As he began to doze contentedly, Liz fell into a deeper, darker sleep.

CHAPTER 13

THE AIR WAS CRISP AND cold by the loch side. It was early autumn and the heather on the hills and mountains surrounding Libran's Loch resembled a patchwork quilt of mottled red and vivid purple heather blossom. The leaves on the trees had begun to turn golden and red, shining and rustling like bags of copper pennies in the morning breeze.

The village shepherd was a young self-educated man in his late twenties, with boyish good looks and a sense of humour to match. Although he had often been disciplined during his childhood for not taking life seriously enough, he had grown, into a very diligent and responsible young man, dutifully tending to his family's flock and well respected by his kinsmen and friends. On the surface, he was well known for his cheery disposition, but beneath the surface, there churned a deep, dark current of loneliness, of a love unrequited and the frustration of hopes and dreams unfulfilled. Being the son of a shepherd and a weaver, Iain had grown up wandering the hillsides, herding the sheep, and only venturing into the village to sell them or their wool at the market, and to purchase essential supplies. Since his parent's sudden death two years before,, Iain had spent many a candle lit evening reading the only book they possessed, an old threadbare leather bound bible which had been in his family as far back as he could remember and from which his mother had taught him to read. Then replenished with hope from the scriptures, he'd sleep alone with only the gentle bleat of the sheep outside to disturb his nocturnal dreamtime fantasies of wondrous places he'd never seen, friendly acquaintances he'd never met, adventures beyond his reasoning and of the love he aspired to share.

Each morning, when the sun rose over the mountains and pierced through the split wood of his window shutters, cutting like a golden knife through the darkness inside the cottage, the shepherd would open his eyes to the new day and whisper his first words of the morning, "Please, let today be that day."

But, this morning he awoke earlier than usual, and said nothing. Instead, sitting up beneath the covers, he felt the strongest desire to be near the water and marched purposefully down the hillside towards the Loch, watching the mists roll back as he made his descent. The early morning sun shone on the rippling waters, catching each wave crest and scattering the sunlight like shimmering diamonds upon their surface.

Stripping off his worn and darned shirt which his late mother had sewn for him long ago, and the kilt bequeathed to him from his father, he plodged barefoot and naked into the icy water beside the trees, a safe distance from the village and prying eyes. Bracing himself against the sharp breath taking coldness of the loch, the shepherd held his breath and dived into the shallow waters where the current was weakest. Watching the fish dart this way and that as he glided carefully over the fine pebbled and sandy loch bottom, the shepherd held his breath for as long as possible, until the build up of carbon dioxide in his lungs and the sharp coldness of the crystal clear water stabbing sharply at his chest, forced him back up to the surface to breathe.

Beneath him, more shoals of small fish darted here and there, reflecting the morning sunshine back up into his face.

Catching his breath, and wary of the dangerous currents which had claimed the lives of far stronger swimmers than himself, the shepherd set off to swim parallel to the shore. Ploughing his way through the waters, he swam steadily towards the furthest point of the bay before stopping to tread water and to catch his breath for a while.

Looking far out across the Loch, he could just make out the prow of a small rowing boat breaking the mist from the far bank side. Puzzled, he swam the few short yards towards the rocks, and held on to them for support and concealment as the boat emerged towards the centre of the loch.

Aboard the boat, sat a young girl in her early twenties, with long curled tresses of dark auburn hair, struggling with the oars against the wind and the cross currents. The shepherd watched as her free flowing hair blew wildly in the wind, and her woollen shawl was suddenly ripped heartlessly from her shoulders and blown some distance across the water. Rowing hard towards the drifting shawl, she ventured further and further into the turbulent currents at the heart of the loch, until finally the water drenched garment drifted just within her grasp. Laying down the oars in the bottom of the boat, she stood up to turn around, facing the shepherd hiding in the distance through the dispersing mist.

Standing in the wind with her long skirts stretched tautly behind her like a thick yacht sail, she struggled to retain her balance in the continuously rocking boat. Spray from the Loch lashed against the boat and the front of her dress, causing it to cling tightly to her slender figure. Unaware that her vessel was drifting with the currents nearer and nearer towards the rocks, she knelt forwards on the wooden seat inside the boat, to reach out across the turbulent water. Grasping again and again for the woollen shawl, she reached further and further out of the boat as it pitched and tossed in the tide. Then, as she reached out one last time, hoping to trap the shawl before the weight of the well drenched yarn sent it sinking below the surface, a sudden wave tipped the hull and the young girl's face and sleeve felt the cold, merciless slap of the loch's watery hand.

Stretching defiantly towards the shawl, determined to prevent the loch from stealing her mother's precious handy work, she narrowly missed its edge by barely a finger's length. Suddenly, an almighty crack echoed across the water, as the keel struck a large jagged rock rising up beneath the boat, cracking the old worn timbers. Helplessly, the young girl lost her balance and toppled into the turbulent, treacherous depths. Falling sideways, the young girl's head struck the side of the boat as it recoiled, and her unconscious body rose to the surface, drifting face down in the water, awaiting certain death in the lonely early morning sunshine.

Diving headlong into the waves, the shepherd fought courageously against the current, praying that he would reach the floating body intime. As he struck the water with each slicing stroke of his hands, he could just make out the edge of the boat as it began to sink down into the icy depths of the loch. By the time he was within a few yards of it, the boat had completely disappeared, leaving only himself and its pale unconscious victim, alone to fight the battering waves.

Turning her body over in the water, the shepherd clasped his left arm around her chest, and rested her head against his shoulder, as he fought single handed to bring the young girl safely back to shore. Each wave that crossed his path, sent cold fresh water splashing directly into his face, his mouth and his nose. Spluttering for air, he pushed on undaunted and determined until he felt the rocks at the bottom of the shallows, graze his shins.

Lifting the girl's body carefully over the edge of a large smooth round boulder, he rolled her gently on to her stomach, and slid her head and chest carefully over its edge to let gravity force the water from her stomach and lungs. After a minute of persistent massage, Iain heard the sound he was waiting for. Ejecting the last of the loch water from her mouth, the young girl coughed and choked her way back to consciousness.

Then, suddenly realising his embarrassing predicament, he dashed the short distance across the pebbled shoreline to his heap of discarded clothing, and got dressed. Tucking the old shirt beneath his kilt, the shepherd trotted back to the cold and shivering maiden he had rescued so gallantly from the early morning tide. Liz sat up on the rock, as she felt the wave of pain throb across her temple and flinching as she touched the tender reddened bump with her fingers.

Where was she, she asked herself, as she wiped her face with the wet sleeve of her blouse and blinked hard, her eyes, still bleary from emersion in the loch. The last thing she remembered as her vision came back into focus, was being in York Minster, hearing all the voices and the prayers of a thousand years or more pounding inside her head, and then, blackness. With a look of bizarre puzzlement, Liz gazed across the Loch, which reminded her of a place she had once visited with her family, years ago. But, if this was the same place, it was very, very different to the way she remembered it. The hillside in the distance looked the same, but there was little sign of the village along the shoreline, or the caravan park on the far bank where they had stayed all those years ago. In any event, if this was the place she was thinking of, why was she here? As far as she knew, she had made no conscious suggestion to visit this place, unlike her previous projection, when she had wished herself on to that hot sandy beach? Something else was different about this projection too! Looking down at her long dark wet hair and dripping wet full length dress with layer upon layer of petticoats, she began to realise that she wasn't transparent like before. She had substance. Then, leaning curiously over the edge of the large rock, she gazed at her reflection in the water only to discover that the face staring back at her was not her own. She was inside someone else's body and mind, but whose? And unless, this person had just left a fancy dress party or a period film set, the most important question she needed to ask herself wasn't 'where' she was but, WHEN!

Attempting to stand up in the shallow water along the shoreline, Liz suddenly realised she was barefoot and winced as the plethora of small sharp stones and pebbles stabbed at the souls of her feet like a bed of nails. Pursing her lips with the pain, she tried to hop between the larger flatter stones, until a sudden wave rushed at her ankles, pummelling her feet with shale until she lost her footing and fell sideways into the shallows. The sudden shock of the icy cold water in her face made her gasp and draw in a sharp deep breath which she found hard to exhale, as she tried to stand up. Then, the weight of the water laden petticoats and deeply hemmed overskirt dragged her back down into the water with the retreating wave, despite her best efforts to climb the pebbly slope.

Looking up she noticed the young kilted man with his long dark brown messy hair loosely tied in a pony tail, standing on the bank side roaring with laughter. Liz scowled with a look as black as thunder.

"Never mind laughing, what sort of gentleman are you? How about giving me a hand out of here!" she yelled, but the young man didn't move. "I said, give me a hand!"

Infuriated she stepped forward, unthinking, straight on to the hem of her dress and in an instant came crashing down again as another icy wave lashed against her, filling her mouth and nose with water which she was forced to expel with a noisy snort and splutter. Raising herself up on to her hands and knees, all she could see was the thick curtain of long, dark brown, very wet hair and occasional strands of loch weed that hung down over her face. Embarrassed and despondent, she looked down to see a man's firm hand reaching through her wet mop of hair to grab her wrist.

"Here! Give me your hand!" said the young man, stifling his laughter within his broad Scottish accent.

Surprised, Liz suddenly stood up, and yelped as the tender bump on her head struck something hard. In the same instant, she heard a startled, "arrgggh," as her head caught the young man under his chin, sending him backwards into the water with a hefty splash. Parting her wet hair, Liz looked down at the young man sat in the water with the hem of his kilt floating upwards in the current like a large tartan water lily. This time, it was Liz's turn to mock the blushing shepherd as he clambered back on to his feet, wrestling with his drifting kilt, to preserve his modesty.

"That'll teach you for laughing!" she said, trying to stifle her own reactive giggle.

The shepherd gripped his jaw with his hand, cursing under his breath as he moved it carefully from side to side to assess the level of injury.

"And you should watch where ye put your head!" he retorted. "You damn near broke my jaw!" he moaned.

"What did you expect, sneaking up on me, like that?" she replied defensively. "You made me jump!"

"Aye, I know," he sighed. "

"I'm sorry," she said smiling softly. "Are you okay?"

"Aye, I'll live!" he replied. "And I suppose I'd better introduce myself," he added. "I'm Iain Lachlan, village shepherd and weaver. And you are?"

"Liz, Elizabeth Curran, but all my friends call me Liz. I'm a …." Liz suddenly stopped mid-sentence whilst she thought of something more appropriate to say than 'call centre operator '. "....fortune teller."

"You don't look like a gypsy," Iain remarked as he stepped back and took a good look at her.

"I didn't say I was a gypsy. I said I was a fortune teller. I can read your past and your future," she replied carefully.

"If I were you, I'd keep that to yourself. Strange things happen around here from time to time so many folk are cautious and superstitious. So be careful what you say and do around here," Iain advised.

"Thanks," she replied smiling before asking curiously. "What sort of strange things?"

"We have unusual sudden thunderstorms that arrive one minute and gone the next. We sometimes get strange mists here and green lights above the loch. We even feel the ground shaking sometimes and it takes me hours to calm the sheep down afterwards."

"You get earthquakes here?" she asked.

"That's a good name for them," Iain remarked. "What did you call them? Earthquakes?" he asked.

"Yes."

"Aye we do!" he added.

"Sounds like the area could be highly charged with electromagnetic energy too!" she added.

"E-lec-tro-maggy what?" asked Iain.

"Errrr lightening, thunder, that sort of stuff," she replied quickly.

"What did you call it?" he asked.

"It doesn't matter," she said. "It's not important," she added wondering if she should have said anything.

"You're not from around here are ye?"

"That depends on where here is."

"You're lost?" he asked, puzzled by her response.

"I think so."

"You didn't look so lost before when you were rowing that boat," he remarked. "You seemed to know exactly where you were going."

"What boat?" she asked surprised.

"Aye, what boat indeed!" he declared. "The one that you crashed into the rocks and which now lies at the bottom of the loch!"

"Oh," she sighed and dropped her eyes guiltily.

"Do you not remember?" he asked concerned.

"I just remember waking up on that rock ," she replied.

"Do you remember anything at all, before your accident?"

Liz could remember the Minster and all of the events of the past twenty-four hours quite clearly, but thought wiser of speaking the truth to the stranger.

"I don't remember a thing!"

"That bump on the head must have caused more harm than I thought," he remarked, concerned. "Yet, you remember who you are."

"Where am I?" she asked directly.

"This is Libran's Glen."

"So that must be Libran's Loch!" she said as she surveyed her surroundings. "But it looks different to the way I remember it."

"I think you must be mistaken, m'lady. I've lived here all my life and it's always been this way. The only thing that changes around here, are the seasons."

Then, looking down at her own clothes and those of the stranger she asked,

"Have we just come from some wedding or fancy dress party?"

"That's a strange question to ask!" he replied.

"Not really, when you consider what we're wearing," she

said. "You look like you've just walked off the set of 'Rob Roy MacGregor'!"

Iain threw her an odd, puzzled look.

"I'm not sure I understand what you're saying," he replied. "But I wouldn't speak that name in these lands," advised Iain anxiously, "lest the sheriff clap you in irons for your utterance!"

"What?"

"The mere mention of that name carries the stiffest of penalties in these parts!"

Liz stopped in her tracks as she tried to think of what he was referring to. Then she remembered about the conflict at Glen Fruin in 1603 and the proscription of the MacGregor name until 1775.

"But that was centuries ago and the proscription was lifted in …" replied Liz, before stopping in mid-sentence. "What year is this?"

"I think I better fetch the physician," he remarked, concerned.

"Please tell me! It's important!" she pleaded.

"1746," he replied.

Liz's eyes widened.

"The Battle of Culloden," she whispered. "Maybe that's why I'm here."

"You know about Culloden?"

"Who doesn't? It was one of the most famous battles in Scottish his-tor-y…" she said, her voice trailing off as she saw the strange look on Iain's face. "At least that's what they're saying…" she added, making a quick recovery, and sighing deeply.

This, 'not mentioning the future' business was beginning to be a lot harder than she first thought. In fact, it was beginning to give her a bit of a headache, or was that just the bump on the head, she said to herself. Dumbfounded,

Liz picked up her heavy wet skirts and crawled slowly and painfully on to the grassy bank. Then, sitting down on the grass, she stared bemused, far out across the Loch, her face pale with shock.

Straightening his water logged kilt which now hung low and heavy around his hips, the shepherd looked at the dismayed and sorry looking young woman, shaking his head.

"And what kind of madness was it that drove ye out on to the loch alone this morning? Don't ye know how dangerous the currents are out there?" he asked.

"Like I said before, I don't remember," she whispered softly.

Iain began to eye her suspiciously.

Completely at a loss to understand her presence more than two hundred and sixty years in the past, Liz looked anxiously at the young shepherd as he brushed his hair back away from his face, to reveal the unmistakable and instantly recognisable, rich brown and honey golden eyes she had become quite well acquainted with over the past twenty-four hours. Unable to hide her delight and relief at seeing a familiar face, Liz immediately smiled,

"Oh, it's you!" she exclaimed with delight, unthinking. "I didn't recognise you, especially when you said your name was 'Lachlan'," she added. "What are you doing here?"

"I should be asking you that question!" Iain replied.

Then seeing Iain's raised eyebrows she further added, "Perhaps I'm mistaken."

"Aye I think you must be," he replied. "I would have remembered meeting someone like you," he said as he rubbed his jaw. "but I don't."

Liz smiled in a vain attempt to hide her disappointment. She was sure it was him or at least a close relative. The likeness was too good to be mere coincidence she thought.

Puzzled by her odd questions and the inconsistency in the answers, Iain thought about the nasty bump she'd sustained on her head, and dismissed his suspicions.

"If ye promise not to break my jaw or half drown me again, I'll set ye on your feet, m'lady," Iain said softly, as he proffered a supportive hand to her.

With eyes gleaming in the morning sunlight, Liz reached out and placed her hand in his. As their fingers and palms touched, a strange tingle of energy rippled between them and the time line quivered.

Back in the present, as Iain sat by Liz's bedside and held her pale limp hand in his, a strange shiver ran through his body and the pathway between his past self and the present was forged.

"Now, if ye'll take my advice, you're best coming with me, cos if the sheriff catches ye, he'll be a hangin' you for sure!"

"But why? I haven't done anything wrong, at least not that I remember!" she declared anxiously.

"That doesn't matter 'round here. You're English and that's enough! He does nae care if you're innocent or no! He'll have ye hung for a spy or a smuggler without a doubt!"

"Where will you take me?" she asked curiously.

"Back to my home up on the hillside not far from here," he whispered. "But we best leave now, afore anyone sees us," he instructed. "Come on!"

Turning away from Liz, the shepherd strode away through the long grass, unhindered by the rough weeds and prickles that lay under foot, whilst Liz danced precariously on bare footed tip toe, wincing and wobbling with every step. Looking back and noticing her difficulty, the shepherd shook his head at her strange ineptness and strode back towards her. Then, with no warning or permission, he picked her up and tossed her over his shoulder like a wounded sheep.

"Hey! What the hell do you think you're doing?" she shouted. "Put me down!"

Iain gripped her wriggling body firmly.

"There's no time to argue!" he replied. "If we do it your way there'll be no chance of reaching the cottage afore midnight!" he retorted.

"Do you treat all your women like this?" asked Liz as she hung upside down over his shoulder, confronted by the rhythmic sluggish swaying of his kilt.

"No. Only you," he replied.

"Why is that?" she asked curiously. "Why single me out for this punishment?" she asked.

"Because you're different, unpredictable," he replied. "You're like a lost sheep, certain to find yourself in trouble if there's no one around to help you."

"And why would you want to help me?" Liz replied.

"It's my job, I'm a shepherd," he replied. "It's all I've ever known – to guide and protect."

Liz thought of the Iain in her present and the way he'd behaved since they met barely two days ago and nodded. In over two hundred years he hadn't changed. He was still her shepherd, her protector, leading her away from danger.

"And whereabouts on this fair green isle do ye come from m'lady?"

Liz opened her mouth to reply, but remembered the warning.

"Over the border," she replied coyly.

"Oh aye, tell me something I don't know!" he snapped impatiently. "I mean where exactly, or do ye have a wee hidey-hole up here somewhere?"

Liz shrugged her shoulders.

"You said that I came across the loch in a boat. Perhaps the answer lies over there, across on the other side."

"Now that's the first sensible thing I've heard ye say so

far," Iain remarked. "and I think ye might be right! But first we need to get ye dry and get that bump seen to!" said Iain as they approached his cottage.

Setting Liz carefully down on the ground, Iain stood up again slowly, letting out a deep sigh of relief as he stretched his stiff neck and arms. Whilst Liz regained her composure and the blood flow to the rest of her body, she watched as Iain walked up to the door of the cottage unaware that his water logged kilt had slid so low on his hips that the upper most part of his bottom, lay exposed like a woman's cleavage above the tartan. Iain turned around as he heard her soft laughter.

"My house is no that bad!" he replied defensively. "It's no palace I grant ye, but it's home and it's dry and it's warm. What more can I say?"

"That's not why I'm laughing," she smiled as she watched his kilt droop defiantly down the side of his hip.

Iain followed her eye line and looked down at the sagging wet tartan. Then turning his back on her to hide his blushes, he gathered the wet fabric together with his left hand and pushed open the door with the other.

From the outside, the small low built cottage looked bleak and uninviting, sticking out from the hillside with moss and heather for thatch and creaky wooden shutters to close the glassless windows and provide shelter from the extremes of the valley's weather. But, on entering the dwelling, Liz was greeted with a welcoming atmosphere and hospitality far better than she expected from the humble shepherd.

At the back of the one room cottage was a wide stone ingle-nook housing a roaring fire, lit freshly that morning. A pot hung from a large metal hook bedded into the mantle above the fire, casting out steam and bubbling aromas of a sweet rabbit broth. A small handmade table and two chairs stood in the right hand corner whilst in the other, draped with a course sacking curtain, tied to the roof beams to shut out the cold draughts, stood the fairly large wooden bed.

"This is my humble home, m'lady and until we find out where ye came from and get ye back home, you're a welcome guest here," he declared. "If you give me but a moment, I'll fetch ye a blanket."

Skirting carefully around her in the doorway, the shepherd dashed across to the bed and pulled off one of the covers. Shaking the dust from the blanket and inspecting it for any imperfections, he stretched the woollen sheet out in front of him like the sail on a ship, whilst his now unhanded and un-tethered kilt drooped at half-mast around his muscular thighs.

"If ye care to come closer," he said encouragingly, nipping his knees together to trap the falling tartan. "I'll wrap this around ye."

Liz nervously entered the cottage, her heavily soaked dress releasing a muddy wet wake behind her, as she crossed the stone floor towards him. Iain watched her struggle with the weighty hem of her dress and shuffled forward towards her, to shorten her journey. Looking up and suddenly seeing his outstretched arms around her, Liz cowered in confused uncertainty.

"I won't harm ye, I promise," whispered the shepherd softly. "Let me help ye," he added placing the blanket around her shoulders before swiftly grasping his kilt and leashing it back into place.

"Now the fire's been burnin' well this morning, so ye'll warm up in next to no time," he remarked. "While I chop some more wood outside, for the fire, why don't ye get yourself dry and hang your wet clothes by the fire. You'll feel much better and the dress will dry far quicker." he suggested.

Liz nodded timidly.

Then, grabbing his axe from behind the cottage front door, Iain headed back outside to split some logs.

"I won't be gone long! If you need me, I'm just outside," he said as he carefully closed the cottage door behind him, leaving Liz standing alone in front of the fireplace.

Iain was right, she thought. I need to get out of this dress. Pulling apart the wet laces that fastened the front of her bodice, she tugged and pulled at the stubborn wet fabric of the tightly fitted sleeves, peeling them from her cold shivering skin. Then, dragging the dress down over her hips, she pushed the heavy water drenched skirts and petticoats to the floor and stepped out from the mound of wet cloth. Picking up the wet garments, Liz laid them carefully over the two chairs that stood at either side of the hearth, just far enough away from the flames to prevent any sparks setting them alight. With just the thinnest white cotton camisole and knee length bloomers clinging to her slender body, she stood as close as she dared to the flames and rubbed her goose pimpled bare arms briskly with her cold bare hands. Then, picking up the blanket which had fallen to the floor near her feet, she pulled its opposite corners together around her shoulders like an overly long poor man's cape and stood in front of the fire staring pensively into the serpentine flames that hissed and spat in the hearth.

Whilst appreciating that Iain was the obvious link between this place and time and the present, Liz was less confident about why she had been pulled back to that particular point in his life. As she continued to look deep into the flames, she ran all the possible reasons she could think of, through her head. Was there something else in the present, that tied in with that day in the past? Was it possibly something to do with the girl, and Iain saving her life? But if that was the case, where did Liz fit into all of this? Clearly, there were more pieces to this puzzle which had yet to be revealed, she considered, as her thoughts turned to Iain. She remembered what she'd sensed as they'd danced at the ball the previous evening, that feeling of a once intimate bond rekindled between them. Something, some past chemistry clearly existed between them and one way or another, Liz was determined to find out the truth. Yet, she sensed nothing, no bond at all with this rough handed shepherd. He behaved like a complete stranger towards her. But then, she reminded herself, she was inside someone else's body and maybe this girl didn't interest him. Perhaps this was where it all began, she suggested to herself. Perhaps something was about to happen that day, that would change their lives forever. All she could do was, wait and see.

As the heat from the fire caused the water in her clothing to evaporate, a faint humid cloud of condensation began to develop around the fireplace, shrouding her in an ethereal mist. The smell of damp cloth took her back to the many times as a child, when she had sat and watched her mother as she ironed the slightly damp bed sheets and clothes in the tiny kitchen of their semi-detached house. She missed those far off halcyon days before the madness of bizarre happenings took a hold of her life, those days, when she huddled by the fireplace, with no worries or responsibilities. Smiling at the memories, she removed her wet undergarments and carefully draped them across the front of the chairs to dry.

Just as she did so, Iain carefully pushed open the cottage door with his back, and re-entered the room carrying a stack of logs in his fine toned muscular arms. The sudden draught from the doorway bowed the flames and Liz turned quickly within the humid haze, to face him, snatching the blanket to her chest. Iain stopped in his tracks, stunned by the semi naked figure silhouetted in the firelight. Startled and embarrassed, Liz stepped back into the hearth.

Missing her footing on the rough cooler chunks of blackened part-burned wood, Liz's arms flailed outwards wildly, trying to latch on to something, anything that would break her fall.

"No!" yelled Iain as he dropped the stack of logs he was holding and leapt across the room to catch her. Then, just as it had done back in the school laboratory all those years before, Liz watched everything slow down around her. In that singular moment as the flames reached out to her beckoning with dangerous inevitability, she felt herself floating timelessly, helplessly. Then suddenly, he was there, again, sweeping her away from danger with his strong muscular embrace. Then, as he placed her carefully on the stone floor, and tore off his wet shirt to smother her legs and the burning blanket with the cloth, a sudden bright light filled the cottage behind him. As the room fell strangely silent, and Liz's body fell limp in his arms, the hairs prickled on the back of Iain's neck. Cautiously and slowly, he stood up and turned away from the fireplace to face the light.

Shining in the middle of the room was Liz's projection, triggered by her heightened adrenaline and imminent danger. Made up of a billion tiny stars of light, Liz looked down at her glistening form before gazing at the frightened shepherd as he held up his hand to block out the glare. Through his fingers he could see her crystal like, sapphire blue eyes and the waves of her cascading long golden curls as they swam out around her like a halo and he realised at once that his star maiden had returned.

"You've come back!" he gasped, dropping to his knees with overwhelming surprise and relief.

Liz gazed at him intrigued, puzzled by his unexpected recognition.

"Do you know who I am?" she asked carefully.

"Yes!" he confessed, his eyes sparkling joyously. "It's

been such a long time! I thought I'd never meet you! I thought you were just a dream!"

Gazing up at her, his eyes filled with awe and wonder, he asked, "Where did you come from? Why have you returned?"

"Where I came from, I can't tell you. That's the rules I'm afraid," she sighed. "But maybe you know the reason why I'm here," she suggested. "It feels almost like I was summoned here," she said thinking quickly.

"Who by?" asked Iain.

"One guess."

"But I, ... Why would I...., "he sighed.

"Did you need me?" she asked.

Iain's head dropped. Ever since his mother had told him the story of what happened on the day he was born, he'd never stopped thinking about her. She was the first thing he saw when he closed his eyes at night, sparkling like the starriest sky, reaching out to him in the dark, and she was the first thought that entered his head each morning as he watched the golden sunrise creep over the mountains at daybreak. Liz gazed at him curiously, intrigued by his silent response.

"How did you find me?" he asked curiously.

"This girl, you're holding, has been my physical form since I arrived here," she replied. "When you rescued her, you rescued me too. You brought me here."

"You mean, you were inside her?" he asked amazed.

"Yes."

"Are you a demon, then? " he asked nervously. "Only demons possess people!"

"I'm not a demon! But mind, I must confess, I'm no angel either!" she replied.

"How long have you been inside her body?"

"Not long," she sighed. "That's why I don't remember

what happened before the accident. I arrived here just as you saved her."

Iain sat back on the floor and brought his hands to his mouth in astonishment.

"You've come to protect me again haven't you?"

"Sorry? I don't understand."

"Like the last time, … the day I was born," he replied. "Don't you remember?"

"I remember a lot of things, but not that," she confessed. "Are you saying that I've been here before?" she asked curiously.

"Yes."

"That must be a journey I've yet to make," she muttered to herself.

"You saved our lives!"

Liz shook her head.

"I'm sorry, you'll have to remind me," she sighed. "It's probably the bump on the head. My memory's a bit fuzzy, I'm afraid," she lied. "Why don't you tell me what happened and I might be able to fill in some of the gaps in my head," she suggested.

Iain's eyes opened wide. He'd never spoken of the events that happened that day, bound by a promise he'd made to his mother as a child, all those years ago, until now. Then, staring in wonderment at her ethereal beauty and magic, he recalled the distant memory of a night when his mother had sat at his bedside, cooling his fevered brow, recounting the tale of the day he was born.

"Her eyes were the brightest blue and sparkled like the stars upon the crisp blue waters of the loch, and her hair of long golden curls flowed over her shoulders like the high mountain waterfalls in spring, shining in the golden midday sun. She was the maiden of starlight, born of the heavens, a beauty worthy of Aphrodite's envy who rode into our lives on the back of a storm. With a heart as pure as the crystal blue starlight that shone from her eyes, she came to us in the hour of my birth and saved us from certain death," he said, with a voice as smooth as silk. A voice she knew and deeply adored.

"Such beautiful words," Liz replied softly.

"They were my mother's words, spoken when she described the starlight maiden to me," Iain said fondly. "She said you would return."

"Return?" questioned Liz. "But I can't be her."

"Why, not?" he asked. "You appeared like magic, out of nowhere and you look exactly like her description!"

Seeing the desperation and disappointment in his face, and in the absence of any reasonable explanation to offer him, Liz relented.

"It's probably another glitch in my memory."

"Ahh, yes. The bump on the head," nodded Iain. "That wee bump has a lot to answer for!" Iain added

"Why don't you carry on with your story? I love listening to stories," she added.

"If you think it will help," he said, puzzled by how someone so magical and seemingly all knowing, could not remember that critical time in his life. But, not wishing to disappoint his guardian, Iain sighed deeply and began his tale.

"It was 1726, I was just eight years old," he said. "I remember there was a good fire burning in the hearth that evening, chasing away the icy night time chill with its roaring flames. With the shutters closed, the heat quickly built up inside the cottage, and I was warming my bare legs and feet by the fire when my father sent me to bed.

Dressed in my long night shirt, I trotted barefoot across the stone floor and climbed into my small wooden bed near the back of the cottage. Pulling the coarse woollen blankets up to my chin, I lay back and rested my head on the soft rolled sheepskin, as my mother carried across a candle and placed it on the stool beside my bed. Then carefully sliding on to the covers beside me, she lifted my head on to her lap and lightly combed my hair with her fingers as she began to tell her tale. Staring up at the roof of the cottage, I watched the dancing shadows cast by the fire and the candlelight, as she described the fierce and blustery winds that nipped her cheeks, as she carried the wooden bucket up the hillside to fetch water from the well.

Any way, not long after she arrived there, and just after she'd raised the bucket full of water to the top of the well, she said that the hairs rose on the back of her neck and she felt heavy hot whisky breath on her skin. She described how she heard the sound of metal being slowly drawn, and saw the flash of the polished blade, as her attacker's gloved hand reached around the front of her neck. "

"She must have been terrified," remarked Liz.

"Aye she was," he replied. "Especially when he told her to turn around slowly, and she saw the short, sharp knife in his hand. She was convinced he was going to murder her."

"What did he look like?"

"He was a wee bit shorter than I, and looked a lot older with frown lines furrowed deep into his brow like 'a freshly ploughed field', she said. He wore an odd shaped dark blue coat with trousers that ran right all the way down to his feet. He wore no waistcoat, fine stockings or garters just thick dark stockings and shoes with no buckles, straps or ribbons. Beneath his coat he wore a plain unfrilled white shirt and a strange, flat and narrow, finely striped knotted cravat around his neck. There was no wig, and his silver white hair was cropped quite short."

"Go on."

"Forcing her backwards against the side of the well, he raised the knife to her throat and said he wanted me!"

"You? Did your mother tell you why?"

"He said something quite strange to her, which neither of us could make any sense of," Iain replied.

"What did he say?"

"He told my mother that I was his 'nemesis', and that I had ruined his life, but once I was dead, his life would be restored."

"What do you think he meant by that?" asked Liz.

"I don't know. How could I have ruined his life if I hadn't been born yet?" Iain asked.

Liz thought for a moment.

"Perhaps he was a prophet or fortune teller of some sort, or a visitor like me," suggested Liz.

"Oh, he was nothing like you! Apart from his clothes, he was solid, normal not spirit like at all."

"Well at least he didn't succeed in his plan, or else you wouldn't be here," said Liz positively. "So what happened?"

"My father arrived. There was a struggle and he stabbed my father, nearly killed him too. My mother swore that she watched my father take his last breath moments before her attacker stabbed her. She said he was just about to stab her again, when you arrived."

"That's horrific!" exclaimed Liz. "So what did she…I mean, 'I', do?"

"My mother described how she suddenly saw their attacker thrown backwards, as if a strong wind had taken hold of him and lifted him off the ground. He landed several feet away on the hillside, and my mother described how she turned to see the ghostly figure of a slim young woman with long fair hair that danced like golden waves in the wind. She said you had the purest blue eyes she'd ever seen, as clear and as bright as the loch beneath a summer's sky. She described how your body was almost clear like a spirit, and how you sparkled brightly like a million stars, just like you are now. She said something else too, but that couldn't have been right," said Iain.

"What did she say?" asked Liz curiously.

"She said that the maiden's belly was rounded and full like hers, but that's not what you look like now," he replied.

"Do you mean, she thought I was 'with child'?" Liz asked, choosing her terminology carefully.

"Yes."

Liz shook her head in disbelief. That would have to be a long way off in the future she thought before asking, "What happened after that?"

"You placed your hands on their attacker and he disappeared, vanished."

"What about your parents? What happened to them?"

"My mother described how you approached them and as you touched them, a strange green glow began to surround them both. At first they thought it was some strange magic or poison."

"But it wasn't, was it?" asked Liz smiling.

"When the green mist disappeared, they were healed, completely and then she was gone. She just vanished like their attacker."

"I just disappeared?" asked Liz surprised. "Without a word?"

"Well, not entirely," replied Iain. "You said something to my mother."

"Do you have any idea what that was?"

"No," sighed Iain. "Except, she said, you would return, to protect me."

"Did she?" asked Liz perplexed.

"This is the first time you've returned," sighed Iain.

"Can you remember anything else?" Liz asked intrigued.

"She said something about her wedding ring too, how you had touched it and blessed it as some kind of talisman to protect us from danger."

"So where is it now?"

"Hidden. She was so afraid of losing it and its protection, she hid it in the cottage somewhere."

"Do you know where it is?" Liz asked.

"My father and I have searched for it many times over the years, but we've never managed to find it. My mother said that the spirit protected it from being found, but that one day she'd return and guide me to it."

"Right," sighed Liz, wondering what to say. "Perhaps that's the reason I'm here," she concluded. "You might not be in danger after all. It might be that I'm here to help you find the ring," Liz suggested.

"Without it, I can't fulfil my mother's wish."

"And that was?" asked Liz.

"To give the ring to the woman I'll marry," he mumbled coyly.

"Perhaps this girl is the one you're destined to marry," suggested Liz.

"No," muttered Iain softly.

"What do you mean?" Liz asked curiously. "She's very pretty and she certainly appears to need looking after. You never know, having just saved her from a watery grave, you might have your foot in the door, there!" Liz encouraged.

"No," replied Iain almost insistently. "She's not the one," he said as his eyes searched Liz's for a reaction.

Relieved to be wrong, Liz began to examine her own feelings for the Iain she knew in the present and felt a flutter in her stomach. The feeling took her by surprise. How could she suddenly feel that excitement, that whirling, dizzy breathlessness for a man she hardly knew, she asked herself as her pulse raced under his gaze and the starlight of her face shimmered.

Iain smiled.

"Oh well, bang goes that theory," replied Liz, trying to bring the conversation back on track. "Still, whilst I'm here I suppose I can give it a shot," sighed Liz. "So what did it look like? Did she describe it to you?"

Iain gazed at the beautiful ethereal figure before him and marvelled at the odd endearingly enchanting way she spoke. Her quirky oddness, her puzzling eccentricities and her uniqueness, enticed just as much as her mystical beauty. She was new, novel and Iain had every intention of getting to know her, and finding out, who she truly was.

"My mother said that it was made from one single silver half crown, which my father took to his brother's smithy and had made into the ring. She described how it was a thin plain band of silver with their initials inscribed inside," said Iain

"Okay," Liz sighed as she thought of a plan. "Did your mother have a secret place where she kept her special possessions."

Iain stared wide eyed at Liz.

"Yes she did! It was a hollowed out stone inside the fireplace behind another stone three rows down from the fire hook! I saw her once gently patting the stone back into place." Iain said cautiously. ".But there's nothing there now. I've checked. There's been nothing there for years."

"Now that I'm here," replied Liz. "Humour me. Take another look," she suggested.

Well it sounded good at least, Liz thought to herself, praying that the science theory from her present was right, that the past, present and future really did exist at the same time. If I am the 'starlight maiden' and I plant the thought in my mind now, to convince Iain's mother to hide the ring when I visit her, then maybe it might just be there, she thought. But, what if she wasn't that maiden, Liz asked herself? What if she forgot to make the suggestion during her visit? She'd have to go to plan B, whatever that was.

Smiling confidently at Iain, despite her anxious doubts, Liz watched nervously as he followed her suggestion and went to the fireplace to carefully remove the stone that he had referred to. In the flickering light from the fire he could just make out a small piece of folded leather laid in the hollow of the hidden stone. Removing the parcel and placing it in the centre of his palm, he carefully peeled the leather back. There in the centre, tarnished black from the dampness over the years, lay his mother's ring. Beneath the ring, scratched into the leather were the words 'for my son'. Bemused, Iain carried a stool to where the young girl lay and sat down, speechless in front of Liz. Then taking the ring and rubbing it gently with a small cloth, he removed the black tarnish from the metal to reveal the shiny silver beneath and held it out for Liz to see.

"Is it hers?" asked Liz.

Iain held the ring up to the light so that he could examine the inside, and there running along the centre of the silver band were his mother's and father's initials. Iain nodded, astonished and Liz sighed with relief.

"How is that possible?" Iain asked. "How did you do that? I checked that place many times! There was nothing there, until now!"

"Science!" Liz replied

Iain rubbed the back of his head whilst gazing at Liz's reassuring smile.

"Science? I don't understand." Iain replied.

"Don't worry about it. You will some day," she said.

"What's important is that you now have your mother's ring, just as she told you, you would."

Turning the ring over and over in his hand, marvelling at its bizarre recovery he suddenly said,

"You are the one she spoke of, aren't you?"

"Maybe."

"It's just, well, you're not quite what I imagined a guardian angel to be like," he remarked.

"How do you mean?" Liz asked.

Gazing curiously into her vivid blue eyes and daring to reach out and gently touch her cheek, he said,

"You're so beautiful, magical to behold, just like I imagined you to be. Yet, the way you talk, the things that you say, ..."

"Like I said before, I'm not an angel. In fact I can be a bit of minx at times," she confessed. "I'm sorry if I've shattered your illusions."

"Then who or what are you?"

"I'm like sunlight on water. You can see me, you can marvel at the beauty of my light, you can feel my heat, my healing mist and the tingle of my energy, but you can't hold me, well at least, not in the human sense of the word."

"You still haven't answered my question," said Iain.

Liz took a deep breath and after muttering a silent prayer for guidance, she replied.

"I'm a projection, a kind of ghost if you like. The key difference being that I am a projection of a person who is still alive elsewhere, whereas a ghost is a projection of a dead person's last energy. What you are seeing is an image cast by my active thoughts," Liz explained hesitantly.

"But if you came from a living person, then why haven't you aged twenty-eight years like I have?"

Ah, good question," she said trying to think of an

answer. "I'm not sure quite how to answer that, except to say that I'm just a guest here, a visitor. I don't live here."

"Then where do you live?" he asked.

"Not where. When," she replied. "I'm from the future," she whispered, screwing up her face in expectation of some cataclysmic reaction. When nothing happened, she looked straight at him and asked, "Are you okay with that?"

"Everything about you is so strange, different, magical," he remarked. "When you say you come from the future, why shouldn't I believe you?" he asked.

"Fair point," she replied.

"My mother trusted you. She accepted your presence and the fact that you just appeared in our lives, saved us and then vanished again. So why shouldn't I?" he asked. "There is one question I would like to ask though," he said. "Why did you choose me?" he whispered as he stepped right up close to her and looked directly into her starry pupils.

"I'm not sure I did," she replied. "Like I mentioned before, I feel like I've been summoned here. One minute I was somewhere else, next minute I was here, inside that girl's body. Bit of a mystery really." She confessed. "But if you're right about me being here before, maybe we're connected in some way. Maybe I followed a path which has already been laid," she suggested. "What do you think, Iain?" she asked smiling.

But before he could answer, she had vanished.

Crestfallen, Iain picked up the unconscious girl's body from the floor and carried her across to the bed. Then, sitting on the edge of the mattress, he stared into the fireplace, bemused. The cottage seemed that much darker now that she was gone. He knew she had to be the one that his mother had spoken of and who had haunted his dreams for so long, and she was every inch as beautiful as he'd imagined from his mother's words. Whoever she was, wherever she was, he made up his mind to find her. She was the one.

Then the girl began to stir and sat up slowly on the edge of the bed.

"Are you okay?" asked Liz. "I hope I didn't frighten you."

Startled by her revival Iain sighed disappointedly, as he looked at the brown eyed dark haired girl before him, "No, I'm fine."

"I'm still here you know," she whispered softly. "I haven't disappeared completely."

Iain smiled hopefully as he noticed a sudden flash of crystal blue light, pass across her eyes.

"How long has it been since you first saw me and rescued me from the water?" Liz asked.

"A wee while," replied Iain.

"Then we better hurry," said Liz anxiously. "Whoever she is, she'll be missed."

"I have a small boat that I keep moored near the bay. If you've the courage, we can row across the loch and see what we find there," Iain suggested.

"Good idea," replied Liz.

"But your clothes are still wet and you must be hungry too!"

Liz nodded.

"Then why don't we have some hot broth and give our clothes a chance to dry," Iain suggested as he rose to his feet and ventured across to the fireplace. "We can't do anything until then!"

The mattress was coarse and lumpy, with the odd spike of straw peeping through. Fidgeting beneath the itchy blanket and the spiky mattress, Liz watched whilst the gallant Scottish shepherd leaned across to the pot bubbling above the fire. Then, reaching above the mantle to the narrow ledge, he took down two hand carved bowls and filled them with broth from the pot. Breaking off two husks of bread from the loaf that stood on the table in a small basket, he placed each piece of bread into the bowls and handed one to Liz.

"It's fresh broth.......Made it myself.....Caught the rabbit last night, just up on the hillside yonder. It always makes a canny bowl of broth."

Liz looked into the bowl and gulped at the thought of the once fluffy rabbit that must have bobbed up and down in the heather, but after sniffing the steamy murky liquid, she decided that the aroma was quite pleasant and encouraging.

"Try it.....It will nae bite," he added.

She sipped carefully on the steaming broth as Iain lifted another drier shirt from a wooden peg on the wall and pulled it over his head, discarding the wetter one beneath. Then, disappearing behind the curtain at the edge of the bed, Liz heard the sudden flop and squelch of the wet kilt as it hit the stone floor. Re-appearing shortly afterwards, wearing another dry length of tartan, Iain fetched a small wooden stool from the back of the ingle nook, and sat down on it in front of the fire, facing Liz. With his fine lean figure and well toned muscles, there was a rugged charm about him that she found quite endearing, but just like the Iain she knew, his most attractive assets were his rich dark brown and honey coloured eyes that glistened with the reflection of the flames from the fireplace. Focussing on his eyes she drew comfort and reassurance from their familiarity as she consumed the soothing savoury liquid.

"Good?" he asked, after she'd tasted the broth.

Liz nodded.

"How's your head, now?" he asked.

"Still painful," she replied.

"Aye! I'm no surprised," he remarked. "You gave it a fair crack, enough to knock ye out!"

Liz smiled timidly as she warmed her hands around the wooden bowl and ate the hot broth.

"Ye look half starved lass! Have they no been feedin' ye well?" he asked concerned.

Liz shrugged her shoulders.

"Would ye like some more broth?"

"I'm fine thanks," she replied.

"Sure?"

"Yes," she answered, then added. "Why don't you tell me about yourself?" she asked.

"What's there to tell? I was born and brought up here in Libran's Glen. My mother schooled me and my father taught me to look after the flock, and I've been doing that ever since."

"What happened to your parents?"

"They both died about two years ago," he sighed. "It was so sudden too."

"Was it an accident?"

"Bad water."

"Bad water?" she asked curiously.

"Aye. We lost several sheep that day, too. The sheriff believed that the well had turned bad, and from that day to this, no one has dared to use it. So I fetch my water from the loch every day, after I've bathed."

"So that's how you were down by the loch when I fell in. You were bathing."

"Aye, is there something wrong with that?"

"No," she smiled.

"There's nothing like the cold crisp loch water for awakening your spirit at the start of the day," Iain declared.

"I can think of a few less drastic ways myself," Liz replied.

"And now you've learned something about me, can you tell me anything about yourself?" he asked curiously.

Liz shook her head.

"You must be able to tell me something," he insisted.

"Rules," replied Liz. "If I tell you, it could create a whole mess of problems."

Iain thought for a moment.

"If that was the case, why was my mother able to tell me that you would return, before you did?"

Liz sighed.

"I can't argue with that."

"Maybe some things were always meant to be," suggested Iain.

"Like Fate, you mean? Destiny?" asked Liz.

"Aye that's right," replied Iain.

"Oooh I don't know about that," remarked Liz. "I had no idea that any of this was heading my way. Not even, an inkling, and I certainly didn't plan 1746 as a key life event in my diary. It just doesn't make sense."

"And who set the rules you keep referring to?" Iain asked.

Liz shook her head.

"What sort of a man forbids the telling of prophecies that could give people faith and hope?" he asked. "Tell me?"

"Someone like you," Liz muttered.

"Like me? A shepherd? Who are you talking about?" asked Iain puzzled.

"You!" replied Liz.

There was a stony silence as Iain tried to take it in and Liz screwed up her face again expecting nothing but disaster. Strangely, nothing happened, not even the tiniest of ripples on the timeline, though Liz and Iain were hardly aware of that.

"What do you mean 'me'?" he asked baffled by her unexpected response. "How can that be, I've never met you before today and you said you were from the future!" Iain added.

Liz sat quietly wondering what to say, as Iain began to add things together in his head.

"That means I must be in the future too!" he concluded.

Liz said nothing.

"So why wouldn't I want myself to know what my future will be?" Iain asked himself. "Unless something bad was going to happen and I didn't want you to tell me," Iain replied to his own question.

Again Liz said nothing. What could she say? 'Oh by the way it'll be more than 260 years before we meet each other in the flesh, 'she thought. Then again, Iain had said she should give his past self something to hope for, she recalled, but what?

"Nothing bad is going to happen to you, I promise!" she said.

"And how can you be so sure of that, unless you are my guardian angel and unless you're with me all the way," Iain insisted as he gazed deeply into her eyes and smiled at her continued silence. "That's it isn't it? You're the one!"

"Yes," she replied shakily, as the realisation suddenly struck home. She was the reason he never married and why he had paid such attention to her in the present. As for the reason why he knew how to lead her around the dance floor, that was quite clearly because he knew her already, and he knew her very well. This rule she was given about not telling his earlier self about his future, wasn't just to prevent the likelihood of an unprecedented paradox, she concluded. It was to stop her learning the truth that he was in love with her!

Suddenly, from 93 million miles away at the centre of our universe and nearly twenty-nine hours after the sun released a huge solar flare of accumulated magnetic energy into space, a tremendously powerful solar wave of radiation struck the Earth. As mankind was yet to discover and share in the worldwide understanding and beneficial applications of electricity, life on Earth in 1746 appeared to continue relatively unscathed. There were the odd flocks of birds which suddenly found themselves flying a little off course, and shoals of fish that ventured off the beaten path. There were the sudden eerie sightings of green blue aurora borealis in northern most countries and a few moods and tempers slightly more frayed than usual, but apart from that, life seemed to continue as normal, except for Liz and Iain.

Supercharged with energy ripples from the solar flare, the frequency and strength of the universal wavelength between that moment in 1746 and the present, increased dramatically, channelling energy in both directions simultaneously. Suddenly an arc of the brightest light jumped between Liz's host body and Iain's earlier self, whilst an identical light arced between Liz's unconscious body in the present and Iain's later self, seated by her side.

In that moment, the present and the past were connected in one continuous stream of energy culminating in Liz's body at either end of the stream. In those brief moments, her energy signal doubled, transforming her host body into Liz's true physical form. Iain's star maiden became flesh and blood reality before his eyes. Accepting this as some kind of heavenly miracle, Iain jumped at the opportunity, uncertain of how long it would last. Looking deep into her frightened and confused eyes, Iain took a gentle hold of her left hand.

"What's happening? What did I do?" she asked anxiously.

"I don't know, Liz, but I'm glad," he declared as his deep frustration and suppressed passion rose to the surface, influenced by the solar flare. " … I'm glad that this miracle happened and I will do everything I can, not to lose you!"

"What are you going to do?" Liz asked deeply concerned.

"Stay with me Liz! …. Allow me the chance to repay the debt of honour I owe! Let me protect you, now ….always!" he pleaded whole heartedly as he held out his hand containing his mother's wedding ring.

Liz gasped with astonishment at Iain's unexpected proposal. Then, remembering his mother's words about the rings' alleged magical, protective, properties, she embraced the sentiment behind Iain's actions and allowed him to place the ring on her finger.

Overwhelmed by the energy, excitement and mixed amplified emotions surging through her, Liz felt like she was spiralling faster and faster out of control. Flinging her arms suddenly around Iain's neck and pressing her trembling softly parted lips against his, she kissed him passionately and hung on desperately until the blackness engulfed her and she passed out.

Opening her eyes, Liz looked up at the interwoven roof of branches above her head and wondered, for a moment, where she was. Then she noticed the kindly face of the shepherd as he smiled down at her.

"Are you alright in there?" he asked concerned. "You gave me quite a turn!"

"What happened?" she asked still slightly phased by the experience.

"You appeared as yourself, your flesh and blood self, just for a moment then you were gone," he said, trying hard to mask his heart wrenching disappointment and grief at her disappearance. "You became real in my hands ... and you kissed me," he said softly with a distinct sparkle in his rich honey brown and gold eyes.

Suddenly, as the memory came flooding back, Liz looked down at the wedding finger of her host, but the ring was nowhere to be seen.

"You gave me her ring," said Liz.

"Aye that I did!" he admitted, smiling.

"I know it's kind of sudden for you I guess, but I've been awaiting your return for quite a wee while," he explained. "You're no regretting your answer I hope?" he asked anxiously.

"No. I knew when I met you that there was something between us, some deep, intimate, intense bond. It's just, your proposal, it was so unexpected and now the ring's gone, "she replied. "What happened to it?" she asked confused.

"I think you took it with you, wherever you disappeared to," Iain replied.

"Back to the present?"

"Perhaps," Iain agreed.

Stunned Liz sat up on the edge of the bed and noticed that the sunshine outside was quite bright and high in the sky.

"How long was I out, I mean asleep?" she asked.

"A good while, I'm afraid," admitted Iain. "But at least your clothes are dry now. So, if you'll excuse me m'lady, I will take my leave of you for a short while as you attend to yourself," he said as he rose to his feet. "I'll await you outside when you're ready," Iain added as he left the cottage and closed the door.

Carefully lifting the dry clothes from the chairs in front of the fire, Liz dressed herself and stood for a moment in the centre of the cottage as the huge life changing penny dropped inside her mind.

"I'm engaged!" she gasped. "… in 1746! What the hell do I say to Iain when I get back home, or does he already know?" she asked herself.

Liz's head throbbed with a heavy dull ache and she wasn't so sure whether the pain was due to the bump or to the brain boggling rationalisation she was trying to perform in her mind. What she was sure of was, that Iain loved her enough to wait two and half centuries to be with her. What woman could ever say that they had been loved to that degree she asked herself, smiling. Then as she recalled the words of his proposal, she gazed down at the simple almost insignificant silver band around her finger and the time line rested.

In the present, Iain sat beside her unconscious body and vigilantly watched her every gentle breath. Then, as the veils in the past and present lifted in unison, the softest of whispers passed her lips and Iain pricked his ears to hear her say, "Yes." Then, feeling movement in her left hand, Iain looked down and beheld his mother's ring on her finger.

Pulled back along the universal energy wavelength into the present, Liz's temporarily amplified and displaced matter had returned bringing with it Iain's most valued treasure, lost to him during the interim years since that day in 1746.

Taken back by its sudden reappearance on her finger, and her echoed proposal response, Iain grasped her hand and rested his head gently against it, recognising its significance and connection to that day so many years ago. Tears of joy trickled down his cheek on to her hand and the ring, as he whispered back to her,

"Now we're connected you and I, and the miracle that brought us together will keep us together." Then, lifting his head and gazing into her softly sleeping face he added. "Come home to me, Liz. Come home."

Chapter 14

OUTSIDE THE COTTAGE, IAIN LEANED on the wooden fence that penned his sheep, and looked pensively out towards the loch. Who would have believed that such a morning as this could bring him the adventure he so long craved. Since his mother first told him of the spirit who saved them, he had kept her image alive in his mind, forever hoping that this magical entity would return. Now she had returned and with her she'd brought challenges far beyond his imagining. He thought of his mother's wedding ring now adorning Liz's marriage finger and smiled.

"Soon, Mother," he whispered softly to the gentle midday breeze. "She'll be mine, to have and to hold! I will find her, whatever it takes and when I do, I'll make her my wife, I promise as God is my witness!" he solemnly vowed.

Liz stood silently in the doorway of the cottage, her eyes brimming with tears as she watched her unexpected fiancé gazing far out towards the loch in contemplative thought. She had never known any man who had sworn such an oath of love and devotion to a woman, and no man had ever touched her heart and soul the way he did in that moment. Only she knew the long, arduous and courageous challenge he had set himself. Only she knew the sacrifice he had made for her and her alone. Clutching her mouth with her hand, to stifle her sobbing, she carefully retreated through the door and closed it quietly behind her. Her heart ached with the pain of his longing and she wanted nothing else but to throw caution and sensibility to the Highland winds and run into his arms. She wanted to tell him everything but, she knew, if she did, if she told him the truth, that they would not meet for another 264 years, she might shatter his heart and the hope that had kept him alive all those years indefatigable in his search for her. Leaning with her back against the door, with tears of despair cascading down her cheeks, she too made a solemn pledge.

"Whoever or whatever you are that brought me here, I beseech you, grant me the power and the opportunity to return to him, whenever he needs me. I won't let him make this journey alone. Help me to be there for him. Help him to survive whatever he has to face and keep him safe until that day, when we are finally together," she vowed, then taking a deep breath and wiping the tears from her eyes, she put on her bravest smile and re-opened the door.

Looking far out across the glen, he knew deep inside, that already his life was changing and would never be the same again. The cottage that had always been his home bore no binding ties on him any longer. There was a world out there, a world he didn't know and which he'd been sheltered from for his own protection. But she was out there somewhere. Thinking about Liz and the magical spirit within her who now wore his oath of betrothal, he smiled. She had brought a beacon of light into his soul and opened up his heart. How and why she had found her way to him, he didn't know, but now they had been introduced, he had the strongest feeling that they would stay connected in some way. With deepest determination, he made up his mind that he would do everything he could to find out where she was.

Hearing the door open behind him, Iain turned to see Liz coming out of the cottage wearing the dress that he had found her in. He could tell she didn't feel comfortable as she fidgeted with the bodice and he grinned broadly as he watched her tussle with her clothes. Liz suddenly looked up at him, and he noticed the redness and puffiness around her eyes. Had she been crying? Was she unwell? Iain looked at her concerned.

"Are you alright, m'lady?" he asked.

"Please call me Liz," she smiled softly. "… and yes I'm fine."

"Are you sure?"

"Yes. It's just this damned dress. I think it must have shrunk!" she lied.

"I gather you don't wear such things where you come from."

"Whatever gave you that idea?" she asked rhetorically just as she tripped on her skirt and fell forwards on to the grass.

Iain couldn't help but burst out laughing as he rushed over to her and lifted her up on to her feet. She looked so awkward and enchantingly amusing as she wriggled along like a waddling duck.

"Thanks," she mumbled quite vexed with herself.

"I'm sorry," apologised Iain laughingly. "But the last time I saw anyone wriggle like that, was when Father Thomas accidentally stepped on an anthill as he delivered his Easter sermon by the side of the loch last year. He wriggled so much that he split his britches."

"I'm sure he found it funny," muttered Liz, gritting her teeth as she pulled and tugged at the restrictive bodice.

A sudden gust of wind blew across the loch and up the hillside towards the cottage, causing her hair to tumble over her shoulders and almost blowing her off her feet. Iain grasped her firmly around her waist and steadied her as she regained her balance and composure.

"Steady now! I've got ye! If you're no careful ye'll be flat on your back! Those winds can sneak up on ye before ye even notice," he warned, gazing down at her affectionately.

Liz noted the already apparent change in his personality. There was a warmth in his voice she hadn't noticed before and an openness she could feel deep inside. Gazing up into his beaming face, she saw more of the similarity with his future self than had been evident just an hour before. Had she helped him already, she wondered as she saw the rich melting brown and golden gleam in his eyes. A flash of brilliant blue sapphire suddenly reappeared in her eyes and this time he was ready.

His kiss was warm, soft but persuasive as he parted her lips and cupped her face gently with his hands. Closing his eyes, he saw only the blue eyed spirit in his thoughts and pulled her closely to him. Filled with longing for him but frightened of the possible consequences if she lost control, she reluctantly released herself from him. Hurt and confused he reached out to her as she turned away from him.

"Don't please!" she pleaded with him.

"What is?" he asked baffled by her statement and her rejection.

"You know why?"

"No, I don't!" he insisted vociferously.

"It's not me you're holding and kissing! It's her! This body!" she explained. "Look, there's nothing I'd like better right now than to be with you! Do you understand? But I can't! She will pay the price for our actions and we don't even know who she is!" declared Liz.

Iain thought for a moment. She was right. He wanted Liz. He wanted to hold her, to love her, but how could he do that when the body she occupied belonged to someone else.

"There must be something we can do, some way we can be together!"

"I'm only energy," she replied. "Like I said earlier, you can see me, and you can feel that tingle when we touch, but I'm like the breeze on a summer's day. I can blow cleanly through you and around you, but you cannot hold me the way you would like to. I promise you, there will be a time when we can be together but until then, my heart and my soul is yours but my body remains out of reach!" she sighed, fighting back more tears.

"Can you see my future?" He asked inquisitively. "Can you? For God's sake tell me!"

"Yes, I can!" she cried.

Iain took a firm hold of her and turned her to face him.

"You must tell me!" he commanded. "What is going to happen, to me, to us?"

"I can't! We don't know what it will do!" she pleaded.

"Please Liz! I must know! Tell me something! Anything! Let me know that I'm there with you, wherever and whenever that is!"

"Yes! You're there! We're together!" she relented.

"Where? How?" he begged, grasping her firmly, desperately wanting something, some tangible hope that he could hold on to.

"I can't!" she replied tearfully. "We might never see each other again!"

"Why? I don't understand!"

"Time is delicate, fragile and fleeting like the flat, calm surface of the loch when the tide is about to turn and the winds are still. One word, one action, like dropping a stone into that stillness can cause ripples that become waves that splash against the shore!"

"What riddle is this?" he asked perplexed.

"Please listen to me, carefully! We will be together when

danger surrounds me. You will be there. We will find each other!"

"What danger? When?"

"I can't say."

"Why can't you stay with me?"

"My body can't survive without my spirit, so I must find a way to return to it."

"How long can you stay?"

"Perhaps a few hours, perhaps days, I don't know. But I will visit you again. I will come to you when you need me," she explained. Then, as he gazed at her and noticed the pain in her face, he gently brushed the tears from her eyes and kissed her forehead softly, whispering,

"I understand. We'll find a way, be sure of that. I'm as stubborn as an ox and I won't give up, you hear? I'll find you, whatever it takes, so don't you cry no more tears, now," he said and hugged her close to him.

He had known her only a short while and knew nothing of her background, but that didn't matter to him. She already knew who he was, that was clear enough and her feelings for him were clearer still. Everything he needed to know about her, he knew he would find out in time. For now, he would value every precious moment with her.

Iain scratched his head and Liz smiled.

"Sorry. I always do this when I'm thinking hard about something."

"You still do."

"Aahhhh. So, do I still have hair then? I've no pulled it out of my head with all my yanking?"

"Your hair's fine," she smiled.

"Well that's good news for a start! That means I've either got hair that's as strong as a blacksmith's anvil or we'll be together before it does all come out!"

Liz smiled but said nothing.

"Iain, I think we need to work out why I'm here. This girl, may be part of that reason, so we need to find out who she is."

Exploring her eyes with his gaze he asked,

"What are women like where you are? Are they all like you?"

"How do you mean?"

"Bold.....outspoken...strong willed...!"

"I'm actually quite timid compared to most others..."

"You speak more freely in a man's presence than any woman I've ever known. Are you not punished for that?" he enquired curiously.

Liz laughed.

"I think most men believe we should be....where I come from....but, at the same time, I think men enjoy the challenge rather than an easy conquest." She went on, "From what I know of the women of your time, they were always kept in the background... following behind their men..... feathering the nest...bearing the children...not speaking unless spoken to....I could never be like that!"

"Aye!...and I'm not sure I could imagine you like that either!" he replied, grinning wryly with an impish glint in his eyes, a look that Liz was happily familiar with. This was the Iain she knew, even if he did have a different name now. Only the long hair and his bedraggled attire reminded her that he wasn't. But then, she remembered the sight of him in his dinner suit that previous evening, with his dickie bow tie askew and his suit covered in mud, and smiled.

A sudden loud crack of thunder ripped across the sky above them and Liz noticed a strange gathering of storm clouds on the distant horizon.

"What was that?" she asked.

"Panic ye not...it's only the sound of our fallen kinsmen, rattling their battle shields in the heavens," Iain explained.

Liz smiled.

"You mean thunder!"

"Aye, I do! … It can get quite fierce up here on the hillside."

"Then we'd better get started before the storm arrives," Liz instructed.

"Wait here, now, whilst I fetch something to keep you warm. The winds can be quite cutting out there on the loch," Iain explained, then disappeared back into the cottage to retrieve an old knitted blanket which he wrapped around her shoulders.

"Thanks."

"My mother often used to sit at my bedside to calm me, when great thunderclaps echoed across the loch. To quell my fear of the storm, she'd tell me many a fine tale of ancient battles between good and evil, with the good smiting their enemies. She'd describe in detail the clashing of shining metal blades as the lightening flashed and clattered around the outside of this house."

"She sounds like she loved you very much…"

"Aye, that she did. She had such a way with words that I could just shut my eyes and see the stories she told…" said Iain pensively. "She said that, on the night I was born, a great storm filled the sky. Lightening flashed everywhere across the valley and lit it up so brightly, it was as if it were midday."

"Do you know if that happened before or after I visited her?"

"It must have been later, maybe after you left. Why?"

"Just curious. It might be nothing," she replied.

"Are you thinking that the storm has something to do with you being here?"

"It could just be coincidence but it might be my ticket home."

"How do you mean?" Iain asked inquisitively.

"I think my projection, the image that you saw, is made from a similar energy to lightening. It had to be something like that storm that pulled me here. It may be something like that, that will pull me back. For every action there is an equal and opposite reaction."

"Sorry?"

"Sir Isaac Newton, heard of him?" asked Liz.

"No. My mother schooled me with the words of the bible and poetry she'd learned as a child. She taught me how to count and how to read and my father taught me how to find my way home using the stars, but that's where my schooling ends."

"You can find great discoveries and wisdom in his words, his science. There is a wealth of knowledge out there Iain, and it's all yours to find. Seek it out, find the science that brought me here and it may lead you to me."

Another crack of thunder ripped across the sky.

"We've no time to waste, Iain! I may not have long! We need to go, now!"

"My boat's just down the hill there. Follow me," he replied.

Just as Iain had described, they found the small wooden boat tied firmly to a low branch and tucked just below the heavy leafy boughs of the trees overhanging the loch. As it rocked gently on the late morning tide, Iain lifted Liz into the boat and climbed in after her. Untying the rope that kept it tethered to the boughs and using one of the oars that lay in the bottom of the boat, he pushed them away from the bank side and into the treacherous currents.

Sitting nervously at the back of the boat, Liz watched silently as Iain pulled on the oars with all his might. With hands clenched tightly on each oar and sweat pouring from his brow, Iain pulled for all he was worth to drive the boat through the water. Reaching the turbulent core of the ferocious currents in the middle of the loch, Liz held on tightly as the boat pitched and tossed in all directions. The crest of a large wave crashed down close to Iain, sending a torrent of icy cold freshwater spray into the boat, soaking Iain as he continued to row. Single-mindedly, he ploughed the oars relentlessly into the water, stroke after stroke until finally they reached the shallows on the far bank. Jumping into the clear cold water, Iain took hold of the front of the boat and dragged it on to the pebbled shore. Whilst he secured it for their inevitable return trip, Liz leapt on to the grassy bank.

"And where in God's name have ye been Lorna?" A sharp deep voice cried out from the trees.

Liz froze on the spot as a strong well built middle aged man strode towards her. So that was her name, thought Liz. Iain heard the voice too, and ducked behind some bracken near the boat, biting his lip as the sharp thorns ripped at his arms and legs. Through the mesh of twisted branches he could just see Liz as she faced her inquisitor.

"Forgive me…" she bleated nervously. "I ventured down here to pick fresh blossoms but fell." Liz ran her fingers through her hair and felt the painful bump on the back of her head. "If you don't believe me…feel here."

Vexed but curious at the unusual tone in her voice, the rough looking man clumsily examined her head.

"Aye there's a bump there alright…..but nothing worthy of making such a hullabaloo about…..Now get yourself back up to the house. His lairdship is growing impatient for the ceremony to begin… and you've yet to be bathed and dressed for the occasion."

Liz swallowed hard.

"And nip those cheeks of yours and put on a smiling

face....It's his big day and yours, so be glad of it! Now make haste!"

Picking up her skirts, Liz scurried up the grassy bank in the general direction of the house. The house was quite big with very small windows on the highest floors and resembled a fortress more than a house. As she approached, two maids came rushing across the courtyard.

"Begging your pardon, m'lady but you must be quick. The guests have begun to arrive and once the priest is here, his lairdship will expect the ceremony to begin!"

"Pray tell me why there is such a fuss?" asked Liz, trying hard to imitate their manner of speech.

The two maids stopped in their tracks and looked at each other strangely.

"Begging your pardon m'lady but it is your wedding to his lairdship, a union that will strengthen the alliance between the two clans...of that I'm sure you're well aware and be hopes you only jest at your ignorance of it!"

"I do jest indeed!" Liz lied. "I'm not myself this morning," she mumbled to the maids. "I fell whilst picking blossoms for my bouquet and my thoughts are a little confused." She said quickly.

Smiling relieved, the two maids bobbed a curtsey and dashed back towards the house. Liz followed behind them, pausing for the briefest moment to look back over her shoulder towards the trees and her only hope of rescue.

Creeping stealthily from his prickly hiding place, Iain cautiously ventured towards the house. Staying in the shadows as the morning sun rose high above the trees, he saw Liz in the distance chatting with the maids before disappearing into the house. Some how he had to get in there, but it wasn't going to be easy.

As Liz stepped through the main door of the house, she was greeted with a macabre spectacle of stuffed animal heads mounted on the stone wall ahead of her. Worn and fatigued tapestries and draperies hung from the other walls, depicting triumphant hunting scenes. To her right, a thick drawn back heavy tapestry curtain marked the entrance to the main hall, and just beneath the ties holding back the curtain to the stone wall, she could just make out an old blood stain, which although scrubbed over on a regular basis, had never succeeded in disappearing entirely. She shivered at the thought of some poor unfortunate victim departing this world from that very spot.

Pausing at the foot of the main stone staircase to her left, she noticed that fresh sprigs of heather had been attached below the wall lamps and guessed that this signified the route to her bed chamber. Picking up her skirts once more, she scurried up the winding stairs until she reached the landing on the first floor. Just to her right, she spotted a small window which overlooked the court yard and gazed across to the trees in search of Iain. For a brief moment she thought she saw some bushes moving near the corner wall of the house, and hoped that it was him.

"Look sharp Lorna and make haste…..There's no time to stand gazing out of windows!…You've to be washed and dressed!…..Whatever possessed you to go galloping off into the woods like that?"

Liz turned to face a stout middle aged woman dressed in a dark blue gown and wearing a rather dusty looking grey white wig. Images of amateur pantomimes popped up in her mind and it took all her concentration to remind herself that she wasn't Cinderella even if the person before her struck a remarkable likeness to an ugly sister.

"I warned my brother you were a bad lot!…Still, I don't envy you your wedding bower …..He's a lot older than I… and his gnarled hands will feel like pokers against your youthful skin." She laughed heartlessly. "I'll wager ten guineas that several nights of lustful frolicking with you will see him in his grave before the end of the month!" she added.

Grasping Liz's wrist sharply, her future sister-in-law dragged her into the bedroom across the hall. Jumping to attention from her stool by the fireside, the timid chambermaid bobbed a curtsey and waited for her instructions.

"Agnes,….wash her down and dress her….and be quick about it!"

With that the middle aged crone turned her back on the two of them and strutted like a cockerel back out into the hallway and down the stairs. Agnes scuttled across to the door and closed it.

"Begging your pardon m'lady, but you had us all worried…disappearing in the early hours like that…..We thought someone had kidnapped you for ransom."

"I wanted to pick some wild flowers for my bouquet." She replied. Then she asked curiously, "How old is his lairdship?"

"Begging your pardon m'lady, but some say he is more than three score year and ten….but he guards his appearance well with fine clothes, fine teeth and wigs to look a lot less than his many years." The maid answered. "But surely, you've met him?….I could never marry someone I'd never met!"

"Money and politics," sighed Liz.

"Well,…best get you ready then m'lady."

Liz stood still as Agnes un-tethered her from the trappings of her gown and undergarments, before sponging her down with the water from the pitcher by her bedside.

The water had cooled and chilled her pale naked skin so much, she relished the softness and warmth of her bridal garments. The pleasure was short lived however, as Agnes began to pull and secure the ribbon fastenings of her white corset.

"Breathe in m'lady," instructed Agnes as she performed one last tug before tying off the ribbons. "There now...that's better."

Dropping the wedding dress over Liz's head, Agnes pulled the garment down and into position before fastening the plethora of tiny buttons and loops at the centre back of her bodice.

"Begging your pardon, m'lady you may be grateful of the hindrance and delay that these cause.....By the time he's managed to unfasten these....all he'll want to do is sleep!" chuckled the maid.

Liz could hardly breathe with the corset fastened so tightly. It was no wonder that fainting and swooning were so common as womanly maladies in those days, she thought.

"Oh...and don't forget to plump them up..."

Liz looked at Agnes puzzled.

"You know....these!" she said, gesturing to her breasts.

Liz glowered with disdain. It was bad enough that she felt physically trust up like a Christmas turkey about to be roasted and carved before the hungry hoards, she certainly didn't want to add to the advertisement by presenting her cleavage so overtly, as an h'ordeuvre for groping fingers to vulgarly paw. But, if she wasn't to blow her cover and place Lorna in danger......when in Rome...Then, finally, stepping into her delicate wedding slippers, she was ready to face her torture.

Meanwhile, Iain had managed to sneak round to the rear of the house and hid in the shadows behind the stable door, waiting for an opportunity to present itself. After a few minutes, a young well-to-do gentleman in a fine waistcoat and suit, walked across the kitchen yard to the stables. Standing in the open doorway for a few moments, he retrieved some snuff from a small pouch in his waistcoat. He had just inhaled a small quantity of the snuff powder from his wrist, when he heard the scuttle of small feet approaching. Peering through the gap between the door and its post, Iain watched as the pouting chamber maid with a well ample cleavage willingly displayed, tapped him on the shoulder.

"Oh, Douglas! I've been looking for you everywhere since the master said you'd arrived. My heart's been aching for ye, Douglas! Did ye mean what ye said last we met?" she bleated naively.

"That's a wee secret I'll keep to myself," he teased.

"Oh, please Douglas! I really need to know!"

"I'll no tell you until my wee friend has said hello."

The maid looked over her shoulder quickly, then having checked there was no one around, pulled the young gentleman through the doorway into the darkness, closing the stable door behind them.

Iain gulped in the blackness, clinging closely to the wall and the deep shadows to stay hidden, transfixed by the unavoidable lurid antics of the young man taking advantage of the naïve young maid.

"I've only a few minutes before they'll come looking for me, Douglas." She whispered anxiously.

"That's all I need," sighed the young man as he pushed up her skirts and pinned her to the stable post. The sunlight shining through the wooden beams of the stable door revealed just enough of the vile spectacle to disgust Iain. Riving her breasts out of the girdle that held their burgeoning weight, the young man squeezed and suckled them between his groans of lust, as he thrust and thrust again. Hanging on to the post to steady her, she bit her lip and began to pant like a breathless hound until the groaning stopped and it was over. The young man stepped away from her and straightened his attire as the maid struggled to bring her cleavage back under control. Feeling suitably satisfied and ready to face the world, he approached the stable door oblivious to the maid's dishevelled attentions.

"Douglas, you promised you'd tell me!"

"Tell you what, that you're a penniless half-wit and whore who raptures in the ensnarement of gentlemen such as myself."

The maid stood in the sunlight of the doorway, her hands shaking and her mouth trembling.

"I was no half-wit or whore Sire, when you seeded me with your child!" she wept. "You swore you loved me, and you'd marry me if I gave myself to you! Now you treat me as common trollop! When they find out, I'll lose my job, my home! Please, Douglas! You've got to help me!" she pleaded.

"I'll not help you whore, or any brood you spawn!" he yelled picking up a riding crop and raising it above her cowering vulnerable figure.

Iain had seen and heard enough. It may not have been any of his business, but no woman deserved to be degraded like that. He would never treat Liz like that. In his disgust and anger, Iain leapt from the shadows and struck the young man across the back of the head, with the spade he found near the door. Taken by complete surprise, the young man collapsed on to the straw unconscious as the maid covered her mouth in horror.

"Never mind gawping madam, if you want to teach him a lesson for his crimes and indiscretions, you'll need to lend me a hand," instructed Iain.

In the semi darkness of the empty horse stall, the maid helped Iain strip the man of his fine clothes, leaving him naked save for his brief undergarments to preserve some modesty. Then tying his legs and hands behind his back and placing his knotted handkerchief as a gag around his mouth, they left him buried in the straw. Finding two guineas in the waistcoat pocket of the young man's clothes, Iain handed them to the maid.

"At least this money might help you for a while, but remember, he mustn't be found until I'm well away from here," Iain instructed.

"Thank you, sir!" she replied, wiping the tears from her eyes.

It took several minutes before Iain was able to successfully engineer himself into the stockings and clothes of his benefactor. Then, scooping some water from the trough nearby, he flattened down his hair to fit under the short well coiffured gentlemen's wig. Then, when the water in the trough had calmed once more, he peered down at his reflection and nodded with satisfaction at his passable appearance. Then rolling back his shoulders and standing poised and erect, he copied the walk of his benefactor and headed back towards the house.

Several eminent guests, with their entourage of servants, disembarked from their respective coaches in the court yard as Iain approached the main door at the front of the house. Discreetly integrating himself into the small crowd of new arrivals, he moved with them, into the house and into the main hall.

Being of a miserly disposition, the laird had lavished little money on the ceremony, providing only the basic amenities, wooden pews, for his guests to sit on during the ceremony. There were no prayer cushions to kneel on, much to the consternation of the gentry, who babbled assertive refusals to spoil their stockings by kneeling on the stone floor. There were no flowers to brighten the appearance of the drab dusty old hall, and with the moaning, groaning and gossiping of the already seated guests, Iain could quite easily have mistaken that he was attending a funeral and not a wedding. The main subject of the gossip echoing through the hall, however, was the vast, disgraceful (though to the elderly gentry) enviable age gap between the prospective groom and his bride, accompanied by the less discreet wagers being taken as to whether the groom would last long enough to survive his wedding night.

Iain frowned silently and settled himself down on the edge of a pew just inside the hall door, whilst the remaining members of the gentry in the crowd muttered their disgust about the menial décor, whilst their servants located seating spaces for them on the pews, and cleared away the dust for their masters. Even the sun disappeared behind the clouds, ashamed to shine down on this farce of a matrimonial union.

Suddenly the doorway cleared, to reveal the elderly laird supported by two of his most loyal kinsmen. Less frail than his guests portrayed and less glamorous in his appearance, the laird made his way down the aisle to the temporary altar at the front of the hall. Behind him strode a rather arrogant and odd looking gentleman, dressed in a suit unlike any worn by the other guests present. Whispers rippled through the congregation suggesting that perhaps his oddly styled suit was the latest fashion in the royal courts in France and Italy. In any event, the guests quickly fell silent as he walked by.

"That's the laird's advisor Captain Magnus McGregor ….They say he's the most powerful man between here and Edinburgh…" whispered one guest seated in front of Iain. "They say he duelled his way to wealth and power….and that he's an accomplished swordsman and a fine shot with a pistol." Iain watched the Captain suspiciously from the back of the hall.

Cheers of, "Bravo Sir!" and "Well done!" echoed back through the hall as the Laird reached the altar.

"Where is she?" he snapped at Captain Magnus McGregor.

"Your bride descends to the hall as we speak." He replied gleefully. "I will escort her here momentarily…"

With that, the Captain marched back up the aisle, out of the main hall and across to the foot of the stairs. Liz cautiously made her way down the last few steps as the Captain approached. As she straightened her dress at the bottom of the stairs, the Captain leaned forward and whispered in her ear.

"Run away like that again and I will have your father arrested and carted off to debtor's prison….do you hear me?" he threatened. "He owes me three hundred guineas, which I have graciously decided not to collect yet….on the understanding that you fulfil your father's side of the bargain," he taunted. "You will marry his Lairdship this day, and when he shuffles off his mortal coil, I will expect full repayment with interest from his estate. Of course," he continued as he ran his gloved fingers over her bare shoulders. "I could forget about your father's unpaid debt, if you wed me……as the Laird's widow….. It could be my wedding gift to you," he sneered.

Liz felt sick and her flesh crawled at the proximity of this evil weasel of a man. Now she understood why Lorna had been trying to flee earlier that morning. Not only was she about to marry a decrepit, cantankerous bully, she was quite clearly the sacrificial victim of the Captain's manipulation and blackmail, to secure the Laird's lands and power.

"You'll never get away with this….." muttered Liz in disgust.

Grabbing her wrist tightly and pulling her into the

shadows beneath the staircase, glaring wildly into her frightened eyes, the Captain hissed,

"I don't see anyone trying to stop me…do you?….Try it!…Walk away!…and how far do you think you'll get?….I have powers at my disposal, to find you wherever you go!"

Liz's heart suddenly began pounding hard with fear, and the Captain's gaze lowered to observe the distraction of her rapidly rising and falling cleavage. Un-gloving his right hand, then placing his other still gloved hand around her delicate throat, he gently stroked the side of her face and glided his fingers down her pale neck. As her pulse raced and he felt her pounding heart against his body, he forced his hand inside her low cut bodice and squeezed the delicate, soft warm flesh of her breast. Then smothering her mouth with his course aging lips, he moved his hands to her skirts, his ruthless passion fired by her fear and resistance. He wanted her now and who would care, he said to himself. His aching limb would find sweet comfort between her thighs, and subjugate her rebellious defiance, he thought to himself. The more he convinced himself that her swift deflowering there and then would have its decidedly pleasurable merits, the more determined he ploughed his hands through her voluminous underskirts.

"You're mine…..you little whore!" he muttered frustratedly. "…And be sure to pour the draught into his wine before he retires," he whispered menacingly. "He will wed you but not bed you, do you understand? Your body belongs to me! I shall be the one to relieve you of your chastity," he added forcing his mouth against hers once more.

Liz felt helpless. If this had been her life, this would never have been allowed to happen, she thought. But it wasn't. She knew that anything she said or did would have repercussions for Lorna, long after she'd gone back to the present. She didn't want to do anything that would make Lorna's life harder than it already was. But there had to be something she could do, she thought, cringing as the Captain's hand plundered her cleavage. Perhaps with her modern independence and liberated ways as a 21st century woman, she could force Lorna's villainous mentor to back off, or would this just make things worse, she wondered. Hesitant to act, she felt the coarseness of the Captain's hand as it suddenly found its way through the layers to her inner thigh. Liz gulped hard and pressed herself hard into the wall, praying that it would swallow her up before he did anything. She felt his fingers rive frustratedly at the delicate fabric of her undergarments and tensed as she felt the ripping of the threads and the feel of his hand on her flesh. A delighted, satisfied grin came over the Captain's face as he pressed himself against her, and taunted her with hot breathless whispers.

"There's nowhere you can go and there's nobody else here to help you," he grinned. "You're mine, and you will yield to me now, or I'll throw you to the lions next door and shame you for your lustful advances towards me.

"You bastard!" muttered Liz. "If you do this, I swear I'll kill you!" she said squirming within his grasp.

"Oh please, threaten me more!" he groaned. "There's nothing I like better than a whore who puts up a fight! Their resistance and tension gives me greater satisfaction!"

Liz felt sick as she clenched her host's thighs tightly together, barring entry to the Captain.

"Knock, knock," he drooled sadistically. "My friend wants to come in," he said, as he tried to force her thighs apart.

"I don't think so!" snapped a familiar voice from behind the Captain. "Guests are by invitation only, and you don't have an invitation to this party!" he continued.

Suddenly the Captain felt the heavy dull impact of the Laird's small marble bust against the back of his head and the resounding deafening, reverberation of his skull, as the blackness of unconsciousness descended on him. Liz gasped as his body slid down hers to the floor and an oddly familiar face in less familiar clothes and wig smiled back at her.

"Did you miss me, m'lady?" he asked with eyes gleaming and a broad grin on his face.

Gulping back powerful tears of relief, Liz threw her arms around Iain's neck.

Having witnessed the Captain leave the hall, Iain had discreetly followed him and witnessed his conspiritous dialogue with Liz. Then, when he saw the Captain force Liz into the shadows, he had grabbed the first blunt instrument to hand, the Laird's marble bust located on a short pillar near the hall entrance, and deployed it against the Captain's head.

"Are you alright?" whispered Iain.

Liz nodded shakily, as she straightened her skirts and stepped out from the shadows. Stepping over the Captain's unconscious body lying in a heap on the floor, she couldn't resist the urge to give him something else to think about apart from the lump at the back of his head. The Captain failed to stir and Liz moved her attention back to Iain.

"Why are you dressed like that?" she whispered.

"I had to find a way to get into the house somehow," he replied as he began to scratch his head under the wig. "So I borrowed this from a most undeserving guest."

"From the way you're scratching your head, it looks like you've brought a few uninvited guests with you," she remarked.

"Damned wig!" Iain cursed. "I'd be more comfortable wearing an ant's nest on my head," he added. "Anyway, how'd you manage to get mixed up with that evil swine?"

"This girl's body belongs to someone called Lorna. She's being forced to marry the elderly Laird by this guy," explained Liz. "He's so horrible but what can we do? If we try to do anything or change anything, we could make things worse for her," she added.

"Now, I have an idea about that," grinned Iain, "... but I need to know something from you first."

"What do you need to know?" asked Liz curiously.

"Can you control when you,....." he stopped, unable to remember the word that Liz had used for her starry presence.

"Project?" Liz guessed.

"Aye, that's the one," he replied.

"I think so," she replied.

"Good! Here's my plan," said Iain as he leaned closer to Liz's ear to whisper.

Allowing Iain to sneak discreetly back into the hall first, Liz adjusted her gown and stepped through the door way into the wedding hall, leaving the unconscious Captain on the floor behind her. With the knowledge of the Captain's sinister plan in her head, Liz quickly regained her composure and calmness, determined to thwart his treachery and wreak her revenge. Holding a small bunch of wild flowers tied together with a white ribbon, she took as deep a breath as she could muster in her tight restrictive corset and elegantly began her bridal march towards the altar at the front of the main hall.

Much to Liz's disgust, the ill-mannered majority of the congregation paid little attention to the bride, and even less attention to the Captain's untimely absence as the Laird's supporter. They seemed more pre-occupied with their incessant complaints about the miserly hospitality from their host, and the prospect of an even more dissatisfactory wedding reception, to pay any attention or reverence to the occasion. Liz could feel the tension in the air, as she entered the arena of self serving social predators, like a lamb to the slaughter. Undaunted and oblivious to her ill mannered audience, Liz concentrated intently on focussing her energy, as she made her way down the aisle, discreetly followed at a safe distance, by Iain.

"Hurry up!" snapped the Laird. "We haven't got all day!.......I have other business to attend to.....Make haste!" Then, noticing that the Captain had failed to return, the Laird bellowed, "Where's Magnus?"

Suddenly, the Captain, slightly dazed, dusty, and dishevelled in appearance, staggered into the main hall, clutching his swollen and painful manhood within his hands.

"What is the meaning of this, McGregor?" yelled the elderly Laird, much to the shock of the suddenly attentive congregation.

"Someone attacked me, my lord, someone from this room!"

Gasps of astonishment rippled through the congregation.

"Are you seriously suggesting that one of my guests is responsible for this?"

"Whoever it was, sir, never left this house. They never got past your guards on the outer door!" replied the Captain. "So they must be in here!"

"Then we shall attend to this after my wedding," commanded the Laird. ".. after the alliance has been made! No saboteur shall be allowed to thwart my wedding plans this day, understand?" yelled the Laird.

"Understood my lord!" replied the Captain as he indicated to the guards behind him to stand on either side of the hall doors, before hurriedly resuming his position at the Laird's side.

As she approached the unscrupulous Captain, and her wizened bitter faced groom, Liz took a deep breath and closed her eyes to focus on her projection and the Captain's thoughts. Within seconds, her sparkling starry image appeared in front of the altar, and Lorna's body collapsed at the Captain's feet. Seeing the bride apparently faint at the altar, the guests gasped and huddled into small gossiping groups to observe and pass malicious whispered comment.

Turning to face the altar, the Captain saw Liz's glistening starlight projection hovering in front of him, whilst the Laird beside him stood angrily overlooking the body of his collapsed bride.

"Fetch the physician! Now!" he commanded impatiently.

The Captain stared at the strange shimmering figure and rubbed his eyes in disbelief.

"Listen to me!" shouted Liz. "Heed my warning o Captain! A serpent of avarice surrounds your heart and hisses through every breath you take! If there is a chance to save your soul, you must repent! You must confess your sins before God and this congregation and beg for forgiveness!"

The Captain stared at her wide eyed.

"Who are you? What manner of magic and mischief is this?" he asked.

"What's that you said?" asked the Laird beside him. "Who are you talking too?"

"There, my lord! Do you not see the spirit before the altar?"

"I see nothing McGregor, except your foolish conduct! Have you gone mad, sir?" asked the Laird.

"Can you not see her, standing there, my lord?" asked the Captain perplexed.

The Laird glanced at the altar and then at his guests who all shook their heads.

"I fear sir, that you have lost your mind!"

"But she's there! I'm telling you!" yelled the Captain as Liz glared at him with her piercing blue eyes.

"Confess, dear Captain lest the fires of hell consume you for your evil deeds!" warned Liz, trying to sound as melodramatic and formidable as possible. "Confess! Confess!" she commanded, relishing the look of pure white fear on the Captain's face.

"I will not confess!" barked the Captain suddenly much to the bewilderment of the congregation.

"You have gone completely mad, sir!" yelled the Laird. "Stand fast sir, so that my clansmen may escort you from this place!" he commanded.

Immediately, the two thick set clansmen guarding either side of the hall doors, stepped forward, awaiting instruction.

"What kind of sorcery and treachery is this?" bellowed the Captain, at Liz's ghostly image as he stepped forward and defiantly ran his fingers through her projection. Liz shivered as she felt the cold blackness of his touch cut through her like a knife. Her image flickered momentarily and the Captain began to walk around her, suspiciously, much to the amusement of the congregation and the annoyance of the clan Laird as they watched him strut like a cockerel around the unoccupied space before the altar.

"Who are you?" he demanded. "What do you want?"

"I am your last chance of salvation! Repent! Confess your sins!"

"Poppycock!" he yelled. "You've bewitched me…You're no more an angel of mercy than I am!" he scoffed.

"Guards!" yelled the Laird. "See to the Captain!" he

commanded as the guards moved through the gathered wedding guests towards the altar.

"This is your last chance Captain!" warned Liz as she focused on her thought energy once more.

The captain continued to pace around her, arrogant of his certainty that she was no angel or ghost, but some strange trick of magic. As he poked her for a third time, Liz latched on to his mind. His thoughts were cold and black like his touch, and his sins were many. Searching the archives of his mind, she saw the pain and misery he inflicted on his many victims. She witnessed the ashamed faces of the vulnerable young women he charmed, bedded and ruined, to leave a legacy of his illegitimate spawn in the most wealthy, influential family homes across the country. She even felt his sadistic satisfaction at watching his father, contorted by agonising pain from the poison he'd unwittingly consumed at his son's hands. Begging for help and mercy in the dark and bitter chill of that winter's night, Liz saw how the Captain's father reached out to him in his final moments, only to receive a last rebuke before dying.

"Very well then madam! Let's see the wrath of which you boast or are your threats as empty and transparent as your appearance!" taunted the suspicious unrepentant Captain.

Still feeling his rough hands against her skin and his coarse lips on her mouth, Liz's anger increased rapidly to fever pitch, along with her adrenaline and wavelength energy. Then, remembering how she'd been able to manipulate the thoughts of the soldier in the woods that morning, she had an idea. Focussing hard inside his thoughts, she began her subconscious suggestions.

'You're feeling very hot!'

Suddenly beads of perspiration appeared on the Captain's brow as he gasped and pulled off his suit jacket, much to the avid curiosity of his audience and the guards who immediately halted in their tracks, unsure of what he was planning to do next.

"Your clothes are on fire! They are burning, you must take them off!'

Suddenly the Captain looked down at his fine French tailored suit, and stared wide eyed and terrified at the hot orange and red flames that licked and curled their way up his body.

"I'm on fire!......The witch has cast a spell on me!..... Fetch water NOW!" he yelled at the two guards nearby. "I'm burning!"

The two men looked at each other, then at the Captain, puzzled. Through their eyes and minds, there were no flames real or imaginary engulfing the Captain.

"What are you waiting for!" screamed the Captain as he defied the flames to pull off his trousers and then tossed them on to the floor.

His audience stifled sniggers at his pale hairy calves and bony knees, as Liz switched off her suggestion and returned to Lorna's body, leaving the Captain looking down at his state of semi-undress and the dusty but undamaged trousers lying in a heap on the stone floor.

"What on earth are you doing?" shouted the furious Laird. "How dare you make such an exhibition at my wedding! I suggest that the only attacker and saboteur in this hall, is you, sir!" he yelled. "Guards take him away!"

"It's the witch!" he screamed, pointing at the unconscious bride who now lay in Iain's arms as he knelt on the floor beside her.

"Good God man! How could she have done anything? We all saw her faint!"

"Don't mock me, sir!" snapped the Captain angrily. "She is responsible for this! She's a witch without a doubt!"

"You forget your place Captain! How dare you insult me or my bride in front of my guests! You may have power and money, sir, but they hold little influence in my home... on my land!....And don't you forget that!"

"Influence? What do you know of that, you ignorant old buffoon! I have more power and influence here than you could possibly imagine!" he hissed, glaring at the many eyes of his onlookers who then flinched and shuffled nervously. "Their loyalties are with me sir! Bought and paid for with my sons who feed at their tables, sprung from the bellies of their so-called virtuous daughters who all too willingly welcomed me into their beds," spat the Captain, as the mother's fans fluttered incessantly and their husbands shuffled uncomfortably with shame. "I hold court here, sir! I hold all the cards! They will no more disown me than they would their grandchildren or their social position," he leered then whispered into the Laird's ear. "I'll let you into a secret shall I? After you've wed your sorceress and died from your matrimonial exertions, whilst you lie in the earth festering and feeding the worms, I shall be Laird in your place! I shall wed your widowed whore and seed her with my legitimate sons to populate your lands and consume your wealth!" goaded the Captain. "Observe your guests sir, like vultures attentive to a corpse, as they wager that your wedding bed will be your death knell! I've even wagered ten guineas myself that you will barely last beyond the twelfth stroke of midnight!"

"You brigand, sir!" bellowed the old Laird bravely, striking the Captain's face with his glove. The remaining guests gasped with horror at the Laird's response. "When I meet my maker Sir, I shall not be held in judgement as a purveyor of treachery, a vice you style yourself with, like a gentleman would a tight fitting suit of the poorest quality. You have made an unwise move, sir, and like the flimsiness of your suit, you shall be torn to pieces by your own acts of deceit. Beware the sons you wield as mercenaries on your behalf, for one day, sir, they shall cut you down with your own blade, Judases against their master!"

The Captain laughed and drew his sword from its sheath. Then levering its point at the Laird's scrawny neck he challenged,

"Sir, I would that you were my emissary to convey my repentance to your maker in person, and with this sharp blade I shall dispatch you without delay from this world to the next!" growled the Captain.

In the mean time, having carried Liz carefully up the aisle and laid her carefully to rest on one of the pews near the door, Iain suddenly lunged at the bemused clansman standing to his right and took hold of his Claymore sword, tearing it from its sheath.

"Enough, Captain! Would you be so brave I wonder, pointing your sword at a younger man? You talk with a sharp tongue sir, but are you as sharp and cutting with your blade?" challenged Iain bravely, levelling his blade at the Captain. "With your Lairdship's consent, I would like to teach this tyrant a lesson, Sir, in defence of your Laird's honour and that of your bride!"

"Such fire from one so young, my boy! But can your fire and youth match the skill of this assassin?" asked the elderly Laird.

"I pray that the Lord is on my side to guide my blade strong and true. But, if it is my fate to die this day......then I shall do so, honourably in your defence!" Iain replied.

"Honourable?" scoffed the Captain. "Your no gentleman sir, to bandy such a word as if it were your badge of office! I would not sully my clothes with the blood of such an infamous philandering dandy!"

With that, Iain tore off the white powdered wig and

tossed it to the floor, causing a cloud of white powder to billow upwards into the faces of the retreating audience.

"I am not the womanising dandy you refer to, sir! He lies, as we speak, in yonder stable, bridled for his carnal disgrace! I may not be of noble birth nor of monetary substance, but I am a hard working honourable man, and I do not judge a man by the cut of his cloth or the size of his purse! I judge him by his words and deeds, and you sir are no gentleman by either course!" defended Iain.

"How dare you, sir!" spat the Captain. "You are no sheriff or judge, qualified to serve me with such slander! Who are you sir? Speak, and let us hear the truth that we in turn might pass equal judgement on you!"

All eyes turned to Iain, eagerly awaiting his response. Standing up straight and proud, Iain addressed his audience.

"I am Iain Lachlan from the loch side village across the water," he began, "I am a defender against the Reivers and shepherd of that parish."

Ripples of mocking laughter reverberated around the hall, but Iain held his position without shame. Then, as the Captain regained his composure he sheathed his sword and appealed to the other guests.

"What say you friends? Confess, who has invited this impostor to provide such amusing entertainment this day, and I shall reward him with my thanks for a job well done and worthy applause! Speak!"

Each of the congregation turned to their neighbour shaking their heads.

"Will no one claim the reward for this jest?"

"I shall!" shouted Liz from the back of the hall.

In stunned silence, all eyes followed the voice, and those nearest to her stepped back to reveal the Laird's young bride.

Suddenly springing forwards from her seat, she snatched the dirk from the second clansman.

"This man before you is no jester! He speaks the truth!" she began.

"Good God!" exclaimed the mocking Captain. "What have you done, my lord to allow your bride to disgrace your authority before this company? Who gives you the right, madam, to speak beyond your place and standing? Have we all circumcised our manhood this morning to give you the right to speak like this to your lords and masters?"

Cheers of disapproval and the tapping of canes on the stone floor, spread through the fickle male congregation, as they rallied to the Captain's cause.

"Oh do shut up, you pompous wind bag!" shouted Liz. "What is this, a party political broadcast on behalf of the chauvinist party? If you spoke to a woman like that, where I come from, you'd be lucky if you didn't wind up in court!" she snapped. "And while we're on the subject, if you ever try to touch me again, you'll have more to worry about than your injured manhood, I can tell you!"

Gasps of shock filled the air as she then swung her blade high. Fearing she was about to lash out, the congregation scattered, bumping into each other to get out of her way. Suddenly clouds of white dusty wig powder plumed into the air, as heads bumped together in their stampede away from her position. With faces suddenly whitened by their collusion, the fleeing congregation coughed and spluttered as they blindly pushed each other out of the way. Through the chalky white clouds, the remaining crowd fixed their gaze on her blade and gawped open mouthed, then sighed, relieved, as she dropped the blade behind her back and spliced the laces that fastened her bodice and corset, loosening them to allow her to breathe. Then, with blade in hand, she bravely advanced towards Iain, swinging the blade to her right then to her left, to keep the congregation back.

Iain, watched his fiancée with such immense pride, he couldn't help but show it in the bright sparkle of his eyes and the broad wry grin on his face. She was indeed the one, so different from any other woman he'd ever come across.

"Mistress McKay!" yelled the elderly Laird. "You are completely out of order!"

"And you, sir, have been so completely blind to this monster's acts of treachery towards you and so many others, until now!" she replied. "My intention was not to offend or undermine your authority, my lord, but to save your life!" Liz continued. "This monster would have me poison you this night, to win his handsome wager and manipulate his widow, me, into handing over your estate in return for my father's safety from ruin at his hands!" she added. "He is evil, sir, with no soul or conscience for his actions, interested only in the pursuit of his own ambition and power!" she declared then paused. "Would I dare to place my reputation and my life at such risk from my words and actions, if I wasn't telling the truth?" she implored.

Standing alongside Iain now, with her sword outstretched and a deep fiery anger burning in her host's eyes, the Laird moved forward slowly towards them, clearing the crowd behind him with each step. A deafening silence weighed heavy in the dusty, musty air, and Liz's heart pounded, readying herself for what might happen.

"She speaks the truth!" declared the elderly Laird. "There is no note of guilt or falsehood in her eyes and I myself, have heard, only moments ago, such vile threats from this brigand's own traitorous lips!" Then turning to the humble shepherd, the Laird unsheathed his sword.

Immediately, Iain placed his left arm in front of Liz as he drew back, bringing her with him, certain that the Laird was about to extract some punishment from him. Instead, the Laird carefully took hold of his blade and offered the hilt to the shepherd, much to the astonishment of his onlookers.

"Rid me of this tyrant, Sir!" cheered the elderly Laird. "I accept your honourable engagement in our defence and furthermore, I offer you my sword which carries with it, all the experience of bloody skirmishes and battles well fought, in the hope that it will serve you as well as it has served me," he said. "But, there is one truth, not yet spoken here today, which I must have an answer to. Are you her lover, sir, to defend her with such passion and at great risk to yourself?"

"I love only the woman I am promised to, my lord and she is not your bride," answered Iain. "If this is the time for truth, I must confess that I did rescue your bride from the loch this morning as she tried to cross to the other side. I saved her and offered her shelter for her recovery until I could return her to you," he said. "I have protected her as I would any honourable woman but I must ask, my lord, why she would be so unhappy to flee her wedding day, knowing her father's life to be at risk?"

The Laird pondered his words then turned to Liz.

"Is this true?"

"Yes."

"Am I so monstrous that you would risk death in your escape and threaten the alliance between our two clans, than to take your vows this day?"

"No alliance can be well founded when it is based on blackmail and treachery, my lord and I feared from his reputation, that the Captain would not honour his promise and all would be lost. So I tried to escape to warn my father of the Captain's intent."

"Why did you not come to me, child?"

"You are formidable, sir, and what notice would you have taken of my words, without proof?"

The congregation and the elderly Laird nodded in unison. Silence reigned once more as the Laird considered what to say and do.

"Young man, I must say to this to you, ….. that a sword once drawn must strike, before it is withdrawn. As agreed, you shall defend our honour and in return, I shall pledge an honourable contract of alliance with the McKay's and release this young child from this matrimony."

Suddenly, the Captain let out a yell of opposition.

"No!!!"

Hurriedly pulling on his trousers and unsheathing his long, hand crafted Italian Border Reiver again, the Captain stood defiantly before the temporary altar.

"Make room there, …that I might not soil your furnishings and your guests garments with this peasant's blood!" commanded the Captain.

As instructed, the servants and clansmen quickly cleared the wooden pews to the sides of the hall as Iain and the Captain approached each other.

"Be careful, Iain!" warned Liz. "Watch out for any dirty tricks!"

Iain nodded, still with his gaze fixed on his opponent.

Circling each other in the centre of the hall like rival lions ready to battle for their territory, the two men watched each other, willing each other to make the first move until suddenly, the Captain lunged forward with his sword. There was the sound of metal clashing and scraping against metal, as Iain successfully blocked the attack. Then, there was another strike and another, above and below, but each time, Iain pushed the Laird's sword into their path, watching his opponent closely, deciphering the Captain's attack strategy.

"You make no move, Sir!" goaded the Captain. "Shall I have the musicians strike up a tune that we may continue to dance and keep our guests entertained?"

"Your words cause no wound sir! Perhaps if you struck less with your tongue and more with your blade, we might truly battle!" retorted Iain valiantly.

The Captain glared into Iain's sparkling dark brown eyes. Then, with a sudden verve and vigour, he swept his blade, down and down, right and right, left and right pushing Iain backwards across the hall. The last strike caught the side of Iain's left shoulder, opening up a deep cut that wept a broad sash of red blood down his white sleeve. The Captain grinned with satisfaction and taking advantage of the distraction, he lunged at the shepherd, jabbing the sword towards Iain's chest. Iain leapt backwards and deflected the blade before striking forward and advancing towards his accuser.

"How did you come by your present attire, sir, unless it was that you set upon a gentleman of this household to rob him of his clothes and purse, gain entry to this house and acquire further heavy purses from the Laird's honoured guests!" leered the Captain accusingly.

"I am no cut-purse Sir!" Iain addressed the Laird. "I did borrow this clothing from the un-gentlemanly dandy he mistook me for earlier, to ensure that the my lord's bride had indeed found safe haven here. Then, hearing the Captain's foul plot to murder my lord, and to see him paw your bride and attempt to deflower her before your vows, I was duty bound to defend you both against his treachery!" replied Iain as he struck back at the Captain.

"So it was you who struck me on the head!" concluded the Captain.

"Aye it was, I confess it, and I feel no shame in doing it! It was no more than you deserved!" replied Iain.

"Good God, McGregor! Have you no honour as a gentleman that you would attempt to dishonour my bride?"

"I earned my noble status through the navy Sir, where

I was regularly commissioned in a similar vane to covertly corrupt foreign aristocracy with my seed in a strategy for overseas land acquisition," replied the Captain. "Yes, I do confess that I did dishonour your bride, with great pleasure... and know this too, my lord," hissed the Captain. "I tasted those sweet lips first. I fondled her soft, motherly mounds and will in time envy the suckling of my sons at her breast! And, as well you might have guessed, I have knocked on the door of her chastity and found oh, such sweet delight in her hospitality."

Gasps of horror at the Captain's blatant confession swept through the hall.

"You evil toad!" yelled Liz, unable to control her anger. "You forced yourself on me, that's true! But my chastity remains as intact as on the day I was born!" she defended vehemently.

Iain's face reddened with anger, as he charged forward with his sword and struck a well landed blow diagonally across the Captain's chest, cutting cleanly through his silken shirt. As the shining metal blades flashed the daylight from the window around the room, their swords clashed in time with the cracks of thunder outside the house, that grew ever louder as the storm advanced towards them. Dark clouds crossed the sky above the glen, blotting out the daylight and pitching the hall into sudden darkness as the duellers continued their fight. The wedding guests who had fled into the courtyard, now returned indoors, more fearful of the storm and the ruination of their finery than the debacle in the wedding hall.

Liz stood by and watched helpless to assist in his conflict with the Captain, afraid even to utter words of encouragement lest she distract him from his focus. The Captain struck back angrily again and again, and once more the Laird's blade valiantly withstood each blow. Hoping to tire his opponent, the Captain inhaled deeply and rained down blow after blow in quick succession, until that moment when the hilt of the fine Border Reiver struck the edge of the robust Scottish blade. Locked together, Iain pushed back against the Captain, forcing the Captain's own blade closer and closer towards his throat. His un-laboured arms were no match for the stamina and muscle of the young shepherd, who had borne many a sheep on his back and in his arms. Then with his left fist, the shepherd hooked a firm blow to the Captain's jaw, and sent him reeling backwards on to the stone floor.

With blood dripping from his mouth, the stunned Captain scuttled backwards on his haunches across the floor, eager to put as much space between him and the peasant as he could. Iain marched over to his retreating enemy and brought the bloodied point of his blade down upon the Captain's throat.

"Do you yield sir!" demanded Iain. "Do you retract your accusations?"

"I do not sir!" spat the Captain. "I am not defeated yet!" he gasped breathlessly wiping the blood from his mouth.

"Accept your defeat Captain, and henceforth, consider yourself banished from this land!" declared the Laird. "Sheriffs! Take this villain into your custody!" he commanded the sheriffs, who dressed in their ceremonial tartan, emerged from the centre of the crowd of guests and marched towards the Captain.

Distracted momentarily by their approach, Iain lowered his blade mistakenly, allowing the Captain to spring at his opponent's legs and bring him crashing to the floor. Leaping on top of the shepherd, the Captain gripped Iain's throat with his right hand whilst his left hand grabbed Iain's sword bearing wrist. With his last reserves of energy the Captain smashed Iain's wrist against the stone floor, causing the sword to fall and clatter away into the temporary darkness. Iain fought back as the two sheriffs stood over the brawling bodies of the two men. Then, as Iain gained the upper hand and lay over his accuser, the Captain saw the fires of justice and retribution burn in the young shepherd's eyes moments before his clenched and bloodied fist crunched against the flesh and bone of the Captain's jaw. A deafening silence filled the hall, as the spectators stared in disbelief at the ill-matched victorious shepherd who sat back on the floor as his defeated opponent collapsed limply into unconsciousness.

Liz rushed forward to Iain's side, and tearing a strip of cloth from the underskirt of her dress, she bound his wound tightly to stop the bleeding. Then, slowly climbing to his feet, the shepherd watched as the two sheriffs dragged the body of the Captain out into the hall, before retrieving the sword from the shadows. For a brief moment his eyes met Liz's as she smiled proudly at him, and their hands touched at the hilt, as he held out the sword horizontally to her.

Suddenly a flash of lightening ripped through the main hall window adjacent to the altar and struck the hilt of the sword in their hands. A powerful bright light engulfed them both and for a moment, Iain saw the brief return of the sparkle of deepest blue across her eyes. In the centre of the light, Liz felt the power of the lightening flowing through them both and sensed that something was about to happen. Grasping Iain's hand desperately and whispering the words 'wait for me', Iain saw the pride in her gaze turn to sadness and as the blue light disappeared from her eyes and the bright light vanished, he knew she was gone.

The guests and the elderly Laird gasped as they saw the shepherd unharmed and suddenly un-bloodied, left standing with the frightened and confused young girl. Moving the hand made bandage to assess the wound on his shoulder, he searched with his fingers beneath the torn shirt but found no cut in his skin. The energy from the storm combined with the energy from her projection had healed his wound and he stared in wonder at the smooth undamaged skin as Lorna looked at him questioningly. His heart sank as he thought of her sparkling blue sapphire eyes and the briefest of moments when he held her in his arms and kissed her. His eyes glistened with unspent tears as he replayed her last words, 'wait for me' in his head. She was gone from his life, and her departure left a deep aching void in his heart. There were so many questions he hadn't had the chance to ask her, and he hadn't even had the chance to find out when she would return or even to say goodbye.

Bereft by his loss, the shepherd solemnly returned the sword to the elderly Laird, uncertain of his fate.

"The job is done, my lord," sighed Iain as he handed over the sword.

Carefully taking the sword from the shepherd's hands the Laird declared,

"It was a job well done, my boy! I would be glad of your services in this household as by personal body guard. What do you say?" asked the Laird. "You'll have board and lodging here and a substantial purse for your services."

"I'm a humble shepherd Sir, and no skilled swordsman for you to entrust your life to."

"Nonsense! You fought and won, unconventionally and untrained perhaps, but you can acquire the necessary skills you lack."

"I am grateful for your favour and offer of employment Sir, but my future path lies elsewhere," replied Iain.

"Then, if I can offer you some small reward for your valour and timely exposure of the Captain's treachery, what would that be?" the Laird asked curiously.

Iain thought for a moment and smiled at the frightened bride in her torn dress.

"I would only ask that you keep your promise to release this maid from this forced marriage and clear her father's debt, that she might return home with honour and not shame."

"So, you can marry her, perhaps?" asked the elderly Laird smiling.

"No Sir. As I have already declared, my heart is sworn to another."

"Very well, then! I shall uphold my bargain! You have my word!" answered the Laird nodding approvingly. "But should you ever change your mind, I will always hold a post for you here."

"I thank you Sir!" replied Iain bowing respectfully before making his way out of the house through the stunned white powdered faces of the re-congregated and dishevelled wedding guests.

Wandering down to the Loch as the midday sun shone brightly on the rippling water, causing it to sparkle like a blanket of diamonds upon the blueness, Iain's thoughts returned to Liz. He revisited the images of her in his head and replayed her words over and over again, as he rowed his boat back across the Loch.

When at last, he re-entered the cottage and tended to the dying final glow of the red and orange embers in the fireplace, he paused and thought of his mother's wedding ring on Liz's finger, somewhere in the future and prayed sadly and softly for her return.

For days and weeks after Liz had departed, Iain tended his sheep, walking miles and miles through the rich heather covered hills searching the skies for strange unpredicted storms that might herald her return to him. Each night, disappointed and disheartened, he returned to the cottage and sat alone by the fire holding the blanket he had wrapped around her shoulders that day, desperate to make some kind of connection to her. As the days grew longer with spring turning into summer, his dreams became haunted by his obsession for her sparkling presence. Each morning when he awoke with the bright light shining through his eyelids, he opened his eyes hoping that it was her light that broke his dreams but, instead he found it was always only the morning sunshine peeping through the wooden shutters. Each painful day ran into another, where the undying hope in his heart fought valiantly against the pit of despair in his soul. The memories of those few short hours together occupied his mind all the time as he replayed every word, every sparkle of her mesmerising blue eyes and the tingle of her kiss on his lips. Then, as the nights began to draw in with the end of the summer, and she failed to return to him, Iain realised that he could not face the prospect of the long cold dark days of winter alone. Selling his entire flock of sheep for a good price, he bundled up the few belongings he had, bid the cottage farewell and closed the door behind him as he left.

The sky was a clear crisp blue, with not a cloud to be seen that morning, as he ascended the mountain behind the cottage. With his few worldly belongings bound up in the sheepskin strapped to his back, he climbed the rocky slopes until he reached the highest point of the ridge overlooking Libran's Loch. There, just on the loch side of the ridge, sheltered by a large rock stood two small cairns, one with a strong wooden shepherd's staff embedded in its centre, the other with a small wooden box buried at it's heart, containing his mother's wooden spinning bobbins and a small wooden cross that he had whittled for her as a young boy.

As the strong harsh, winds approached him from behind the ridge, Iain knelt on the softer, heather covered ground at the foot of the two cairns. Placing the bundled belongings beside him, he bowed his head in prayer. Then rising to his feet and staring out over the glen, he savoured his last glimpse of the panoramic view of the verdant valley with its vast shimmering loch sparkling in the sunshine like her unforgettable eyes. Then, picking up his bundle and tossing it on to his back, he turned away from his parents, from the glen and the only home he'd ever known and set off west ward alone in search off a new life, a new education and most importantly, Liz.

CHAPTER 15

WHEN LIZ OPENED HER EYES, it took her a few moments to focus on her surroundings, but as her blurry vision began to clear, she realised that she didn't know where she was or what had happened? Had she passed out and just been dreaming or had she really been projected back to 1746? As she blinked her eyes, she looked around at the unfamiliar surroundings, and a sudden anxiety took hold of her. Where was she? The room was too modern for her still to be at the Laird's 18th century mansion house. So, where was she and what year was this?

Thinking back to what she could remember just before her projection, Liz recalled standing in the Minster, her head pounding with thousands of voices and thoughts, and then everything went black. Wherever she was, it wasn't the Minster and it wasn't a hospital either. With its dusty old fashioned heavy drapes, old wooden utility furniture and rattling wooden sash window frames, nobody could have blamed her for thinking that she had been projected back to the 1940s. Who was she this time she wondered, as she examined her clothes and her hands …… Then she saw it, the small silver ring shining on her wedding finger and she realised that she hadn't been dreaming.

Someone was sitting beside her on the bed where she lay, and as her eyes focussed more clearly, she began to make out the welcoming, smiling handsome face of the one person she really wanted to see – Iain. She was home again, well at least back in the present and more importantly, he was with her. Sitting up suddenly in the bed, she flung her arms around him and squeezed him tightly. Unable to hold back her overwhelming relief at being back and her excitement at discovering the miracle that he really was, Liz pressed her mouth to his with a passion that would have melted the ice caps at the North Pole.

"Welcome back!" he said choking cheerily. "Whoa ! Hey! Not so tight! I need to breathe!" he said rather surprised by her reaction.

Tears of joy cascaded uncontrollably down her cheeks as she sobbed into his shoulder.

"Hey," he whispered softly. "It's okay. We're safe. What's wrong, Liz?"

"I'm so sorry, Iain!" I didn't want to leave you! I couldn't stop it! The storm came and I held on to you as long as I could, ... but then, I found myself back here," she explained.

Iain nodded, smiling softly as Liz released him slowly, and sat back, gazing at him through tear filled eyes.

"It was you wasn't it?" asked Liz hopefully. "You rescued me from the Loch."

"Yes," he sighed. "I was humble Iain Lachlan back then," he replied. "I've had a few names and a few different identities since then," he said. "That way, I managed to avoid a lot of awkward questions."

"You changed your hairstyle too!" Liz smiled as she fingered the edges of his rich dark hair.

"Hmmn. So what did you think of my rugged Highland shepherd phase? Was I daring, dashing and ....."

"Desirable?" Liz interrupted.

Iain looked at her sideways, and a little puzzled.

"Definitely," she whispered teasingly.

Iain grinned wryly as he worked out where and when

she'd spent the last few hours and gently lifted her left hand towards the light.

"So matter can time travel," he remarked. "I was here with you when it materialised," he explained.

Liz fingered the ring carefully and tried to remove it to examine it more closely but it wouldn't budge.

"It's stuck!" she said as she pulled at the ring. "I can't get it off!"

"Have you changed your mind?" asked Iain sounding suddenly disappointed.

Liz suddenly stopped, realising what her actions must have looked like.

"Oh no!" she said embarrassed. "I just wanted to look at the initials again inside the ring, but I can't get it off!"

"Perhaps you weren't meant to," sighed Iain. "Perhaps it's become your lucky time travelling talisman," he suggested.

"And perhaps it's still an engagement ring, if you're still interested after all these years," she beamed.

"That's my girl!" he cheered as this time he pulled her into his arms and kissed his bride to be. Deep inside her, she could feel her soul lifted like never before, and as his gentle but protective arms encased her, she knew she never wanted to be with anyone else.

"You seem to like men in kilts don't you?" he asked cheekily, when they finally surfaced for air.

"Just one man," she whispered, as her eyes twinkled with delight in the afternoon sunlight.

"That was our first meeting," recalled Iain. "I can remember every detail as though it were yesterday," he said enthusiastically. "I rescued you from the Loch and brought you back to my cottage. Then you damn near frightened the hell out of me that day, when you did your projection thing!" he remarked. "I'm used to it now though. But back then, phew! It was really scary stuff! Though as I remember, you were exquisitely beautiful, just like you were last night when I first saw you at the ball," he smiled. "Why on earth you wanted to tag along with me…."

"As I recall, you didn't give me a choice!" Liz replied.

"Right," he nodded.

"I would never have guessed you were a shepherd," Liz smiled.

"That was my father's job, and I just followed in his footsteps. It's what you did in those days. You did what your parents did and you never stepped outside of your social circle or class."

"But you did, didn't you, to get here? You even passed yourself off as a gentleman that day, wearing a fine suit and a white powdered wig."

"Yeh, I remember. Disgusting!" he remarked.

"Sorry?"

"That damned wig! I was scratching my head for days after that! The damn thing was so alive it nearly crawled away on its own! Change the subject quick, it's got me scratching already!" he cringed as he began scratching the top of his head.

"Where did you get it from, anyway?" she asked curiously. "You did look rather pompous!"

"That was the idea!" he replied. "I borrowed the outfit from a rather obliging oaf who I caught indulging in carnal favours in the stable where I was hiding."

"Carnal favours?" she asked naively.

"He was getting intimate with the chamber maid," he explained delicately.

"Oh."

"So what happened after I left?"

"Not a lot really. The Captain was arrested and the last I heard, he was headed out on a convict ship bound for the colonies. As for Lorna, I convinced the Laird to release her from the marriage contract and he promised to restore her reputation and put right the damage done by the Captain."

"What about you?"

"Me? I returned to the cottage for a short while, hoping that you might appear again but when you didn't, I packed up my belongings, sold the sheep at the market and headed out into the big wide world."

"So what should I call you? Iain Sinclair, or Iain Lachlan?" Liz asked.

"Sinclair is probably the safest. It might trigger too many questions otherwise."

"I really didn't want to leave you that day, Iain. God knows I wanted to stay," she said sadly.

"I know," he whispered softly as he opened his arms towards her and held her close. "There wasn't anything either of us could do to stop it. The storm came and then you were gone. Part of me thought I'd never see you again, but I never gave up hope. I remember the last words you said to me, 'wait for me', and I did. Anyway, that's the past. We're here now, together, and that's what really matters," he said as he kissed her forehead. "How are you feeling?"

"Tired….and a little confused," Liz replied.

"Why do you feel confused?" Iain asked.

"Well if my body was here all the time, how is it that, at one point, I wasn't just a projection back there, ….. I was real?" she asked.

"I once asked Fraser the same question."

"Fraser?"

"That's where we are now, ….at Fraser's house," explained Iain.

"And what did he say?"

"Well he ran some data through his computer to do with unusual storms, and weather conditions, recorded back over time. Apparently it was about that time when there was a mention of strange electrical storms, earth tremors and sightings of strange green blue auroras in the sky above Glasgow and the Trossachs. He reckons that they may have been caused by a significant solar flare," replied Iain. "Perhaps the energy from the sun powered up your connection enough, between the past and the present, to strengthen your projection and allow the interchange of matter. At least, the wedding ring is certainly proof of that," he suggested.

"Now, I know you said before that I visited you several times in your past, but it never really registered what that meant. It wasn't until I heard you make that pledge back then, that I realised how you felt, how you must feel, now. You've been searching for me and waiting for me all these years haven't you?"

Iain nodded silently, his rich brown and honey golden eyes staring deeply into hers. Then leaning forward towards her, as Liz's heart pounded nervously and excitedly in her chest, Iain pressed his mouth against hers, tasting the salt of her fresh tears on her lips, and feeling happier than he'd ever dreamt he could feel. She hadn't needed to say it, he could see it in her eyes, and he had felt it all those years ago when his mouth had tingled with her first kiss. It was that instinct and longing he'd seen in her deep blue sparkling eyes that had kindled his passion and kept him hoping through the years. But to hear her say 'yes' to his proposal in the past as well as the present was more than he could ever have wished for. He wanted to make love to her right there and then and it took all his self control to stop himself from giving in to his desires for her.

Reeling and breathless from his kiss, she gazed into the depths of his captivating eyes, almost as if she was reading his mind. Then, smiling with her eyes sparkling brighter

than he'd ever seen them before, she slowly removed her
t-shirt, followed by her trousers and stretched out before him
on the bed. Needing no further invitation and unable to find
any just reason why he shouldn't, he swiftly removed his
own clothes and tossed them on to the floor, before sliding
along the bed next to her. Tracing his fingers gently up her
legs, and over her hips, he rested his head on the pillow
next to hers and dived into the inviting watery blue depths
of her eyes. There was so much more to their captivating
blueness, he thought as their almost hypnotic effect drew
him in. As his mind opened up to her and drew closer to her
consciousness, he felt strangely refreshed as if rejuvenated by
their deep blue energy.

Liz had had relationships before but never like this.
The men in her life had always laid down the terms of their
relationship from the outset with their likes and dislikes,
no compromise and extreme lack of sensitivity. As for
'love', it seemed to be little more than a dirty word in their
vocabulary, never to be spoken and must definitely never to
be displayed…..except from her. They were never interested
in what she had to say, to them, she was their listening ear
and playmate but not much more. But this?

Inside she felt so different. It was as if her first journey
back into his past had changed her from a hap hazard palm
and thought reader, into a more sophisticated and electro
sensitive energy channeller. Her gift and her consciousness
were evolving.

She expected to feel nervous and self conscious during
her first intimate moments with Iain, after all, he was still
very much a stranger to her and she wasn't the kind of girl
to open her intimate boundaries to anyone. But now, lying
beside him, she didn't feel nervous at all. She could feel his
closeness and his openness to her, as if her journey between
his two conscious minds, sealed by his physical contact

with her, had opened up a strong neuro-electrical channel between them. She knew there was nothing to fear from him. Everything he did, he did for her, and as the feeling of calmness and serenity grew within her, the doors to her consciousness and her soul opened.

Something magical was happening to her before his eyes, he could see it in the way she responded to him and he could sense it in the air around them like a low voltage energy field protecting them. He gazed in awe as she stretched out along his body like a butterfly emerging from its cocoon, stretching out its fragile glistening beauty in the sunlight. Sensing her fragility, he removed his hand from her, frightened that his touch might shatter her into a million pieces. She touched his hand with hers and smiled with a radiance that melted his fears immediately. Although this was a new experience to her, Liz felt strangely as though she'd made love this way with Iain, many times before. Perhaps it was the excitement from these events in her future that she was feeling, compounding her elation and desires. Whatever it was, she felt instinctively guided as she connected with his field energy. Merging with his consciousness she could feel every thought, every desire he'd ever had for her since their first meeting. She bathed herself in his emotional warmth and he felt it and responded. He could see her too in his mind's eye, no longer a dream, she was a real presence. She hadn't just returned the part of his soul which she'd taken with her when she vanished that day, she was giving him so much more. Her trust in him and her unconditional love seeped into his soul like fine golden honey, sweetening his bitter memories of the years they'd spent apart. The noise of the city just outside their window seemed to disappear as they lay in the afternoon sunshine, silent and undisturbed by the world around them. Even time held its breath in that exquisite moment, as the merger of his centuries old wavelength with hers broke the boundaries of time and space, and transmitted a unique pulse of powerful positive energy radiating outwards across the universe and across time. No words could describe the power and breathless exaltation of their union as they lay in each others arms joined across time.

"I love you ……always have," he whispered close to her softly parted lips.

"I know," she sighed. "I've sensed it," she smiled. "And I think I …" she began, but Iain placed his finger gently across her lips and silenced her confession with the softest of kisses.

The low voltage electrical field which Iain had sensed, faded quickly, taking with it the green aura that he had become accustomed to over the years whenever there was any physical contact between them. Feeling an overwhelming sense of relief and fulfilment, Iain gently rolled on to his back beside her, and gazed across the bed into her beautiful haunting eyes that glistened with joyous tears of delight. Love had always been an elusive unattainable dream for her, forever locked away in a fortified vault that she had no access to. But now, she felt like she had been reborn into a light and depth of feeling that made her past life seem so plain and unimportant. She wanted to scream like a child on a fairground ride, enjoying the breathless thrill of being whisked up to exalted heights before dropping speedily back down to earth. She wanted to share everything with him, be every where, do everything. She wanted to cry an ocean of tears, to release the overwhelming feelings she held for him, like a shaken bottle of champagne about to pop its cork. Wanting to say so much to him but unable to speak, Iain stared into her wildly excited eyes and pulled her close, calming her trembling lips with his.

It was early evening and the sunset cast its golden red glow through the window, bathing Iain and Liz in a fiery light, as she lay facing him and ran her excited fingers gently down his handsome toned body. Opening his eyes, he admired her beauty and grinned wryly, elated in the knowledge that he was home at last. She was his shelter, his comfort from the storm. She quelled the emotional frustration and fire that burned within him. She was the one!

Liz looked at him, and could sense his contentment and peace as he reached out to her and drew her closer to him.

"I know you've only just met me, but I've known you most of my life," Iain confessed. "After searching and waiting for you for so long, it suddenly seems so strange that you're here at last, changing my life again. It's almost unnerving, trying to break those habits that have been my life for so many years," he continued. "I don't need to hope for you to appear any more. You're here. I don't need to convince myself to be happy, because I am," he sighed. "That halcyon future time I've dreamed of, being with you, waking up with you beside me, touching you, kissing you. That time is right here, right now."

"I hope I haven't disappointed you?" she whispered softly.

"You? Disappoint me?" he asked rhetorically. "If I had to wait a million years for this moment, you'd still never disappoint me," he answered. "In fact, you've surpassed my expectations, and they were pretty high," he said, grinning from ear to ear, his rich brown and honey golden eyes gleaming with delight, as he pulled her suddenly into his arms and kissed her.

When he finally let her go, noticing that the sun was finally setting he declared, "It's starting to get dark outside. We better get dressed and see what Steve and Fraser are doing downstairs." Then, added. "We decided to rest here until you'd had a chance to recover and to wait for darkness so that we could sneak across the city to our rendezvous point," Iain replied. "Incidentally, how's the arm?" he asked.

Liz could barely remember the car chase, the bullet wound or their escape through York Minster, as she examined the dressing on her arm. Peeling back the dressing carefully, Liz stared at her clean undamaged arm underneath the dressing, in bewilderment, as Steve knocked on the door of the bedroom.

"Just a minute," Liz called out, as they hurriedly got dressed. "I don't understand," she replied. "I thought I'd been shot."

"You were," Iain replied.

"Then where…"

"You must have healed yourself, just as you healed me, back there," he explained. "One good turn deserves another," smiled Iain.

Presently, they heard the heavy creaking of the wooden staircase and Steve appeared in the doorway alongside Fraser.

"Welcome, young lady! I'm Professor Fraser Hughes," he introduced himself politely. "How's the wound?"

"It's healed completely," said Iain.

"Did she do it?" asked the Professor.

"Seems that way," said Iain

"How did you know?" Liz asked the Professor.

"He told me all about it!" chirped Fraser as he looked at Iain. "He's told me all about your visits to him. Which one was it this time?" Fraser asked Iain.

"Libran's Loch. Her first visit to the cottage," Iain replied.

"Aaah yes. That was your introduction to young Iain wasn't it?"

Liz nodded.

"Marvellous!" Fraser remarked. "And what about, the infamous Magnus McGregor?"

"Who?" chorused Liz and Steve.

"The Captain!" answered Iain as he pretended to fight with an invisible sword, much to Steve's bewilderment.

"Oh him!" Liz sighed, nodding. "Totally evil! Loathsome! Made my flesh crawl!" she said as she pulled a face.

"Who the hell is Magnus McGregor? Who's young Iain and where on earth is Libran's Loch?" demanded Steve perplexed. "Did I just step off this planet for half a day? Is anybody going to fill me in here, or am I going to be kept guessing?" he frowned frustratingly.

"Whilst she was resting, Liz made her first ever visit back to the past. To be precise, back to Iain's past," explained Fraser.

"I was actually christened Iain Lachlan back in 1718. I adopted the name of Iain Sinclair some years ago when I moved to England," Iain added. "Liz has just used her ability to project her thought energy, to send herself back to my past, to 1746."

"Look! Never mind the jokes!" snapped Steve.

"It's no joke," said Liz. "I didn't know I could do it. I still don't know how I did it or whether something or someone else was responsible. But it happened, and here's his mother's wedding ring to prove it!"

Fraser's eyebrows raised in astonishment, and Steve's jaw dropped.

"So let me get this straight," said Steve. "You can time travel using your mind," he said to Liz.

Liz nodded.

"And you're 292 years old!" he said to Iain.

"I'll be 293 in April," Iain replied.

"But that's impossible!" declared Steve shaking his head.

"What did you do, take a drink from the fountain of eternal youth?"

"Not quite," smiled Iain as he looked at Liz.

"I better explain," interrupted Fraser. "When she was a child, going through adolescence, Liz had an accident that altered the electrical frequency in her body and isolated the positive and negative electrical charges in each of her cells. As a result, she has developed an ability to store tremendous amounts of electrical energy without spontaneously discharging it into her environment, as we all do."

"I don't follow," said Steve.

"Ever pulled on a nylon sweater and heard it crackle or felt a static shock and noticed your hair stand on end?"

"Yeh," Steve answered nodding his head.

"But when it happens to Liz, she stores that energy. Not wishing to sound insensitive, my dear, but you behave rather like a rechargeable battery but more efficient. When Liz has sufficient energy or too much energy in her body, she can project herself into people's thoughts, or to different places or even to different times, by tuning her thought energy waves into what we call the universal wavelength and using it as her mode of transport, if you will, to get her to her intended destination," Fraser continued. "Oh, I nearly forgot! If she touches you whilst she's in the process of projecting her thought energy, she also has the novel ability to recharge you, to restore your cells to their optimum condition."

"Are you talking about rejuvenation?" asked Steve.

"Exactly! And every time Liz has come into contact with Iain……"

"She's made him younger?" asked Steve.

"Well done, young man! Now you're getting the picture!"

"How did he work all this out?" whispered Liz to Iain.

"I captured all the details of your visits in my journals,

along with every word or phrase that you said, which I remembered. After I talked to Fraser about you, he asked to read the journals and carried out some analysis for me," explained Iain. "You even left me a note in my journal once," he smiled.

"Can I see it?" Liz asked excitedly.

"Sorry. It's out of bounds to you I'm afraid, except if the entry becomes retrospective for you," Iain replied.

"Something to do with paradoxes perhaps?" she whispered.

"Good girl! You're catching on!" Iain smiled.

"It's all true Steve," said Liz calmly as she looked across at Steve.

Steve stared at the delicate, slender and stunningly blue eyed and beautiful young lady before and shook his head in stunned, disbelief.

"Every time we met after that, your act of returning to the present rejuvenated me. It was as if it was your parting gift to me, to help me to await your return," added Iain. "At first your visits were short but frequent. Then they became longer and less frequent. Between each visit I would age gradually. Sometimes you cried to see me grow old. Then you'd hold me in your arms, a glowing light would surround us and the years of age would just drift away from me," Iain said, then he added. "When I saw you yesterday in the classroom, it was only the second time I had ever seen you in your physical form."

"You mean, you recognised me under all that student gear?"

"I'd recognise you anywhere," Iain smiled.

"How have you survived for so long? Did anybody else know?" asked Steve.

"I always kept it a secret. After Liz's visits, I always moved on, to prevent any awkward questions about my rejuvenation. Most of the time, when I moved on I adopted a new name and identity, which worked fine until the turn of the last century, when public record keeping really started to take off. After that, I had to be very careful and creative. I didn't share my secret with anyone until about forty years ago. That's when I met Professor Fraser Hughes for the very first time. We studied together at Edinburgh University. We were both studying physics at the time and we became really good friends, and have remained friends ever since. He's grown older of course, but he's always been there for me, helping me to work out who you were and where I might find you. We've also been working together to find some answers to your abilities, Liz."

"So what's this business with the ring then?" asked Steve.

"Long story, but essentially, Liz was able to locate my mother's missing wedding ring back then and, ….. " Iain paused.

"He asked me to marry him, and I said 'yes'!" interrupted Liz delightedly.

"But you don't even know this guy!" said Steve concerned.

"Cheers!" remarked Iain.

"Sorry, no offense, but it's true!" added Steve.

"Look Steve, I know you're only trying to protect me here, and I thank you for that. But, you need to pull yourself back and see the bigger picture here," began Liz. "For some strange, miraculous reason, if there is one, Iain and I met and became connected across time. Something very powerful pulled us together. Since meeting Iain, I've never felt so protected, so loved as I do when I'm with him. It's like we've always been together, and which girl do you know who could not love a man who has waited so long to be with her."

"Okay I get that, and I suppose with that kind of exceptional pedigree for loyalty, patience and endurance in a relationship, I accept what you're saying. But how can you be in love with Iain, when you've only known him two days?"

Liz turned to look at Iain, whose smile and knowing gaze aroused a deep warm glow within her, and she knew without a doubt, as he could quite plainly see in her sparkling eyes, that she was well and truly hooked.

"It just happened and I've never been happier," she replied. "Have you managed to work out why I was sent to you, back then?" she asked Iain.

"That's a very good question. Something I've thought about for a long time now, "he replied. "And in all honesty, I don't know, but Fraser and I are with you now, and together we'll figure this out, won't we Professor?" asked Iain.

"Yes my dear. Leave it in our capable hands and we'll get there eventually, brains and technology permitting, of course!"

Liz smiled, knowing she was in the company of three loyal and honourable friends, who cared for her very much.

"Wonderful!" said Fraser rubbing his hands. "Now we've got all that out of the way, who's for a nice pot of tea?" he asked.

"Lead the way Professor!" they all chorused and followed Fraser out of the bedroom door.

As they settled themselves down in the living room, Fraser disappeared for a few minutes and returned carrying a tray containing a steaming teapot dressed in a brightly coloured knitted tea-cosy, four cups, a bowl of sugar and a small jug of milk. As he placed the tray on the table near the fire, Fraser caught a glimpse of Liz's bright glowing eyes as she gazed at Iain and broke into a broad smile.

"I see you've managed to make a miraculous recovery young lady, no doubt due to Iain's excellent care!"

"Yes, I'm feeling fine now, thank you Professor!" Liz replied.

"I know this has all been thrown at you rather suddenly, but I can assure you, if there was anyone I'd recommend to take really good care of you, it would be Iain!" cheered the Professor.

Iain fidgeted uncomfortably, uneasy at Fraser's words of commendation.

"Are you sure that's what you want, Liz?" asked Steve.

"More sure, than I've ever been about anything in my entire life! It feels right, and I know it's the right thing to do! Please be happy for me."

"I just don't want to see you get hurt," said Steve solemnly. "and this whole situation just doesn't add up in my head."

"It's not meant to," replied Fraser. "It defies normal rational reasoning. But this is not a normal situation is it? Our brains haven't developed enough to comprehend concepts that lie on the fringe of our current knowledge and experience. You only have to think back about five hundred years or so to the point where we believed that the world was flat. It wasn't until we succeeded in making that first round the world trip that we truly began to believe that world wasn't flat. Similarly, up until now, we've only ever understood time on one plane. We've lacked the technology and the ability to prove the existence of any other alternative. But now that Liz has made her first successful voyage into the past, more journeys will become possible and the information gathered from those journeys will provide the foundation blocks to our better understanding and use of time, "explained Fraser.

"What about you Fraser? How are you able to accept it?" asked Steve curiously.

"I've known Iain for many years and I have witnessed his 'youthening' several times. I've met Liz before too," he whispered to Steve. "But that's our secret, for the moment."

With his head pounding and with an overwhelming eagerness to get back to a reality which he understood, Steve decided to change the subject.

"In case you'd forgotten, we do have an urgent rendezvous to keep at the river!" interrupted Steve as he drank his cup of tea.

"Whereabouts on the river?" asked Fraser.

"Near the Grand Opera House."

The Professor thought for a moment.

"You'll need a map of the old ginnels." He said.

"The ginnels?" asked Steve.

"They're the hidden old narrow back streets that run through the centre of York," said Iain."

"You can get from here to the Opera House using the ginnels for most of the way, without being seen from the main streets. That's probably your best chance." suggested the Professor.

"We don't need a map, "said Steve. "I can use the satellite navigation on my mobile phone. Give me a second while I punch in the details."

Finishing their tea and taking Steve's cue to head out into the hallway, the Professor handed all three of them some old coats from the hall stand and took hold of Iain's and Liz's hands.

"For so many years, you've been a good friend to me Iain, almost a father figure in fact. You even introduced me to my late wife," said the Professor. "It seems so strange now, not only to see you looking as young as you did back then, when we first met in Edinburgh, but sending you off on your way, with the one you've been searching for. "He went on, "My dear child, I don't know any other man in the entire world who has been through as much as Iain has, for the sake of a woman. You're in the best possible hands and I wish you both, all the luck in the world."

"Thank you," she replied.

"Okay, I've got the directions. Are we ready to go?" asked Steve as he concentrated on the screen of his mobile phone.

"As ready as we'll ever be," said Iain.

CHAPTER 16

THE AIR WAS FILLED WITH the sound of birds gossiping and cooing as they roosted high in the trees and on roof tops throughout the city. The three fugitives stepped with trepidation out into the darkness of the backyard, grateful of the birds incessant twittering to mask the sound of their feet on the ancient cobbles. With the exception of a nearby supermarket, who proudly displayed a large white banner proclaiming in big red letters: "Open 24 hours", the retail sector of the city had long since 'shut up shop' and gone home. Small groups of laughing and chattering revellers strolled along the narrow streets surrounding the Minster, occasionally disappearing into the open doors of the various public houses and restaurants that were open for business around the city. Luminescent footlights lit up the walls of the Minster with their golden glow, adding to the majestic magnificence of its dominating presence at the heart of the city.

A tall street lamp at the end of the back lane provided just enough light to enable them to see their way across the yard to the back gate. Sliding back the bolt and lifting the lever quietly, Steve opened the gate and peered out into the lane. Nothing stirred.

"Come on," he whispered. "It looks clear."

Edging their way along the cold damp red brick wall, they ventured the few yards towards the main road, with Iain holding Liz's hand reassuringly and smiling softly, his eyes glinting gold as they caught the light from the over head street lamp. Still trembling with excitement and her heart palpitating with the thrill of adventure, Liz's face brimmed with a happiness she couldn't hide, a happiness they could all feel. But deep below the surface, hidden within her subconscious, fears regarding her limited ability to control her gift and concerns as to what it might do to her, began to germinate the first seeds of doubt and dread.

Just as they were about to creep around the corner, a small silver car turned on to the road at the end of the lane. Quickly they flattened themselves against the wall and hid in the shadows until the car had driven past. Then, inching their way forward again, Steve checked for any other traffic on Lord Mayor's Walk, before beckoning to Iain and Liz to cross the road quickly. A row of parked cars on the other side of the road provided them with additional cover, as they kept to the shadows and crept their way along the street. The steep grassy bank and the medieval city walls towered over them cloaking their escape route in darkness until they reached several small shops near the crossroads marking the entrance to Goodramgate. Turning the corner, the three fugitives headed through the battle and weather worn historic archway within the city wall, with Steve leading the way to the streets beyond.

"We need to head straight down this road until we hit the crossroad for Low Petergate," said Steve, as he checked the satellite navigation on his phone.

Sticking close to the walls and shop fronts on the left side of the narrow street, avoiding the occasional drips from broken guttering and drainpipes, Liz and Iain trotted stealthily along beside Steve, watching every where for any signs of their pursuers. As they approached the crossroad leading to Low Petergate, they could feel the air becoming increasingly more humid and heavy. Looking ahead, a hundred yards or so, they could see the street disappearing into a thick clinging mist.

"Nice to see someone's on our side," commented Iain.

Liz shivered beneath the oversized duffle coat that Fraser had given her.

"Looks creepy to me," she whispered. "All we need is a pipe, a magnifying glass and a deerstalker and we're set. It's like a scene from a gothic novel."

"That mist will provide us with just the cover we need as we head down towards the river," explained Iain.

"We'll need to keep very close together though," cautioned Steve. "If we get split up, we'll have a devil of a job trying to find each other."

"Good point," said Iain. "Stay close Liz," he said as he reached for her hand again and squeezed it affectionately, determined not to lose contact with her. Entering the mist warily, the increased humidity that hung around them, clung to their hair and clothes like a wet blanket, and slowed progress as their breathing became laboured. Steve kept wiping the moisture from the screen of his mobile phone, trying to keep the phone as dry as possible, conscious that if it got too damp......

"Damn!"

"What's wrong Steve?" asked Iain.

"The phone's died on me, "he moaned. "It's the dampness.."

"No need to panic! Help is at hand! I know York like the back of my hand, well not quite like the back of my hand, but pretty well enough, I think. Sometimes there are hidden advantages to being dragged along on boring academic pub crawls in search of obscure and cryptic trail clues. Being able to remember the pubs and their locations by the end of one of those evenings is an exceptional skill by anyone's standards, especially after several pints of real ale!" chirped

Iain. "If I've got my bearings right and my memory serves me correctly, we can cross this square just ahead, and that will take us into the Shambles. Then if we follow straight through to the other side, the streets start to slope down towards the river, so it shouldn't be too difficult to find our way there," said Iain encouragingly. "The mist should increase in density as we walk down the hill. The thicker the mist, the nearer we are to the river, simple! Then we just toddle along the river path to the rendezvous point. Stay close and take it slowly though. This kind of mist deadens most sounds in the same way snow does. If we're not careful and we take a wrong turning, we could wind up, well ….. in the river itself!" advised Iain.

"The visibility is dropping fast, "muttered Steve.

"I can barely make out where I'm walking now," remarked Liz.

"We need to stay alert," added Iain, pricking his ears as he heard just a faint sound some distance behind them. "We might not be alone down here."

"What do you mean?" asked Liz. "Do you think they're around here somewhere?"

"Just a hunch. Could be nothing, but on the other hand….."

"Iain's right. I suggest we keep our voices down to a whisper ……. Just in case we walk straight into them," said Steve.

"Good idea," replied Iain. "Just keep really close."

Quickly, crossing the small square, Iain pointed in the direction of a narrow lane leading away from them into Little Shambles. The houses on the lane were extremely old and defied gravity as they leaned in towards each other, threatening to crash down on to their heads. Liz noticed that some of the windows had been twisted completely out of shape, but miraculously hadn't broken. Some of the doorways carried the same distortion, with the angles of some door frames pushed to acute and obtuse extremes, giving the impression that if something heavy pushed the houses in the direction of the lean, the entire lane would collapse like a pack of cards. On the front of the houses and small shops on either side of the lane, they could see the original dark oak facia timbers, pock marked with lots of tiny holes.

"This is like stepping back in time by about three or four hundred years," whispered Liz.

"You should feel quite at home then!" joked Steve to Iain.

"Nice to see you haven't entirely lost your sense of humour then," whispered Iain as he frowned at Steve.

"Now, now boys, play nicely. We're in this together, remember," whispered Liz, trying to ease the tension between them.

Steve's overly protective behaviour towards Liz, together with his cynical scepticism of Iain's past was beginning to irritate Iain immensely, especially when he kept dropping back behind Iain, obviously to check that Liz was okay. Seeing that Liz was still safely with them, and sensing Iain's annoyance, Steve remembered what Liz had said, and took the lead again. He knew she was right. They needed to work together as a team if they were ever going to get through all of this, and petty squabbles, for whatever reasons would only serve to distract them, a luxury they could ill afford whilst danger lay close at hand.

Liz could feel their writhing hostility towards each other and shook her head as she thought of Steve with his suspicions of Iain as some con man trying to deceive and exploit Liz for her remarkable gifts. Then she thought of Iain, justifiably annoyed at Steve's evident failure to protect Liz, and his own suspicions of Steve as the other man in her life. Jealousy versus mistrust, a highly explosive combination Liz thought. Then suddenly, cold leather gloved hands closed around her mouth and waist, and she felt herself being pulled back through the swirling mist, away from Iain and Steve, by her yet unknown abductor.

"It's remarkable that these buildings are still standing, especially when you consider how often York becomes flooded. They've defied everything that's been thrown at them," whispered Iain as he turned to Liz, but she was gone.

"Liz? Liz? Where are you?" shouted Iain, as he reached out behind him where she'd been, and fumbled in the mist desperately trying to re-establish physical contact. "Liz? Liz?" He yelled out into the mist, as he felt a wave of panic over come him.

"Ssshhh!" commanded Steve. "We need to listen! If someone's got her, we might be able to make out which direction they've taken her!" For a minute, they stood still and held their breath, concentrating on any sound that might give them a clue as to Liz's whereabouts.

She could feel the hard metal belt buckle pressing into the centre of her back and his hot stale breath prickled the hairs on the side of her neck, as her abductor pulled her hard against his chest. She tried to struggle and twist, but he held her fast, gripping her so tightly she could hardly breathe. As they waited in the misty darkness, she could hear Iain's faint cries in the distance and the muffled clatter of shoes on the cobbles as Iain and Steve ran this way and that way trying to find her. "Over here!" she tried to scream through the gloved hand, but the only sound that left her mouth was an inaudible smothered mumble. With her right hand free, she clawed at the hand around her mouth until her captor's other hand grabbed her throat.

"Struggle like that again, and I'll snap your neck!" he grunted.

Liz knew he wouldn't. Whatever his threats, someone wanted her alive, to know what she knew, to obtain her gift. From the fading sound of their voices, Iain and Steve were getting further away, so it was all down to her to do something. Armed with only her wits and pressed firmly against her abductor, she did the only thing she could. Stamping her heel as hard as she could on his right foot then his left, he crumpled temporarily, allowing her to bring her right foot up quickly underneath her and kicked as hard as she could into his groin. A deep groan echoed from her captor as he crumpled even more. Then flicking the heel of her foot up sharply, she wacked the underside of his chin and kicked him backwards, forcing him reluctantly to release his grasp on her. Then, after turning briefly to see him double up in agony, she sped off into the mist ahead of her, and ran straight into Iain, coming towards her.

"What happened to you? Where'd you go?" he asked breathlessly and concerned.

"Someone grabbed me from behind and started to drag me away! He threatened to kill me!"

"Whoa, calm down!" said Iain as he could see the panicked distressed look on her face. "What did he look like?"

"Don't know! Once I got him off me, I didn't bother to hang around and find out!" she gasped.

"Good girl! Let's get out of here! There may be others!" he shouted to Steve.

Holding on to each other in the intense mist, they sped off along the narrowest, mistiest and darkest of the old streets, slipping occasionally on the medieval cobbles until they emerged on to one of the main roads heading down towards Coppergate. Hearing the clatter of several heavy boots not far behind them, they sprinted down Coppergate until they came to King Street, a narrow cobbled lane leading down to the river.

"There's a bridge to the right, at the bottom of this lane," gasped Iain. "Come on, they're right behind us!"

Unable to stop for breath, the three fugitives fled down King Street and took a sharp turn right towards the bridge.

"Quickly, down to the river!" commanded Iain.

Puzzled, Steve and Liz followed him down to the edge of the quay.

"Quickly, slide over the edge," instructed Iain. "The water's at low tide. If we can just hang on here, they'll never find us in this mist. They'll think we've headed towards the bridge." Iain continued.

Climbing between the chains of the safety rail at the edge of the quay, Iain, Steve and Liz, slid on to their stomachs and lowered themselves over the edge. Holding on tightly by their fingertips, the three clung to the side of the slippery, cold, wet stone quay, their feet only inches above the water, as the clatter of the boots on the cobbles became louder and louder above them. Torch lights streaked across the river behind them, and all three suddenly realised that their pursuers stood directly above them. Looking up from the shadows of the quay wall and holding their breath, they clung on in fearful silence.

"Looks like they headed for the bridge, Sir!" a young male voice shouted out.

"Spread out!" boomed a deep commanding voice. "Yaslo, stay here on the quay!"

"Yes, Sir!" barked an eastern European voice.

There was more clattering of heavy boots fading into the distance, whilst one man marched slowly back and forth along the quay.

"I can't hold on much longer," whispered Liz to Iain. "I'm going to fall."

Cautiously, Iain pulled himself up just enough to see over the top of the quay. A younger man dressed in black and carrying a handgun was about six feet away from him, walking away. Gesturing to the other two to stay still, Iain pulled himself up and slid on his stomach, back on to the quay. Quietly, creeping up behind the gunman, Iain kicked out at the back of the gunman's knees, bringing him crashing down and causing the gun to fall from his hands and skid across the cobbles. Rolling on to his side with blood streaming from the side of his head, the gunman tried to struggle to his feet. Leaping away from him, Iain grabbed the gun and pointed it at the young man.

"Get up Yaslo!" Iain commanded, as Steve climbed back on to the quay and began to help Liz.

"Are you alright, Liz?" Steve asked.

"Nothing that a good hot shower couldn't fix!" she replied.

"You're coming with us!" said Iain to the gunman. "You're Yaslo, right?"

Yaslo nodded. "Now, move it!"

Together, the three fugitives and the gunman headed away from the bridge and along the riverside until they were well out of sight. The mist lay thick and heavy making their progress slow and treacherous. Then, just ahead, where the mist became patchy, they could just make out a long boat moored at the quay. As they got closer, the words on its bow read, 'The Blue Rose'.

"We've found it!" whispered Steve. "Let's get onboard!"

Iain pointed to Yaslo with the gun, and indicated for him to climb down first on to the boat. Yaslo did as he was told and waited on the deck of the boat as Iain, Liz and Steve made their descent.

Suddenly, a bald headed, unshaven muscular man in his late thirties popped his head up from the far end of the boat. A gun barrel gleamed in his hand as it pointed towards them.

"Where the hell have you been? You're late! I'm Jackson." he barked. "I should've taken off hours ago! Who the hell is he?" he demanded, pointing the gun at Yaslo.

"Collateral and information!" answered Iain.

"Where's Grant?"

"Dead! He never made it I'm afraid." said Steve.

"Get inside quickly!" he commanded. "I'll cast off. Oh, and for God's sake, get the 'collateral' tied up. Grant was a decent guy, and if he gets in my way…."

"We get the picture," replied Steve.

Yaslo skulked his way inside the boat with Steve, Iain and Liz behind him. Presently, as they watched from the windows and saw the boat pull away from the quay, their captain peered through the cabin doors.

"There's a bathroom at the far end of the cabin, help yourselves. There's sleeping quarters as well. You might want to get some rest. We've got a long journey ahead of us!"

"I'll keep an eye on our guest here," said Steve. "You two get yourselves cleaned up."

"Aye, aye!" They chorused.

Handing Steve the gun, Iain led Liz along to the far end of the boat into the bathroom. Inside there was a shower, a sink and a toilet, with fresh towels draped from rails on the back of the door. Above the sink was a tiny window with very short curtains kept in place at the top and bottom by flexible white plastic coated wire. As she pulled the curtains together for privacy, she felt Iain's hands around her waist and his hot breath against her neck. Her skin tingled to his touch as he ran his fingers down her arms. Turning to face him, her eyes radiated the unabashed joy she felt deeply inside.

"I think you better wait next door," she whispered. "I'll let you know when I'm done.

"I said, I'd never let you out of my sight again. Remember?" Iain said.

"Well unless someone comes flying through this tiny window to whisk me away, I think I'll be pretty safe," she replied.

"Really?" he said holding her tightly and grinning like a Cheshire cat. "Do you think so?"

Liz wrapped her arms around his neck and nipped the skin on the back of her hand making her wince.

"What on earth are you doing?"

"Just checking."

"Checking what?" he asked curiously.

"Checking that I'm not dreaming all of this," she replied.

"Women! You really are the strangest of creatures," he laughed.

"I bet you've met quite a few in your time," she said curiously.

"Hmmn yeh, one or two."

"Did you like any of them?"

"Hmmn," he nodded.

"And you never married," Liz added.

"Thought about it once, then changed my mind."

"Why?"

"Ooohh I don't know. Perhaps it was because she wasn't you," he sighed.

Liz blushed.

"You're not having second thoughts, about me, are you?"

"No way! You're stuck with me now!" she cheered.

Iain smiled. He'd never met a woman quite like her. Not only did she have some pretty remarkable gifts but she was warm, funny, caring with just a touch of eccentricity to add a little spice. She was definitely the one!

"You better sit over there then whilst I pop in the shower," she said as she began to peel off her t-shirt.

Iain turned away politely.

"You weren't so gentlemanly this afternoon," she teased.

"Aaah, yes well. That was different," he coughed still with his back to her. "I think I can be forgiven for slipping up on that occasion. After all, you were pushing all the right buttons as I remember."

Liz said nothing. There wasn't a sound.

"Liz?"

Iain turned around quickly, panicking at the thought that she might have disappeared again, but there she stood, in the shower, peeping out from behind the curtain with a broad school-girlish grin on her face, and every inch the woman he adored.

"Gotcha!" she grinned.

"Don't do that! You nearly gave me a heart attack!" he gasped.

"Sorry! Couldn't resist!" she said as she pulled the curtain around her.

Within seconds of turning on the hot shower, the bathroom filled with steam whilst Iain sat on a stool in the far corner, just able to make out her fuzzy silhouette through the curtain. Squirting some shower gel on to a sponge and lathered up the sweet smelling lotion on her body, Liz cleansed herself of the residue of the pond stench and the dirt from the quayside.

"Are you alright in there?" asked Iain after a few minutes.

"Water's lovely and hot!" she replied.

"Like me?" came a whisper in her ear.

Iain had climbed into the shower behind her and was resting his chin on her shoulder as he draped his arms around her body. His soft hands caressed her as he kissed the back of her neck, sending shivers down her spine.

"You can't tease a man like that and not expect some kind of reaction," he whispered provocatively.

"I bet you were a real Casanova back then!" she remarked teasingly.

"I had my moments," he admitted grinning. "Just like, I'm having one right now."

"I could say no," she sighed as he pressed her body against his.

"Yes, you could," he grinned cheekily as he turned her around to look at him, with eyes gleaming brightly.

Liz slid away from him and climbed out of the shower.

"Hey, where're you going? What did I say?" he asked, baffled by her sudden rejection of his seductive charms.

"Not here," she whispered. "It's not ….private." Then she added. "When we find somewhere to stay, I might change my mind."

"You're right." He sighed dejected. "But, you can't blame a hot blooded Scotsman like myself, for trying!"

"Suppose not!" she replied.

"Maybe I should wear my kilt next time, to gild the lily, as it were!" he teased.

"You and lilies?" she replied shaking her head and trying not to laugh as she recalled their first encounter at the loch, and the image of Iain sat in the shallow loch water with his kilt floating around him, popped into her head.

"I didn't mean…"

"Gotcha again!" she laughed, but then her laughter stopped. Something was wrong. A greyness suddenly descended over her face and the lustre disappeared from her eyes as she stumbled across the bathroom to the door and then collapsed.

Grabbing a bath towel and vaulting out of the shower, he wrapped the towel around himself and rushed to Liz's side. Sliding on to the floor, he pulled her towel wrapped body carefully into his arms and cradled her gently.

"What's wrong Liz? What's happening? Are you in pain? Did that guy hurt you back there?" Iain asked.

"They're coming!" she replied. "I can feel their anger! They're close!"

"What can I do?" he asked helplessly.

"I'm scared Iain! Hold me, I feel dizzy and weak like I'm being drained of all my energy."

"I'm here Liz and I won't leave you," he whispered softly. "Jackson will get us out of here, don't worry. We'll just sit here for a few minutes while you rest. It's been a long day and you're exhausted," he said as he swept the wet hair from her face and held her close.

Suddenly a host of tiny stars surrounded her, as her thought energy fought to stay within her body and her protective blue / green aura engulfed them. As he held her in his arms, Iain watched as the aura expanded beyond the bathroom, much to the alarm of the others onboard. He could hear their cries as the luminescent field spread throughout the boat. Looking down into her face, Iain watched helplessly as Liz's eyes paled and closed.

"Something is trying to pull me away," she whispered weakly. "Don't let it take me!"

"No no no!" Iain yelled. "Liz open your eyes! Look at me! Fight it! You've got to fight it!"

"I'm trying to," she whispered.

Iain had a sudden thought.

"Liz, listen to me carefully. Whoever is doing this must have a fix on your position. They must be able to tune into your thought waves! I'm not exactly sure how! You're only chance may be if you project yourself somewhere, far enough away, or somewhere out of this time zone! Do it now!"

"I can't! I won't leave you!" she cried weakly.

"You have to! I'll find you, I promise!" he insisted, gripping her hand tightly.

"I won't leave you!"

"You've got to!" he whispered. Rocking her gently in his arms with her head pressed against his heart, he rested his cheek against her hair and prayed for a miracle.

The energy drain she had been feeling was exactly that. Something was generating a powerful receiver beacon drawing her energy like a magnet. Subconsciously generating her own electromagnetic defensive field around the boat, she drew on every ounce of energy she could from within herself and everything around her. Iain felt suddenly weakened and for just one moment she had the energy she needed. With her last breath she projected, knocking out all the power on the boat, and plunging them into darkness. Everything was still and silent. Everyone onboard the boat froze, paralysed with fear. Then suddenly the boat began to pitch and toss, just like his tiny wooden boat on the loch. Liz's hand slipped to the floor limply and lifeless. She was gone.

"No!" Iain screamed. "You can't take her, not now! Steve!" he screamed, lifting Liz's limp body in his arms and kicking open the bathroom door. "Steve! Help me!"

"What happened? What's wrong?" he asked.

"Who put the lights out?" yelled Jackson.

"Is there a defibrillator on board?" asked Iain desperately.

Steve looked at Liz in Iain's arms.

"She's gone Iain!"

"Not if I can help it!" he yelled crossly. "Jackson! Defibrillator! Where is it?"

"Under the sofa! What you want one of them for?"

"Get it!" ordered Iain.

Steve nodded and shot across the cabin to retrieve it, whilst Iain laid Liz carefully on the wooden table. Pinching her nose and opening her mouth, Iain breathed air into her lungs and began massaging her chest. Steve checked the defibrillator which had its own inbuilt backup power supply. Placing his ear on her chest Iain listened for her heart beat, but there was nothing. Once again he pinched her nose and repeated the process, but still there was nothing.

"Is it charged?" Iain yelled at Steve.

"Yes!"

"Give it here!" Iain snapped.

"Are you sure you know what you're doing?" asked Steve concerned.

"I used to be a doctor! Don't argue!" he yelled and grabbed the paddles. "Now, stand clear!"

Concentrating hard and focussing all his thoughts on Liz, he placed the paddles carefully on her. The jolt lifted her body off the table before releasing her again. Iain listened and felt for her pulse, but there was nothing. Then, placing the paddles on her again, he dispensed a second jolt. Praying as hard as he could, he rested his head on her chest and listened. He wasn't sure whether it was his desperate wishful thinking or not, but faintly there was something. Checking her pulse he nodded his head.

"Steve take a listen!" Iain instructed.

Steve placed his ear carefully on her chest. There was a slow steady beat and it was getting stronger with every second.

"You did it! You brought her back!"

As he stood over her deathly pale face, a warm soft salty tear fell from his eyes on to hers as he clutched her hand in his and gently stroked her hair.

Her eyelids flickered open, and as she slowly began to pull round, she could see the pain and desperation in his frightened helpless eyes. Relieved and exhausted, Iain collapsed on the small sofa next to the table and rested his head in his hands.

"I nearly lost you for good that time!" he sighed.

Weakly, at first, she lifted her hand and ran her fingers gently through his hair. Turning his face towards her, he kissed the palm of her hand and it was her turn to wipe the tears from his eyes.

"What's going on!" bellowed Jackson as he came striding through the darkened cabin. "All the instruments on my panel have gone dead! My phone's gone dead too!"

"So has mine," said Steve, as he gestured to Jackson to be quiet.

"What's wrong?" asked Jackson.

"Liz collapsed. Iain had to revive her," explained Steve. "We think she's going to be okay now."

"Liz collapsed when she got out of the shower. She was complaining of feeling that her energy was being drained away from her, then the green mist surrounded us. It's kind of her defence mechanism, like a protective electromagnetic blanket. I could see her projection being pulled from her body but she managed to hold it back," explained Iain.

"So what knocked out all the power?" Steve asked.

"My best guess? I think she did. I asked her to project herself further away, out of range of whatever was after her. I think she didn't have enough energy to do that, so she drew on all the energy around onboard this boat. Unfortunately, whatever she did, didn't work. She didn't project but at least she's still alive…. and here."

Steve gazed at Liz with deepening concern.

"That depends on what you mean by 'here'," remarked Jackson. "That's what I came in to tell you."

"Tell us what?" asked Iain.

"We're not there anymore. We're not on the river. We're out at sea!"

"What?" exclaimed Iain.

"That's impossible!" remarked Steve.

"If you don't believe me, take a look for yourself! I'll go and see if I can restart the engine."

"This is becoming more like science fiction by the minute!" Steve exclaimed.

"Ssshhh," commanded Iain.

Yaslo had been sitting watching the drama play out before him and listening intently to their conversation. Suspiciously, Steve approached him on his way up on to the deck, eyeing him curiously. "You know something about this don't you?"

Yaslo didn't flinch.

"I'm guessing here, but couldn't this be part of the reason you're after Liz?"

Yaslo looked straight ahead.

"Answer me!" Steve barked.

"Electro magnetic energy," muttered Yaslo.

"Sorry? What was that you said?" asked Steve.

"The blue / green light we saw. I've seen it before. Back in the laboratories I have seen them create this light by colliding particles along the magnetic field around an object. But that's all I know." replied Yaslo.

"So why was she generating electro magnetic energy?" Steve asked Iain as he approached.

"Like I said before, I think that's how she generates her own personal force field, or defence mechanism"

"But that's impossible!" replied Steve.

"So is everything about her and me and this situation, but it doesn't mean that it isn't happening!" declared Iain.

"You can say that again!" remarked Jackson, raising his head out of the engine compartment and climbing back up into the main cabin. "One minute we were on the river, now we're in the English Channel!"

Puzzled, Iain and Steve clambered their way up on to the deck followed by the Jackson. As they stepped up on to the deck, they expected to see the river banks on either side, and the buildings and bridges that crossed the river as it headed out of York. Instead, the sight that met their eyes, left them shaking in disbelief. Whatever it was that had affected Liz had also affected the boat and everyone on board. Turning to see the characteristically famous White Cliffs behind them, they realised that they were now sailing away from Dover, far out to sea.

"What the hell?" exclaimed Steve.

Iain dashed back down below deck and ran across to where Liz lay recovering. Sitting beside her and squeezing her hand lightly, Iain asked her a question.

"Liz? I know you're tired but I need to ask you something. Did you do this? Did you bring us here?"

"Yes," she answered. "I didn't know if I could do it, but I couldn't leave you all behind."

"So you used your energy to project us electromagnetically out of danger."

"Yes," she replied.

"Do you remember what you were thinking just before it happened?" asked Iain.

"Why is that important?" asked Steve as he re-entered the main cabin.

"Sometimes we overlook what we initially regard as irrelevant or insignificant in our search for an answer, only to discover that they are in fact, critical to the event," Iain explained.

"You're beginning to sound like the Professor!" remarked Steve.

"Ssshhh," replied Iain. "Liz, do you remember what you were thinking?"

"Romantic thoughts, especially when you kissed me," she said.

"Eureka! That's it!" cheered Iain.

"I don't get it," said Steve.

"Who'd have believed it? The power of love!" answered Iain grinning wryly.

Steve shook his head.

"Look, unlike us, Liz has the ability to charge up electrical energy in her body and that's what she uses to project herself. When she realised she didn't have enough energy to do what she needed to do, she began to draw electrical energy from the boat, knocking off all the power as she did it – a bit like an EMP pulse. Unfortunately that still wasn't enough, but when I kissed her and made physical contact, she was able to draw that little extra piece of energy she needed from me," Iain explained. "Now that's what I call power! What do you think?"

"So Liz transported us here?" asked Steve.

"Yeh, brilliant isn't it?" cheered Iain. "It's just a theory I know, but how else could you explain it, and it was just what we needed, right?" replied Iain. "USS Eldridge, eat your heart out!" he grinned as he dashed back to the bathroom, re-emerging a minute later, fully dressed in warm fresh clothing and carrying a bundle of clothes for Liz.

"USS Eldridge?" queried Steve.

"Crikey, call yourself a detective? Come on! Don't tell me you haven't heard about one of the most confounding scientific mysteries of the 20th Century? The Philadelphia Experiment – Project Rainbow," replied Iain.

Steve looked puzzled.

"Seventy years ago, just before Oppenheimer split the atom, the US Navy were rumoured to have conducted experiments using super electromagnetic fields to make their ships invisible to radar. Such an experiment was apparently conducted on a ship called the USS Eldridge, though they still go to great pains to deny it. According to witness accounts of what happened, the powerful electromagnetic field generated by two super coils, one at either end of the ship, generated a green glow around the entire ship, just like the one Liz created, only hundreds of times larger. The ship apparently disappeared leaving only the impression of the ship's displacement in the water. Meanwhile, in Philadelphia harbour, a couple of hundred miles further north, the ship apparently reappeared there for a short time before disappearing again and returning to its original location." said Iain.

"So, you're saying that Liz generated enough electromagnetic energy to transport us nearly 300 miles along the Earth's magnetic field lines to the English Channel," replied Steve. "One question."

"Yes?"

"If the ship returned to its original location, will we?" asked Steve.

"Good question," answered Iain scratching his head. "If we do, I don't think they'll be expecting us. If we don't, well, we've escaped, definitely a win-win scenario in my book!"

"And how exactly did this happen again?" asked Jackson.

"I suppose you could say it all boils down to Liz's 'magnetic personality of sorts." replied Iain. Then realising the humour and irony of his response, he laughed. "I like

that! Magnetic personalities! Mmmmmn. Of course, that
is just my theory, I might be wrong but what else could it
be?"

"But why her? And why you?" asked Steve still searching
for a satisfactory answer. "It's bad enough trying to weigh up
the odds of two strangers meeting in the present, but across
260 or so years of time? There has to be something else.
There has to be something connecting you two, something
that sets you apart from everyone else. There has to be a
reason!"

"Does there?" asked Iain. "We always try to look for
order in chaos, don't we? We can't just accept chance or
serendipity."

"Ok Einstein, explain this one if you will. How the hell
could you two link up across time? What was it that pulled
her to you?"

Iain sat down on the edge of the seat and began to
pull together every scrap of evidence and every piece of
information he'd gathered in his head over the centuries.
His audience waited silently. If anyone was qualified to come
up with an answer, it could only be him. Only he knew all
the occasions when Liz had visited him, the circumstances
surrounding those visits, and the outcomes which had sent
her winging back to the present. Leaning back against the
cushion, he stretched out his long legs in front of him and
rested his chin on his chest. The Channel waves lapped
rhythmically against the hull of the boat, rocking it back
and forth like the pointer on a metronome.

"I knew he didn't have an answer!" remarked Steve.

Iain looked up sharply at Steve, his rich honey brown
eyes turning dark and bitter.

"You're right. I don't have an answer, at least not just
yet. We don't have all the pieces to this puzzle, so how can
I make any rational conclusions? We don't know who tried

to have Liz killed in the first place. We don't know who that squad of goons are and whether or not they're working for the same person. These situations didn't occur within a controlled environment, so we don't exactly know what we're dealing with here!" replied Iain. "Have you got any suggestions?"

Steve didn't answer.

"You don't like me much, do you?" asked Iain.

"Now you're deflecting!" retorted Steve.

"But I'm right, aren't I?" probed Iain. "Ever since you turned up, you've resented my involvement with Liz."

"Why does that surprise you?" asked Steve.

"It doesn't."

"I've been protecting Liz for months now, keeping her safe…"

"Oh, and by keeping her safe, you mean exactly what, sitting up there, miles away in your ivory tower, whilst she dangles from the end of the hook, waiting for the sharks to strike!"

"That's not strictly true! Grant was watching over her!"

"She was bait, for who? Have you found out who they are? No? I didn't think so! So I guess that makes us about even! I'm trying to find answers and so are you!"

Steve moved towards Iain, as fury blazed in each of their eyes.

"Stop It! Both of you!" Liz yelled as she tried to sit up. "What's wrong with you?"

"How can he put you through all this Liz? If it really is true about old Methuselah here, couldn't he just be using you to continue the cycle of rejuvenation, to harvest your power? You're keeping him alive, but at what price to you? Everyone has to pay the piper some time. What price will you have to pay for saving his sorry ass? We nearly lost you this time!"

Liz's eyes filled with tears. Although, she knew how much she loved him and believed in his love and devotion to her, she couldn't deny that Steve had made a pretty valid point. Was Iain using her? Was there something that Iain wasn't telling her? Was there something else he was holding back? Was he the real power and the reason behind Liz being pulled back to his past? No. She didn't believe that. She couldn't. But how could she convince Steve otherwise? She could feel Steve's pain, his grief. He cared for her too. She could feel his fire and resentment that Iain was the one she chose. Liz opened her eyes and looked at Steve. She could see his wounded pride and understood now, the truth behind his attitude and actions. Gently placing her right hand against his cheek, she felt his pain like a thousand tiny knives slashing away at him deep inside. He reached for her wrist and carefully removed her hand.

"I didn't know!" she said.

"What's there to know?" he said coldly. "I'm just trying to protect you, Liz and so far, we haven't done a very good job have we?"

"But I'd be dead if it wasn't for you, Iain, Jackson and the Professor. So you must be doing something right!" she sighed. "It's not your fault, it's this damn gift! If I didn't have it, I probably wouldn't be in this position and neither would you!"

"Look, let's just all calm down," sighed Iain. "The only way we're going to get through this is if we work together. We have to trust each other. We're all we've got!"

"He's right, we do need to work together. We're all very tired too, it's been a hell of day," agreed Steve as he held out his hand towards Iain. "Sorry! I guess I have been putting you under a lot of pressure. No hard feelings?"

Iain looked at Steve, and at the olive branch of

reconciliation extended towards him. Slowly he reached out and grasped Steve's hand.

"Thanks for saving Liz, and I'm sorry I had my doubts about you. I guess I've found all of this a bit too much to swallow, to be quite frank! I'll never fully appreciate what you've been through over the years. I'm not sure I could have survived the way you have." Steve confessed. "And I know now, you'll never let any harm come to Liz!" announced Steve.

Iain dropped his head, sure of his memories from the past but uncertain of their place in the sequence of present events.

"I can only try," he sighed heavily.

Taking the focus away from Iain, Steve looked at Yaslo.

"You! Yaslo!" he said.

Yaslo sat to attention.

"Take everything off!" said Steve.

All eyes looked curiously in his direction.

"We're stuck out here in the middle of the Channel, right? But we've still got his lot hunting us down! They shouldn't have a clue where we are, so let's keep the advantage! He might be carrying a transmitter!" explained Steve.

"Good point!" agreed Iain. "We don't exactly want to make it easy for them to find us again, do we? "

"Just do it! Now!" commanded Steve.

"I better go and get dressed," said Liz as she carefully sat up and lowered herself on to the floor, still wrapped in the towel.

"I'll follow you," added Iain, as the walked towards the sleeping quarters in the cabin.

Yaslo began pulling off his clothes until he stood naked and shivering in the centre of the deck.

"Throw me your clothes!" ordered Steve.

Yaslo did as he was told.

"There's some spare clothes just in the cupboard behind you," said Jackson.

Carefully, turning his back on Steve and Jackson, Yaslo reached into the cupboard, and pulled out some trousers, a shirt and a sweater, which he put on.

Throwing Yaslo's clothes to Jackson, Steve said, "Chuck them overboard! We don't want anybody tracing us!"

Jackson nodded.

"So what do we do now?" asked Jackson.

"We head back to the south coast," replied Steve.

"And where are we heading?" asked Jackson.

"Southampton docks."

"Southampton it is!" confirmed the Jackson, as he began to bring the Blue Rose about.

CHAPTER 17

IAIN AND LIZ CAREFULLY MADE their way through the main cabin as the boat pitched and tossed in all directions as a result of the high Channel swell. The berth at the front of the cabin, next to the bathroom, was quite small, with just enough room to accommodate a small double bed and some wood panelled shallow shelved cupboards. With Iain giving a supporting hand, Liz entered the room and sat down on the bed. Offering her the small pile of clean clothes he'd gathered up from the bathroom, as well as a helpful hand, Liz began to dress.

"Can I ask a question?" said Liz, as Iain helped her pull on the trousers.

"Fire away....." said Iain.

"I know and I understand why you can't tell me things that relate to my future. But is there anything else that you're keeping from me?" she asked.

Iain didn't answer.

"Presumably ... over the years, you've tried to figure out why I have these abilities, how they work and what the connection is between us. I agree with what Steve said. There has to be something more to this. What I mean is, it can't just be a bizarre series of coincidences, can it? What have you been able to find out up to now?" she asked, desperate for some answers.

Iain sat down on the bed next to Liz.

"Back then, science knowledge was extremely limited

and highly suspected by less educated people. Religion was more high profile in those days too. Ask the wrong questions, of the wrong people…. and very soon, you could find yourself in some rather tricky situations. But then you know that, you were there." He said.

"I've only visited you once so far," remarked Liz, shaking her head.

Iain nodded pensively before replying, "You've got a very busy schedule ahead of you."

"How many times have I visited you?"

"Thankfully, so many times….that I can't place an exact figure on it. Then, there were the long gaps, the many years that you didn't visit!"

"Did you ever get any warning of my visits?"

"Hmmn. Personally? No. Meteorologically speaking? It's like you're the storm's daughter. You always seem to ride in and out of my life on the back of a storm, like you're connected to it or your presence causes some major atmospheric or electromagnetic interference. I know my head buzzes and my heart rate goes up too, when you're on your way!" Iain replied.

"Was there a storm that day, when you saved me?"

"It was difficult to tell. There was so much mist on the loch that morning I couldn't see the sky at all, but there was one hell of a storm when you left."

"Yeh, I remember that," she agreed. "Has the Professor had any ideas about it?"

"Fraser and I agree that after your first arrival and departure, a clear electromagnetic link must have been established between us. But as for the initial push or pull of energy, bringing you through to the past, that's still a mystery. I've walked those hills and the banks of Libran's Loch so many times and found nothing, although the geology of the area does suggest that it has a high conductivity factor for electromagnetic energy. In fact the mineral deposits, particularly the high quantities of gold and silver in the mines around there, create a kind of superconductive triangle of converging electromagnetic energy fields, or vile vortex," explained Iain. "If you then add that to the increase in seismic activity every time there's a solar flare or increase in solar activity, the glen can become a pretty interesting crucible of electromagnetic energy," Iain explained.

"So how would that affect me?" she asked curiously.

"Just like the moon can affect the tides, plant growth and people's moods, so can the sun," began Iain.

"Ahh you're talking about sunlight deficiency affecting people's moods and ability to produce certain vitamins," she replied confidently. "I don't think that applies to me except when I get a bit grumpy during the winter."

"Yeh, what you're saying is true, but there's a lot more to it than that," said Iain.

"As you know the Earth has a molten magnetic core and two poles, north and south which radiate lines of magnetic force."

"Yeh, that's junior school stuff," Liz replied.

"But in addition to that there's the Equator where the magnetic field lines are weaker and further apart."

"Yeh, I know that too," she replied impatiently.

"Have you heard of the expression, 'being in the doldrums'?" he asked.

Liz nodded.

"That's where I am most of the time, when I'm at work," she remarked. "Fed up, depressed, with nothing to look forward too."

"Working in a call centre can do that people," he smirked.

"Hoy, don't be so cheeky," she smiled.

"Anyway, the doldrums are a large area of low pressure

just north of the Equator at a point where the winds from the northern and southern hemispheres mix. Combined with the heat around the equator this is the place where nothing happens, ... Ships find themselves becalmed," explain Iain.

Liz listened hoping Iain would get to the point very soon.

"But, just above and just below the equator on the edge of the tropics of cancer and Capricorn are ten known points around the Earth, where the magnetic field lines converge over land or over water, creating strange field anomalies called vile vortices," explained Iain. "And there's the north and south poles, of course, making twelve altogether."

Liz's eyebrows raised curiously.

"Vile vortices? Sounds like a mediaeval illness," replied Liz. "So what do these vortices do?"

"Well, they allegedly make ships and planes disappear, possibly to another dimension or time," whispered Iain in a mysterious tone.

"Sounds like the Bermuda Triangle to me," Liz remarked.

"That's it exactly!" replied Iain. "The Bermuda Triangle is the most well known one but there's also one in Pakistan; Hawaii, off the coast of Japan; in the South Atlantic......."

"So what are you trying to say here?" Liz asked. "... that Libran's Glen could be another vortices."

"It certainly has potential, but for geological and seismic energy reasons," he replied.

"So what about the sun?" she asked.

"Three things really," he began. "Firstly when the sun erupts, releasing huge quantities of electromagnetic radiation into space, this can affect satellite communications; TVs; radio; the national grid, sometimes blacking out whole areas or causing super-storms, …. like the one back in 1859, which shorted out telegraph wires right across the United States and Europe," he explained before pausing for a moment. "Secondly, Fraser has been working on a theory that the massive electromagnetic interference caused by the solar flare, can trigger seismic activity, increasing the likelihood of eruptions or earthquakes during peaks of solar activity. But more personally, it has been shown to affect mass animal migration, interfering with their internal body compasses and behaviours, sending fish or animals miles off course or causing flocks of birds to drop out of the sky. And of course, "he added. "It can affect human behaviour too, provoking mass social tension and riots."

"And where do I fit into this picture?" Liz asked.

"Do you react to the weather?" Iain asked.

"I'm like a weather vane," she sighed. "About two hours before a storm, I suffer from blinding headaches until the air pressure breaks. I can smell snow in the air about four days before it arrives and when a sub-zero cold front is about to move in, my joints ache and stiffen up," she explained.

"Fraser believes that your accident occurred during a period of increased solar activity, which probably should have blown the power source you were attached to, but which discharged into you instead," he explained.

"Yeh, tell me about it."

"You're lucky you weren't killed!" remarked Iain.

"I know."

"But because of that, something happened to your personal magnetic field, somehow making it stronger and more sensitive to electromagnetically influenced climatic changes. It could also explain how you can pull peoples' thought energies to you or how you sense things about places and objects," he continued. "However, because you're more magnetically switched on, as it were, you not only attract energy towards you, you become more attracted to other more powerful energy sources," explained Iain. "Fraser believes that there was powerful solar activity throughout 1746 and phenomenal electromagnetic energy in the Glen that sent out energy ripples through everything, including time and which managed to hook on to you, pulling you back towards its source. Then, as we've also had our own period of increased solar activity here in the present, Fraser believes that this may have been responsible for pulling you back to the present.

Liz sat quietly for a moment, trying to take it all in, then slowly she began to smile as the pieces of information, like the pieces of a puzzle, began to drop into place.

"Do you know, some of that actually makes a lot of sense," she said nodding her head. "Who would have thought it? Electromagnetic energy causing time travel!"

"It's been known to move ships too, like the USS Eldridge, allegedly."

"Oh yes, that was the Philadelphia Experiment wasn't it?"

"Sometimes referred to as Project Rainbow," replied Iain. "Back in 1941, that experiment caused the ship to disappear and re-appear a couple of hundred miles further north, before reappearing back in its original spot about ten minutes later."

"So what do I do now? How do I learn to control it?" asked Liz intrigued.

"How do you control any electro magnet?" replied Iain.

"Switch it off."

"Or find a way to block the energy."

"What, do you mean I'd have to walk around all day in a rubber suit?" she asked as she shook her head, rejecting the idea.

"We'll work something out," replied Iain smiling reassuringly. "But for now, you need to rest," he instructed.

"So, do you think Fraser's theory makes sense?" asked Liz.

"I don't see why not. We're going far beyond the realms of known science here, and the one thing that is common throughout time since the universe began, is of course, the sun! So, if you're on its radiation wavelength, a wavelength, which connects everything in the universe, then why not? You could go anywhere or to any time!"

Liz thought for a moment as she processed more of the information inside her head.

"You said that the Glen was prone to seismic activity."

"Oh yes! We have earthquakes, lots of them. Minor ones of course. The west side of Scotland has some very powerful fault lines where the land mass crashed into England eons ago. In fact, there are areas down the west side of England that are absolutely riddled with fault lines, like the Lake District," explained Iain.

"And I thought we lived in an earthquake free zone," Liz remarked.

"Far from it," replied Iain. "There's even a long fault line that stretches right across the country from Bristol, through London and along the Thames, and. there's two more fault lines running through the English Channel," added Iain.

Liz lay back against the pillows and closed her eyes, mulling over all the information in her head.

"So do you think Fraser's right that Libran's Loch is some kind of seismic electromagnetic epicentre?" she asked.

"Yes, I'd say so," he agreed. "But we need to take a look at a geological map to be sure.

Opening her eyes again and carefully sitting up, Liz smiled at Iain excitedly and said, "Come on then. There's bound to be a map or two onboard this boat. Why don't we find one, and check it out?"

"Okay, but you've got to take it easy," he said concerned. "You've just been through one hell of an ordeal. I nearly lost you."

"You're right," she sighed. "Incidentally, thanks for saving me."

"Don't mention it."

"How exactly did you know what to do?" she asked curiously.

"I was a doctor for many years, before I went into psychology."

"You're a pretty handy person to have around," Liz remarked. "Any other talents I should know about?" she smiled cheekily.

"One or two," he replied candidly before whispering, "but if I told you, reality might come crashing down around our ears."

Liz looked deeply into his smiling, shining rich brown eyes, and she knew that there was far more to her fiancée, that she was yet to discover, only inflamed his appeal to her, adding to his enigmatic charm.

"You weren't a spy at one time, were you?" she asked, unable to resist the question that had sprung into her mind, when she had visited him in the future, when he helped her escape from the mine.

Iain's eyebrows raised.

"How do you get from doctor to spy?" he asked intrigued.

"There's just something about you, far different from that day in the Laird's mansion. I don't know whether it's just because, over the years you've perhaps found yourself in a lot of similar situations. But especially, in the future when, you….."

"Don't say it!"

"Okay, I'll put it this way then, "she sighed. "You seem to handle yourself very well and very professionally in a crisis, like you've been trained."

Iain said nothing. He couldn't tell her the truth about that! He couldn't tell her about Paris or Tokyo. They were in her future. They hadn't happened yet.

"I'm right aren't I?" she asked.

"Drop it Liz, please," he implored. "This is a dangerous conversation for us to be having, far more dangerous than if this boat was filled with C4. Don't!"

"Okay, you'll just have to find something to keep my mind off it."

"Sounds fine by me," replied Iain. "Let's see if we can find a map," he said as they left the bedroom to re-join the others in the main cabin.

"Captain, have we got any maps anywhere onboard?" asked Iain.

"Course I have. Nautical, obviously, but I do have others. If you look in the large drawer below the long sofa, you'll find them all in there."

"Cheers!" replied Iain.

"What's up? "asked Jackson a little concerned.

"Just exploring a few ideas!" he answered.

Jackson frowned. "I hope she's not going to beam us somewhere else!"

Kneeling on the floor in front of the long wooden drawer, Iain pulled it open. Inside, there were small maps, large maps, folded maps and scrolled maps. Fumbling through them one by one, unfolding them and unrolling them, Iain eventually found the maps he was looking for.

"Eureka!" he exclaimed." One's a geological map of the United Kingdom and the other is a geological map of the world."

Rising to his feet, Iain walked across to the table in the centre cabin and carefully laid out the maps on its surface. Then spying a pencil and couple of pens stored in a jar on a nearby shelf, he emptied the contents of the jar into his hand and came back to the table. As Liz held down the two furthest corners of the map with her fingers, Iain used the limited utensils at his disposal, to mark dots on the map and then drew lines on the map of Scotland, pointing from north east down to the south west. Liz looked at all the lines and dots on both map, puzzled as to what they could mean. Iain stepped back with a satisfied grin on his face.

"What's going on?" asked Steve. "Come on what's the big secret?"

Iain stood proudly next to Liz, placed his arm around her shoulders and squeezed her affectionately.

"It's no secret. I was just explaining Fraser's theory to Liz," replied Iain.

"The Professor thinks that I am being attracted to peaks of electromagnetic and seismic energy emanating from an epicentre at the heart of Libran's Glen in Scotland."

Steve looked at them both, somewhat bemused.

"Liz, this is what I was talking about!" said Iain pointing at the area from Libran's Loch northwards towards Fort William and eastwards towards Aberfeldy and Pitlochry. "This is the Great Glen Fault."

Steve and Liz looked down at the map and followed Iain's finger as he traced the fault line down from Inverness southwards.

"The Great Glen Fault is a fault line that stretches down from Inverness, down through Loch Ness to Fort William and beyond," Iain explained. "Below that, towards the top of Libran's Loch and running not quite parallel, is the Highland Boundary Fault. Above the Great Glen Fault you have the Moine Thrust which runs almost along the entire north west coast line. Between these three fault lines, down the mid west and the west coast of Scotland, there have been many documented recordings of seismic activity, or earthquakes, " he continued. "The mountains mark a cross hatch of fault lines where there have been clusters of seismic activity." Iain explained.

"How do you know this?" asked Liz.

"Research and reading. I've done a lot of reading over the past 260 years or so," replied Iain.

"So, these dots on the maps, what do they mean?" asked Steve.

"They mark certain key critical events that took place during my life."

"Liz's visits?" Steve asked.

Liz lifted her eyes from the map and saw the stony expression on Iain's face that said, 'don't go there'.

"Are these places where you experienced tremors, or electrical storms of some kind?" asked Liz delicately.

Iain sighed, "Yes," realising that Liz was now beginning to take his warnings seriously and picking up on her cue to field their questions technically rather than personally. " If you notice, the area around Libran's Loch is the only place where several seismic events have occurred in such close proximity to each other, which means it could be, as Fraser suggested, the source of the mystery, the source of the energy that's attracting you."

"I'm sorry, I'm not a geologist. So what's the significance?" asked Steve.

"I'm not a geologist either. I just studied and travelled with one for a while. Anyway, back to the point." He paused. "Silver is the highest conductor of electricity. You add to that, the fact that the three mines in that area form a triangle of frequent seismic activity and what have you got?" Iain asked.

Steve shook his head.

"I don't know, some kind of seismically activated electromagnetic transmitter?"

"Give that man a star!" cheered Iain.

"Transmitting what, though?" asked Steve.

"An anomaly, or portal that could connect right back to the big bang itself and as far forward as the end of time."

"Great! More science fiction! I might have guessed," sighed Steve. "When are you going to tell me something that makes any real sense? This is all kooky theoretical stuff that you'll never be able to prove even if you are right!"

"Steve," began Iain. "I don't know you, I don't know what your beliefs and influences are and to be quite honest, I haven't got time to pander to your scepticism. I'm not a visionary like the Professor, I'm a scientist dealing just with the cold hard geological facts and drawing informed conclusions that might just pull us all out of this mess. Conclusions that might help us and help Liz particularly, to understand what's happening to her, why and making an educated guess as to where this is all going!" Iain declared. "Fact! We're all connected. Everything is connected. We all began life as one mass of gases, chemicals and matter, with perhaps one common electrical frequency, before the big bang split and scattered everything across space and new frequencies developed. Despite everything that has changed and evolved since then, we all carry that original underpinning frequency – the spark that triggered the big bang, if you will – which connects us but which we've overlooked and not tapped into, until now. I'm guessing here, but I think Liz's accident at school, exposed that pure energy signal within her, allowing it to override every other frequency, giving her a master key to open doors to every place and every moment in time since the universe began. And when you consider her ability to store energy far beyond man's normal tolerance, she has her own power source to project that signal and herself, anywhere, "explained Iain.

"But why me?" asked Liz.

"Serendipity! You just happened to be in the right place at the right time when something highly improbable but not impossible, happened. Increased solar activity resulting in the interference with our planet's electrical fields could have caused the sudden electrical surge through the national grid which, in turn, blasted you across the school laboratory. Then think about what happened in the Minster when you collapsed. Again, you were the right person, at the right place at the right time. Fraser did have a point back there. You must have been flooded with enough thought energy in that cathedral to take you to the moon and back! But instead, it must have pushed your signal straight towards the nearest receiver – Libran's Loch!" concluded Iain.

"I thought you said it was a transmitter?" questioned Steve.

"It is, when the conditions are right. But it could just as easily become and electromagnetic receiver under reverse conditions – low tides, no seismic activity, no powerful solar activity, …"

"Solar activity?" asked Steve.

"Don't ask," whispered Liz. "But why wasn't I pulled back to a different place in the world or to a different time or person?" she asked, desperately trying to find a tangible link.

Placing his hands gently on her shoulders and looking deep into her tired, eyes, he answered.

"You're assuming that all of this has some personal connection, I don't think it has other than whoever it is who is interested in you, Liz, and who quite clearly wants what you have to offer. I think Fraser's theory is probably about as close as we're going to get for the moment, but there may be other clues out there which we just haven't found yet. I do know this though, whoever, or whatever brought you to me, whether it was chance or deliberate intention, I have no regrets! Have you?" He asked.

"I would have preferred not to be a fugitive. I had quite a nice settled life before, and I wouldn't mind returning to it someday," Liz replied.

"Oh come on! Where's your sense of adventure! You can't tell me that you were really happy in that call centre. You can do far better than that!" Iain replied.

Liz's mouth dropped open.

"What?" Iain asked, as he saw the look on her face.

"There you go again! I never told you I worked in a call centre," said Liz.

"Aaah," sighed Iain, realising he'd said something he perhaps shouldn't of.

Liz could see that he was hiding something.

"How long have you known about me, where I live, what I do?" she asked.

"Not long," Iain replied sheepishly.

"How long?" she insisted.

"Just a few months. Fraser convinced me to wait, to minimise the risk of causing a paradox."

"So are you trying to tell me, you never attempted to seek me out?" Liz asked curiously.

"Aaah," Iain's eyes glistened guiltily.

"You did, didn't you? You found me," she concluded.

Iain looked honestly into her suspicious eyes.

"I saw you, once," he confessed.

"Where? When?"

"I came into the pub, last year. It was shortly after Christmas. New Year's Eve, in fact! I had a couple of drinks, listened to the highland piper playing his bagpipes and then

left," Iain replied. "What was the name of the pub again...
oh, yes. ...The Jolly Drovers?"

"You were there, that night? The night that guy was
going to kill me?"

"Ooohh, a lot earlier on. I left about 9, 9:30. I remember,
you were heavily occupied reading people's palms, one
after another. They never seemed to give you a break!" Iain
replied.

"I don't remember seeing you," Liz replied.

"Oh I was there, tucked away in the far corner of the
pub, beside the old range, and when I went to the bar, I
could barely see you through the heaving crowd."

"Why didn't you approach me? Why didn't you say
anything?" she asked curiously and a little disappointed.
"You could have asked me to read your palm and I wouldn't
have known ....." she stopped as the penny dropped. "You
didn't want me to know who you were. You didn't want
me to see what would happen," she began. "You thought
it might change everything, didn't you? Still, I imagine,
having come that far, the temptation to make contact must
have been tremendous! How did you fight the urge to say
something? What stopped you from breaking the rules?"
she asked curiously.

Iain took her hands in his.

"Something inside me, told me, it wasn't the right time,"
he replied. "Call it an instinct, if you like. It just suddenly
felt very wrong."

"That must have hurt you though, to walk away, when
you'd waited so long to meet me," Liz remarked.

Iain said nothing, but Liz noticed the seriousness in
his eyes and figured that it must have indeed been, a very
painful decision for him to make. She sensed something
too. Perhaps it was the degree of pain that lingered just that
little bit too long in his eyes but, she knew that there was

something else. Something he was holding back, a dark secret perhaps? A truth she wasn't yet meant to know?

"What matters most, is how we go forward from here," Iain answered, carefully deflecting the topic. "I promised you, I would help you to find the answers to all this and we will see it through together," he declared.

Liz looked pensive and a tense silence spread through the cabin, with only the steady chug of the engine and the lashing of the waves against the outside of the hull, providing the background noise, as the boat headed towards shore.

"If you'll excuse me gentlemen, I'd like to talk to Liz alone, up on deck." requested Iain.

The three men looked at each other puzzled, but nodded their agreement, and the Captain resumed his navigation of the Channel as Iain led Liz on to the deck.

The Channel wind buffeted the boat and blew Liz's long wavy blond hair randomly in all directions, making it almost impossible for her to see where she was going, as they stepped up on to the deck.

"Be careful Liz," warned Iain. "Hold on to the rail."

Liz did as she was asked and took a firm hold of the metal rail above the cabin door.

"What is it Iain?" she asked. "What's wrong?"

"You looked disappointed back there," he said carefully. "Have I upset you?"

Liz thought for a moment as the boat rocked sharply backwards and forwards.

"No, not really," she began. "It's kind of difficult to explain."

"Try me."

"Steve has a point. I know very little about you other than what we've been through in the last couple of days, and you can't tell me a lot about your past because of what might happen. But don't you understand, without those pieces of the puzzle, how can I move forward? How can I unfold your personality and really get to know you as a person when you have to censor everything you tell me. It's like opening Pandora's box, I don't know what you're going to do or say next, because everything I know about you is artificial. It's only what you're allowing me to know. At least back in 1746, you were you. Your words and your reactions were real. Seeing you now, I'm not sure I know you at all. You're not the same person who impulsively took a gamble and proposed to a stranger on an emotional whim. Can you understand how confused it makes me feel?" she asked. "I know you're just trying to protect us, but life is full of risks whatever we do. How do you know that sharing your experiences with me wasn't what was meant to happen naturally in the first place? How do you know that maybe we're supposed to cause some reaction that alters the future on to a path that it was intended to go on? How do you know that your controlled and guarded words won't cause the paradox anyway? How ...."

Iain suddenly pulled her trembling body into his arms and looked down into the tearful pools that showed the emotional torment she felt inside. Each of them felt the strain, the pressure and the responsibility that Time and Reality had placed on their shoulders, a responsibility which ironically threatened to split the bond that time and serendipity had brought together.

"I'm sorry," he sighed. "I've been a complete idiot. I've been so obsessed with trying to protect what we had and what we will have, that I forgot about what matters most, and that is what we have now!" he confessed. "I don't want to lose you," he said staring deep into the darkness, beyond the mesmerising blueness of her eyes. Then, taking a deep breath he said, "I need you! I love you! I always have, and I thought, I felt back then, and all those times you came to me, all the times we made love, that you loved me too! You were my wife!

Stunned by the revelation, Liz stepped away from his embrace. Her head spinning with his words that repeated over and over again in her mind.

"That's what you meant when you said the ring wasn't meant to come off, didn't you?"

"Yes," replied Iain after some hesitation.

"When did this happen? When did we get married?" she asked.

"You wouldn't tell me."

"Why, because of the paradox?"

"Sort of."

"Why then?"

"You like surprises, …. that's all you said."

"That kind of knocks on the head everything I've just said to you, doesn't it?"

"Hmmn," he nodded. "It just goes to show, that sometimes we don't even know ourselves."

"And did you mean what you said before, about us being lovers in your past?"

"Yes. Does that bother you?"

"I don't know. You're telling me that sometime in the future, I will be married to you whilst having an affair with your earlier self. I would love to be student in your psychology class when you try and explain the behaviours and moral argument behind that one!" she replied. "And I know this might sound a stupid question, but how will you feel when that happens? How will you feel when I disappear and you know that I'm with him, your earlier self? Will you feel jealous? Will you reject me when I return? And God forbid if I fall pregnant! How am I going to know who the father is?"

Iain gazed at her silently as the wild Channel winds

blew all around them. He didn't disagree with any of the points she had made. He tried to think what he could say to her, to help her cope with the inevitable certainty that her future was destined to be split between loving who he was now and loving his earlier self.

"You're not having an affair with another man Liz," he began. "I am the man you loved, who shared your bed and who loves you now. I know when and where you're going, and yes, you're right, I do know what you'll get up to. But don't you see, those events happened to me, they're in my memory, they're who I am. They don't involve another person, they involve me and I love you, probably more than you'll ever know or understand. And yes, you will become pregnant with our child and whether it is sired by my earlier self or me, it is still <u>me</u>, my DNA, my flesh and blood, our child and you'll make me the proudest husband and father, ever!" he declared with such honesty and sincerity, that all her stony doubts and worries crumbled into dust.

Disarmed by his truth and the irresistible reality of his unwavering dedication, loyalty and love for her, Liz melted into his arms. Her kissed exuded a warmth and depth of feeling that reassured him of her reciprocated love. Yielding to his embrace, she opened her mind completely to him and allowed the flow of her thought energy to pass between their two minds.

For the first time, Iain felt and understood the crushing loneliness of her life and her ability. He felt the pain of her isolation and understood its devastating effect, as it had done in his own life for more than two centuries. Though they came from two different centuries, they were more alike than even Iain had understood. Hearing her secret, private, intimate thoughts and desires inside his head, the anxiety of her rejection dissolved into a solitary tear that ran down his cheek til the sharp sea wind caught it and whipped its fragile liquid into the turbulent fray. His happiness was boundless as he held her face in his hands and returned her kiss with a passion so unchecked and unrestrained, Liz felt like she was being swept away by the Channel winds themselves.

Suddenly, snapshots of their love making from Iain's mind, filled her head. She could feel his elation and desperate need for her and the completeness and satisfaction he felt after each intimate moment they shared across time, only to have his world and his heart ripped apart again, each inevitable time she was pulled back to the present. Then she saw his memory of his York cottage, standing outside the bedroom door, cursing himself for his moral restraint in not attempting to seduce her. He was, indeed a gentleman, she thought, as Iain gently released her.

"Why was that?"

"Sorry?"

"I mean, back at your cottage near York. If you knew we'd made love before, why did you decline my advances?"

"For you, it would have been the first time. I wanted you to know that I respected you. That I wasn't going to take advantage of you in that situation. I wanted you to want me for all the right reasons and not because you felt you had to be grateful for me saving your life. I didn't want you to confuse your excitement and release from fear, with any genuine feelings you might have had for me, and I wanted your first time with me, to be as special as my first time with you. I wanted you to know who I really was, to love me for everything that I am and not just for the façade I've had to maintain," he explained.

"Was I your first?" she asked delicately.

"You showed me how," he whispered softly in her ear before kissing her neck gently, making the hairs on her skin, stand up and tingle.

More images began to fill her head as he held her tightly

in his arms. She could feel his heart pounding in his chest close to hers as she buried her head in his shoulders.

It was a few days after their first meeting. The sunshine had felt quite hot that morning as Iain solemnly carried out his regular daily regime of heading down to the loch to bathe. Removing his clothes and placing them on the large rock at the edge of the bay, he dived into the sparkling crisp clear water, trying to drive the thoughts of her out of his mind. The coldness of the water numbed his skin momentarily, but he quickly adapted after swimming a few strokes beneath the surface. Pacing his breath and hovering carefully above the pebbled ground, Iain explored the loch bed for freshwater mussels.

Eventually, forced up to the surface to breathe, Iain wiped his blurry water filled eyes to see a pale figure watching him from the shoreline. At first he thought he was dreaming, but as his vision became clear and he called out her name, the crystal blue sapphire eyes that had captured his heart days before, stared across the water towards him. Liz was back.

Standing chest deep in the water, he watched fascinated as she removed her strange clothes and he saw her nakedness for the first time. He'd never seen any woman naked before and tried not to stare at her soft and pert, well rounded breasts as she waded into the water towards him. Then, suddenly she was gone, disappeared beneath surface. Had she slipped? Was she drowning? Had he even seen her at all? Iain couldn't say.

Suddenly the water broke in front of him, and there she was, with eyes gleaming brightly in the morning sunshine, her wet long blond hair, draped like liquid honey over her shoulders. Iain was speechless. There were so many things he wanted to say to her, but every time he tried to speak, the words just faded into dust.

Wading closer towards him, with the loch water on her

eyelashes glistening like tiny diamonds, she threw her arms around his neck and pressed her soft wet body against his. Pressing her gently parted lips against his and giving Iain a long, wet, hot kiss, Iain felt the softness of her breasts crushed against his chest as her hips locked around his. Gently placing his arms around her, he felt her soft pale skin beneath his fingers and the uninterrupted flow of her thought energy passing through his body and his mind. For just a moment, he thought he could see the waves of an open sea stretched out before him as a brief mental link to his 21st century self was made. Just as his current self indulged in the pleasure of her mind and bodily contact, so did his earlier self in a strange time defying embrace before Liz vanished completely into the past.

For Iain's earlier self the reaction caused by her curvaceous body pressing intimately against his, was instantaneous. It wasn't the first time he'd ever displayed such prominent manhood. Just dreaming of her some nights, was enough to provoke that response, but this time she was there in person, just as she had been for those few moments when he'd proposed. This time, there was no hiding what he felt for her, and he saw her cheeks flush a light hot pink, as he backed away embarrassed. Taking his hand and wading right up close to him, she whispered,

"It's okay, Iain. There's nothing to be shamed of."

Iain gulped as Liz pulled him closer and stroked him gently beneath the water. His eyes closed in incontrollable ecstasy at the delicateness of his touch, and he suddenly wanted her so much, that nothing else seemed to matter.

"Liz!" was all he could say as he kissed her desperately and picked her up his arms, wading eagerly through the water to a flat submerged rock, where sat down carefully with Liz resting gently on his thighs.

Not even the cold crisp loch water could cool their

feelings for each other as she lowered herself carefully and he penetrated her deeply. Suddenly, he felt her warm, tight intimate grip around him and as he gasped with unspeakable pleasure, Liz arched her back and heaved a sigh of deep, contented delight. No words were spoken, but many thoughts and dreams were shared in that moment. Gently caressing her breast with his fingers, Iain watched her responses to his touch with deepening interest. As she gently rocked backwards and forwards, she guided Iain's hands over her body until suddenly, with an unexpected gasp of shock and excitement, he opened his eyes wide, and experienced an ecstasy and contentment he'd never felt before. All his frustrations and tension were gone as he stroked the wet hair gently from her face and gazed deeply into the dark pools of her blissful, peaceful loving soul, before kissing her softly. Closing his eyes, he enjoyed the sweetness and heat of her breath before feeling the touch of lips and the weight of her body on his, lighten. Anxious that she might be leaving again, he opened his eyes, but it was too late. Every evidence of her existence, including the clothes she had discarded on the shore, were gone.

Wrenched from the summit of exalted pleasure and happiness, to the depths of grief and pain at her loss once more, Iain clenched his fists and roared a resounding," Liz!!!" that echoed across the loch and across time to her conscious mind in the present.

"Liz, Liz," whispered Iain as he gently shook her.

Liz opened her eyes slowly, and blinked several times until her vision came back into focus. Sitting up sharply, unsure of where she was, she could see three figures just in front of her.

"Where am I? What happened?" she asked, as she could now see Iain quite clearly on his knees by her side, with Steve and Jackson close by.

"You're on the boat Liz. You're with friends. You're with me, and you're safe," replied Iain.

"What happened? I remember being on deck with you, then this."

Seeing the three white faced men in front of her sporting very concerned expressions, Liz guessed she must have fainted.

"Did I pass out or something?" she asked curiously.

"Pass out?" exclaimed Jackson. "Passed out of existence completely!" he said scratching his head. "You just vanished!"

"Ssshhh," said Iain. "It's okay Liz. You're back," Iain said reassuringly. I don't want to alarm you, but Jackson is right. One minute you were in my arms. We'd been talking about my past, we were kissing, and the next thing I knew I was holding fresh air. You vanished completely," explained Iain. "Do you remember where you went to?" he asked concerned.

"I thought I was just watching one of your memory snapshots in my head as we kissed. Then I thought I was dreaming," she said, trying to recall what had happened to her.

"Can you remember what you saw?" asked Iain.

Liz blushed and whispered the details in Iain's ear. Steve and Jackson watched as Iain's face turned scarlet and thought better of asking to hear the details for themselves. Iain coughed with embarrassment and declared, "It's okay, she wasn't in any danger."

"I think we figured that one out," smirked Jackson.

"I think we should leave them alone for few minutes," suggested Steve as he patted Jackson on the shoulder and they both headed towards the stairs leading on to the deck. When they were out of earshot, Iain whispered.

"I told you it was special."

"How did it end? What happened after we......."

"You disappeared again," he replied. "I couldn't tell you about it because you barely said a handful of words to me. I didn't know where or when you came from. I didn't even know if it was real or imagined until now. You were as gentle as a dream and so beautiful in the morning sunshine. You made it impossible to resist you," he confessed.

"You make it sound as if were torture," Liz remarked disappointed as her pounding heart began to slow and calm.

"If that was torture, then sentence me to an eternity of punishment," he smiled broadly. "You were pretty hot stuff, especially for those times," he continued. "The hardest thing was the terrible grief I felt at your loss," he sighed. "I wanted you so much it nearly drove me out of my head."

"I'm so sorry," she sighed deeply.

"Don't be," he smiled reassuringly. "I got over it once I began to realise that it meant that you would return to me. It gave me hope, apart from an incredible ... well I think you know what I'm talking about."

Liz blushed.

"But, how could I be physically there, Iain? How did that happen?" she asked desperate for a tangible answer.

"Well, "he sighed. "If I was to hazard a guess, I would have to say it had something to do with how weak you were following your collapse. I think it also had something to do with how you felt about what you saw in my mind and what you wanted to happen. ..... And thirdly, I think being out on the open sea may have given you a clearer reception to where you wanted your signal to go."

"But I disappeared completely?"

"I know," he sighed. "Remember, I was there with you at both ends of your journey."

"Just like you were back at the Minster and at Fraser's," she replied.

"Ahh, you might have a point there," remarked Iain. "It might have something to do with our physical and mental connection."

"I hope it doesn't happen every time we make love," she whispered.

"It didn't happen when we made love at Fraser's. You actually projected when we were in the Minster, when you'd lost some blood from the bullet wound and you were in mild shock. You were vulnerable then and it was when I sat with you and held your hand, whilst you were unconscious at Fraser's, that the ring appeared on your finger and I felt the strangest tingle of energy pass between us," Iain explained.

"I'm afraid there was more than a tingle when we ......"

"I know, remember?" he asked rhetorically. "I was there."

"So what happens now?"

"We're going to have to keep a constant vigil over you. You're very vulnerable at the moment and other than for the reasons I've suggested, I'm not exactly sure if it will happen again and if we can stop it."

"Surely there's a reason why all this is happening? I can't believe that this is just all down to chance?"

"Liz, you're looking for fate," Iain replied. "It's a natural reaction. If we believe in fate, we are saying to ourselves that there is a plan, there is a future, especially now that we've passed the Millennium and outlived just about every prediction about our destruction. We need to feel that there is certainty here and out there in space, and if what scientists are saying about the past, present and future existing simultaneously, then maybe our lives are sealed in the same instant we are born and die."

"You say it like you don't believe that there is an order to things."

"I didn't say that. Order comes from within us. It is the constancy of our deep seated behaviours and beliefs that make us who we are, that under pins our lives and sets the pattern, as well as the trend for our actions and reactions. As we grow older and we learn what brings us success and what doesn't, we reject the neural pathways to failure and retread those that bring us success, making them stronger until they become almost automatic, constant."

"And that's why you can't teach an old dog, new tricks?" she asked.

"You can, it's just harder the more entrenched our thoughts and habits become. It takes a lot of effort to break away from the established path, and that makes us feel uncomfortable. But it doesn't mean that it's impossible. We just choose to select the path of least resistance and effort, and that's where we begin to confuse our predictability with destiny, fate."

"You can hardly apply that to us," remarked Liz.

"Oh we can. You are developing an ability that is derived from your need to survive following your accident. When you lost the normal controls for discharging energy from your body, you had to create new ones. Your brain worked out that there were two possible outcomes to your accident. You either died, or you found a way to deal with that excess electricity, an escape route for the energy, which you did, in the form of your projection. Once your brain realised that this pathway solved the problem, every time the energy levels got too high, either because you were excited or frightened, you projected. But that's not all. You're now faced with two choices of behaviour. Do you lock yourself away from situations that generate the energy which makes you project, so that you can go on living what you perceive to be a normal life or, does your deep seated curiosity and daring, that caused the accident in the first place, drive you towards the energy, to see how your projections and abilities develop. The more you project, the more you want to project and the more you are drawn to the energy and danger you need to fulfil the cycle. Like the saying goes, we become prisoners to our own success," Iain explained. "You've just proved with your rapid development from thought to physical projection through time, that your brain is hard wiring itself into a successful developmental regime. Where it will take you, or take us, I just don't know, but I'm not jumping off the horse until we cross the finish line, okay?"

"So basically I'm trapped," Liz concluded. "I can't stop this from happening?"

"You're only trapped if you want to be. Only if you choose not to learn to control your ability but let it take control of you. I can help you to train your mind. To bring order to your chaos, but you have to trust me."

"Okay."

"The first step is to identify the trigger, the missing piece of the puzzle, the source of the connection that pulled your projection through to my past. Once we know what that is and how it operates, you can learn to fight it. Then you can control when you project and perhaps, where, just like you did today. You fought against whoever or whatever was trying to pull you away and you found a way to turn that 'pulling' energy into a powerful 'push' away from the danger. You did it! Can you see that?" asked Iain excitedly as he surprised himself with his own revelationary conclusions.

Liz gazed at the wonder in his eyes, shocked by the discovery he laid before her.

"You overrode the pattern of your deep seated behaviour and broke the cycle. Then, when you saw and thought about us together in the past and felt the urge to complete what you felt was unfinished business, you were there! You called the shots! What happens now is up to you. You can go where you want to go, not where habit dictates."

"Are you saying that it was the desire I kindled for your earlier self that pushed me back to you?" asked Liz.

"I think you're asking the wrong person that question," he smiled." You should be asking that of yourself," replied Iain. "Now if you said, did I have a strong enough need and desire for you, to pull you back to me, then I would have to say, yes," he confessed. "I wanted you so much, that when you left that day, I felt so devastatingly empty," he added pausing for a moment. "Maybe it was that powerful combined push and pull in the same direction that brought you back to me! I do know, that after your sensational return, after we made love that morning, something happened to me. I changed. I became stronger. I knew then, how strongly you felt for me. I knew how much you loved me and you gave me a hope that I've been hanging on to all these years."

"Weren't you worried that I wouldn't come back?" asked Liz.

"I felt a tremendous connection with you, and also, there's something I didn't realise until now," he began.

"What's that?"

"When we made love, you shared something with me. You showed me, just for a second or two, this moment in time. I saw you as you are now, on this boat. You gave me the gift to see through my own eyes, what the future held in store," he said softly. "That's how I really knew, we'd meet again, and until that moment happened, just now, I knew you'd always return to me."

Stunned by his touching and significant revelation of his feelings for her and the unique and special bond they shared across time, Liz grasped a renewed faith in her future and the certainty that Iain would always be there for her, whatever they had to face.

Iain waited patiently, watching the crystal blueness of her eyes dazzle with a deep sparkle as she blossomed from the maiden of mediocrity into his bride of beatific bewitching beguilement. Then, as her radiance lit up the cabin, she instinctively held up her left hand towards Iain and he reciprocated, gently pressing his palm against hers, entwining their fingers together as if in some symbolic gesture of the bridge that held them together through time.

"I love you" she whispered, as tiny, pinpoint stars of light began to glisten around her body and face. Iain reached out with his other hand and gently touched the starlight on her cheek.

"Stay with me Liz," he whispered through the brightness of her aura. "Direct your power to where you want to be," he added as a dark cloud of anxious doubt crossed his face, and worry wasn't far behind.

Instinctively, gripping her hand and the ring that bound them together, Iain willed himself to hold Liz in his gaze, to not blink in case even the visual detachment from her was enough to allow her to slip away. Steve and Jackson, curious of the sudden bright light inside the cabin, crept silently down the steps and watched in awe and wonderment as the galaxy of tiny stars engulfed the star maiden and her shepherd.

"What's going on," whispered Jackson to Steve. "Is she an alien?"

"No. Ssssh," whispered Steve mesmerised by Liz's extraordinary beauty.

Seeing and sensing his anxiety, Liz felt his negativity and doubt trickle over her like a cool shower on a hot summer's day and her aura softened. Then leaning towards her, his lips suddenly engulfed hers, and she felt his slow, steady heart beat close to hers. Gradually, the frequency of her own excited heart beat began to slow and with it the brightness began to dim, until finally the last of the tiny stars disappeared into her eyes.

It hadn't worked to keep in her in the past, but he hoped his calming contact this time would strengthen her anchor in the present. He knew that keeping her calm and energy neutral was vital to her sustained existence in the present, and now he'd given them both proof of that. Together, they could hold the pull of Time at bay.

"Good girl," Iain whispered, whilst heaving a sigh of immense relief. Then, as he slid along the seat beside her and rested her head on his shoulder, Liz nestled into his warm and protective embrace.

"I don't ever want to leave you again," she whispered softly into his chest. "I want to always be with you here, now, in the present."

"I know. But to make that possible, there's a price we have to pay," Iain replied. "To keep us together, here in the present, you must travel back to me in the past. Your future visits are what kept me alive until now. If you choose not to, I won't survive. It's a catch twenty-two situation. If you want to be with me in the present, you've also got to be with me in the past." Iain explained.

"And those visits have already happened?"

"Yes."

"You mentioned before that you believed my thoughts and feelings triggered my return to your past?"

"I think they can trigger your projection anywhere at any time," Iain replied.

"Ah, right. So that's why you kissed me."

"Your joy was literally charging you up with excitement and positivity."

"Yes I know."

"And with high positivity and excitement comes high adrenaline – your internal energy source. You were charging yourself up, ready to project," he explained. "If I hadn't calmed you down, you could have disappeared again, just like you did before."

"So does that mean I'm sentenced to a life of sobriety?"

"Of course not," he smiled. "You need to disappear literally, from time to time, to perpetuate our relationship, but your ability to stay calm should allow you to have greater control over when those disappearances occur."

"Right, I get it!" she replied. "So, excitement, anger, pain, they're all out if I want to stay put?"

"That about sums it up, yes."

"But if I can't stop it and I do disappear, I will turn up where I most want to be?"

"Unless, there is some stronger influence over you, then yes."

"And you and Fraser believe that Libran's Loch is acting like a homing beacon, if I have no conscious coordinates when I disappear?"

"Mmmm, that's an interesting way to put it," Iain remarked.

"It just so hard to believe, that this all started because of one naïve mistake I made as a kid that happened to coincide with an electromagnetic surge of solar activity."

"So it would seem."

"You couldn't make that one up if you tried!"

"Well, you could," replied Iain.

"Yeh, but no one would believe you. I'm not sure if I believe me, except that you're here when you shouldn't be and somebody else believes me too, or else why would they be after me?"

"I think, we agree that the answer to all our questions lie

somewhere near Libran's Loch and the only way we'll find out for certain is if we go back there, together."

"What would we be looking for?" she asked curiously.

"A pulling point. A beacon perhaps, or something that would act as the concentration point for all the electromagnetic energy, once it's been seismically or atmospherically triggered. We also need to check if you have any other connection with the village, like an ancestor perhaps," replied Ian. "You mentioned when you first visited me in 1746, that you had visited Libran's Loch before?"

"My parents took me there once for a weekend break," she said.

"Go on," said Iain listening intently.

"We had arranged to stay in the Loch View hotel at the top of the village. The hotel was lovely with a wood panelled lounge bar and restaurant on the ground floor. We had a big family bedroom on the first floor, overlooking the lane. That first afternoon, after we arrived, I did a bit of exploring into the village and came across the old church."

"Lachlan Kirk."

"That's right," Liz acknowledged.

"I went inside and had a look around. I'd been wandering around for about twenty minutes when, I suddenly found it incredibly hard to breathe. It was as if all the air had been sucked out of the church and I honestly thought I was going to collapse."

"Sounds similar to what happened at the Minster," remarked Iain. "Go on. What happened?"

"I had to leave, and I headed down towards the Loch, hoping that the fresh air would calm me down and make it easier for me to breathe. But it didn't. As I stood on the banks of the Loch, my throat and my lungs seemed to close. I couldn't breathe and I felt as heavy as lead. Then I experienced something really spooky!"

"I'm listening," said Iain eagerly.

"I suddenly felt as though I was surrounded by a crowd of hundreds of people. Perhaps thousands! I felt them all around me, pressing against me, touching me, and they kept saying the same thing over and over again. 'The clan must return to the village and five generations will be born there'."

Iain sat bolt upright, stunned by Liz's unexpected revelation.

"What's wrong?" she asked.

"The clan you're talking about is my family. They're the original clan that founded the village, hence the name Lachlan, meaning 'of the loch'. For reasons I don't fully understand myself, the clan gradually left the village and, as far as I'm aware, I don't think they ever returned. But it has been a few years since I was last there."

"It doesn't end there," added Liz. "It was about two years later, we went back there to see the Clan Gathering."

"It's been a long time since I last attended the Gathering," replied Iain.

"That's what they said."

"Who?"

"The organisers of the event. They said it had been well over a century since the last one!" Then she added. "When I mentioned my spooky experience and the message I was given, the look on their faces was an absolute picture."

"I'm not surprised. They probably thought you were one farthing short of a guinea!"

"I might have expected that too, but that wasn't the look I was getting," replied Liz. "Stunned, they all sat in silence across the table from us, looking at each other, like they each wanted to say something but were afraid to. Then, eventually, Andrew the historian and clan guide spoke. He asked when it was I'd received the message, and when I told them, they all gasped with surprise. Turns out, he got the idea for the Gathering about the same time. One or two others around the table had also had some kind of message too."

"Collective consciousness," said Iain. "Or perhaps they were 'tuned in' to the message wavelength like you."

"What do you mean by 'collective consciousness'?"

"If you were all blood descendants from the original clan, it's possible that some electrical signal homed in on that link in your DNA," suggested Iain.

"Theirs perhaps," replied Liz. "But I don't think I have any ancestors there. My Dad's family were originally Scottish but not from around that area."

"Do you know that for sure?" asked Iain.

"I guess not."

"It maybe that way, way back, before records were kept, possibly as far back as before I was born, one of your Dad's ancestors may have married one of my ancestors. Maybe there's a DNA link without us really knowing it," suggested Iain. "Remind me to ask Fraser to compare our DNA next time we meet him."

Liz nodded.

"So where does the mine fit into all of this?" Liz asked.

"Oh, you mean the mine from your projection into the future?"

"Yes."

"Well, there's three mines in that area, like I said to Steve. Each one of them contains gold, precious stones and silver with the potential, when their electromagnetic fields combine, to become a superconductor or transmitter," Iain explained. "Or in your case, that alone could most likely be the beacon that pulls you in."

Suddenly, Iain's eyebrows raised, as more pieces of the puzzle began to click together. Liz could now travel backwards and forwards in time. Someone was already clearly knowledgeable of her abilities, to want to either harm her or use her abilities, he thought. But how could they know? Liz's abilities had only really developed in the last couple of days, and other than when she disappeared into the past, Iain had never left her side. So how was it possible, Iain asked himself. It didn't make sense, unless the person who was looking for her had met her and knew what she could do. But that person would have to be from Iain's past, where they could have met Liz during one of her visits or they were from her future. Either way, the person who was the key to her attempted abduction or murder, had to be a time traveller too. But who?

"Time," he mumbled. "Time! The beacon! That's it!"

"What do you mean?" asked Liz, intrigued by Iain's sudden outburst.

"Paradox! Someone's trying to stop us!" declared Iain.

"Stop us from doing what?"

"Everything points to Libran's Loch. Your time travel, our meeting, your beacon and the mines! My God, why didn't I think of this before? Where's Fraser when you need him?"

"Why?"

"I think someone's trying to create a vortex just like one of the vile vortices!"

Liz looked puzzled.

"The glen is a central point between all three mines. The loch is directly above a fault line, and any major fluctuations in the loch's volume of water, like summer droughts or winter floods, can trigger seismic activity," explained Iain.

Still Liz looked puzzled.

"In the past, when there have been quakes in the area, a strange luminescent anomaly has been well known to appear in the sky above the loch, created by the upward burst of electromagnetic radiation hitting the convergence of the combined electromagnetic fields from the three mines," continued Iain. "You said in that in your visit to the future, we were escaping from a mine that was flooding?"

"Yes, and the ground was shaking too from all the explosions."

"Are you sure that they were all explosions?"

"The tunnel and shaft were shaking so much and then the water began to rise so fast, I don't know."

"So it's possible that the explosions may have triggered a quake or at least caused a rupture in the loch bed to flood the mine and then trigger a quake!" suggested Iain excitedly.

"Are you saying, that someone is going to deliberately blow up the mine to cause an earth quake? But, why?"

"Possibly to create a bigger electromagnetic anomaly. A bigger beacon or transmitter," Iain replied.

"But, why?"

"To do what you can do naturally," concluded Iain. "Someone's found a way to time travel through the vortex! Someone's found a way to tap into the energy and time wavelength, like you! That's why they want you. You've been using the natural anomaly all the time without realising it," cheered Iain. "It explains why you appeared in the loch that first time. Lorna, like you just happened to be in the right place at the right time when your thought energy materialised. Then, when you returned to me, you appeared on the loch shore. You couldn't project into me though, which might have been quite interesting, because I was still conscious. There was no vacancy in my conscious thoughts for you to occupy, and obviously, there must have been no one else in range, so you were forced to physically materialise. The fact that you came back means, like Fraser's theory suggests, that you have created a two-way pathway through the anomaly, linking the present with the past and the future. Someone knows you're the key and either needs your abilities or wants to stop you, because of something you do in the future or something you did in my past!"

"Is that really possible?" she asked.

"Fraser would know the answer to that one," admitted Iain.

"Well the only person I've met so far from the future, was you, Iain, and the only person I've met in your past is, …." Liz paused as the grotesque image of Captain Magnus McGregor appeared in her thoughts. "Oh no! Not him! That's not possible! You said he was arrested and transported to the Colonies for what he did!"

"That's right!"

"Then who is it?"

"I don't know, but I'm guessing we'll find out very soon. When whoever it is, is eager and wealthy enough to send a private army of mercenaries after us, I don't think they've got any intention of giving up," he said. "And if that person is up to something at Libran's Loch, we'll find out who it is when we get there."

"Won't we be walking into the lion's den?"

"Yes, you're right," he agreed. "But now this paints a whole new picture of the situation," he continued. "We're not just trying to find answers, we're now trying to save this country."

"What do you mean?" she asked deeply concerned.

"If this person is trying to trigger a big enough earthquake to create and contain the anomaly, he will trigger a whole chain reaction along the fault lines that could pull this country apart!"

"So what do we do now?" asked Liz.

"We need to get to Libran's Loch quickly," replied Iain. "before events have an opportunity to escalate out of control.

Apart from transporting us here, have you ever projected to another place, instead of another time?" he asked.

"Yes."

"Do you remember how you were able to do that?"

"All I remember was that I was resting at the time."

"Okay. I need you to trust me." He said seriously.

"Why? What're you going to do?"

"First I'm going to take you back to the cabin and then, with your permission, I'm going to help you relax and drift into a semi-sleep like state and see if you can reach out to Libran's Loch now, in the present, and find out what it is or who it is that connects us . Are you okay with that?"

Liz looked at Iain. She knew how important this was to both of them. If he was right, and they were able to identify the link across time, then maybe she could learn to control her gift. Nodding, her approval, Iain took her hand and led her back below deck to the cabin, before a shocked and very curious Jackson, Steve and Yaslo, now seated in the main living area.

"What's going on?" asked Steve, feeling left out of the loop once again.

"We'll tell you later," whispered Liz. "Don't worry."

As they entered the cabin near the bathroom, Liz sat down on the bed.

"What do I need to do?"

"Just lie back on the bed and relax," instructed Iain. "I want you to close your eyes and focus on your breathing. When I tell you, I want you to take a deep breath in and then breathe out. Are you ready?"

"Yes."

"Okay. Breathe in.......and out.......and in.......and out. I want you to clear your mind and focus just on your breathing.....in......and out......in.....and out."

Suddenly, the cabin door opened behind him and Steve

was standing in the door way, insatiably curious at their secrecy.

"What's going on?" whispered Steve. "Are you serious about what you said out there?"

"Ssshhh. Come in and sit down quietly. Liz is about to go on a little journey."

Steve did as he was instructed and sat on the floor with his back resting against one of the cupboards for support, watching Liz on the bed.

"I'm going to count back from one hundred Liz, and whilst I'm doing that, I want you to focus on the cottage, my home. We'll use that as a safe anchor point for you to latch on to. I just want you to reach out with your thoughts. I don't want you to fully project. You need to stay here where you'll be safe. It's only your thoughts I want you to project to the cottage, to explore it and the surrounding area. That way we should be able to get a safe 'heads up' on what's going on up there," Iain instructed. "If you're ready, here we go. One hundred. Ninety-nine. Ninety-eight. Ninety-seven, ninety-six…….."

Liz's eyes became heavy as she relaxed deeper and deeper into the bed. As he counted back from one hundred, her breathing became steady and slow as she began to slip away from her conscious world and into her sub-conscious. In the distance, she could just make out the faint sound of Iain's voice counting slowly and rhythmically in time with her breathing. She was at peace.

Walking through the darkness of her mind, she began to focus on the small shepherd's cottage built into the hillside overlooking Libran's Loch. The image of the cottage gradually became much clearer in her head, and she began to feel the cold wind coming down from the mountain tops. She was there.

"Can you see the cottage?" asked Iain softly, his voice drifting towards her on the hillside.

Looking at the cottage, she suddenly saw the image crumble, until all that lay before her were a few moss and bracken covered stones marking the walls of the cottage, and the remains of the fireplace half buried beneath the bushes that now covered that part of the hillside.

Walking across the threshold of the cottage, Liz began to remember her first meeting with Iain wearing his kilt and his old Ghillie shirt. She smiled.

"Can you see the cottage?" asked Iain again.

"Yes."

"What does it look like?"

"There's not much of it left. It's just a ruin. There's no roof. The walls have gone, except for a few remaining moss covered stones." She answered.

"Is there anything there that you feel drawn or pulled to?"

Liz carefully walked back and forth over the ruins.

"No, there's nothing."

"Try outside the cottage. Take a walk around it. Tell me what you see or what you feel."

Liz stepped outside of the ruins and carefully made her way around the outside of the cottage, drifting through the bracken, thistles and ferns that covered the pen where the sheep had been kept. Then, climbing slowly up the hill, past the cottage, she looked back towards the Loch and marvelled at the beautiful view. In the distance she could see all the rich reds and purples of the heather on the far hillside leading down to the Loch.

"It's beautiful, Iain. The colours are so stunning and vivid."

"Okay Liz, I want you to open your mind and focus

on the source of energy that's pulling you in. Can you do that?" asked Iain.

"Yes."

"Now follow that feeling to where it really feels strong."

Slowly, with her eyes closed, Liz turned around full circle, trying to pick up any sensation she could. Then turning with her back to the ruined remains of the cottage, she set off along the hillside. Just ahead of her she noticed a small cluster of bushes and decided to investigate.

"Have you found anything?" asked Iain.

"Not really. There's nothing here. There's some odd looking bushes just up ahead. I'm going to take a look."

"Whereabouts are you?"

"I'm a few hundred yards behind and above the cottage."

Iain thought for a moment.

"Be careful. You might be near the old well." Iain warned.

Liz approached the bushes slowly. As she drew closer, she could just make out some stone work buried under thick tightly entangled bracken. Stepping effortlessly and spirit like through the bracken to the top of the well, she peered down into the deep dark abyss that was overgrown with weeds.

"I'm at the well," she whispered.

"How do you feel?" asked Iain.

"Curious."

"That's natural. Do you want to explore the well?" he asked

"Yes."

"Okay. Travel down to the bottom of the well, carefully. If you start to feel anything strange, tell me," instructed Iain.

"What's happening?" asked Steve quietly.

"I think Liz has found something. It could be part of the source that's been pulling her through time. I may have been incidental to her abilities, if my suspicions are right," whispered Iain.

"What do you think it is?"

"Liz responds to electromagnetic energy and absorbs it from people, surroundings and or events. It's what helps her to generate sufficient power to project her thoughts."

"Okay, I get that."

"I'm trying to get her to home in on the energy signal that is acting like a beacon for her thought projections," explained Iain.

"So she's currently projecting her thoughts down some old well, in search of some energy? Is it safe for her to do that? If the source is powerful, will she be able to come back to us?" asked Steve concerned. "

"It's just her thought energy that's being transmitted into that place."

"Yes I know. But if that place is powerful enough to pull her to it through time, don't you think it's powerful enough to keep her there?" warned Steve.

Iain nodded and quickly turned to Liz lying on the bed.

"Liz," he said softly. "I want you to turn back."

"Wait, I can see something, a channel leading away from the well. It looks as though it's been hand hewn. I can see the silver thread leading back along the shaft. It's getting bigger and brighter…."

Her voice trailed off.

"Liz, Liz, what's happening? What's wrong?"

"It's the noise, like an ear piercing scream inside my head, squealing continuously! It's hurting! The pain!!!!" she cried.

"Get out of there now, Liz! Come back to me!" Iain pleaded as he took her limp body in his arms. "Liz! Liz!" he called out desperately, gently shaking her shoulders. "How could I be so stupid!!!!" he yelled, annoyed at his own ignorance.

"Calm down Iain! How's her pulse?" asked Steve.

Feeling her neck with his fingers, he counted the beats in his head.

"It's racing!" he replied.

"Try to bring her out of the trance," suggested Steve. "That might be enough to pull her back!"

Iain nodded, as beads of perspiration trickled down his face. Then, taking a deep breath to calm himself, he spoke slowly and deliberately into Liz's ear.

"Liz, I'm going to wake you up now. I'm going to count down from five through to one, and then you'll wake up feeling relaxed and refreshed. Five, four, three, two, one….. wake up Liz!" Iain instructed.

Liz lay still and silent in his arms. Was she unconscious? Was she sleeping? Or had something happened? Iain and Steve looked at each other, each uncertain of what to say or do next. Then they heard it, the voice that sent a chill down Iain's back, a voice he remembered but which he hoped had disintegrated into the distant past. It was the chilling vengeful voice of his duelling adversary – Mad Magnus McGregor!

"I know you can hear me Lachlan! I may not be able to project as prettily as your little whore, but I can reach you just like she can!"

Out of the shadows in the confined cabin, stepped Captain Magnus McGregor, still decadent in his attire but very much up to date with his taste in fashion and looking barely a day older than he did all those years ago, at his moment of defeat. His eyes were still cold and soulless, his voice still as sharp as the words he spoke.

"Where the hell did you come from? You were arrested and sent for transportation!" said Iain.

"Do you know him?" asked Steve.

"He knows me alright!" sneered Magnus. "He robbed me of my well earned title and my bride! He ruined me! Three long months I spent in that rat infested cell before they pushed me onboard that pox ridden ship bound for the new colonies. But every dog has his day! I've waited a long time for this, and I'm going to enjoy every last moment of your pathetic life!"

"Where is she?" asked Iain angrily.

"That witch is here with me, trapped where she can't escape! If you want to see her restored again, you'll need to bring her body to me!" Magnus commanded.

"How did you find us?" asked Iain.

"I've been tracking your movements for quite a long time now. It's easy to trace someone who seldom ages much and who does little to change his appearance, even if he changes his identity. And I suppose you want to know how I acquired my gifts since we last met." He suggested coyly. "A freak storm hit the transportation ship before we sighted land. A bizarre accident freed me from my incarceration and when the crew panicked as the lightening engulfed the ship, I made my move. I and the other prisoners took control of the ship and set most of the crew adrift. When the storm passed and the strange mist cleared, we found ourselves adrift on a different sea, near the coast of Japan. Not only had we moved from one ocean to another, we had also moved forward in time. For a while, we earned a living pirating across the Pacific until I raised enough capital and made enough influential connections to set up my salvage and development company! Then, I found you, a solitary picture in an old geological article, just as you're looking now. I knew then, that your whore, with her magic, must have found a way to transport you to the future or to keep you alive!"

Iain leapt angrily across the room towards Magnus' image, but Steve grabbed hold of him and pulled him back.

"Where is she? Where's Liz?" asked Steve.

"You have her body and I have her mind in a very safe place, for the moment!" he declared. "You thought you'd escaped when you transported out of York, but I've been tuned into Liz's frequency for quite a while now, watching and waiting for you to make an appearance in her life. You didn't need to worry about us following you. I knew where you were all along. Oh, and that reminds me, Professor Hughes sends his regards! It's ironic isn't it, all those students volunteering for his research as willing victims for the advancement of science. Now, a victim of his own success, and of course, a victim of his association with you, he is now the unwilling victim of my scientific endeavours! Well, better go, I have a previous engagement with a rather beautiful young lady who I find quite illuminating!" he laughed haughtily. "She might just bring some spark back into my life, what do you think?"

With that, the projection faded into the shadows and the two men sat bewildered on the bed next to Liz's unconscious body.

"What the hell was that all about, and where's he keeping Liz?" asked Steve.

"He was there, the day Liz and I first met . She had projected into the mind of Lorna McKay, a young woman who Captain Magnus McGregor had blackmailed into an arranged marriage with the local elderly Laird. Magnus intended murdering the Laird after the wedding and marrying the girl for himself, whilst commandeering the childless Laird's estate left to his widow. We ruined his plans. As for where he has her imprisoned, I'm guessing, but judging from where we lost contact with her, I'd say she's being held in that mine. He must have figured out the mine's real power.!" declared Iain. "Tell Jackson to head to shore immediately! Have we a computer onboard?" asked Iain.

"I think Jackson's got a small laptop to help him with his navigation," replied Steve.

"Good," answered Iain. "Try and track down two charter companies, one to fly Liz and I by private helicopter up to Libran's Loch, the other to fly you and Yaslo by commercial internal flight to Glasgow."

"That's going to be expensive!"

"Bill it to me," said Iain. "Don't worry, I've got money. There have to be some plusses for having an extended career life!"

"Sounds like you've got a plan." said Steve.

"I'm not the naive hillside shepherd he takes me for!" replied Iain. "He may have been time hopping to get where he is, but he still hasn't learned anything! He's still the greedy arrogant and self obsessed extortionist I met back then. But I've made the most of my prolonged existence and invested wisely in my global education. This is what we need to do." said Iain.

CHAPTER 18

THE SMALL HELICOPTER ZIPPED STEALTHILY through the cloudy early morning sky, just clearing the trees that covered the lower slopes of the Scottish mountains, like a yellow and black dragonfly searching for a safe resting place. Iain sat behind the pilot, monitoring Liz's vital signs throughout the flight, from the portable monitor that had been attached to her body prior to take off. Employing his past medical experience and Steve's contacts in the Air Emergency Service, Iain had been able to charter a flight, to transport Liz safely to a landing field near the base of Libran's Loch. With a medical assistant on hand, Liz had been placed on board the helicopter attached to a drip to maintain her hydration whilst she lay unconscious in a coma-like state, disconnected from her thought energy. Thanks to the skilful careful flying by the pilot, Liz remained stable throughout the journey whilst a distraught Iain sat alongside her, with her hand clasped close to his chest.

"Hang in there Liz," he whispered softly in her ear, as the weight of his self imposed guilt pressed heavily on his conscience.

He couldn't have known that from such a meagre conflict with Captain Magnus McGregor, all those years before, such a colossal obsession with revenge would develop. Was this the price he had to pay for interfering with the events of that day, he wondered. Had Lorna really been meant to drown in the Loch? And if Liz did have an ancestral connection with the village, did they all owe their existence to the paradox he, himself had created by rescuing Lorna and Liz? If he could find the family connection then all he had to do was work out, why Liz was meant to preserve her family line and why were Liz and himself so important? Something or someone was driving all of these events but who and why, thought Iain. Why were his ancestors so desperate to ensure that the future generations of the clan would return to Libran's Loch? Iain shivered as the realisation suddenly struck him. Something big was about to happen to the loch and the village, and somehow he and Liz were tied up into it. Was it really his stubborn persistence that was driving him towards the answer to his questions or was fate suddenly the uninvited guest in his life and in his thoughts? Being able to solve this complex intricate web of events and time was a quest for another day, he thought. Saving Liz was the most important challenge and priority in his life right now, and he was on his way to face it.

Steve's idea about chartering the helicopter had been a stroke of genius. Not only were they able to transport Liz speedily and safely but, there was an added bonus too. The helicopter could fly low enough through the Scottish glens and mountain ranges, using the Nap of the Earth to remain virtually undetectable to radar. Relying on their invisibility to radar to get as close as possible before being discovered, Iain hoped that the combination of this stealthy approach and Liz's disconnected state, might at least give them the element of surprise. Steve also had his instructions to rally reinforcements via Glasgow, and provided Yaslo cooperated, Iain believed that their joint efforts and two prong attack might just work. Iain knew that they needed to be quick and decisive, if Liz was going to be able to return to her body safely, with her thought energy intact.

Liz's projection hovered in the centre of the detention

chamber, suspended within the electromagnetic cross field convergence anomaly about a metre off the ground.

"Ingenious isn't it?" gloated the rough deep voice of her arrogant captor. "No handcuffs or physical restraints required. You're being held in place, like any other magnetic oddity, caught between the directional fields. You're my puppet, and I can do anything I want with you! If I increase the strength of the magnetic field on any wall or the floor or the ceiling like this, "he said playing with the electrical current controls. "You tell me what happens!"

Suddenly Liz was pulled to the wall behind her. Then, just as quickly, she was pulled across to the other side of the room and then back to the centre.

"Even this window contains electro magnetically charged particles that will repel your energy. I can hold you there indefinitely!" declared Magnus from his viewing room.

"Stop it please! You don't know what you're doing!" pleaded Liz.

"Oh I think I do!" Magnus sneered.

"I just hope you're wearing radiation suits! Do you realise how much electromagnetic radiation you must be belting out here?" asked Liz.

"I think I'll be safe enough wearing this suit!" Magnus replied.

"What about its affect on the atmosphere?" she asked. "I hope you've got your wellies and a brolly handy, cos this place will act like one hell of a beacon for some pretty crazy weather."

Magnus grinned at her through the cell window.

"Is that what he told you, your Professor, Mr Lachlan?"

"He said you might be mad enough to try and construct another Bermuda Triangle here, but he also warned that you'd probably wipe out the British Isles in the process, causing massive quakes and the like," she replied. "But then, why should I expect anything less from you! The only person you care about is yourself!" Liz snapped. "Oh, yes and while we're on the subject, how is your dynasty of illegitimacy doing? Judging by the ugly mugs of your hired thugs, it wouldn't surprise me if you've kept your mercenary antics within the family, so to speak!"

Magnus scowled.

"A viper after my own heart," he muttered. "Just as venomous and defiant, as I remember. Such a pity you backed the wrong side my dear. With your abilities and feisty spirit, we'd have made a good match back there," he hissed.

"Never!" she yelled. "Dream on! Oh, and I don't think a few bolts of lightening and a rattle of the thunder drums is going to be enough to create your vortex!" she yelled at him.

"You're absolutely right, my dear. Thunder and lightening are only the spark to light the fuse!" Magnus sneered.

"So what are you going to do, stomp around outside doing some kind of pathetic rain dance?"

"Actually I've got a machine to do that for me!" Magnus replied. "It's sonic frequency will cause such a powerful vibration through the rock, you'll almost see it ripple like water. Add a few explosive devices and millions of tons of displaced loch water, and you've got the makings of a super quake that will indeed, tear this country apart!." He boasted. "Oh and the cherry on the cake is, when the earth's crust begins to split and sends out a stream of powerful magnetic energy straight up into the magnetic field anomaly above, it will create a vortex more powerful than the Devil's Triangle. It will create a portal for travelling anywhere through time and space. I will be able to re-mould history to my own personal design! I will have complete control over every event since the world was born and the future will be mine to steer as I will!"

"Just graduated from the high school for bad acting megalomaniacs have we? Swallowed a few delusional maniac pills? Come on, do you really think your plan is going to work?" Liz snapped.

"Enough!"

"Ooooo Touchy are we!!" yelled Liz.

Then she heard the buzz as the Captain turned up the power of the magnetic current, which crushed at the atoms of her projected image. She screamed. The pain was like nothing she'd ever felt before. Not only could she sense her thought energy being crushed, it was as though all her nerves were on fire, searing through her projected body like hot knives. Then it stopped and the voice bellowed through the speakers.

"Insult me again and I'll destroy you right now!"

Recovering her composure, Liz began to think. If Magnus was holding her underground in one of the silver mines and they had to wear suits to protect themselves against the electromagnetic radiation, that meant that her cell was acting like an electrical beacon, amplified by the silver and other highly conductive ores in the mountain. If Iain was trying to find her, the increased electrical pulses could be detected from outside. She knew it was risky, but she also knew that antagonising Magnus might be her only way of getting a signal to the outside world.

"You wouldn't do that though, would you?" she replied. "The fact that you're holding me here now, means you either need me for my ability or you need me as bait to reel in Iain!"

"Why have one, when I can have both!" he grinned,

sadistically. "When the time comes, you're going to help me project through the vortex."

"What if I refuse?"

"Then Mr Lachlan will cease to exist once and for all!"

The daylight of realisation suddenly dawned in her mind.

"It was you, wasn't it, who tried to kill Iain and his parents?" She yelled.

"Aaah yes," Magnus sighed. ".. my maiden voyage back into the past. That was part of my earlier experiments. Pity, I was only able to project there for a few minutes. But, it did prove that it could be done!" Then he asked, "Have you made that visit yet? Of course you haven't! You looked a little older back then," he concluded. "A little fuller in figure perhaps! Of course, if I decide that I don't need you after all, I could kill you and you'd never make that visit! And if you don't make that visit, poor Mr Lachlan and his darling parents won't be saved, will they?" he laughed.

"You bastard!" she screamed.

"If I were you, you should try being just that little bit nicer to me, your husband to be!"

"I'd rather bathe in a pit of scorpions than marry you!" she yelled.

"I've warned you!" he screamed down the microphone. "Test my patience again and you'll fry!"

"You want me, that's what this is all about, isn't it? You want revenge against Iain for not being able to have Lorna! But Iain made sure you couldn't have her!" she taunted. "You failed, and now she's long gone!"

"Enough!!!!" he shrieked.

Then she heard the high pitched buzz.

"There it goes again?" shouted the helicopter pilot above the sound of the rotors.

"What?" asked Iain.

"A minute or so ago, there was a blip on the EM detector for a couple of seconds, but then it was gone. Now it's happened again and it's a lot bigger, look!"

Iain left his seat beside Liz's unconscious body and looked at the small EM monitoring screen. Just towards the North West, he could see a steady blip on the screen.

"Where's that coming from?" asked Iain.

"It's coming from just over the next ridge, about three miles away," answered the pilot.

"Do you know what it is?"

"It could be a generator of some sort, but it's only just appeared, like it's been switched on, then off, then on again."

As he spoke, the blip disappeared.

"I'm sorry, it's gone," said the pilot.

Iain thought for a moment as he looked ahead out of the cockpit window to the mountain in front of them. Below them was a forest of trees stretching up from the Loch to the lower slopes. Further down the Loch, he could just make out the peripheral cottages of his home village emerging near the shoreline.

"That has to be it!" he exclaimed. "That has to be where they're keeping her! She could even be trying to signal us!" suggested Iain. "Try and find a place to land!"

"Okay!"

With that, the pilot brought the helicopter over the top of the trees and down on to level ground, about a third of the way up the mountain. Turning to Liz, Iain softly kissed her before addressing the nurse beside her, "Take good care of her! If I'm not back within two hours, fly her back to Glasgow Infirmary!"

The nurse nodded. Then sliding open the door of the helicopter, Iain leapt out on to the heather covered hillside. Crouching low and buffeted by the wind from the rotors, he carefully made his way up the mountainside, away from the helicopter. Behind him, the Loch stretched out like a long dark ink stain on the grassy bottom of the glen. With the strong cold wind biting at his face, he recalled the countless times he had shepherded his sheep along the mountainside all those years ago. The ground ahead of him was ascending steeply now, as he dug the spikes of his mountain boots into the ground, to anchor him against the elements. Armed with little more than a climber's rope, a tazor, a small handgun, a good measure of hope and the certainty that Liz would survive, Iain was ready to find and take on his adversary!

Liz opened her eyes. She was still trapped in her cell, still projecting her image, but her light had faded to only half of its previous brightness. Just below her, strutting around like a territorial cockerel in his protective suit was Captain Magnus McGregor,

"As the first occupant of my electro magnetic suspension cell, what do you think, Miss Curran? It's ideal for holding violent prisoners! No need for straight jackets, just throw them in the cell and switch on! Several organisations have already signed contracts and placed orders in readiness for their full scale production. Each cell wall encases electro magnetic field transmitters which direct their fields inside the room. The object or person is placed in the centre of the room and once the power is switched on, the fields converge and form an electro magnetic cage around them at the centre of the room, suspending them at the optimum convergence point. As you've already found out, if I increase the power to any of the walls, floor or ceiling, the extra field energy pushes you away from that transmitter towards the opposite wall. All we do, is establish what your personal field frequency is and we program our transmitters accordingly, to repel you into the centre of the room. It's already been used on a lot smaller scale to transport fragile substances, and it can even trap thought energy projections like you!" explained Magnus proudly. "Of course, the real deterrent is the room itself. As you rightly identified, any time spent in the room, unprotected will irradiate your body. The more time you spend here, the more likely you are to suffer long term side effects. Spend too long in here and death will become the only real escape from the tormenting agony!"

"You're evil! Far worse than you were, back then. Then, it was just power and greed that drove you," she cringed.

"So you think I've changed?"

"I think your experiments and whatever brought you through to the present, has twisted your mind tighter than an over-wound spring. I pity you your insanity, it will bring you more pain than this cell could ever inflict!"

"…Says she, whose body and brain will start to die, in a little over two hours!"

"You won't let that happen! I know you won't! You wouldn't destroy what you desire! You need my body to help your project, just as much as I do! Your threats are empty and wasted!" she replied. "If I'm right, you've had to strike a deal haven't you? Iain's on his way with my body isn't he?" asked Liz.

"Well done my dear! I can see that threats alone will not keep you in line, but perhaps what I have lined up for you will make you more malleable!" he grinned.

"What do you mean?" she snapped.

"I have a rather interesting associate, a former ship mate of mine who travelled with me onboard the transportation ship. Unfortunately, I'm afraid he didn't travel well through the vortex. Seizures are his frequent and painful torment, but, when he is stable, he has a remarkable ability for projecting his thoughts into your mind. With his taste for brutality, rape and murder, I've no doubt that once I've introduced you to each other, you'll never be the same again, "gloated the arrogant tyrant unaffected by the electromagnetic fields, as he pulled a small remote device from his pocket.

Pressing a couple of buttons, Liz began to lower to the ground. This time, Magnus walked through her projection, disrupting her energy flow. Even though she couldn't sense his thoughts and his feelings through his protective suit, the mere idea of him invading her space and her virtual body made her feel sick.

"Looks like you've lost a bit of your sparkle with your last act of defiance!" he remarked.

Liz hovered helplessly. Even if she wasn't suspended between the fields of energy, without mass, there was little, if anything, she could do to either retaliate or escape. If there was ever a hell for ghosts, this was it. She felt like she was enclosed in an invisible suit which was pressing firmly against her from all directions.

"You look a little older than I remember you," remarked Liz carefully.

"Unlike your partner who is able to rejuvenate from your power, I have aged normally during the physical days, months and years that have lapsed in real time, since our last encounter. It is only time herself who has accelerated and aged nearly three centuries since that day. I have been spared the physical ravages and psychological fatigue that your partner has been forced to endure. Only he has been forced to repeat the cycle of growing older and growing old, to know again and again the agonies and frustrating physical inabilities that dog the twilight of our years." replied Captain Magnus McGregor with a distasteful falseness and sarcasm in his voice. "But once your body is reunited with your thought energy, you will pay me the same courtesy and return my youth to me or you'll remain incarcerated here forever!"

"What if it doesn't work?" asked Liz carefully.

"What do you mean?" snapped Magnus.

"We still haven't figured out exactly what drew Iain and I together or why I'm able to rejuvenate him. What if you're not compatible? What if something else happens instead? What if there's a missing piece to the puzzle that we haven't found yet? Are you really ready to take that risk?" warned Liz.

The Captain frowned. He knew she was right, and in the absence of any evidence to the contrary, was he really prepared to gamble his life against the chance of rejuvenation without any hard proof? But who was she to countermand him. She was after all, only a woman and by 18th Century values and traditions, which still coursed prominently through his veins, the only rights she had, were the expectations of being bedded and spawning his blood thirsty heirs.

"Enough!"

This time Liz was ready for it. In her visual examination of her surroundings, she had seen little evidence that any sound-proofing had been applied to her cell. Hoping and praying that her assumptions were right, and remembering some very basic principles in relation to sound waves and electromagnetic fields, she let go and screamed loud and low for all she was worth. As the electromagnetic fields crushed her fragile projection, she hoped that the audible sound frequency of her scream would break through them and disrupt them just enough to either set her free or to carry her voice beyond the boundaries of her confinement.

Two miles away above ground, another blip appeared on the helicopter's monitor. Using the small portable radio handset in front of him, the pilot opened the frequency.

"Delta One! Delta One! Are you receiving? Over."

There was short crackle on the radio, then the pilot heard Iain's voice reply,

"Delta One receiving. Any news?. Over."

"Another blip's appeared on the monitor less than a mile North of your current position. Over."

"Got that! Maintain radio silence from here on in. I'll contact you. Over!" instructed Iain.

"Roger that, Delta One. Over," replied the helicopter pilot before replacing the radio on the control panel in front of him. A second later, a high velocity bullet pierced the helicopter's cockpit screen and the pilot's helmet visor, forcing his head backwards. In an instant, the inside of the visor was splashed with blood as the bullet drove deep through his right temple, into his brain. As the medical assistant jumped in reaction to the unexpected gunfire, a second shot pierced the side window and struck her throat, sending blood spurting on to the floor as the impact threw her hard against the cabin wall.

A few seconds later, the door of the helicopter slid open and two of Captain McGregor's men climbed onboard. Unhooking Liz's drip from it's vertical stand, the soldier held the container and the tube carefully as his colleague un-strapped Liz from her stretcher and lifted her up in his arms. Moving towards the door, the soldier handed Liz over to two of his companions standing outside the helicopter. Then carrying her between them in a portable stretcher, the four soldiers marched quickly back to the waiting van and lifted her carefully into the back, before making their escape via a private disused hillside road.

Perturbed by the volume and intensity of her scream, Magnus backed away, uncertain of what she was trying to achieve. As the pain coursed through her projection, she switched from trying to repel the field energy, to drawing on it, absorbing it. The walls suddenly began to flicker and shudder intermittently as she disrupted the flow of the electromagnetic energy. As the power of the electrical charge grew within her, the brightness of her projection increased until it sparkled like diamonds captured in sunlight. Magnus could tell something was wrong and backed away towards the cell door, shielding his eyes from the bright glare.

Thinking back to that day in her school physics laboratory, Liz opened herself up to the full force of the energy until suddenly bursts of white lightening discharged from her, striking the only object in the cell capable of receiving the energy – Captain Magnus McGregor. Although his suit protected him from the radiation, it did not protect the remote device he held in his hand. As the high voltage electrical charge struck the small black box in his hand, there was a short sizzling noise and the power to the electromagnetic fields died. All of the circuits in the remote had been obliterated. Liz was free.

Unable to immediately understand how Liz had broken the fields, and uncertain of what other party tricks she could perform, Captain Magnus McGregor turned away from her towards the door of the cell, as he screamed into his headset for assistance. Liz made her move and lunged at him as the door began to open. Surging past him, she found herself outside the cell, in one of the main corridors. She was free! Quickly, composing her thoughts, she focussed her mind on Iain.

Having reached the ridge of the mountain, high above Libran's Loch, Iain zipped up his insulated camouflage jacket against the searing winds before heading towards the steep slope that descended rapidly towards the old silver mine. Keeping low to the ground, and retrieving a small pair of binoculars from one of the jacket pockets, he sat and observed the mine entrance for two or three minutes.

In front of the mine were several plain covered trucks with a small troop of armed mercenaries unloading boxes and placing them on to smaller trailers. Then a small unmarked van arrived. The two soldiers seated in the front seats of the van, climbed out and headed round to the rear doors. Opening them up, the two soldiers helped their companions to disembark with the portable stretcher containing Liz's body.

Iain's heart pounded ferociously in his chest, as he imagined what must have taken place back at the helicopter. He pulled the radio from his pocket and flicked the switch.

"Delta Two! Delta Two! Are you receiving? Over," he asked anxiously, but the radio just whistled and crackled with no reply. "I say again! Delta Two! Delta Two! Are you receiving? Over!" he repeated, but still there was no response. Iain suddenly felt sick as the van doors were closed again. With no other prisoners to escort, Iain realised that the pilot and his medical assistant must be dead.

Watching helplessly through his binoculars as the soldiers below carried Liz's body into the mine entrance, Iain suddenly felt the cold steel of a gun barrel against the back of his neck. Thinking quickly, he launched the binoculars straight at his captor standing immediately behind him, before turning quickly to grab his captor's ankles. Pulling them sharply towards him as the mercenary reeled from the blow of the binoculars striking his nose, he succeeded in bringing the soldier crashing down to the ground. Bashing the soldiers hand against a nearby rock, Iain watched as the gun dislodged itself from the soldier's grip to fall into the heather several feet away to his left. Launching himself into the springy heather, Iain scrabbled for the gun as the slightly concussed soldier began to quickly unsheathe his sharp short bladed knife.

Picking up the gun, his mouth dry with fear, Iain rolled on to his back and pointed the gun at his knife bearing assailant. As the knife blade left the soldier's hand and pierced Iain's shoulder, a single shot was discharged from the gun, hitting the soldier directly in the chest. Although he wore a bullet-proofed vest, the force of the close range shot was strong enough to blow him backwards on to the ground. With blood soaking through his jacket, Iain gritted his teeth as he removed the knife from his shoulder. Then with the gun in one hand and the bloody knife in the other, he scrambled across the hillside towards the falling soldier. Sliding on his back down the heather covered slope, the soldier fell head first towards the edge of a narrow crag. Unable to latch on to anything that might prevent his descent, the soldier grasped desperately at the edge of the sharp rocks as his body swung out and over the precipice, before crashing downwards against the face of the crag. Clambering down towards the crag, Iain flipped the safety catch on the gun and stowed the weapon inside his jacket before placing the knife in the back pocket of his trousers. Lying down on his stomach at the edge of the rock face, Iain reached down and grasped the arm of the dangling soldier.

"Hang on!" he shouted. "I'm going to try and pull you up!"

The soldier looked up into Iain's face as he leaned slightly further of the edge to get a firmer grip on the soldier. Managing to set the toe of his right boot on to a narrow lip on the rock face, the soldier grasped upwards at the edge of the crag with his second hand, whilst Iain pulled him upwards. The pain of his knife wound seared through his shoulder as he dug his feet firmly into the ground to anchor him whilst he pulled the soldier to safety.

In the three centuries that Iain had been alive, he prided himself on never having seriously wounded or killed anyone, even in self-defence. Today, however, he had a gut instinct that he might not be able to avoid it. As the soldier finally managed to pull his chest up and on to the edge of the crag, Iain released his grip and sat up exhausted.

"That was a very valiant effort Professor!" declared a voice from behind him. Iain spun around to see a tall thick set soldier standing over him with an automatic rifle. The face was rugged with short spiky blond hair. "Unfortunately, unlike you Professor, we don't reward failure with second chances!"

Pointing the rifle at the unarmed soldier's head, the sergeant fired. Death was instantaneous, and the corpse flipped backwards with the impact before falling lifelessly over the edge of the crag. Iain froze in terror, the fear distracting him from the pain of the wound in his shoulder.

"The gun! Drop it over the edge!" ordered the sergeant.

Iain carefully reached inside his jacket and retrieved the gun.

"Over the edge!" repeated the sergeant. Iain complied. "Now the knife!"

Iain slid his hand slowly behind his back and retrieved the short blade from his trouser pocket.

"Easy does it!" directed the sergeant. "Now drop it carefully over the edge." Again Iain complied. "Now get up, slowly and keep your hands where I can see them!"

Iain raised his hands as he rose to his feet.

"Iain" whispered a sweet familiar voice, softly in his head. "Iain, it's me. I'm okay, but I must reconnect with my body," said Liz. "So I can't stay in your mind very long. I can sense your pain. Are you hurt?" she asked.

"Just a scratch," he replied inside his head. "There's nothing to worry about." He lied. There was a pause.

"There's damage to the muscle tissue where the knife went in, but you're very lucky. The blade narrowly missed the main artery and the lungs but you'll need my help to stop the bleeding," she said.

"How on earth do you know that?" he replied with surprise and just a little guilt from having lied to her.

"I can sense the disruption in the flow of adrenaline through your shoulder. He's managed to snag a couple of your nerves, so your fingers will probably feel a bit tingly or numb," she replied. "Let the guard bring you in," she instructed.

"Why?" he asked curiously.

"There's something big going on down here in the mine. The whole place is riddled with electronics and fields generators as well as explosives. It's Captain Magnus McGregor, he's back and he's out for revenge! Something tells me that it will take our combined efforts to stop him. Must go…. I can sense my body is close," she said.

"They've taken your body into the mine, Liz," whispered Iain silently inside his head. "Be careful!"

"I will!" she replied, and her presence disappeared from his mind. Iain sighed. At least she was still alive, and he had no doubt that this sergeant had every intention of reuniting him with her soon.

"Move it!" commanded the mercenary. "Down the slope!" Iain obliged.

Liz closed her eyes and focussed on locating her body within the mine. The slow steady beat of her heart pounded out its rhythm towards her, getting louder and louder as she drew nearer. Then, suddenly, her thought energy was there, home sweet home. Thankfully her lengthy thought energy absence hadn't caused any lasting damage, other than a few misfiring recent memory connections which would recover in time. Not wishing to alert her captors that she was complete and conscious again, Liz resisted the urge to open her eyes whilst she was still on the move.

Her carriers had placed her on to a wheeled hospital trolley with a slightly sticky right front wheel which juddered irritatingly every few metres. Judging by the relative smoothness of the ride, with the exception of the wobbly wheel, Liz deduced that she was being transported along a gradually downward sloping long corridor, leading deeper into the mine. Suddenly she began to detect the faint damp odour of wet stone, and the rattling of her trolley, previously muffled, now echoed around her as the temperature dropped rapidly. They were in some kind of cavern, in close proximity to the Loch. Liz tried hard not to shiver, as the soldiers finally brought her trolley to a halt.

"Your report Abrams?" commanded a surly familiar voice.

"We secured the body from the helicopter as ordered, Sir!" replied Abrams.

"Witnesses?"

"Two sir! The pilot and a medical assistant, both extinguished!"

"Good!"

Liz stifled a gasp of horror as she continued to lie motionless on the trolley.

"Any reports of her energy presence?" asked Magnus.

"None Sir!" replied Abrams.

"Take the girl's body down to the lab!" instructed Magnus.

Suddenly Liz heard the crackle of a radio receiver.

"What is it?" he snapped.

"Intruder captured at the outer perimeter, Sir!" said the voice.

"Who is it?"

"It's Professor Lachlan, Sir!" replied the voice.

"Good! Excellent!" drawled Magnus gleefully. "Bring him down to the lab! I think it's about time these two lovebirds were re-united!" he ordered. I'm going to really enjoy this! But keep a watch out for anything unusual! The prisoner's thought energy has escaped! If anyone starts behaving suspiciously, bring them to me at once!"

"Yes Sir!" the voice replied.

Liz suddenly felt a cold familiar touch on her leg and fought to stay relaxed as Magnus ran his hand over her body, before the soldiers moved off towards the lab. The sound of extra foot falls behind her, told Liz that Magnus was following them to the laboratory.

After two or three more minutes, Liz felt the impact of the heavy plastic curtains striking the trolley as they entered the laboratory and the trolley finally came to rest.

"Leave us!" ordered Magnus.

Liz heard the marching of boots as they faded away into the distance, and realised she was alone with Magnus. Her nerves and senses on hyper alert, she listened as his softer foot falls approached the trolley and she felt his hot moist breath close to her ear.

"It won't be long until your spirit returns to you and we can begin the process," he whispered. "Then I'll make you mine and you'll rejuvenate this tired body!"

Leaning over her face, Magnus kissed her hard on her mouth and it took all her concentration and self control for her not to betray her conscious revulsion and disgust. He hadn't changed at all since their last meeting, she thought as she felt his invasive fingers explore the soft skin beneath her shirt. 'You'll pay for that big time Mister', she said to herself, then Magnus stopped, sensing a sudden tension beneath his fingers. Liz forced herself to stay calm as she felt his suspicious eyes burning into her, observing every breath she took. She wanted to strike him, but she knew if she did, she would face a far worse torment. Silently and motionless, she maintained her sleeping pretence as Magnus scrutinised her carefully.

Brushing his hand over her skin, he could feel her inner warmth. She was back. How dare she take him for some stupid imbecile, he thought, and was about to expose her failed deception, when he had an idea. Curious, to see how long and how far she was prepared to go, Magnus ventured across the lab to his make shift office and wandered towards the glass tank adjacent to his desk. In the tank crouched a large well fed tarantula. Picking up his thick gloves from beside the tank and tucking them into his pocket, Magnus picked up the small rectangular tank and carried it back through to the lab.

Concentrating hard on Magnus' thoughts, Liz suddenly turned cold and clammy as she saw the large spider in Magnus' mind. She hated spiders, always had, ever since one had bitten her as a child as she'd fished it out of their empty bath with her fingers. What was he planning to do with it, she wondered, as she heard his footsteps returning.

"I'd like you to meet a very good friend of mine, Liz," began Magnus. "It's such a pity you're not awake, or you'd see how handsome he looks, at least to other lady spiders anyway," he continued. "I call him Juan, after Don Juan because he loves the ladies and whilst we've been down here he's been somewhat starved of their company," explained Magnus. "I brought him back with me from Hong Kong and I keep him in my office. For a long time miners kept canaries down the mines to detect poisonous gases. Me, I have Juan, here. He can sense most changes in air pressure, but most importantly, he's my early warning system for detecting seismic vibration. Juan is so sensitive to vibration and movement that he starts to dance around long before my sensors detect anything," added Magnus.

Putting on his protective gloves, Magnus carefully

reached into the tank and carefully lifted out Juan and placed him on Liz's chest. Immediately, Liz could feel the eight hairy legs on her soft smooth skin. Staying as still as she could, Liz began to think fast. If everything in the universe was connected like Iain suggested, if she tuned in to the right frequency, maybe she could communicate to the spider, she thought.

Whilst Juan sat motionless on her chest, adjusting to his new warmer surroundings, Liz focused her energy on the spider but nothing happened. Then, as she tried to contact Iain, and his image appeared in her mind, Juan began to move. Trying to blot out her anxious thoughts about the spider, Liz willed herself to believe that the spider was actually Iain, gently caressing her body. As her sensuality replaced her fear, the spider began to respond.

Watching the spider intently, Magnus loosened Liz's shirt, to allow Juan to crawl over her exposed naked skin. Carefully lifting its front legs into the air, Magnus observed Juan's dextrous movements with strange fascination. Juan had never behaved like this before, Magnus thought. What was he doing? Whilst Liz lay calmly imagining Iain's gentlest caresses, Juan began to detect her sexual attraction, absorbing the pheromones secreted through her skin, into his feet. As Liz produced more and more pheromones, Juan became excited.

Liz's experiment was working. Although, her pheromones were different to those of a female spider, they were still just within the zone to make Juan feel quite frisky. Adding to the subtle electrical flow of adrenaline beneath the surface of her skin, Juan began his ritual mating dance, raising four of his legs into the air and gently moving backwards and forwards across Liz's stomach. Magnus began to frown frustratedly and moved towards the spider. Immediately, sensing Magnus' aggression as a threat towards himself and his rather larger surrogate female, Juan dropped his front legs and prepared to defend his territory.

"What the hell is the matter with you Juan!" snapped Magnus. "You're supposed to bite her not dance her to death!"

Suddenly the spider recoiled and launched itself at Magnus. Magnus raised his arms as the angry hairy tarantula flew at him. Knocking the arachnid to the ground whilst cursing under his breath, Magnus quickly grabbed a sharp scalpel from the laboratory table adjacent to Liz's trolley and flicked it at the floor. As Juan landed on the floor and recoiled ready to strike again, the pointed metal blade pierced his bulbous abdomen and pinned him to the ground.

"Take that you vicious swine!" yelled Magnus. "That'll teach you for trying to take a chunk out of me!"

Liz guessed that the spider had suffered some miserable consequence at Magnus' hands and felt sorry for him, despite her phobia. Then, taking advantage of Magnus' otherwise distracted thoughts, she stealthily slipped into his mind, and began probing for information about his plans.

Images of the mine walls vibrating and crumbling, flashed before her in his mind. There were images too of huge amounts of water rushing into the shafts from the Loch above. The whole mine was shaking as the massive water displacement pushed the pressure levels above the fault line to critical, triggering the earthquake. Reaching out beyond the present, she saw his future reality. She saw the devastation, of the shock waves cascading down the west coast, through the heart of the Lake District and down towards Wales. She witnessed the tidal backlash from the Atlantic Ocean converging in the Irish Sea to form a tsunami of monumental proportions, sweeping inland, laying waste to villages and towns that fell in its path. Trees collapsed like toothpicks. People ran in all directions, only to disappear beneath the swamping wave. Then as the weight of water reached further inland, the ground began to shake and split. Mountain tops crumbled, sending boulders into the valleys below. Winding roads high up in the Pennines twisted and buckled, sending motorists and walkers plummeting down the mountainside. Pulling back from the scenes of carnage and devastation, she watched as the mainland of the British Isles split along its major fault lines. As the earthquakes reached the Welsh Fault System and the Variscan Front, crossing southern England from Bristol, through Greater London to Dover, she watched as the major cities crumbled into unimaginable anarchy and chaos.

Liz lay horrified beyond imagining, unable to grasp the enormity of the global catastrophe that Magnus was intent on creating. Frantically trying to remember every detail of the electronic equipment and its layout in the mine, she resigned herself to find a way to shut down the devices permanently.

Turning back towards Liz now, and noticing a marked increase in her breathing, he touched her arm and felt the rapid rise in her heart rate, throbbing beneath his fingers, Magnus grinned. Strapping her arms and legs to the trolley, he began wiring up electrodes to her scalp and her forehead. The surgical spirit felt icy on her skin as Magnus prepared each site for contact with the electrodes. Then, hearing the rapid clicking of a keyboard near by, Liz deduced that she was now hooked up to some kind of computer analysis machine to interpret her brain wave patterns, perhaps like the top secret system she had seen in the soldier's mind on that fateful New Year's Eve.

"Well, well!" announced Magnus with sadistic pleasure in his voice. "According to my equipment here you can give up the pretence, Liz! I know you're in there! Open your eyes!" he ordered.

Slowly, Liz opened her eyes and squinted to adjust to the bright lights in the laboratory.

"So you thought you could fool me!" he sneered. "Your pounding heart betrayed you my dear! What was it that got you excited? My touch perhaps? Or was it your fear of my little arachnid friend, now deceased?"

"You're a monster!" she yelled at him. "I saw what you are planning to do! Millions of lives will be lost, for what? You're seriously prepared to commit global mass murder and possibly destroy the planet in the process just so you can be in control! You're not just mad, you're completely deranged!"

Magnus' brow furrowed deep and red with ferocious anger as he slapped her hard across her face, leaving a reddened impression of his hand print on her cheek. The blow stung and burned, but that was just what she needed to keep her alert.

"Get your hands off her?" yelled Iain, as he struggled to try and free himself from his escorts' grasp as they dragged him into the laboratory. A sudden sharp blow of the rifle butt striking the side of his head sent him crashing to his knees. "If you've done anything to harm her, I swear I'll kill you!" threatened Iain.

"Oh, rest assured my dear Professor. I haven't harmed a hair on her head, yet!" Magnus snarled. "Now fetch Professor Hughes!" ordered Magnus. "After all, this is a reunion of sorts, isn't it?" he teased.

"You'll never get away with this!" shouted Iain.

"Oh, I think I will!"

"What do you want with the old guy anyway? You don't even know him!" enquired Iain. "What's he done to you?"

"You're right! I don't know him, but he is the closest thing to family that you have, isn't he?"

"Leverage! Is that it? If I don't comply, you'll extract what you need to know from him!"

Magnus laughed.

"You rate yourself too highly!" he teased.

"So it's his information and knowledge that you want!" Iain concluded. "So what am I?"

"Deliciously expendable, after, of course, I've got what I want from the Professor!" he grinned. "You've got no idea, how many ways I've thought about tormenting you, over the years! The schemes that have run through my head! I've tortured you and killed you a thousand times since our last meeting! But now, finally you're here as my prisoner! Everything you took away from me, I will relish extracting from you! Every frustrating torment I've suffered, you'll suffer too! But more than that! I will have the absolute pleasure of seeing you suffer! I've been watching you for years waiting for just the right moment, and now, it's here! The balance of our lives will be restored! What was once yours is now mine!" he taunted running his fingers over Liz's writhing body. "Beautiful isn't she? Highly spirited! But she'll soon tire and weaken under my control and then she'll be mine!" he grinned again, his dark pupils sparkling with excitement.

"Let her go! Let them both go!" yelled Iain. "It's me you really want!"

"And I have you, right where I want you!" Magnus replied.

"Do you? I wonder?"

"What do you mean?" asked Magnus.

"A victory is empty and meaningless if it isn't fought for and earned," remarked Iain.

"Do you really think I'm bothered about that?" snapped Magnus.

"Oh you will be, when everyone around you realises how spineless and gutless you are," replied Iain.

"Such are the desperate pleas of the condemned man!" hissed Magnus. "I've waited too long for this, and I will have it! I will see you suffer!" bellowed Magnus apoplectically. Then, facing Iain, he leaned over Liz and kissed her pursed unresponsive lips passionately. Iain pulled on his handcuffs wildly, desperate to break free, but his efforts were futile.

"Get off her, right NOW!!" Iain commanded. "Or I swear I'll kill you!"

Magnus stood up and paced across to where Iain stood between the two guards. With years of vengeful frustration and anger pent up inside him, Magnus unleashed his wrath, with a solid right punch to Iain's stomach followed by a hard punch to Iain's face. Iain crumbled with each impact and a cut opened up at the side of his mouth, adding to his involuntary blood letting.

"Remember your place shepherd!" growled Magnus McGregor. "I'm in control here, not you! You answer to me! She is mine! Mine to manipulate! Mine to touch! Mine to corrupt, if I so wish!"

"I wouldn't be so sure about that!" replied Iain.

"Words! Are they the only weapons you have? Well they don't cut me!" grinned Magnus.

"I know her future! I know my past! She's there with me and you can't tear us apart!" replied Iain.

"Maybe in one reality, but events can be changed! I know! I've been there! If it hadn't been for this bitch here, you and your parents would have died the day you were born!" Magnus declared.

"But that's the whole point! We didn't! She stopped you! You didn't change anything! She has an inbuilt ability to find the abnormalities in time and restore them to the way they were meant to be! And no matter what you try to do, we will stop you!" insisted Iain.

"Maybe she'll stop you too!" leered Magnus. "You're a freak of time yourself! Your energy should have died long ago! Once she's with me, once I make her my wife your future and your past are doomed to disappear, to unravel," remarked Magnus. "That's why I have no intention of killing you, at least not until I've broken the tie with you through the vortex. But, like I said before, I will enjoy torturing you!" he continued. "Oh and one more thing, if I kill her now, you both die! Get the picture?"

Moments later, the escorts returned with Professor Hughes.

"Welcome to the reunion Professor! As you need no introduction to my other guests, it leaves me just to introduce myself!" said Magnus.

"Don't bother! I know who you are, Captain! Iain told me about you years ago!" replied Fraser. "What I would like to know is, what the hell do you think you're playing at?" he asked.

"Come on Professor let's see that brain of yours in action! You're the genius here, you tell me!" challenged Magnus.

At Magnus' bidding, the escorts released Fraser and watched as he unruffled himself before beginning his analysis. Looking around, he observed the large pipes carrying the power cables through the laboratory and beyond. He observed the silvery streaks in the mine walls and remembered passing the soldiers pushing the crates of explosives and detonators down the various east bound sloping shafts of the mine.

"Well? I'm waiting Professor!" taunted Magnus.

"This isn't the only mine in this area that you have control of, is it?" asked the Professor.

"Yes."

"All of the mines around here are, or at least were, rich in precious metals, particularly gold and silver. You're also feeding tremendous electrical power deep into the mine, far more than you would need to power standard lighting and machines. You have a lot of electromagnetic field monitoring equipment situated around this laboratory, and that's apart from the system you're using here, for mind control." said the Professor.

Magnus feigned a yawn.

"Come on Professor! The longer you procrastinate the longer your friends here suffer!"

"How dare you, sir! I am in no way responsible or accountable for your heinous actions, and yes I can guess what you're up to!" he replied. "Each of the mines contains enough highly conductive silver and other ores to generate a powerful electromagnetic field. You're using the mines to triangulate their super-conductive energy fields towards one central point, to form an electromagnetic anomaly. But even with the power you've brought into the mine it won't be enough to do what you want to do......unless the devices and explosives you've placed at the heart of the mine are meant to trigger a seismic event below the converging field energy. The burst of potential energy from a large rupture in the earth's crust hitting the anomaly will rip apart the atoms and background frequency waves to form a hole, a vortex which will increase the earth's magnetic fields, altering the moon's orbit around us, pulling it in, nearer to our atmosphere. As the moon is pulled closer, the tides around the world will become more powerful. The sea currents will become disrupted and the skies will increase their electrical potential and that's apart from the massive seismic shifts you'll trigger!" explained the Professor. "What you're doing could at the very least, upset the earth's orbit and at worst, bring the moon crashing through our atmosphere! You're trying to bring about the end of the world!"

"Stop being so melodramatic Professor! You've ignored the real value from what I'm doing here!"

The professor approached a portable whiteboard near the monitor that had been used to record various formulae and equations far beyond Iain's level of understanding. Cleaning the board with a convenient cloth, Fraser began to draw a diagram on the board.

"This is the Earth." He said, as he drew a circle and bisected it with horizontal and vertical lines. "The horizontal line is the Equator, equidistant from the North and South magnetic poles." Then he drew several crosses above and below the Equator line, running parallel to it. "These are the current magnetic vortices that exist above and below the Equator to form two separate rings of magnetic anomalous energy." He continued. "These anomalies act as anchors or stabilisers, steadying the Earth's orbit. Gravity keeps the moon from flying off into space whilst the Earth's magnetic fields keep it at just the right distance from the Earth's atmosphere. Yes the Earth is prone to 'wobble' occasionally and that's when the moon gets that little bit closer. If you disrupt the electromagnetic fields around the Earth with such an event as you're planning," he said as he drew a red cross on the diagram. "You will upset the electromagnetic balancing act around the girth of this planet. And this will happen….." announced Fraser as he drew a second diagram showing the moon pulled towards the northern hemisphere and the earth tipping on its axis, destabilising the magnetic vortices.

"The Earth's orbit will destabilise as a result of the directional shift caused by the additional pull and convergence in the magnetic fields. Like ball bearings that spin around the circumference of a skateboard wheel when it travels too fast, the vortices will clump together causing an orbital wobble and the moon could be pulled towards the new vortex in the Northern hemisphere!"

Iain gasped in horror and noted the look of absolute fear and terror on the faces of the stationary escorting guards.

"Scientists! Huh! Always over dramatising the negatives! If we listened to all your doom and gloom, we wouldn't ever make any technological advances!" Magnus remarked. "And besides, you haven't mentioned the best bit, have you?" he grinned.

"You mean there's something good that comes out of all of this?"

"If you're referring to the possible convergence of the vortices towards the new event, causing a singular larger electromagnetic anomaly, the size of London which could cause the disappearance of matter into another level of existence, suspended outside reality as we know it?" suggested the Fraser.

"That's it!!!!" exclaimed Magnus jubilantly.

"You're insane! Absolutely insane!" gasped Iain.

"Extremely unlikely. No one can really accurately predict the multiple and co-dependent escalating impacts from such an event! We still have no firm proof that something else beyond our current scientific knowledge might occur! You would risk the destruction of this world and possibly others in the universe on such a risky and highly improbable outcome? I'm afraid, Iain's right, you are insane! Your time jaunts have seriously mis-configured your brain's reasoning capacity!"

Silence fell over the entire laboratory as every witness to Captain Magnus McGregor's insane plans trembled with fear. They watched as this arrogant selfish and short sighted mad man carried on his duties coolly, untouched by the terror and destruction he remorselessly intended to wield.

"You two" Magnus yelled to the guards." Release the girl and take the prisoners down to the oscillation chamber NOW!"

Liz's eyes burned angrily like ice on fire, as one of the guards untied her from the trolley and pulled her on to her feet

"If you're thinking of trying anything rash, my dear, you might want to think twice," Magnus suggested sarcastically as he retrieved a radio remote control from within his laboratory coat. "This device is linked to the Molecule Oscillating Velocity Equipment, explosives and the electromagnetic field generators deep within the mine. If you try anything heroic, I'll blow the lot!! So I suggest that you back off right now!"

"You wouldn't do that!" said Liz. "We'd all die, you included!"

"Don't gamble with fools!" advised Iain. "Do as he says, Liz!"

Liz stood her ground as Iain reached out and took her hand, squeezing it affectionately.

"Now move it!!" ordered Magnus to his men.

The two guards slipped behind the trio, prodding and pushing them with their weapons in the direction of the main shaft. Magnus watched them warily as they were marched past him, before he followed behind.

Chapter 19

As they left the laboratory and headed across to the main shaft, Iain noticed the conveyor belt that ran down the full length of it. Unlike the usual conveyor belts he expected to see, this one was shiny, new looking and meticulously clean, instead of being covered in coal dust, broken ore and debris.

"That must be how he transported the explosives and equipment to the deepest part of the mine," whispered Fraser to Iain.

"That's right Professor! Now climb on to it, all of you!" ordered Magnus.

The two guards nudged the three prisoners on to the conveyor belt as Magnus pressed the overhead starter button to set the belt in motion. There was an initial judder as the conveyor belt sparked into life, before it began to pick up a moderate speed. The aged and pensive Professor sat at the front of the line, followed by Liz, then Iain, the two guards and finally Captain Magnus McGregor himself. Several metres into the shaft, the walls and ceiling began to narrow and pull in around them. The air was cold, heavy and musty with the smell of damp rock causing Liz to shiver as she bumped along the conveyor belt between the Professor and Iain. Iain took off his outer jacket and placed it around Liz's shoulders.

"There's a small electric stun device in the left inside

437

pocket, keep it handy whilst I think of a way to stop this thing," whispered Iain.

The blunt cold metal tip of a rifle barrel glanced against the side of Iain's head.

"Hey, watch where you're sticking that thing!" yelled Iain.

"Keep away from the girl," ordered the guard.

"Okay! Okay!" replied Iain, as he settled back on the conveyor belt, his hands folded over his knees, discreetly watching the overhead lamps that hung from heavy chains suspended from the ceiling of the shaft at regular intervals. He counted quietly in his head, and established that they passed underneath each lamp about every five seconds. Then he noticed that the incline of the shaft was increasing as it descended more rapidly towards the deepest level of the mine. Suddenly he had an idea. Quickly sliding nearer to Liz, he leaned forward and whispered,

"Be ready to jump off the conveyor belt when I shout, and pass the message on to Fraser."

"What are you going to do?"

"Just be ready to jump when I say," answered Iain quietly.

"Okay," whispered Liz before sliding herself carefully towards the Professor and whispering the message into his ear.

Waiting a minute or so whilst he watched and timed the overhead lamps, Iain suddenly leapt up from the conveyor belt, and grabbed the chain above the next approaching lamp. Then swinging quickly backwards, he kicked the rifle out of the first guard's hand before landing a kick fairly and squarely on the guard's jaw. The guard reeled backwards covering the second guard's gun. Iain smashed the light bulb, plunging them into momentary darkness as the conveyor belt continued to move forward.

"NOW!!!" yelled Iain as he swung out again. His foot struck something solid and then there were two shots fired and a deep groan. When the conveyor belt emerged from the darkness, the first guard lay limply across the belt itself, covered with blood and very dead. The second guard was nowhere to be seen and Iain had disappeared too!

Before they fell within the light of the approaching lamp, Liz and the Professor jumped off the conveyor belt, colliding in the dust and dirt. Liz felt a firm hand on her shoulder and the barrel of a handgun against the back of her neck. She flinched.

"Get up!" commanded Magnus. "Move it!"

Liz and the Professor slowly got to their feet, but there was no sign of Iain. Still suspended from the lamp chain in the darkness, Iain watched as Magnus marched Liz and the Professor down the final stretch of the shaft.

Suddenly, a pair of firm hands closed around his ankles and yanked hard, bringing Iain down on to the conveyor belt with a crash, his chest, stomach and arms taking the full impact. Flicking his feet quickly backwards and then upwards, he caught the second guard in the chest and the chin, sending him staggering backwards against the mine wall. Turning over, then jumping off the conveyor belt, and feeling fitter and more agile than ever before, he grabbed hold of a protruding rock in the wall close to the collapsing guard and swung both of his legs up towards the guard's chest. As the guard's right hand raised, with a gleaming sharp knife in his grasp, Iain caught the guard's chin and wrist with his feet, sending the knife flying and clattering into the dust beneath the conveyor belt. As Iain's feet touched the rocky ground, the guard kicked them out from under him, sending Iain backwards into the dust. Coughing and spluttering, he clambered back to his feet ready for the guard's next move.

The guard disappeared on his hands and knees scrabbling in the dark and the dirt to find his knife. Unarmed, Iain slid his broad leather belt from his trousers and folded it in his hands, ready to lash out. Finding the knife, the guard lunged directly at Iain with his arm fully outstretched. Trapping the guard's wrist within the loop of the belt, using both of his hands, Iain snapped the belt against the guard's skin and twisted it. The twisting leather nipped the skin around his wrist, twisting and cutting it like a sharp knife, just enough to force him to drop his weapon. Then, loosening the belt and holding it at its tip, Iain whipped the buckle end of the belt across the guard's face. Catching the buckle with his hand, the guard latched onto the belt and pulled hard, yanking Iain forwards into the wall. As he turned towards the guard, Iain could just make out the guard's raised hands holding a fairly large rough edged boulder.

Suddenly, from quite a distance behind the guard, Iain heard the echo of a single gunshot and a short whistling sound, before the inevitable dull squelch as the bullet impacted against soft flesh. Blood cascaded from the front of the guard's throat as the bullet exited and struck the mine wall. A second shot followed as the guard grasped at his throat. This time, he dropped to his knees, his chest soaked with blood. In a moment, he was dead. But who had fired the shot, thought Iain anxiously. Were they friend or foe?

"You're a hard man to find!" exclaimed Steve as he came running forward out of the distant shadows.

"God, am I glad to see you!" cheered Iain, grabbing Steve and giving him a firm slap on the back.

"You didn't think you were going to leave me out of all the excitement did you?" asked Steve.

"Course not! You're just in time for the best bit! Come on!" said Iain. "How'd you find me?"

"When we turned up at the rendezvous point and found

the helicopter with the pilot and assistant dead, but you and Liz missing, we assumed that there must have been another route around the hill. We found it and followed it until we came to the mine." explained Steve.

"You managed to get reinforcements then?" asked Iain.

"Let's just say, we encountered a Territorial Army base on our way up here, and they were happy to oblige, weren't you Corporal?" asked Steve.

"Yes Sir!" came back the response from the Corporal followed by a handful of his men. "Leave this to us now, Sir!"

"He's got two hostages, the Professor and Liz! He's also got a remote detonator! If you go storming in there, he's threatened to blow the lot!"

"What's he up to Iain?" asked Steve.

Under the light from an overhead lamp, Iain drew a large triangle with arrows pointing towards the centre.

"The three points of the triangle represent the three silver mines in this area. Magnus has set up electromagnetic field generators in each of the mines, which he can set off using his remote device. These generators will radiate powerful super conductive magnetic fields that will converge in the centre of the triangle, above Libran's Loch," Iain explained. "Below the Loch, at the bottom of the deepest shaft in this mine, he's planted a powerful vibration device to shake up the solid rock so much that it will start to move. Backed up with enough explosives to blow a massive hole through to the Loch, he intends to flood all the shafts and underground caves in this entire area. If he succeeds, the weight of all that displaced water will cause a considerable seismic event which could result in earthquakes up and down the country. If he succeeds, the seismic shock will transmit a wave that will knock out everything electrical within a ten mile or more radius of the impact zone. He's hoping that the electromagnetic field anomaly generated above Libran's Loch will act like an inter-dimensional portal. The problem is, with all that seismic and magnetic field activity, it might have far reaching global consequences!"

"You're not serious, are you?" asked the Corporal.

"Oh he's serious alright!" replied Iain.

"I suggest we send three separate squads out to knock out the field generators and the power in each of the mines, Sir?" proposed the Corporal.

"You read my mind Corporal!" replied Iain. "If he's got no power, he can't activate the fields or the vibration device! But how do you intend to deal with the explosives, Corporal?"

"We're going to need a decoy to distract Captain McGregor and give us enough time to get in there and disarm the explosives!" the Corporal explained.

"How long do you need?" asked Iain.

"About thirty minutes!"

Iain looked at Steve.

"Well? You said you didn't want to miss out on the excitement! Are you game?" asked Iain.

"Of course I'm game! What do you want me to do?" replied Steve.

"Right! First, I'll walk in there, unarmed and give myself up."

"What's to stop him shooting you on the spot?"

"Nothing! Except.....he gets a huge kick out of seeing me suffer," said Iain.

"If you say so, but you're taking one hell of a risk!"

"Remember, Liz's down there with the Professor. I've got to get them out of there!" replied Iain. "What I need you to do is, to free the Professor and get him out of there. Get to Liz, free her, then I need you to get her to project into me so that when Magnus McGregor gets close enough to kill me, she can do her stuff!"

"Okay!" nodded Steve.

"You might need this," suggested the Corporal, handing Steve a small hand gun. Steve fingered it carefully.

"Thanks!"

"Incidentally, who do I have to thank for dealing with him?" asked Iain, nodding in the direction of the dead guard.

"That would be me," admitted the Corporal.

"Cracking shot!" praised Iain. "Oh, and how will we know that you've disarmed the devices and the explosives?"

"We'll cut the power last!" said the Corporal. "If we cut the power first, it may trigger the devices."

"So, when the lights go out, game's over!" confirmed Iain.

The Corporal nodded.

After synchronising their watches, the Corporal radioed his orders to the other squads and gave Iain a nod, before making his way down the shaft followed by five more soldiers.

"Right then, Steve! Ready?"

"Ready!" answered Steve with the hand gun in one hand and a torch in the other.

Fumbling their way down to the bottom of the shaft, Steve led the way, armed with his hand gun whilst Iain crept along side. Where the conveyor belt came to an end, the shaft levelled off, with four passageways leading eventually to four other chambers spread out beneath the Loch, each containing explosives ready to be detonated. A fifth passageway, just to their right, led to the central chamber containing the earth vibrating device. Close to the base of the conveyor belt was the entrance to another steeper shaft containing an older, well used rock conveyor, for moving the mined ore to the upper levels of the mine. Covered in dust and the remnants of the last ore extraction, the conveyor looked as though it hadn't been touched in more than thirty years.

Iain suddenly raised his nose into the air and began sniffing.

"What is it?" whispered Steve.

"It's Liz." replied Iain. "In this confined space, I can smell her scent."

"You must have a very keen nose." remarked Steve. "I can't smell a thing!"

"Being able to smell and identify a woman by her perfume before you see her has allowed me to avoid several unwanted confrontations over the years. It works with men's aftershaves too" explained Iain.

Steve raised a puzzled eyebrow.

"I'll not ask why!" replied Steve.

"Good!" said Iain. "Jardin de Chinoise (Chinese Garden)…..that's the perfume Liz wears." said Iain sniffing the air again quickly. "Come on, this way!"

Following the passageway around several bends, Steve and Iain suddenly began to hear voices echoing from the chamber just ahead.

"Stay here, "instructed Iain quietly. "Give me five minutes, then make your move……and keep low."

With that, Iain straightened up and brushed himself down, until he was reasonably satisfied with his appearance. Then raising his hands and clearing his throat, he walked towards the sound of the voices.

"Hello!" he greeted them cheerily. "Thought you'd got rid of me did you? No chance of that! I'm like a bad penny…..I just keep on turning up! Room for one more?" he enquired teasingly.

Magnus fumed deeply like a volcano about to blow.

"Where are the guards?" he growled.

"Oh, you mean Fred and Ginger!" Iain teased again."
Well Fred, I'm afraid, lost his footing on the conveyor belt.
He couldn't quite get the hang of the four shoe shuffle and
got the bullet, literally. As for Ginger, he never saw what was
coming next! Bit the dust, so to speak! Anyway, how are we
all doing?" asked Iain, as he perused the situation.

Liz was cuffed to an overhead pipe with heavy duty
plastic ties, whilst her feet rested on an upturned crate. The
Professor was sat on the ground with his hands cuffed to the
base of the molecule oscillating velocity equipment.

"They say three times is a charm!" declared Magnus.
"This time I will have the pleasure of killing you and your
friend!" he taunted, pointing his gun at Iain and Fraser. "In
twenty minutes, this generator will be at its optimum power
and will begin to send an electromagnetic wave through the
rock, agitating the molecules enough to provoke a seismic
event along the fault line beneath the Loch. Carefully timed
explosives will then be detonated to amplify the seismic
effects which will see the lower levels of this mine and the
others, fill with water! You and your friends, Mr Lachlan,
will either drown or be crushed to death!"

"It's not 'Mr Lachlan', it's Professor Lachlan if you don't
mind!" corrected Iain.

"I couldn't care what you call yourself! Get over there!"
ordered Magnus pointing to another empty crate near the
wall of the chamber. "Climb up and cuff yourself to the
pipe!" he ordered throwing a set of plastic ties to Iain. "Do
it!"

"Look, why don't you let Liz and the Professor go! We
both know it's me you want! It's so obvious that you want
revenge for Lorna, so why don't you let them go? This is
between you and me!" replied Iain.

"Oh I'll have my revenge and they're part of it!" Magnus

bellowed. "As for Lorna, well I think I've found a far better prize don't you agree?" he teased as he approached Liz and pawed her with his roughened hands. "I'll make her my lap dog, malleable to my commands, subservient to my advances."

"I think you're a bit late for that, old man!" Iain taunted.

"What do you mean?"

"How much did you pay your goons to spy on me? Whatever it was, it evidently wasn't enough!" Iain added. "Sometimes, if you want a job doing properly, you just have to do it yourself and you might want to get your eyes tested while you're at it because you're observation skills are pretty abysmally! "

"What are you talking about?" Magnus demanded.

Iain grinned, his eyes sparkling mischievously.

Magnus pulled out a scalpel from inside his laboratory coat and rolled up Liz's trouser leg, just above her ankle.

"Tell me now or I'll cut her and you can watch her bleed to death!"

"Oh please, not that old threat again!" moaned Iain. "Come on, credit me with more intelligence than that! You're not going to hurt Liz, she's too valuable to you! We all know that! Without her, you've got no control over the vortex you're trying to create!"

"Very well!" Magnus replied as he approached the Professor sat on the floor and held the scalpel blade to Fraser's throat.

"Tell me right now!"

"We're married!" announced Iain. "We got married on board the boat! If you don't believe me, she's wearing my mother's wedding ring!"

"That's not possible!" Magnus bellowed. "It can't be!"

Bemused by Iain's announcement, Liz twisted her left

wrist just enough to view the fingers of her left hand, and flashed it towards Magnus.

"It's true!" Liz replied as she glanced across at Iain. "Look!"

Magnus stared upwards at her cuffed hands and noticed the plain, slightly dull silver band on her wedding finger.

"You're lying, both of you!"

Magnus's face turned a rather dark shade of purple.

"You'll pay for that, Lachlan!" bellowed Magnus as he noted something in Iain's gaze, a flash of sincerity that betrayed some truth to his statement.

"I hate sore losers, don't you?" asked Iain rhetorically.

'You're playing with fire. Back off before we all get burned,' warned Liz's voice inside his head.

'Just trust me. I know what I'm doing,' Iain replied with his thoughts.

Magnus fumed as he watched Iain stand on the crate and cuff himself to the pipe.

"You're lying!" Magnus snapped as he yanked the crate out from underneath Iain's feet, leaving him hanging from the pipe. "I know maritime law! You couldn't have been married onboard that boat!"

"Not normally, I agree," remarked Iain as he grimaced at the pain of his wrenched arm muscles. "But because your goons chased us into the Minster, we were able to recruit a very important member of the clergy into our ranks," Iain lied. "It wasn't a bad service either. Although the sea was just a bit, choppy for my liking. Slightly spoiled the rhythm of our vows didn't it Liz," he lied confidently.

Liz nodded as Steve crept into the chamber behind Magnus and hid behind the cabinet containing the power circuits for the molecule oscillating velocity equipment.

"But it didn't stop us from cementing our relationship," teased Iain.

Magnus checked his watch. He was slightly behind schedule.

"Don't you want to stick around to make sure we don't escape?" asked Iain.

"When this device starts to rock and roll, even if you do break free, you'll never make it to the surface in time." laughed Magnus.

"What about Liz?" asked Iain.

"If what you say is right, she's damaged goods now, and she's no use to me! She can die alongside you, Professor Lachlan!" replied Magnus. "I don't really need her help to guide me through the vortex. I have a device that mimics and transmits her thought frequency so I can go wherever I want to, whenever I want to! All I have to do is go back in time and I can undo everything you've done Professor! She maybe your wife right here, right now but for eternity, she'll be mine!"

Suddenly, there was a tremendous thundering noise and the debris from the ceiling of the chamber began to fall all around them.

"Someone must be trying to disarm the explosives!" shouted Magnus above the noise of the rumbling ground. "They're booby trapped against any sabotage attempts!"

Iain frowned. There was no way that he could communicate any warning to the Corporal and the rest of his squad. Steve, however, had a small radio receiver in his back pocket. Squatting out of sight behind the cabinet he switched on the radio quietly and began tapping his fingers gently against the microphone.

Feeling the rumble in one of the other chambers, the Corporal pulled out his radio to check the status of his crew in the other chambers. As he was about to open the receiver, he could just make out the sound of a faint rhythmic tapping noise.

"Sounds like morse code, Corporal Sir." said the Private standing close by.

"Ssshhh!" ordered the Corporal. "I'm listening!.... Explosives rigged stop. Will try to secure remote detonator stop. Get out while you can stop. Fifteen minutes left," translated the Corporal. "Okay listen up! The explosives have been rigged to blow if we tamper with them. Johnson! Spencer! We haven't got a lot of time! Radio the lads in the jeep and get them to bring the anti-impact canisters down here NOW!"

"Yes Sir!"

"We're going to encase the explosives with the impact foam! It won't stop the explosion but it should reduce the effects of the blast. Alert Mitchell, Sinclair and Braddock likewise!" commanded the Corporal. "Now move! Henderson, come with me, we've got civilians to rescue!"

"Yes Sir!"

Gradually, the rumbling stopped in the chamber and Magnus checked the settings on the equipment, before turning back to face Iain.

"Alright! Who was responsible for that? I want to know right now!" Magnus bellowed.

"Honestly? I don't know!" replied Iain.

"Who else is here? You must know!" yelled Magnus.

"Well, I can hazard a guess! Get it? Hazard a guess? Never mind!"

"I've no time for pathetic superfluous jokes!"

"I think reinforcements have arrived to put a stop to all this. Perhaps it's the military! Fraser does have one or two connections," suggested Iain.

"Shut up! I need to think!" snapped Magnus.

"Better think quickly then, I reckon there's only about ten minutes left!" Iain teased whilst Liz and the Professor stayed silent, anxiously awaiting their fate. "You'll never make it out in time, unless you delay the detonations."

Boosting the power to the molecule oscillating velocity equipment, Magnus stepped back from the controls grinning as a deep low hum began resonating from the device, increasing in intensity every few seconds.

"When the device hits maximum output, the vibration will trip the booby traps in the other chambers and the whole lot will go up. But I'll just keep this remote with me for insurance!" he yelled above the hum.

Steve peered around the side of the cabinet and noticed Liz and Iain suspended from the overhead pipe, and the Professor handcuffed to the device.

'There goes that plan!' he thought to himself. 'What the hell do I do now?"

"Pity I have to leave you here my dear!" yelled Magnus as he turned to make his hasty departure. "Maybe we're just not meant to be, not in this lifetime! But in another time, another place, we'll meet again! I'll make sure of that!" he sneered before turning and running out of the chamber and back along to the main shaft.

As the hum became deeper and louder, more debris began to crumble and fall from the ceiling and walls as the chamber shook vigorously. Steve leapt out from his hiding place as a muffled explosion went off in one of the other chambers. Then, suddenly the walls began to split apart and they could hear the sound of water rushing towards the chamber from a distance.

"Hang on! There's got to be something I can use to set you free!" shouted Steve.

"Try inside the cabinets!" yelled Iain.

Quickly Steve went from cabinet to cabinet till he found a small pair of electricians' wire cutters.

"They'll do!" shouted Iain. "Quickly, set the Professor free first, the water is getting closer!" instructed Iain.

Dashing over to the Professor, Steve got down on his knees and carefully slid the cutters between the Professor's skin and the plastic ties. The Professor winced as Steve twisted the tie trying to get the cutting edge hard against the plastic, just as the cold murky loch water began to rush into the chamber.

Within seconds the water was several inches deep and rising, sweeping the crate away from underneath Liz, causing her to drop suddenly like Iain. With the full force of their combined weights pulling on the ceiling brackets that kept the overhead pipe in place, the pipe began to bend.

"Try and swing yourself along the pipe towards the cabinets Liz!" shouted Iain, as more water rushed into the chamber.

Meanwhile, the Professor struggled to keep his face above the water as Steve pulled and twisted at the plastic ties. Suddenly the plastic split and the Professor was catapulted forward into the strong flowing current.

"Are you okay?" shouted Steve.

The Professor struggled to his feet, completely soaked from head to foot.

"I'm fine! We need to help Liz and Iain!"

Rushing towards them, the Professor took Liz's weight on his shoulders and pulled her the final two metres towards the cabinet, whilst Steve supported Iain's weight and pulled him across. The pipe creaked and groaned as Iain finally set down on the top of the cabinet. Clambering up beside them as the water rose to three feet, Steve cut Iain free before passing the wire cutters to the Professor to cut Liz loose.

"We need to move quickly before the water reaches the power cables, or else we'll be left in the dark! Let's move!" commanded Iain.

Jumping into the freezing cold water, Iain led the way followed closely by the others. Linking hands, they struggled through the strong rising current along the winding passageway towards the conveyor belt. As they entered the main chamber the Corporal and Henderson waded towards them.

"Are you okay?"

"Yes Corporal!" yelled Iain above the noise of the rushing water. "Lead the way, we'll follow!"

Wading across the chamber to the start of the ascending shaft, the Corporal and the Private pulled the Professor up on to dry ground, followed by Steve, as Liz and Iain struggled towards them. Suddenly, there was another detonation and the four men were forced to dive to higher ground further up the shaft, as the ceiling of the tunnel collapsed behind them, trapping Liz and Iain in the chamber. Fortunately, part of the ceiling near the passageway that they'd just come from, also collapsed blocking that entrance into the main chamber.

"What are we going to do?" shouted Liz.

"The water's stopped rising for the minute! The passageway behind us is blocked. That should buy us enough time to find a way out of here!" explained Iain as he pointed to the old mine shaft.

The lights above their head began to flicker.

"Quickly! The water must be about to hit the main power lines! We'll be plunged into darkness! Climb on to the old conveyor!" Iain instructed. Liz did as she was asked.

Several metres into the old shaft, the lights behind them flickered and died. In her soaked shoes, slipping on the dusty chunks of ore that littered the old conveyor belt, Liz lost her footing in the darkness and fell, dashing her forehead against a boulder just above her. Her eyes closed as a trickle of blood ran down her brow, and the rushing noise of the water turned to silence. She was unconscious.

Where am I and why is it so dark? Liz thought to herself as she stirred back to consciousness. A faint smell of Loch water filled the air around her, in what appeared to be a long, steep and humid tunnel. Running beneath her, up the full length of the tunnel was a narrow track carrying an old heavy duty conveyor belt, on which she was lying. Ahead of her and behind her were rocks of various sizes and shapes, which lay along the conveyor, covered in dust as if they'd laid there for centuries. Further up the shaft and every twenty feet or so after that, a small caged lamp shed an almost halcyon glow along the tunnel, just bright enough to light the way. Shivers ran down her spine, as a sense of dread and danger dominated her thoughts. How had she got here and where was she going? She didn't know. Yet something seemed strangely familiar about this place. Had she dreamt of this place? Or perhaps this was just a dream itself. Picking up one of the many small pieces of rock just ahead of her, she turned it over and over in her hands. It was about eight inches long and rough to the touch. Liz sniffed the slightly damp rock. The odour was unmistakably Loch water with some metallic undertones. She hesitated, convinced most certainly that she'd performed this act before. Trying to understand why she was sitting in a tunnel leading away from, what seemed to her to be a partly submersed mine, she looked down at herself, examining her appearance for any further clues. The jeans she wore were unusual and definitely not what she would have bought. In fact, on further inspection in the half light, she realised she was wearing a man's pair of jeans. The shirt too, also belonged to a man, which she deduced from the way the shirt was buttoned. Looking at her hands, she noticed that her wrists were a little sore and swollen, as well as appearing red and badly grazed, almost as if they had been bound. Looking at her wedding finger she noticed the plain silver band. Definitely not her taste in jewellery she thought, but it did tell her that she must be married. Yet, she couldn't remember! A wedding day was the most important day in most women's calendars but obviously not important enough to Liz, if she was able to wipe it from her memory so easily. Every second she sat on the conveyor belt revealed more and more perplexing information about her current predicament. Lifting up her head, she peered a short distance ahead of her, to see a figure sharing this journey with her. Turning around to look back down the tunnel towards her, Liz could just make out the handsome features of a slim built man in his thirties. This stranger looked at her as if he knew her, and appeared puzzled by her lack of progress up the conveyor belt.

"What have you stopped for? Come on.......if that last one blows, this shaft will flood pretty fast!...Come on!!!"

This wasn't a dream, she thought. This was a nightmare... ..a bit more realistic than other nightmares admittedly she thought, but a nightmare nevertheless! Who on earth was that man and what exactly was going on? Or maybe she'd wake up, safe in her bed and write this off as another one of those frustration dreams that lurk in your subconscious ready to re-emerge and thwart a peaceful night's rest, just when you needed it most.

The ground began to shudder beneath her feet, causing the lamps to swing violently, smashing several of the bulbs in the process. Taking a deep breath, she reached forward and began to crawl over the rocks ahead of her on the conveyor belt. Just as she was within arms length of the stranger, the tunnel shook with the impact of a not too distant explosion. The blinding light from the blast lit up the whole tunnel as Liz clapped her hands over her ears. The force of the blast ripped through the shaft, snapping the conveyor belt and scattering the rocks in all directions. Liz and the stranger were thrown against the wall of the tunnel.

"Well that's put pay to that!" he said in between coughing and spluttering amid the dust. "Are you okay, Liz?" he asked.

"Still in one piece.......I think."

"We've got to get out of here NOW!"

With that, the stranger began climbing again. Liz followed behind him. Who was he, she asked herself. He clearly knew who she was, he knew her name, but she had no recollection of ever having met this handsome stranger before. If she had met him, there were no doubts in her mind, that with looks like his, she wouldn't have forgotten that face ever! He also had a smooth educated Scottish lilt to his voice. If this was a nightmare, she thought, at least she was glad to be in the company of such a charming, handsome man. Like Alice In Wonderland, she felt an insatiable and understandable curiosity about her current plight, but now, was not the time to ask twenty questions. Escaping the perilous danger behind them, was their top priority. She could ask all the questions she liked later, when they were safe. Placing her trust in the charming stranger, she resigned herself to the fact that she must have suffered a blow to her head causing her to suffer from temporary amnesia, and followed his instructions unquestioningly.

Another explosion ripped through the tunnel, extinguishing most of the remaining lights and reducing the visibility even further. Through the darkness and dust that enveloped them now, Liz heard the voice again.

"Keep going Liz! We're nearly there......Reach for my hand!"

She fumbled her way towards the stranger as her eyes grew more accustomed to the darkness. Her arms and knees were sore and scraped from clambering over the rough and often sharp rocks. Finally her fingers touched the warm soft skin of his hand and felt his grip, as he pulled her towards him. His was not the hesitant or nervous touch of a stranger, his was the touch of a caring concerned friend or partner. She mused for a second which one she was…

"There's a ladder up ahead. It should take us to the next level," he said.

Liz looked deep into his eyes for a moment, oblivious to the chaos that surrounded her. Friend or partner, she wondered.

"Liz, stay with me…….I know you're confused……….. You said this would happen, "he continued. Then taking hold of her firmly with both hands, he said," Try to remember……You know me……I'm Iain."

"I said this would happen?…I don't understand."

"You've projected here from your past, …but there's no time to explain right now. I need you to trust me!"

The tunnel shook again, but this time, it wasn't an explosion. This was an earthquake. Fractures began to appear in the walls of the tunnel and now they were completely in the dark. Iain held on to Liz.

"Move!"

"I can't see anything!"

"I've got your hand! Don't let go! We've got to reach that ladder!"

With her left hand, Liz kept a tight grip on Iain's hand whilst clambering over the rocks and twisted metal beneath her. The air was thickening with dust all around them as they struggled onwards and upwards for what seemed an eternity. Then, Iain paused for a moment as his hand touched something metallic and smooth along the side of the tunnel. Running his hand over the metal, he could feel the grooved rungs of the ladder.

"I've found it!" he shouted over the noise of the rumbling and crashing in the tunnel.

But his words came too late as the icy cold water submersed them. Gasping for air and fighting against the force of the water, the stranger grabbed desperately at the ladder. Gritting his teeth as every muscle in his arms strained agonisingly, he fought to pull Liz against the current towards him. Spluttering and gasping for air, she grasped on to his upper arm before grasping the ladder itself. Pulling her between him and the ladder to protect her against the force of the water, the stranger guided her upwards. Climbing closely behind her, Liz and the stranger began their vertical ascent to the upper level.

With wet feet sliding on the metal rungs, Liz climbed slowly and carefully from rung to rung as she heard the roaring water rushing along beneath them.

Thinking quickly, the stranger undid his old faithful trouser belt which had been his only weapon in the fight against Magnus' guards. Lashing it around the handrail that ran the full height of the ladder, he fed the belt back through two of the waistband loops on the right hip of his trousers and re-fastened the belt buckle.

"Liz," he shouted again. "Undo your belt and loop it round the ladder handrail to your left."

Liz reached out and felt along the wall for the handrail, then, unfastening and sliding ff her belt, she did as she was asked.

"Have you done that?"

"Yes!"

"Now slide the belt back through the hip loops on your trousers and re-fasten it…….This should help to keep us on the ladder, if the tunnel shakes again!"

"Done!" she replied after fastening her buckle.

"You go first and I'll follow behind. Now climb!"

Liz slid her hands up the handrails on either side of the ladder and pulled herself up on to the rungs. She looked upwards as she began to climb but, it was still too dark to see anything. She could feel the vibration of Iain ascending the ladder behind her, reassuring her that she was not alone in this terrifying hell. 'Keep climbing', she kept saying to herself in her head as each foot found its way on to the next rung and the next rung, higher and higher up the ladder. Iain followed close behind, careful to avoid Liz's feet just above his head. The sounds from the tunnel began to change, becoming a little distant as they now climbed further and further up a vertical escape tunnel leading to the higher level.

"We're in a connecting tunnel!" shouted Iain. "I reckon we've got about another thirty feet to climb until we reach the hatch!"

The tunnel below them suddenly began to rumble and shake violently, followed by the sound of rushing water. Liz's feet slipped off the rung, leaving her hanging precariously from the handrails. Holding on tightly, she searched the air with her dextrously balletic feet until she was able to find the nearest rung again with the toes of her shoes. Her heart was pounding fast.

"Are you alright?" shouted Iain, who had felt the ladder wobble as Liz slipped.

"I'm okay!"

Steadying herself again, she resumed her ascent cautiously, sliding her hands up the rails as she went. Rung after rung she climbed, wondering if they would ever come to an end. Then she began to feel the walls of the connecting tunnel closing around her.

"We should be getting close to the hatch now! Reach carefully above you as you climb……you should be able to feel the handle!"

Liz nervously lifted her left hand off the rail and reached into the darkness above her head. Nothing. She climbed another rung and tried again. Her hand hit something hard.

"I think I've found it," she shouted down to Iain.

"Stay where you are! I'll climb up beside you!"

Liz felt Iain's body brush against her as he climbed up the final few rungs to reach the hatch. In the darkness, she could feel his warm breath against her face, as he stood level with her on the ladder. His closeness to her made her tingle all over and again she had the eerie feeling that she knew him a lot better than she first thought. Her heart was pounding so fast now and the heat from her blushes felt so intense, she feared she would alert him to her highly excited state. Reaching above his head to the hatch above, Iain's face was very close to hers.

"I need you to steady me while I grasp the hatch with both hands," Iain instructed. "I want you to hook your left arm through the rail and link up with your right hand around my waist. Ready?"

Hesitantly, Liz wrapped her arms around his waist and held on tight. Suddenly, Iain could feel her heart pounding close to him and puzzled at her curious reaction. Then, he realised that her nervousness was not due to her fear, but due to the fact that he was a stranger to her. Her past self had projected into her own body and this projection was how she would remember him. Pausing for a moment, he leaned towards her and kissed her trembling lips. Panicking like she'd just been thrown into a plunge pool of icy cold water, Liz suddenly let go of him. Catching hold of her quickly, Iain could feel her trembling nervously in his arms and whispered, "For luck." She'll not forget that in a hurry, he thought, grinning wryly to himself.

Trying to regain her calm and composure, and failing

miserably, she hesitated momentarily as she wrapped her arms around his waist again.

"Are you okay?" he asked teasingly.

"I'm fine, really!" she answered shakily.

Reaching up above his head, Iain could feel the round turning handle on the door of the hatch and tried to turn it. Holding his breath and exerting every ounce of strength he could muster, Iain pulled on the handle. He gasped and took a deep breath, before trying again. They could hear a faint grinding of metal, as the mechanism within the hatch door slowly began to move. Climbing up another rung, with Liz clinging tightly around his hips, Iain pushed his shoulder hard against the hatch as he turned and pulled on the handle again.

"Liz, I want you to carefully climb up and push the hatch as hard as you can!"

"Okay!" she replied nervously.

Climbing up in front of him until her head was touching the hatch door, she reached up and pushed. There was an eerie deep groan coming from the metal door, then suddenly it opened.

"Keep on pushing!" he gasped as they both pushed against the heavy hatch door until it opened completely. A sudden rush of cool dust free air hit their faces as the light blinded them momentarily. Blearily, Liz pulled herself up through the hatch and sat on the floor of the upper corridor coughing and catching her breath, while Iain pulled himself up.

The corridor shook violently causing the hatch to clash down suddenly and unexpectedly, narrowly missing Iain's ankles, which he managed to pull out of the way just in time.

"That was close." Iain sighed. "Right, where are we?" he asked as he gazed at Liz's shy and embarrassed face. For the first time in her life, she could see his handsome features smiling back at her, and his captivating rich brown and honey golden eyes sparkling brightly.

"I think it's a main passageway," Liz replied.

Iain scanned the passageway, looking for clues and a way out. Almost eighty metres away a small motorised maintenance cart stood idle against the mine wall.

"We must be in a main access corridor …….not far from the entrance," he said. "Let's grab that cart and get out of here," he continued, pointing to the maintenance cart.

Dusting themselves down as they stood up, Liz and Iain could hear the sound of heavy boots heading in their direction. Without any further hesitation, they sped off in the direction of the cart, as a small patrol of three armed guards, approached the hatch.

"Shoot them!......Both of them!" yelled the leading guard as he took aim with his hand gun.

"Don't look back, Liz! Keep running!" shouted Iain.

The guards opened fire and several bullets whistled towards them as they fled towards the cart.

"Get behind the cart! I'll get in and try to start it!" Iain instructed.

The first bullet missed her head by millimetres, impacting against the wall of the passageway just in front of her. She ducked behind the cart as a second bullet whizzed above her back, missing her by a split second. Iain dived into the foot-well of the cart as a third bullet struck the side. Rummaging under the dashboard of the cart, his fingers located the starter motor's ignition wires and he yanked them free. Splitting the plastic coating of each wire to expose the copper underneath, he shouted to Liz.

"Get ready to jump in!"

The guards advanced quickly towards the cart as Iain

brushed one of the bare wires against the other, jolting the cart into life.

"Get in and stay down!" he shouted.

Liz slipped into the passenger foot-well of the cart just as Iain pushed down the accelerator peddle with his right foot. Leaning low over the driver's seat he peered carefully over the back of the cart at the guards rushing towards them. Another round of bullets shot towards them at lightening speed. Iain ducked and turned quickly to look ahead of them through the steering wheel. Crouched in the foot well, Liz spotted some containers of machine oil just behind the driver's seat. If she could only reach them, she could tip them out of the back of the cart, she thought. Peering carefully around the side of her seat, she saw the guards trying to catch up to them. In an instant, she slipped around the side of her seat and into the back of the cart, where there was a box filled with an assortment of oil containers and paint tins. She grabbed the oil canister nearest to her, unscrewed the lid and poured the contents in different directions on to the passageway floor behind the cart as they sped along. As they approached the start of the oil spillage, the guards came to a halt and resumed their aim at Liz and Iain before opening fire once more. Suddenly, the whole mine began shake violently.

"It feels like this whole mine is about to come down on our heads any second!" yelled Iain as he pressed the accelerator pedal to the floor.

Debris fell from the walls and the ceiling around them, and Iain twisted the steering wheel this way and that to avoid the clumps of rock that struck the floor of the passageway just ahead of them. Liz hung on tightly. Turning a bend in the main passageway, Iain began to recognise his surroundings as they merged with a familiar looking corridor that led to the main entrance.

"Not far now!" he yelled to Liz over the noise of the trembling ground and falling rocks. "Hang on!!"

About two hundred metres away he could see the Professor, Steve and the Corporal running out into the daylight. Then the electromagnetic super conducted wave blew invisibly through the entire mine with a deep low sonic hum.

"What on earth was that?" yelled Liz, as she struggled to maintain her balance. Iain looked back briefly into the mine and stared in horror as a ripple of distorted light hit the soldiers behind them and they disappeared instantly.

"It's the vortex! I can't believe he actually did it!" yelled Iain, quickly turning back and focussing on the entrance to the mine.

"What is it? What does it do?" asked Liz.

"It's a powerful convergence of electromagnetic energy that is capable of pulling in matter and catapulting it into another time or dimension."

"Like a black hole?"

"It's not as powerful, thankfully! A black hole will even pull in light. This vortex can't! It's not on the same atomical frequency, but we are! If we don't get out of its path, we'll find out exactly what it does, personally!" Iain yelled.

With the vortex advancing towards them at a higher velocity, Liz turned quickly to look at Iain, instinctively knowing that they weren't going to make it in time and flung her arms around him. Whatever was about to happen to them, wherever they were going to go, she knew they needed to be together.

Turning to look back at the entrance of the mine, the Professor, Steve and the Corporal watched as Iain and Liz sped towards them on the maintenance trolley. Then, as they stood catching their breath and looking back towards the mine, the wave of energy from the vortex overtook Liz and Iain as they reached the mine entrance, and as Steve, the Professor and the Corporal looked on in horror, in an instant the star maiden and her shepherd were gone.

CHAPTER 20

THE MAINTENANCE TROLLEY CARRIED ON out of the entrance and crashed into the high wire fence just a few metres from the mine. Striking the fence head on, Iain and Liz were catapulted head first into the fence and landed on the hard ground close by. Iain groaned as he rolled over on the ground and crawled to where Liz lay.

"Liz, are you alright?" he asked as he brushed the dust from her face and mouth, and checked for a pulse. Opening her eyes, the first thing she saw was his relieved and welcoming smile looking down at her.

"Where are we?" she asked a little confused.

"Outside the mine entrance, "replied Iain.

"How'd we get here?"

"On that thing," Iain replied indicating to the mangled maintenance trolley that was now partially swaddled in the wire fencing.

Liz shook her head even more confused and then winced with pain.

"What's wrong?" asked Iain concerned.

"The last thing I remember was losing my footing on that dusty old conveyor belt and then this," she replied rubbing the bump on the side of her head.

"How's your vision?"

"Fine. I just don't remember what happened? Was I unconscious? How long was I out?" she asked bemused, trying to find answers which might help her make some sense of their current situation.

Iain sat back in the dust beside her, deep in thought, re-running the events in his head.

"I think you were out for quite a while," he replied eventually with an odd roguish smile on his face.

"What?" she asked as she noticed his odd expression. "Come on! There's something you're not telling me! And why are you looking at me like that? What did I do?"

"I met you," he said softly.

Liz sat up straight and stared at his peculiar, almost mischievous, secretive expression, as if he had the words, 'I know something you don't know' tattooed on his forehead.

"That's a strange thing for you to say!" Liz remarked. "I met you too, two days ago. What's going on?"

"No," Iain replied smiling as he gazed at her concerned face. "You honestly don't know, do you?"

"Know what?" she asked frowning and irritated by his cryptic response.

Iain's face opened up into a broad wry grin.

"Think Liz!" he beamed as he held her at arms length and gazed curiously into her eyes. "What was the last thing you remember before you blacked out?"

Liz sighed deeply.

"I remember we got cut off from Fraser, Steve and the Corporal. Then we found that old shaft and climbed on to that conveyor belt. I remember trying to climb over the rocks, stumbling, ... and then this!"

Iain said nothing, but just gazed warmly and encouragingly at her, trying to get her to arrive at the same conclusions he'd made, on her own. Liz recognised his expression and searched frantically in her own mind to find the missing link. Then, she shrugged, clueless.

"Sorry. What am I missing here?"

"One word," he replied. "Vision."

"Vision?" she asked puzzled, then a couple of seconds later, the large penny dropped. "Oh, that vision!"

"Only it wasn't a vision, was it? You didn't project your thoughts into your future self……"

"I was there….." She interrupted, with a wide eyed look of discovery on her face. "That explains why I woke up in bed covered in bruises and dirt!"

"Did you?" he asked curiously.

"Yes!"

"You're right! It does explain that!" he replied. "Think about the start of your 'vision' and when it ended. Does it fit into the gap in your memory?"

Liz thought for a moment then smiled and nodded vigorously.

"Yeh! It fits perfectly!" she replied. "How the hell did you figure that one out?"

"I was there," he said smiling. "You changed."

"Changed? How?"

" When I saw you fall and went back to help you, but before I got there, you were already on the move."

"Go on."

"There was something about you that just wasn't right. I thought at first it might have been the bump on the head making you a little confused and disorientated. But then, I could see in your eyes, you really didn't know me!" he continued. "You looked really scared like you'd suddenly been dropped into the middle of a nightmare."

"That's certainly how I felt!"

"I wanted to hold you, to reassure you, but judging by the look on your face, I think that would have frightened the hell out of you," said Iain. "Then I suddenly remembered what you'd told me about your vision, the mine…the explosions…..our escape and how confused and frightened you'd felt. So, I put two and two together and I talked to you and you took my hand."

Liz listened attentively.

"Look, I'll tell you what happened. You compare it to your 'vision', and hopefully, it should all make sense!"

"Okay," replied Liz.

"I managed to get you on to the ladder leading to the emergency access shaft and the upper levels. There were explosions going off way back down the shaft. Then an almighty wave of water came rushing at us, filling the shaft. I grabbed on to the ladder and managed to pull you through the water. I guided you on to the ladder and then we began to climb towards the top of the access shaft. You nearly fell once or twice as the whole place shook, but we managed to make it to the hatch at the top of the shaft."

Liz nodded in agreement.

"Then, I kissed you," Iain confessed.

"You did what?" Liz exclaimed.

"I kissed you," Iain smiled.

"I don't remember that bit!"

"Maybe you forgot."

"Oh I think I would have remembered that…How did I react?"

"Surprised. Embarrassed. In fact if I hadn't caught you and hung on to you in my arms it could have been pretty disastrous," Iain explained. "That wasn't a vision you had. That was the first time you met me, wasn't it?" he asked. "You were so shy like a teenager on their first date," he said grinning, then, added. "The more I think about it, you were quite charming and endearing. Sweet," he confessed with a wide wry grin.

"Sweet? Me?" she questioned.

"Well you were, back there!"

"Oh, and I'm not now?" she frowned.

"Well, after what we've been through in the last couple of days ...... It also explains a lot about why you behaved the way you did in my lecture room."

"I was just trying to keep a low profile," Liz replied. "I thought I was doing a pretty good job too!"

"Until I got up close to you," Iain grinned again.

Liz frowned.

"Oh come on! It was cute. I was flattered. An attractive looking student with a crush on her lecturer, it's enough to boost any man's ego!"

Liz dropped her head in embarrassment.

"I could feel your heart pounding through the table. What was I supposed to think, ...that you were about to have heart attack or something? And your face, the way you hid it. Come on, admit it….You were blushing!"

"I didn't know what to do," whispered Liz. "I remembered that I'd seen you before somewhere, but I couldn't think where. I didn't make the connection with the vision until later," she explained. "I was embarrassed because I couldn't remember how I knew you. You could have been an ex-boyfriend or something. I just couldn't remember! And I didn't know how you'd react or if you remembered. Worse still, if it was because of something embarrassing, I didn't want to make a scene!"

"Anyway," he sighed. "That was the past! It wouldn't have made any difference how you reacted to me, that day! You took me completely by surprise!" he confessed. "When I saw your eyes, I knew exactly who you were! In fact, I had a hell of a job trying to hide how I felt for you, but I think I managed," he beamed. "There wasn't a single thing about you that I missed that day. You had my fullest attention," he sighed. "I was already in love with you, couldn't you tell?"

Liz suddenly looked up into his shining brown and

golden eyes, and could see immediately that he was speaking the truth.

"That's where this whole thing began, isn't it? Back there in the shaft!" Iain asked.

"How do you mean?"

"Your attempted abduction and your first visit back to me in the past, they happened later didn't they?"

"You're right!" answered Liz nodding in confirmation.

"I'm just guessing here but, that was where we first connected isn't it?" he asked. "That's the precise moment in time when, "Iain paused. "…..when you first fell in love with me?" he whispered softly, his sparkling eyes searching her bemused expression for a reaction.

"I …," Liz didn't know what to say. She knew he was right. She didn't remember anything about a kiss though. He obviously added that change, she thought, but she couldn't deny that her feelings towards Iain all seemed to emanate from that point.

"Why did you kiss me?" she asked. "You didn't do that before."

"I couldn't resist. I'd missed you so much when you projected from the boat and I thought I'd lost you. Then, after we escaped from the lab, that was the first opportunity I had to be close to you again and you were there, with your arms wrapped around my waist, holding on tightly, trusting me, a perfect stranger to keep you safe. I'd missed your touch so much. Could you honestly blame me?"

"I guess not," Liz replied. "

Liz thought about what Iain said, turning his words over and over in her head.

"So, let me get this straight," she began. "That wasn't a vision or even my first thought projection. ……That was my first physical projection… into the future."

"Yes." Iain replied beaming with delight. "You just didn't realise it!"

"But why?" she asked puzzled. "It must have been something pretty powerful that pulled me physically into the future!"

"But it was!" replied Iain. "It was the vortex!"

"But the vortex is just an energy source! It's not human! It doesn't know me personally! So, why me?"

"That's why we decided to come here, before the vortex and before your thought projection, remember? There must be something else that we're missing, an ancient family connection perhaps."

"I don't know. This whole time thing's got my head spinning. It's like yesterday, today, tomorrow, they're all out of sync! I don't know where I am any more. There's no anchor point for me to hold on to, no starting point from where I can get my bearings. My life, my direction, my future it's all spinning out of control like a compass in an electrical storm!" she sighed.

"That's it! That's it exactly!" Iain exclaimed.

"What? What did I say?"

"You hit the nail right on the head!" Iain replied excitedly.

"I don't understand!"

"Up to the point that you had your accident, just like the rest of us, you were anchored by your DNA, and your own electromagnetic field. You knew where you were in the world and the world related to you. Everything was in its rightful place, rooted, anchored. But when you had that accident, something must have happened to weaken those anchors. Like an oar less boat adrift on the Loch, I think the accident caused you to float on that frequency. To drift wherever the universal wavelength took you," suggested Iain. "I think something in our future is sent a strong wave

471

along that frequency, back to my past and I think you got swept along with it! If it turns out that you also have a distant ancestral link to my village, it could mean that wherever there is a strong DNA link to you, that may also influence the energy current, pulling you towards key places and events connected to your extended ancestry. Up until now, whilst your emotional and blood ties were strongest in the present, they continued to pull you back. But the more visits you make elsewhere, and the longer you spend away from the present, the more lost you could become!" explained Iain.

Stunned by his revelation, Liz sat in silence absorbing the enormity of his words.

"We must get you home, Liz." whispered Ian sensitively.

"If your right, what about Magnus and his plans? What about the reason why we're here? What about the reason we came together in the first place?"

Iain thought for a moment.

"First thing's first. We need to know exactly 'when' we are before we can figure out the 'why'," replied Iain. "Do you remember when you had your 'vision'?"

"Not exactly. Eight months ago? A year perhaps? My memory's not that good."

"Okay, we need to find something to pinpoint where we are now," instructed Iain. "I know there were trucks here when they brought me in."

"But they're not here now," remarked Liz.

"Yeh, interesting that? How could those trucks disappear without leaving any tracks?" Iain asked himself. "Unless, they haven't been here, yet. We must have travelled back at least a few months to a point before the whole project was set up here," Iain concluded.

Looking around for more clues, Iain suddenly noticed

the back of a large red metal plaque attached to the outside of the fence with a padlock and chains keeping the metal gate shut. Deciding to get a better look at the notice, Iain headed back towards the fence and began to climb.

"What are you doing?" asked Liz.

"The notice on the other side of this fence could give us a clue. Give me your hand and I'll help you climb over," replied Iain.

Carefully they scaled the metal fence and dropped down to the ground on the outside. Approaching the metal notice, they read: 'WARNING – STRICTLY PRIVATE. LAND DEVELOPMENT IN PROGRESS. TRESPASSERS WILL BE PROSECUTED. ACCESS TO AUTHORISED PERSONNEL ONLY. By order of PROTON Inc. 1st May 2009.'

"That's just over a year ago," said Liz. "...and this definitely wasn't here when they brought you in?" she asked.

"Definitely! I would have remembered having to climb it. This fence must have been a temporary measure until they started to move the equipment and the troops in. Once they were in, there would have been guards at the entrance."

Iain's mind began to whirl. Memories of this time in his immediate past, began to resurface. He remembered the last time he'd visited that part of the world, and he suddenly recalled a secret too, which he wished had stayed forgotten. A secret which even Fraser didn't know. Questions suddenly filled his mind. Was he here now, again, to put that matter right or was he meant to make sure that it never happened? He'd already changed Liz's 'vision' with a kiss, according to her. Did that mean that events could be changed, that we could change our future, he thought. Was he meant to change that event too? Iain thought about the events in question and shook his head. They didn't seem

Abbygail Donaldson

that important to warrant pulling both himself and Liz through to that moment in time, he thought. There had to be another reason. The vortex may have driven them here, he considered, but Iain's instincts were telling him that somewhere at the bottom of all this mess there had to be some blood ties and links to their future. Everything seemed to point in that direction.

Liz rubbed her dusty scraped hands against her jeans and noticed the ring still on her wedding finger.

"You were right about the ring," she said. "I don't think it is meant to come off." Iain smiled.

"Like I said, perhaps it's meant to stay there for a reason."

Liz looked at him seriously as a sudden idea flashed into his mind.

"What's wrong Iain?" Liz asked.

"I've just had a sudden thought," he replied with a glint in his eye. "What if we are at the same point in the past as when you had your vision, your first projection?"

"What difference would that make?"

"Well, for a start, there would be two of you on the same time plane with the same unique energy frequency and the same DNA, obviously," said Iain.

"And."

"One of you remembers the projection whilst the other experiences it."

"Is there a point to this?"

"Just hear me out," replied Iain. "What if your presence here and your memory of the event triggered your other self to make the physical projection. No identical matter can occupy the same space at the same point in time. Maybe if we hadn't landed here, you wouldn't have physically projected. Maybe our disappearance here caused an energy

474

gap in the present which had to be filled, and because there were now two of you here, one of you had to go."

"So my earlier self plugged the energy gap?"

"Mmmm. Pretty much I think," Iain nodded.

"But, what about my bump on the head, and my loss of consciousness?" she asked.

"Maybe that was another trigger," he began. "Maybe, that was what facilitated the exchange. At that moment of vulnerability and unconsciousness, and within 'ground zero' of the vortex's creation, maybe it was able to perform a straight swap. Your earlier self was pinged into the gap left by your future self and your future self pinged here, hey presto, you've created a perpetual time loop. The universal energy balance is restored," Iain explained.

"Phew! That's a real head banger of a theory!" remarked Liz. "If that was really true, how come it hasn't happened to other people?" she asked.

"Because, they weren't caught up in the creation of a time vortex," Iain replied.

"But what about you? Why didn't you have the same kind of 'vision' or 'physical projection'?" she asked.

"Because, I don't have your ability."

"But, using your theory, that would mean that you left a gap in the present, wouldn't it?" she asked.

"Good question," he replied and paused to think of answer. "Maybe because you unnaturally extended my life, I was surplus to requirements….. I wasn't supposed to be there?"

"But your existence would leave a wake of impacts on events and people's lives!"

"That's true," he nodded. "Even I don't know the answer to that one. Maybe that's just one of the many universal mysteries of time and space we've yet to explore and understand."

"Great!" replied Liz.

"It's just a theory. I'm no expert in this field. I might be wrong, who knows?" Iain replied. "But, one thing I do know is, that the universe is all about balance and counterbalance, actions that have equal and opposite reactions. It certainly fits most of the pieces of our puzzle together."

"So how do we get back to the present, Einstein?" asked Liz.

"We find a way to stop the event from happening. If we succeed, the vortex was never created and we never travelled through it. If the event never happened then the energy exchange never occurred and you never had the vision or projection. Simple!"

"If you say so. My brain's feeling like scrambled egg at the minute just trying to understand all this!" sighed Liz. "I really don't like people and situations messing up my head," she complained. "So, in simple terms, if we stop Magnus from rigging the mine, we get to go home, yes?"

"Yes," replied Iain.

"Okay, I buy that," said Liz. "…but, what about us?"

"What about us?" Iain repeated.

"Won't that destroy the link between us and undo events so we never meet?"

"Perhaps."

"Well it strikes me that, if the event doesn't happen, I don't have the vision or make that projection, and I don't meet you for the first time. And if we stop the event early enough, would we also stop the attempted abduction and murder?"

"Hmmn. It's possible."

"And if those events don't happen, I won't go into witness protection and I won't even meet you at the university. In fact we might never meet at all!" Liz sighed.

"I think there has to be something else that connects

us, something totally unlinked to the vortex," replied Iain reassuringly. "Don't worry Liz. Whatever it takes, we'll work it out! I have no intention of disappearing from your life and losing you again, ever!" declared Iain as he held her in his arms. "We'll find the answer and we'll get you back home, I promise!"

"So what do we do now?" asked Liz.

"We need to get some help. We can't do this on our own. We need Fraser," replied Iain.

"Do you think we have enough time now?"

"We have the advantage that, we know what's going to happen, how he's planning to do it, and when, but we still need to be careful and think things through. We need to work out what the impact will be if we try to change anything." advised Iain. "You managed to change my past and my future for the better. I'm pretty certain we can stop Magnus too!"

Reaching into his trouser pocket, Iain pulled out his mobile phone. It was damp from their escape through the flooded mine.

"Damn!" he frowned, then a thought flashed across his mind. "No, it's okay!"

"What do you mean?" asked Liz.

"When we were in the mine, I had my phone in my pocket and it got wet and cut out!" he said.

"Yes."

"When the E.M.P. hit, it wouldn't have affected the phone because it was already out of commission! If I can just dry out the components, I should be able to get it going again! In the mean time, I suggest we find some place to stay and some dry clothes. It can get pretty fierce up here when the sun goes down."

Then fumbling inside his shirt, he fingered a small

waterproof pouch containing his bank cards and sighed with relief.

"That's okay then."

"What's okay?"

"Before we left my cottage I stashed my wallet in a rubberised pouch inside my shirt just in case. So, the hotel's on me tonight! And I think we deserve a decent meal too! What do you say?"

Liz smiled, prompting Iain to give her an affectionate squeeze.

"That's better! Think of it as a short holiday. The only difference being we've travelled to a different time instead of a different country. But we can still treat it as a break away from our normal lives, and I know just the place where we can stay. It's only about two miles from here. Come on!"

Striding off down the old country track, Iain and Liz squelched along in their well sodden clothes and shoes, eager to reach the sanctuary of a warm comfortable hotel. Iain looked down at himself and Liz and had another thought.

"Liz, if anybody asks any questions I think we should have an alibi of some sort, just in case."

"What do you suggest?"

"Well, we wouldn't look out of place as a couple of hikers, albeit very wet ones. We can say we fell in the Loch....it happens quite a lot around here, people falling out of boats or off jetties! Yes! It's simple and straight forward."

"Do you think anybody will be interested?" Liz asked.

"Probably not, but if they ask....we've got our answer! The fewer questions we raise in people's minds, the less memorable we will be and the less impact we will make. Okay?"

"Okay."

As they turned the corner and headed around the base of the mountain, a strong wind struck them from the direction of the Loch. Liz shivered, but for Iain, being the hardy Scottish shepherd that he was, the sharp cold wind held no challenge for him. Liz looked across at Iain admiringly.

"I guess this brings back memories for you, does it? Roaming through the countryside near your home?"

"I used to walk the flock through here many times, when there was no track at all." He replied.

"I can just imagine you in your kilt, tending to your flock. It must have been very lonely for you out here on your own."

"When you're watching sheep, it's like watching over children. Take your eyes off them for a second and they can wander off or get up to mischief. You really have your hands full. You don't have the time to feel lonely. Well perhaps a little, when you're sitting watching them graze."

"How did you cope then?" she asked.

"I dreamed of my future."

"I bet it didn't look anything like this!" she laughed.

"Oh I don't know. I dreamed about visiting different places in the world......and I've done that. I dreamed about different careers I could have away from the homestead....... and I've done those too!"

"What about friends and family?"

"Oh I've had plenty of friends over the years," replied Iain. "Some were like brothers.....but like everyone else, they grew old and died."

"I'm sorry."

"Don't be. I have lots of happy memories of them. Memories I'll share with you over time, when this is all over and we settle down somewhere."

"Was it true what you said back there, about me being pregnant when I saved you and your parents on the night you were born?"

"No, I made it up," he replied.

Then he noticed the disappointed look in her eyes.

"Of course, if that's what you want." added Iain.

"I'd love to have children," replied Liz.

"Well then, I'll just have to see what I can do," he grinned wryly.

"Do you think we'll ever be allowed to settle down?" she asked.

Iain stopped and he looked at Liz's tired face.

"I hope so! But if hope isn't enough, I'll find a way to make it happen!"

Just ahead of them, through the trees, they could just make out the main road. The traffic was quite fast in both directions, and Iain and Liz had to sprint across the lanes to reach the other side of the road.

"Through here," he said. "This road will take us into the village. It's only about a mile away."

"I recognise it! It's been a long time, but I still remember this road," she said.

"Come on then! It's not far! I'll race you!" he grinned, as he turned and jogged away down the road.

"You're mad!" she yelled after him.

"I maybe mad," he shouted back to her. "But I'm also hungry! Come on!"

So with her shoes and clothes still moderately sodden, she sprinted and squelched her way along the road after Iain.

A large opening in the dry stone wall marked the beginning of the car park adjacent to the hotel. The Hotel itself was a big white building, built in 1846 with a big dark green sign emblazoned with gold lettering, declaring that this was The Lachlan Arms Hotel. Positioned overlooking the junction where the lane into the village began, Liz stood at the corner of the building and looked down the lane towards the picturesque cottages with small pretty rose gardens that stood on either side of the road leading down towards the Loch.

"Nice view isn't it?" asked Iain as he caught his breath. "If we wander down to the shops at the bottom of the lane, provided you don't mind wearing tartan, I'm sure we'll be able to get fixed up with some fresh clothes," suggested Iain.

Passing one or two bemused looking walkers dressed in waterproof clothing and carrying rucksacks, Liz and Iain headed down the lane towards the small village shops displaying all manner of souvenirs depicting the Scottish Highlands. There were boxes of shortbread, butter fudge and sticks of rock in the window, and draped over the doorway were small sheepskin rugs, children's kilts and one or two hand knitted jumpers. Stepping across the threshold a young girl walked towards Iain carrying a silver tray containing two china plates. On each plate lay a delicate white paper doily on which was placed pieces of creamy fudge on one and warm buttery shortbread on the other. The rich buttery aroma drifted under their noses, making their mouths water.

"Good afternoon! Would you like to try some warm shortbread, Sir?" the young girl asked.

"Mmmmmn Thanks!" replied Iain as he reached out towards the plate and took a rectangular finger of the shortbread and popped into his mouth. "Delicious!" he sighed, as he chewed away at its rich crumbly texture.

"Thank you," said Liz as she popped a piece into her mouth, and enjoyed the buttery crumbly taste as the shortbread melted on her tongue.

"Actually," began Iain as he struggled to finish the last remnants of shortbread that were stuck to the back of his teeth, "I was wondering if you could help us."

"I'll try," the girl replied timidly.

"We had a bit of a tumble in the Loch this afternoon and were wondering if you had any suitable clothes we could buy, the warmer the better."

"We do sell clothes, but they tend to be touristy if you know what I mean."

"Oh, we don't mind that! What have you got?"

"We have a selection of kilts, locally made in the Lachlan tartan. We have polo shirts and sweatshirts for the golfing enthusiasts. We have some hand made Arran jumpers. If you need socks, we've got thick knee high Arran socks to wear with the kilt and we have some standard cotton rich socks too!"

"Lead on!" requested Iain, and they followed the young girl through the shop, down a short flight of stairs and into the basement level where most of the clothes were stored.

"I'm afraid we only have one fitting room," confessed the young girl.

"That's okay!" said Iain. "We'll take turns."

For the next half an hour or so, they searched through the hangers, baskets and shelves for the various items they needed before taking their turn behind the tartan curtain, in the small fitting room. Liz stepped out first from behind the curtains wearing a narrow leg pair of discreet predominantly dark blue and black tartan trousers with a dark blue sweatshirt displaying a small Scottish flag just below her left shoulder. Then, came Iain, sporting a medium weight kilt in his family's tartan, knee length woollen socks, a soft cotton Ghillie shirt topped with a beautifully cabled Arran jumper.

"You carry the kilt well, Sir," commented the young girl. "Have you ever worn a kilt before?"

Iain smiled at Liz as he replied. "Yes, I've worn kilts for years. What do you think, Liz?"

Liz smiled as she stepped back to view the full ensemble.

"You wouldn't look out of place on the cover of Scottish Country Life," she replied. "You've also got an incredibly sexy pair of legs," she whispered to him as they followed the girl towards the till. "What I want to know is, are you wearing it in the traditional manner?" asked Liz as she playfully ran her fingers over the pleats of his kilt.

"Now that's a time honoured secret," he whispered teasingly. "I suggest we walk back up to the hotel and get ourselves checked in," said Iain as he pushed his bank card into the card reading device and punched in his PIN number. Then, when the transaction was complete, Liz and Iain bid their farewells and made their way back up the lane towards the hotel, each carrying a large carrier bag containing their wet clothes.

The double glass doors stood open as they approached the hotel.

Liz suddenly grabbed Iain's arm.

"Wait," she said.

"What's wrong?" he asked warily.

"Nothing......it's just you've forgotten to remove one of the price tags from your jumper," she explained as she snapped the thin thread between her fingers that kept the white oval cardboard tag attached to the neck of the jumper. "There, you're okay now," she said as she stuffed the tag in her pocket.

Iain smiled, "Thanks."

His eyes sparkled as they caught the afternoon sun peeping down on them through the trees and Liz smiled too. She was hooked. Never in her life had she experienced so many thrills, dangers, and excitement. She had to admit, she was actually enjoying the whole adventure. As long as she was with Iain, nothing else seemed to matter. She knew that some day she might tire of the turmoil and continuous change, but for now, she was enjoying every precious minute.

Approaching the small dark oak check-in counter, midway down the hall, adjacent to the lounge bar entrance, a smart young lady dressed in a simple dark blue blazer, skirt and crisp starched white blouse stood behind its counter.

"Good afternoon. How can I help you?"

"We'd like to book a double room please," answered Iain.

"I'm afraid most of the double rooms have been taken except for the large room at the front of the hotel, just above the bar. It's slightly dearer than the standard doubles but has full en suite facilities and a fine view of the village," she said.

"We'll take it," said Iain handing over his bank card.

"For how many nights?"

"Three please."

"The tariff includes breakfast in the main restaurant just behind you and evening meal bookings are available too. Alternatively, we have a good selection of bar meals available all day til 9pm."

"Can I book a table for 8pm?" asked Iain.

"Yes sir. Will that be all?"

"I think so," answered Iain, punching in his PIN number into the card holder.

"If you can just sign the register, I'll take you up to your room."

Iain nodded, and taking the sturdy ball point pen offered by the receptionist, Iain scrawled his signature and his address into the book, as the receptionist stepped around the side of the counter.

"This way," she said and led them up the thick carpeted creaky stairs leading to the first floor. Reaching the first floor landing, the receptionist turned to her left and led them through a narrow corridor to the door of their room. Turning the large metal key in the old mortise lock, the receptionist opened the door to the large spacious double room.

"If there's anything else you need, just let me know," she said as she left them to settle in.

A large king size bed rested against the back wall of the room and pointed straight towards the three tall sash windows that overlooked the crossroads leading into the village. A door adjacent to the bed led into the bathroom.

"Tea! That's what we need! Some hot sweet tea!" said Iain as he spied a cream plastic kettle on the table below the windows, along with a tray of essentials.

Liz looked across at the complimentary tray which contained two sets of cups and saucers, and a china bowl containing coffee, sugar and milk sachets and several individually wrapped tea bags. Picking up the kettle, Iain disappeared into the bathroom to fill it with water before replacing it on its stand and flicking the switch. The kettle chugged and hissed rhythmically as the electrical element heated the cold Highland water. Gradually the bubbling of the water increased until finally the plastic switch, on the top of the handle, clicked off. Dropping a tea bag into each cup, Iain poured in the boiling water, added a sachet of sugar and milk to each cup, and gave them a quick stir with the teaspoon provided.

"Nothing like a hot cup of tea made with pure Highland water to heal all ills and calm the worried soul!" he said, offering a cup to Liz as she sat on one of the easy chairs near the windows. Iain sat down in the other chair beside her, and together, almost simultaneously, they clutched the hot cups in their cold pale hands before blowing on the steaming liquid and ingesting their comforting fluid.

"Iain, I've been thinking," said Liz suddenly looking concerned. "Don't you think you should contact your other self, here, to let him know that you're spending his money, or we might find some unwanted uniformed visitors banging on our door."

Iain scratched his head again.

"You're right. But I won't be able to reach him on his mobile, because it's the same phone as mine, and if I try to ring him on his land line, what exactly am I going to say? Hello Iain, it's me Iain from the future! I hope you don't mind but I'm a bit strapped for cash. So I've used our bank card! Hope it's okay. Thanks. That'll really go down well, won't it!"

"What about contacting Fraser and explaining to him what's happened and get him to set up a meeting. We're going to need his help anyway to sort this whole thing out, and he might be able to figure out what connected us in the first place!" suggested Liz.

"Brilliant idea!" replied Iain. "How about, you go and freshen up, while I contact Fraser. When I'm done, I'll join you. How does that sound?"

Liz smiled and sighed.

"That's my girl! One way or another we'll get to the bottom of this, I promise!"

Finishing her tea, Liz got up and disappeared into the bathroom.

Picking up his mobile, Iain selected Fraser from his list of contacts and hit the call button on his touch-screen. The phone rang again and again until finally there was a click and a familiar voice at the other end.

"Iain?"

"Hello Fraser!"

"Have you changed your mind, already?"

"About what?"

"The fishing trip of course? Ten minutes ago you said......"

"That wasn't me!......Well it was me...but not ME!" answered Iain.

"Iain, you're not making sense! Are we still going?" asked Fraser.

"That's not why I am ringing!"

"Why are you ringing?"

"It's possible Fraser! We've done it!" exclaimed Iain excitedly.

"What is? Iain calm down and start from the beginning!"

"Time travel!"

"Oh, that! We've always known it was possible it's proving it that's the hard part!"

"I'm proof! Liz and I have done it!"

"Sorry?"

"Liz and I have travelled back in time!"

"How's that possible? You haven't met Liz yet! Or has she projected to you again?"

"No! About a year from now, I meet Liz. There's a whole load of stuff happens, which I'll tell you about later. Then, she and I get zapped back here!" explained Iain.

There was a profound silence on the other end of the phone.

"You haven't been drinking that punch again have you? I've warned you about that before! Terrible stuff! Good for stripping paint off walls though! God knows what it does to your stomach!"

"I haven't been drinking, Fraser!"

"That's even more worrying," Iain heard Fraser mutter on the other end of the phone. "Look, I know you've been stressing a lot lately about Liz," he sighed compassionately. "But you know how delicate the timeline is. If you try to force your hand, something could go disastrously wrong. You just have to be patient."

"Fraser, I'm not stressed!" he snapped. "Okay, I am stressed, but not about what you think!" Iain continued. "Please Fraser, think! Have I ever rung you like this before?"

There was a pause then Fraser replied," Well, there was that time you managed to lock yourself in the janitor's cupboard trying to escape Handy Hannah the Faculty Secretary."

"Oh come on! You know what she was like at that party! She damn near took my eyes out with that mistletoe! Then, she followed me into the gents! She didn't leave me any choice! I had to hide somewhere til she cooled down!" Iain replied defensively.

"Oh, so that was the reason you had your face buried in Cynthia's cleavage when I opened the cupboard door!"

"How the hell did I know she was in there trying to escape Crawford, and you know how small that cupboard was! Cynthia and I could barely breathe!"

"Oh so that's your excuse for all that funny noise. You were gasping for air were you? Pull the other one!" Fraser replied sarcastically.

"Okay! Okay! I had the hots for her, I admit it! But this is something else! You have to believe me! We need your help!" replied Iain desperately. "We need to stop the anomalous event!"

There was a stunned pause on the other end of the phone.

"Okay, go on. I'm listening. What kind of anomalous event?"

"If I said 'super-conductors', 'converging electromagnetic energy fields', and artificially induced major seismic activity, what springs into your mind?" asked Iain.

"This isn't April the first is it?"

"Not on my calendar," replied Iain.

"Where are you?" asked Fraser curiously.

"Libran's Loch."

"Isn't that your old stomping ground?"

"That's right."

"There's a few mineral mines round that neck of the woods, gold, silver, precious and semi-precious stones. Major fault lines too!"

"Yeh, tell me about it! Very moving!"

"I want you to meet us here, in Lachlan village next to the Loch. Oh, and you'll need to contact Iain ….your Iain. He's probably in his office about now, marking student papers. I want you to explain what's happened and tell him I've had to use some money from our account…..I didn't have any cash on me when we arrived here…..and!" instructed Iain.

There was silence on the other end of the line.

"Look if this is some kind of joke!"

"No Fraser! This is no joke! I'm deadly serious and a lot of lives depend on what we do now! But I'll explain everything when you get here!"

"Where are you staying?"

"The Lachlan Arms."

"It'll take about five hours to drive up there!" answered Fraser.

"I appreciate this, honestly! I'll get you booked in for the night! Thanks Fraser! I owe you one!"

"Do we need to find Liz and bring her with us?" asked Fraser.

"That could prove interesting, but I don't think you should! Besides you might not be able to find her."

"Why? Has something happened to her?"

"It's complicated and there's no time to explain it right now."

"Understood! I'll contact Iain and we'll get there as quickly as we can!"

"Thanks!"

Iain ended the call and thought hard for a moment. They had barely been there a couple of hours and already their actions were causing problems. Finishing his tea, he remembered that Liz was waiting for him in the shower and headed for the bathroom.

Liz had turned on the shower and slipped out of her clothes, which she had piled neatly on the stool next to the radiator. Then, climbing into the bath, she placed the plug in its hole and sat down, huddled under the warm water bombarding her from above. The heat from the water soothed her aching body, comforting her like a warm blanket. Resting her head on her knees, she closed her eyes and breathed in deeply. So many thoughts ran through her head. Was she really here? Was this really happening or would she open her eyes and find herself safely tucked up in bed, back home? Her eyelids suddenly felt very heavy and in a moment, her tired arms slumped limply by her sides. Exhausted, with her head resting on her knees, she drifted off to sleep.

"Liz? Are you okay in there?"

There was no reply, only the sound of running water.

"Liz?"

Still, there was no reply. Rushing into the bathroom, Iain found Liz sitting in the bath, slumped over her knees. Checking her pulse anxiously, he realised she was just sleeping and sighed with relief. Then, stripping his clothes off and switching off the shower, he climbed into the bath behind her, and drew her gently into his arms in the soothing hot water that filled the bath around them. Leaning back against the end of the bath, Iain rested Liz's head on his chest and swept her wet hair from her face as she slept.

"It's alright Liz….Everything's going to be okay," he whispered.

CHAPTER 21

An hour passed before Liz's eyes flickered open and she stared at the unfamiliar white ornate ceiling above the bed. Still wrapped in the towel that he had placed around her, Liz turned towards Iain who lay alongside her. His deep brown and golden eyes glowed enticingly as he delicately un-wrapped her soft and warm body. Though he didn't speak, her head was filled with his rich charming voice, as if chanting some magical spell inside her mind. Closing her eyes she felt his warm soft mouth caress hers as he lay close to her and she felt his gentle sensitive touch against her skin. Sliding over her slender hips, she felt him press against her and reached out to him, pulling him closer.

The village fell quiet outside the hotel and the air felt heavy with a strange sense of expectancy, whilst in their room, only the sound of their breathless excitement, broke the overwhelming silence. Gazing up at him, she admired the suppleness of his body and held her breath as she gripped him tightly. Looking down into the deep sparkling blue ocean of her eyes, he found himself free-falling deeper into her soul.

"I need you," he smiled unsurprisingly as the aurora engulfed them, invigorating their senses and tingling their nerves. He could feel every cell in his body awakening to her life giving energy, and just when he felt his passionate energy waning, he suddenly had so much more to give. She was exhilarating, addictive and to know that she loved him made all those years of desperate waiting and longing, worthwhile. Closing his eyes, and gripping her gently but firmly, he held his breath too. As the seconds passed by, the wave of blissful contentment washed over them and the timeline rippled gently.

"I love you Iain," she whispered softly.

"I would never have guessed," he grinned cheekily, with his rich brown eyes gleaming with delight.

"Oh, you!" she laughed and bounced one of the pillows off him softly. "You're just a big tease!"

"Aim to tease, aim to please!" he laughed. "Anyway, food! I'm starving!"

"Me," too!"

"Let's go down to the bar and grab a bite to eat!"

Re-energised, Iain jumped out of the bed and dashed into the bathroom. After a couple of minutes and a couple of bumping noises and muttered curses, he emerged, smart and distinguished in his recently acquired Scottish attire. Following his example and drying her hair into a soft wavy style that flowed gently like a golden waterfall over her shoulders, Liz emerged and followed Iain out of the room and down to the large lounge bar.

At the far end of the bar was a small open fireplace, piled high on either side with small, neatly stacked logs of wood. Several day trippers sat at the tables running the full length of the bar, downing pints and devouring hot tasty food. Iain strode decisively up to the bar. A young barman stood behind the counter eagerly ready to serve.

"Yes, sir."

"Any chance of some food?" asked Iain.

"Yes , sir….The menu board is just in front of you if you can just tell me what you would like and which table you're sitting at."

Liz located a table near the window at the front of the hotel, and sat down.

"What's the table number?" asked Iain.

"Eight," replied Liz.

"Are you ready to order?" asked the barman.

"Fisherman's pie please......What would you like Liz?"

"The same please."

"So that's two fisherman's pies. Anything else?"

"No, that's fine thanks." Acknowledged Iain.

"While we're waiting for the order, can I have a pint of your best ale please, and my young lady will have?...."

"Whisky and dry ginger please....no ice."

"Thank you.......I'll bring your drinks over to you as soon as I can."

Iain walked over to the table in the window and sat opposite Liz. Within a minute or so, the barman approached with a tray containing their drinks.

"Here's your beer, and your whisky and dry ginger, Sir."

"Thanks," said Iain and placed the tumbler of golden amber liquid in front of Liz, and kept the dark brown beer in front of himself.

"May the tides of time bring us safely to our home's shore," toasted Iain quietly as he clinked his glass against Liz's.

"To the tides of time," whispered Liz.

After a short wait, their two meals arrived, piping hot and the two hungry travellers ate heartily, content in their momentary lull from the dramas they'd left behind them and from those yet to come.

The sky was dark, and the birds were cooing their evening roosting song when Fraser and the younger Iain arrived in Iain's small dark green vintage MG sports car. The noise of the old reverberating exhaust sounded like music to Iain's ears as he watched his prized automobile slowly negotiate the car park's gravelled entrance. Looking out of the window, Liz and Iain watched the headlights of the car as it came to a halt, before rising from their seats to meet Fraser in the car park.

"There's something I should tell you, Liz," said Iain as they made their way out of the bar and towards the door of the hotel.

"And what's that?"

"He's here, too."

"Who?"

"The other me," confessed Iain.

"Ohhh," she said stopping dead in her tracks. "How are you going to get around that one?" she asked curiously.

"Easy. I just say he's my twin brother."

"I guessed that!" she replied. "I wasn't talking about that. I mean, how's he going to take it? Think back. How would you have felt if you'd suddenly been introduced to me by your future self?" she asked.

"Good point," he replied pensively.

Then she had a sudden thought.

"Do you remember any of this, meeting up with your future self?"

"What are you getting at?" he asked.

"Well, this is your past. If science was right about the past, present, future thing, then this has already happened for you. You'd remember it, wouldn't you?" Liz elaborated.

"Clever girl! Yes you're absolutely right!"

"Well then?"

"What?"

"Do you remember anything about tonight?"

"Nothing. Not a sausage!" he replied, but then paused. "No wait, I do remember something,"

"What is it?"

"Fraser said something on the phone about a fishing trip which I backed out of.......I'm trying to remember why, " he said as he chewed on his bottom lip, perplexed. "Why did I back out of the fishing trip?" he mumbled.

"I'm just guessing here, but if it was about a year ago, do you remember what happened at last year's summer ball? Perhaps you had a hot date? Why else would you turn down a fishing trip?" she teased.

"Mmmm," he pondered. "Yes, I remember now."

"Dare I ask?" she said curiously.

"Let's just say, I'd rather forget that weekend. Complete disaster! I would have been better off going on the fishing trip after all."

"Why?" she probed curiously.

"Please, don't ask. You don't really want know," Iain replied guiltily. "And anyway, it won't happen now will it, because I'm here instead. So it doesn't matter," he sighed.

"Oh come on! Of course it matters! We've changed your future. There may be consequences! ......and besides, you've got me guessing now!"

Iain said nothing.

"Oh, I see," Liz said nodding as she began putting the pieces of the puzzle together in her head. "Was it really that embarrassing?" she teased. The temptation to look into his thoughts and find out the truth, seemed irresistible to her. What had he done that he felt so ashamed of, she asked herself. Then the penny dropped. Iain saw the look of wide eyed astonishment on her face and dropped his gaze.

"Oh no!" Liz concluded. "You didn't? It wasn't you, was it?"

"What?"

"The fluorescent bra on the top of the university building?"

Iain's face flushed a deep shade of red.

"Yes, okay? It was me! I was the one that was on the roof that night with Janice. But she was the one who tied her luminous bra to that mast! Alright? Satisfied?"

Liz burst out laughing.

"It's not funny! She followed me everywhere that night, and my bum!"

"What about it?"

"She wouldn't leave it alone," he added. "She squeezed my bum so much, the bruises looked like a satellite map of the world, big blue and green patches where her pincer fingers had been. I could hardly sit down for two days!"

Liz stifled another laugh.

"So why did you go with her?" she asked curiously, "I thought you were saving yourself for me?"

"Look, I'm a passionate hot blooded Scotsman, not a damn monk! I never said I'd been celibate."

"I wouldn't have expected you to be," she replied sympathetically. "Just tell me why you went with her."

"I got drunk, very, very drunk and I remember trying to lose her in the corridors. It was an absolute nightmare! Talk about man-eaters! She makes jaws look like a vegetarian! The more I tried to lose her, the more desperate she was to find me!"

"So why did you .....you know?"

"Like I said, I was very, very drunk. I just remember seeing her blond hair and desperately wanting you!"

"Oh," she replied.

"I wish I hadn't, but I can't change that now," Iain sighed.

"So you've invited your younger self here, knowing how desperate he is to meet me! Isn't that like putting a red rag to a bull?"

"It could be. I'm sorry, okay! But what was I supposed

to do? Fraser doesn't have a car. He needed me to drive him here."

"Okay, so how do we deal with this? Only you know how he'll react!"

"Let's just see what happens. It might be okay," replied Iain unconvincingly.

"How would you feel?" asked Liz carefully.

"Devastated, probably. Desperate, definitely!"

"Maybe I should stay out the way," Liz suggested.

"No, he needs to see you. He needs to know that you're not a dream. He needs you!"

"That's what I'm worried about," she replied.

Iain sighed deeply and smiled.

"Just be yourself. Give him the hope he needs to keep going, Liz. As much as we need him and Fraser, he needs us right now. If he gives up and loses hope, I won't exist anymore and the event will still happen," Iain whispered softly.

In the dim light from the external hotel lamps and the low solar powered foot lights near the wall of the hotel, Liz and Iain approached the car. Standing silhouetted by the lights behind him, Iain senior watched quietly as his younger self climbed out of the driving seat. A strange heavy silence hung in the air between them like an invisible mist, as Iain's younger self viewed his silhouette beside Liz, with caution and suspicion.

"I think it's best if we discuss matters away from enquiring eyes, don't you?" suggested Fraser. "We don't want to draw any unnecessary attention now do we? Have you got us booked in Iain?" Fraser asked Iain senior.

"Yes. You're both in a twin room on the first floor, just along the corridor from us." replied Iain senior.

"What name have you used for Iain here, seeing as you've no doubt used your own name to register?"

"John Sinclair......You're my twin brother if anyone asks."

Iain's younger self nodded silently and watched in awe as he saw Liz standing beside the dark silhouette of his future self. Her long golden hair floated softly in the late evening breeze, haloed by the antique street lamp that cast its halcyon glow behind her. Even though he couldn't see her face in the darkness, he knew it was her and his heart pounded wildly as her sweet scent filled the air. As she stepped back nervously into the light, overwhelmed, frightened and confused by his excitement, he smiled as he saw the beauty of her vivid blue eyes sparkling magically just as he'd remembered. He watched as she trembled and faltered, longing to run to her and sweep her up in his arms. Then she stepped back into the shadows again, afraid of him, afraid of the repressed passion that reached out desperately in the darkness towards her, a passion that screamed out of his thoughts and into her mind. He worshipped her and wanted her desperately, like a man possessed. He was dangerous, but only to her.

This hadn't been planned. He'd had no coaching from Fraser on how to handle his feelings for Liz and his emotions were raw and unleashed. Iain senior noted the look in both their eyes and knew that Liz was right to be concerned. Being carbon copies of the same man, how would she know the difference between them? Iain senior fidgeted uncomfortably, remembering how desperate he'd felt a year ago, the night he'd thought about ending it all.

Fraser sighed, helpless to resolve his dear friend's emotional quandary. Scientific theory he could handle, but its impact on people's feelings and sensibilities went far beyond his abilities and understanding. This was a situation that even the most qualified of psychology professionals would take years to unravel. Sensing the growing tension, Fraser placed his arm around Iain senior's expectant shoulder.

"I think you and I should go inside, Iain whilst Liz talks to 'John'," said Fraser guiding Iain back towards the hotel. Iain looked back over his shoulder at Liz, deeply and justifiably concerned. Was it wise to leave his younger desperate self alone with her, he wondered?

"She'll be okay," said Fraser reassuringly. "But then, you know that, already," guessed Fraser.

"That's the whole point, I don't know," replied Iain anxiously. "This didn't happen. We've changed the past."

"She loves you, Iain. Never question that," reassured Fraser. "But this is a very delicate situation and you need to tread carefully. If you or Liz do anything that changes his view of the future or destroys his hope, everything may be lost."

"But he's me and she loves me. She loves him. What do I do?"

"You have to trust her. She'll find a way to get you both through this and as you pointed out yourself, you are both the same man. What happens to him, you will feel and remember too. His new experiences will integrate themselves into your mind. She is with you, she's not with another man.

"I didn't believe it at first, until I saw you," said 'John'. "I thought it was somebody's elaborate idea of a hoax, until now," he said as he slowly approached Liz with his heart pounding and his mind racing.

Trembling nervously and confused she backed deeper and deeper into the shadows of the hotel, frightened of his thoughts and feelings for her. Worse still, she was frightened of her own feelings for him and with every moment she was in his presence, she found it harder and harder not to see him as the man she was in love with, who made her body come alive in his arms.

"Liz," he whispered softly as she backed up hard against

the wall of the hotel with her heart pounding wildly. "Liz, talk to me please. I need to hear your voice," he whispered as he gently stroked her soft velvety cheek and looked closely into the bewitching vivid blue eyes that haunted his dreams. "I've missed you so much!" he pleaded as he noticed the pools of fearful tears welling up in her eyes.

"Please don't," she whispered weakly. "I'm scared."

"I'm not going to hurt you. There's nothing to be scared of."

"Yes there is," she replied as he brought his mouth close to hers.

"What are you frightened of?" he asked as his hands softly rested on her shoulders and his lips brushed lightly against hers.

"Me," she replied, as he pressed his mouth firmly against hers.

His kiss was eager, hungry and hot, as her mind whirled with confusion and fear. She could feel his heart racing against hers. She could feel the strange electrical tingle between them, just as it had happened back in the cottage. This was Iain. This was the man who had waited so gallantly for so many years, to be with her. This was the man she was in love with and she wanted him.

Inside the hotel, Iain felt a strange shiver run through him and a look of instant concern flashed across his face.

"What's wrong Iain?" asked Fraser.

"He's ….." Iain began to explain but stopped. "I have to go! I'll be back in a minute!" he said as he dashed off down the hallway and back out of the hotel.

"Just hold me Liz. I need you. I want you so much," he pleaded, helplessly out of control as he kissed her again. He wanted her now, more than anything else in the world and he knew she wanted him too.

Trying desperately to fight against the current

of incontrollable passion between them, she gasped unconfidently, "I'm not the Liz you're meant to be with. She's out there somewhere waiting for you."

Confused by the fear in her voice, the pounding of her excited heart, and the taste of salty tears on her lips, Iain's younger self (John) weakened. Sensing the desperate longing in his mind, and his strongest desire to make love to her, she pushed hard against him, trying to resist, but his warm lips silenced her protestations once more. Then, Iain, her Iain appeared behind his younger self. Seeing the additional reflection in Liz's eyes, his younger self turned to see his older self standing calmly behind him. Liz cowered in the shadows, tearful and confused from her ordeal.

"Liz, are you okay?" asked Iain senior.

"Yes," she replied shakily.

Handing her the room key he added," Go on up to our room, I need to talk to 'John'."

Taking the room key, she flitted through the shadows to the hotel door and disappeared. Once she was out of sight, Iain senior spoke.

"Before you say anything, I want you to listen to what I have to say," began Iain senior. "I should be angry and if it was anybody else and not this situation, I would be, but I know what you're going through.," Iain senior explained. "I know what you're thinking. I know what you're feeling for Liz. Can't you see what this is doing to her right now? You're forcing her to choose between you and me, and we're the same person. I know how much you want to have her right here, right now and if I hadn't stopped you, you'd have destroyed all her illusions of you."

"What do you mean?" his younger self asked. "She wanted me too! She's in love with me, don't you think I can tell that?"

"You're me but you're not me and this situation wasn't

meant to happen. She's only ever known the caring, sensitive and gentle side to me. What you were about to do, was to show her the beast beneath surface!"

"How do you know that that's not what she wants?" his younger self asked, just as the penny began to drop. "Oh I get it! You've slept with her haven't you? But I'm not allowed to!"

"Shut up and grow up!"

"Right! So what am I supposed to do, pretend she doesn't exist? Pretend that I haven't waited nearly three centuries to be with her? You're the one who dangled her in front of me! What kind of a sadist are you?"

"I'm sorry!" apologised Iain senior. "I'm really sorry! If I could have avoided this I would have done! But I couldn't!"

"So what happens now? Do you go back to your cosy love nest upstairs? And what happens to me?"

"Please, all I'm asking is, that you don't do anything we'll all regret! You are better than this and she is special! She is precious and fragile! This didn't happen a year ago! I didn't do this and neither should you!"

"That's easy for you to say," snapped his younger self.

"For God's sake! Stop thinking with your Thomas and think with your brain! You weren't intended to meet her now, but you will meet her soon, when it's right. If you screw things up now, you screw up the future for all of us!"

"You don't need me to do that for you! Looks like you've done a pretty good job of screwing it up all on your own! Why else would you be here, trying to put things right?"

"This wasn't our fault! We were trying to stop Magnus and this was where we wound up!"

"Magnus? What's he got to do with it?"

"It's a long story."

"So why do you need my help?" asked the younger Iain.

"We could have two Magnus' to deal with and an extra version of me might just come in handy," replied Iain senior.

"Great!"

A few minutes later as Liz came back down the stairs, she watched both Iain's enter the lobby of the hotel chattering away to each other about the car. Seeing Liz at the far end of the hall, standing anxiously at the base of the stairs, both Iain's smiled apologetically. With Iain senior close behind him, the younger Iain advanced towards Liz and pulled her gently to one side beneath the shadows of the archway leading to the kitchens beyond. Staring frantically over his shoulder at Iain senior, Liz saw him nod and mouth the words, 'it's okay'.

"I'm sorry Liz," he sighed. "I was bang out of order back there. I didn't mean to hurt you. I guess it was the shock, the excitement. I'm really sorry," said the younger Iain.

"I know," she whispered trembling.

"I wouldn't hurt you for the world, you know that don't you?" he asked anxiously.

Liz nodded.

"I don't expect you to forgive me, but will you at least let me buy you a drink? You look like you could do with one."

"I think we could all do with a stiff drink!" added Fraser as he escorted Liz, Iain senior and 'John' into the bar.

"John! I've got us checked in," said Fraser as Liz and Iain senior went to find a table. "Did you manage to sort something out with your 'brother'?" asked Fraser.

Iain's younger self nodded.

"Are you okay?" asked Fraser concerned.

"I'll be fine," he sighed. "I just need a drink, a large one," he added drawing the barman's attention. "A double single malt please, no ice."

After a couple of drinks, the receptionist collected them, to escort them to their pre-booked table in the restaurant. Settling down in the far corner next to the window, Liz and Iain senior sat across the table from Fraser and Iain's younger self. Over the course of the meal and one or two bottles of wine, Liz and Iain senior recounted the events in the mine that had led up to their arrival at the loch that day.

"The strange thing is, if Magnus was going to stick to his plan, why hasn't he started preparing the mine? When we arrived through the vortex, there was nothing. No signs of any work in progress, just the wire fence around the entrance."

"Do you think he's changed his mind?" asked the younger Iain, as he watched Liz discreetly.

"That's a point!" replied Iain senior. "Could he have changed his mind, Fraser?"

"It's possible!" concluded the Professor. "But from what you've described he seems pretty determined to create that vortex. You also have to consider that to go against his original plan, something must have changed."

"Do you think he's here already?" asked Iain senior.

"I would say so," answered Fraser.

"How long?" asked Liz.

"Long enough to have an influence," suggested Fraser.

"Then there's a good chance he knows we're here," concluded Iain senior. "How?" asked Liz, puzzled. "We only got here today."

"If I'm right about Magnus, he's probably been tracking us some how or he's got spies here," replied Iain senior.

"So what do we do?" asked Liz.

"Are there any other energy sources around here where

Magnus might try to construct an alternative vortex?" asked Fraser.

"He might try to base it in one of the other mines, but they don't go directly under the loch," suggested the younger Iain.

"Too obvious," said Fraser. "If he's as wily as you say, he won't make it easy for you. In fact he'd have a better chance of hiding it if it was right under your nose."

"That's it!" said Liz.

"Ssshhhh," the three men chorused.

"What do you mean?" asked Iain senior.

"Do you remember what happened when we were in the Minster?" she asked.

"The Minster?" questioned Fraser and the younger Iain.

"Sorry, privileged information," replied Iain senior. "Fraser warned me about divulging details about the future," he explained, before answering Liz. "Okay, yes, I remember, Liz. What about it?"

"All that prayer and thought energy concentrated in one place," she suggested.

"Do you mean the old village church?" asked Iain senior.

"Why not? Who would suspect a church?" she explained.

"She does have a point," remarked Iain's younger self.

"Could she be right Fraser?" asked Iain senior.

"Unlikely, but not impossible!" Fraser replied. "What's the geology like around there?"

"Like everywhere else near the loch, rich in minerals." Iain's younger self replied.

"What about the strata? Has there been any evidence of seismic activity?"

Both Iain's thought for a moment before chorusing in stereo,

"Easter, 1736. The whole village was inside the church listening to Reverend Mackie when the whole building shook."

"A massive crack appeared in the spire wall and we all ran outside fearing the church was about to come crashing down on us," recalled Iain senior.

"I was thinking, a little more recently that that?" asked Fraser.

"Let's just say that the village has been known to move with the times," grinned Iain senior wryly.

Fraser began nodding as he worked out the probability, and the pros and cons in his head.

"If there's sufficient seismic activity beneath the church and Magnus is aware of that fact, then you may be right Liz," said Fraser.

Iain leaned across the table towards Fraser and dropped his voice to a whisper.

"If we manage to stop the vortex being created, will we get to go home?"

Fraser thought for a moment.

"You said earlier, that the mine where the vortex was created hadn't been developed.

"That's right," replied Iain senior.

"Technically speaking, if the original vortex isn't constructed or delayed, it will create a paradox with original outcome. Neither of you should be here, unless, he has managed to create an alternative vortex very close by within the same time frame or possibly earlier. In which case, if you stop this one from becoming active, then yes, you might return home," explained Fraser. "Incidentally, do you remember any of these events from your past?" Fraser asked Iain senior.

"That's what Liz asked me earlier. No. I have memories of this time, but not these ones."

"Interesting," Fraser commented. "The vortex seems to preserve memories and events prior to its creation."

"What does that mean?" asked Liz.

"Ohhh the obvious one is, that the vortex is itself, an epicentre of timeline diversity radiating different branches split from the original timeline into an infinite number of possibilities of which this is only one answer."

"I bet you wish you'd never asked," whispered Iain senior to Liz.

"So if we're here, what's happened to us on the other side of the vortex?" she asked.

"Hmmn. At a guess, I would say, you have just disappeared like the mysterious flight 19 that disappeared in the Bermuda Triangle, concluded Fraser. "Speaking of mysterious disappearances, did you find out what happened to Magnus after you came through the vortex?"

"There was no sign of him or the guards who disappeared just before us," replied Liz.

"Think. I need to know exactly what happened when the vortex was created and where you were when you disappeared?" asked Fraser.

"We 'disappeared' near the entrance to the mine, "said Iain senior. "Another few feet, and we would have made it."

"Okay. Now tell me what happened leading up to that," said the Professor.

"That's the complicated bit," confessed Iain senior. "It wasn't just a case of us trying to escape from the blasts and the rapidly flooding mine, though that was a nightmare in itself," he replied, as he looked at Liz. "Something else happened, I would say, more or less around the time the vortex happened."

Fraser raised his eyebrows.

"Go on," he encouraged.

"Liz changed."

"Changed? How exactly?" asked Fraser, further intrigued.

Iain explained his theory as simply as he could.

"It would certainly explain why she didn't recognise me or have any idea where she was," concluded Iain senior.

"And what do you remember of the actual event?" Fraser asked Liz.

"Nothing."

"Nothing?" he asked puzzled.

"I fell on the conveyor belt and hit my head. The next thing I knew, I was outside the mine with Iain. I couldn't remember a thing."

Fraser pondered the incident in his head.

"Was Liz confused in any way?" he asked.

"She wasn't concussed, if that's what you're driving at," answered Iain. "She was fully conscious and coherent. She was just different, like I was a complete stranger to her," Iain recalled.

"She'd physically changed places?" asked Fraser.

"I believe so," replied Iain senior.

"So, you believe the vortex caused Liz to trade places, a matter exchange," nodded Fraser. "And you switched back. Interesting," remarked Fraser. "What I can't understand, is why Iain came with you," added Fraser puzzled. "Something else must have happened to connect you in some way. Did Iain tell you what happened whilst you had been unconscious?"

"Yes."

"Was it exactly like your vision?" asked Fraser curiously.

"More or less," replied Liz.

"What do you mean, 'more or less'? Was it the same as your vision or not?" asked Fraser. "This is very important."

"It was exactly the same except for the kiss," she blushed.

"The kiss?" questioned Fraser and Iain's younger self.

"In my vision, Iain never kissed me whilst we were climbing out of the shaft, but when it actually happened, he apparently did."

Scratching his head again, Fraser asked.

"Did you tell Iain about your vision before the event happened?"

"Yes." she replied.

Fraser looked at Iain senior.

"What did I do?" Iain senior shrugged. "It was just a kiss!"

"We know what you did. Why did you change the event?" asked Fraser.

"I didn't know I'd changed anything until she told me afterwards. I just thought she left out that little detail originally, to avoid any embarrassment."

"Okay. Now tell me why you kissed her?"

"She was frightened. She needed a distraction from the danger. We were very close and I wanted to kiss her," Iain senior replied.

"So you didn't intentionally try to change anything?"

"Well, not exactly," he replied.

"Go on."

"The thought did cross my mind, that if I kissed her, it might make me more memorable," he confessed. "It was only a kiss. Okay, I admit, it was probably one of my better ones, but at the end of the day it was just a kiss. That's all."

Fraser shook his head.

"That's all?" muttered Fraser.

"What? I don't understand," said Iain senior quizzically.

"What happens when you kiss someone?" asked Fraser.

"What do you think happens? Lips meet! What else?" replied Iain.

"Exactly!" exclaimed Fraser.

"Eh?"

"If there was moisture on your lips, DNA could have been exchanged," Fraser explained.

"When you put it like that…" Iain remarked. "Talk about muddying an otherwise purely romantic gesture."

"I couldn't have put it better myself," laughed Fraser. "Muddying! That's exactly what you did! At a crucial point of time and during an energy exchange between Liz and her earlier self, you muddied her DNA. You transferred some of your DNA to her."

"We'd already done that earlier on," Iain muttered.

Fraser looked at Iain in disbelief.

"What? How the hell was I supposed to know we'd wind up in a vortex? Why does it matter that we exchanged DNA, as you put it?"

"With anybody else it probably wouldn't matter, but with you two, Liz is from the present, your DNA is originally from the 18th century. When you exchanged DNA, you exchanged time and wavelength boundaries within the jurisdiction of an equivalent time processor. If I'm right, both your DNA has now been corrupted or bonded together. Wherever one goes, the other will follow, to wherever and whoever the DNA link is strongest."

Iain and Liz looked at each other and then, thinking exactly the same thing, they looked down at the ring on Liz's wedding finger with suspicion.

Fraser saw the look on their faces.

"You did something else too, didn't you?" asked Fraser.

"Give a guy a break, will you!" Iain replied.

"What did he do Liz?"

Liz looked at Iain senior and lay down her left hand on the table in front of her.

"When I visited Iain back in 1746, he proposed to me. Iain placed his mother's wedding ring on my finger and I can't take it off!"

"Your mother's wedding ring?" asked Fraser.

"Yes!"

"18th century?"

"Yes!"

"With perhaps a little of your mother's DNA for good measure?" asked Fraser.

"Okay, okay! I get your point! I screwed up big time!" moaned Iain senior. "But I didn't know anything back then. How was I supposed to know that what I did in the heat of the moment would have consequences?" pleaded Iain senior. " So, what does it mean? What did I do?" he asked concerned.

"One of you may not be going home, no matter what happens. If Liz's DNA has stronger ties in the present then, when the timeline is 'restored' you'll both return to Liz's present. But if your DNA is stronger, then you could both end up back in the 18th century," explained Fraser.

Everyone around the table fell silent as the enormity of Fraser's words sank in.

"And you thought Magnus was the problem!" remarked Iain's younger self.

"Ssshh, I'm thinking," snapped Fraser. "So you two were right on the edge of the vortex whilst Magnus and his men were further in the mine, closer to the source?"

"Yes," replied Iain senior.

"Hmmn," sighed Fraser.

"Fraser, what are you thinking?" asked Iain senior.

"I think that kiss involving Liz's past self, also created the link to this time."

"But why here?" she asked.

"Iain's DNA link with the village and his home must be really strong. Are your parents buried here?" asked Fraser.

"In the old churchyard," chorused both Iain's looking at each other.

"There you are then!" concluded Fraser. "That's why you're here. Unless there's something else you haven't mentioned.

Liz looked at Iain.

"I don't think so."

"So how do we tackle Magnus?" asked Iain senior.

"Difficult to say," answered Fraser. "We can only guess at the moment. We need more information and some solid facts about what he's up to before we can plan anything. I suggest, that in the morning we do some investigation in the village and we check out the church," proposed Fraser. "But be warned, he could be nearby or he could have his spies out there," said Fraser. "I suggest we sleep on it, and meet again at breakfast to decide where we check out first. Agreed?" asked Fraser.

"Agreed." They chorused.

"If it's alright with you Liz," said Iain senior. "I need to stretch my legs and clear my head."

"I'll come with you," she replied.

"I think it would be safer if you stayed here in the hotel, Liz. I promise I won't be long. One of us should check the perimeter anyway, just in case there's anyone out there."

"I'll get my coat," said Iain's younger self.

"I don't think that's a good idea," said Fraser. "Both

of you together? That would be making it too easy for Magnus."

"I'll be fine," said Iain senior. "Don't worry."

" Liz, you look tired, "remarked Fraser. "I think it's time we retired for the evening."

"You're right, Fraser," she replied and rose obediently from the table, looking at each Iain in turn before making her departure. Iain's younger self trailed along behind them, leaving Ian senior heading out into the hallway alone.

"Will he be alright?" asked Liz anxiously, as she looked back over her shoulder at him as he stepped out of the hotel into the blackness.

"Liz, my dear, Iain just needs to sort out a few things in his head. Don't worry. It's important that we all get a good night's sleep tonight if we're to think with clear heads in the morning," he replied. "Try and rest."

"I will," she said as they reached the top of the stairs.

"Goodnight," said Fraser as they parted company.

"Goodnight Professor," replied Liz as she turned and headed off towards their room.

Minutes later, Liz had climbed into the large bed and lay staring up at the ceiling contemplating what Iain must be thinking as he walked alone, outside in the darkness. But as the moon rose high over Loch and shone down on the windows of their room, fatigue finally won its inevitable victory over her conscious mind and sleep prevailed.

Some time later, in the deep darkness and quiet of the night, Liz felt Iain's soft warm lips touch hers. She felt the silky light touch of his fingers against her skin and she responded unhesitant, like a willow gently moving and swaying in a summer breeze. Even in her semi sleepy state she could sense his excitement and his passionate thoughts. Remembering the thrill of their earlier union, she encouraged his attentions, reaching out to him dreamily in the darkness and welcoming him deep within her intimate realm. Then, as the moon cascaded its light through the windows, she watched his silhouetted body tower magnificently over her, with his face masked enigmatically by the shadows. A shiver of excitement rippled through her body, and Iain placed his fingers softly over her lips, fearing she might cry out. Then, gazing down at the magical crystal blueness of her eyes, he let go of all the despair and desperation he'd held locked up inside him. Tears of intense relief filled his eyes as he realised his dream.

Liz tore at the sheets with her hands, gasping at the ecstasy that pushed her pleasure to the point of pain. Unable to breathe in, Iain kissed her, filling her with his warm breath. Then, opening her eyes she stared wildly into the deep dark pools that led to his soul. Bound together, physically and spiritually, Liz felt complete and unburdened, yet something was minutely different. Tired and unsure that her instincts weren't just some kind of imaginary paranoia arising from the exceptional ordeals of the past few days, she chose to ignore them and drifted back into a blissfully contented sleep.

As she sighed deeply and turned on to her side, Iain's younger self quietly dressed and returned to the twin room he shared with Fraser. Then, climbing quietly into the single bed, he stared up at the ceiling, smiling with intimate satisfaction and delight.

Outside the hotel, gazing up at their bedroom window from the dry stone wall across the road, Iain senior sat nursing his raw, intimate, and emotional wounds beneath the shadows of the old village oak tree.

As he had returned from his thought clearing walk, Iain had spied the shadowy naked silhouette of his other self through the un-curtained bedroom window. Drawn by some bizarre, compulsive fascination, he had sat on top of the meadow wall, transfixed by the intimate betrayal being played out before him. Closing his eyes, he could see Liz clearly through the eyes of his younger self as he shared the new memory of that moment, that was now being transplanted into his mind. He was there too. He could see and remember the fire inside him. He could feel the softness of her skin beneath his touch and the smell her sweetness like springtime after the rain. He felt her body yielding to his and he gasped in unison with his younger self, as they shared that singular crescendo of intimate pleasure. This wasn't someone else making love to Liz. He was making love to her.

Despite his warnings, Iain's younger self had succumbed to temptation and seized his opportunity. Iain senior knew instinctively, that Liz was ignorant of the betrayal and vowed never to expose it. Gasping with despair at his unique plight, he stared teary eyed into the night sky, praying for an answer to the disturbing conundrum in his head.

"You bloody fool," he whispered softly to himself. "She warned you of the risks and you just let it happen," he chastised himself.

All he could do for her now, was to hope for her continued ignorance of the betrayal. For himself, he prayed for forgiveness, the purging of his memory and the absolution of his shame.

CHAPTER 22

As HIS EYES BLURRED WITH the pools of his shame a sharp edged familiar voice reached out from the night to him.

"Painful, isn't it to watch your life torn apart piece by piece? It claws at your insides like a farmer's rake!"

Iain ignored the voice, believing it to be nothing more than his own aggrieved broken heart seeking revenge. Then he felt the course fibrous knot of the old fisherman's rope as it dragged across his bare skin at the front of his neck. Jumping to his feet in surprise, he felt the rope rapidly tighten and burn his skin as the voice, just as coarse, burned his ears with its spite.

"Where I come from, this is how we treat traitors, we give them good measure of a hangman's rope!"

Iain struggled and tried to swallow as the knot crushed like a stone against his throat. This was not the voice of his heart seeking revenge. This was the voice of his black hearted soulless nemesis, Mad Magnus McGregor!

"Easy now! We don't want that pretty neck of yours broken before I've had a chance to enjoy the sweet taste of revenge!"

"Revenge! I thought you tried that already," mocked Iain. "and as I recall, you failed miserably! You failed at my birthday! You failed with Liz! You failed back there, in the mine! You don't seem to be having much luck on that score, do you?" teased Iain. "Why don't you just give it a rest? Accept defeat gracefully and retire."

"I won't give up until you and yours are wiped off the face of this planet!"

"Now that's where you keep making your biggest mistake," remarked Iain. "You take things far too personally!"

"You made this personal when you took her from me!"

"You mean, Lorna?" asked Iain.

"Yes!" Magnus growled.

"I didn't 'take' her. I rescued her."

"You ruined my plans!"

"Aaah, now that I do agree with. Guilty as charged, and proud of it!" Iain grinned wryly, pushing his despair to the back of his mind.

"You'll not be grinning when you see what I have in store for your lady friend," Magnus sneered.

"You love to torture your women, don't you? Has nobody ever told you that just a few words of flattery, and a nice bunch of flowers go a long way on a first date, far better than threats and cold hearted brutality. They just don't cut the mustard I'm afraid!" Iain teased. "You could tidy yourself up a bit too. A good haircut, a clean shave, smart outfit ….They could do wonders for your image!"

"Shut up!"

"Speaking of brutal, ill mannered, ugly and evil megalomaniacs, where's your other half? Busy winning first prize in a gurning competition is he?"

"You'll find out soon enough," sneered Magnus.

"Right then, what are we waiting for?" asked Iain. "I'm here! You're here! Let's get the party started!" he teased as Magnus towered over him.

"Enough!" barked Magnus knocking Iain down on to his knees.

"Touchy, aren't we!" replied Iain.

"I said enough!" yelled Magnus vehemently. "You ruined my life, both of you and now it's time for some pay back!"

"Wait a minute! We didn't ruin your life! You did that to yourself!" retorted Iain awkwardly just as Magnus tightened the rope. "Trying to choke me won't change the truth!" spluttered Iain. "It was your deceit, your villainy that brought us here! Wherever you came from, whoever you were. We had no part in that! The credit is all yours!" he continued as Magnus began to seethe.

Iain's eyes began to sparkle as he looked up at his determined and embittered foe.

"That's it isn't it! You were a monster long before Lorna or I came on the scene. Something happened that flipped you into the monster you are today! What happened? Did somebody humiliate you?"

Magnus' face blackened and his right fist shot out reactively, powerful in its rage, hitting Iain squarely on the jaw and knocking him backwards.

"Push me too far, and I will kill you right here, right now!" growled Magnus.

"Promises, promises! That's all you're good for, but it doesn't mean that you'll do it, does it?" goaded Iain, preparing himself for another attack. "You're like a pair of badly hemmed trousers….. just a big let down!"

Magnus grabbed Iain by the rope around his neck and pulled Iain's face close to his.

"So you think I don't enjoy killing people and watching them die? Well, you're wrong!" Magnus hissed into Iain's face. "Nothing will give me the greatest pleasure more than watching you die!" he confessed. "Except, perhaps, seeing your agony when your lover knows the truth about your darker side!"

"And what 'truth' is it that, Magnus? What is it that you

think you know about me?" growled Iain deeply, like a lion disturbed from his slumber.

"I have eyes! I have ears to witness your pathetic dark betrayal this night! What fool walks away and allows his substitute to rape his woman? I've watched you! I've watched them! I saw the little drama in the car park earlier on! You've inflicted more pain on yourself this night with your irresponsible neglect, than I could ever dream of inflicting on you in a century of physical torture!" gloated Magnus.

Iain said nothing. He had no intention of feeding the ears and mouth of such an evil contemptible soul. Neither was he foolish enough to believe that he could obtain absolution from this purveyor of evil. Whatever punishment he was owed for his actions, Iain was determined to face it head on, even if it meant losing the most important person in his life. Dragging the already tormented and defeated shepherd into the middle of the road in front of the hotel, Magnus signalled to his men to come out from behind the dry stone wall behind him.

"You know what to do!" He commanded, and watched as the dozen or so men broke through the front door of the hotel and proceeded up the stairs to the rooms on the first floor.

"Been here long?" asked Iain curiously. "You almost look as if you had this all planned out!"

"Thanks to your sabotage, I've been here three years, with ample time to plan what I'd do when you appeared!" confessed Magnus.

"Indulge me. How exactly did you know we'd turn up here, now?"

"I'm surprised you haven't figured it out for yourself, Mr Lachlan! I knew when you turned up, you'd most likely try to contact yourself or your professor friend to help you.

It was simply a case of placing a tap on your phone and the professor's and waiting," sneered Magnus.

"Well, at least you haven't got around to the mine yet," muttered Iain.

"Did you really think I'd make the same mistake twice?"

"What do you mean?" asked Iain anxiously.

"The real power behind this valley isn't just the superconductive properties of the mines around here, it is the transverse fault line that runs beneath the Loch itself and the old village church, before passing beneath your cottage and up into the mountain. The leak of seismic electromagnetic energy into the centre of the loch bed is what gives the loch its powerful currents. The church marks the epicentre of that leak," explained Magnus.

"That must be why Liz was able to pick up their message," Iain mumbled to himself, as the pieces of the puzzle clicked together in his head. The energy radiating out from the epicentre beneath the church must have boosted the signal from the residue thought energy in his ancestor's graves and combined it with the conscious prayer energy trapped within the building itself, he concluded. With no mass and no gravity to affect it, his ancestor's energy signal could travel whenever and wherever it liked. It could also act as a homing beacon pulling other energy in. But why pull Liz in? Why had his ancestors picked her? Was she simply just the first person with the right ability to pick up their signal? Was he simply the first Lachlan to possess the right qualities to assure the future of his family into the next millennium? But more curiously, if he was right, how could they have known how he'd feel about her?

Suddenly motivated away from his guilt he rose to his feet defiantly, with renewed vigour and determination.

Curious of his sudden recovery from his self imposed despair, Magnus gripped Iain's leash and watched him suspiciously.

Iain watched as the light came on in their bedroom and he listened to the shrillness of her screams and the bellowing of their voices, as Liz was awoken and forced around the room. Suddenly she appeared at the window briefly and began banging on the glass and screaming out his name. Then almost immediately, they pulled her back and dragged her down the stairs behind a bleary eyed Fraser and his defiant younger self. One by one the rest of the lights in the other hotel rooms came on, as the residents awoke to the sounds of tramping boots stampeding along the corridor and down the stairs.

Suddenly, Liz, Fraser and his younger self emerged from the hotel, the guards pushing them along with the butts of their guns, towards Iain. Kicking the backs of Iain's legs, Magnus forced him back down on to his knees as Liz screamed, "No!" and ran towards him. Magnus tightened the rope around Iain's neck and Liz stopped in her tracks, as the guards flanked her on either side and restrained her.

"You bastard, Magnus! Let him go! Let him go right now!" Liz demanded angrily.

Magnus handed the rope to one of his guards and strolled arrogantly towards her. Liz's bright blues sparkled fiercely with the glow from the old street lamp, as she glared vehemently at their loathsome self-sworn enemy. As Magnus neared her, she lurched forward but the guards pulled her back. Magnus lifted his head and sniffed the air like a blood hound homing in on his wounded prize, as he slowly and predatorily paced around her.

"Mmmmmn There's nothing quite like the smell of a woman's fear and vulnerability in the presence of a man," remarked Magnus as he lifted some of her wavy hair with his fingers and inhaled its scent. "Can't you smell it Mr Lachlan?

You've certainly seen that look before haven't you?" Magnus announced as he gently stroked her soft tear stained cheek before grasping her chin between his fingers and parting her salty lips with his. Liz bit sharply and snagged the corner of Magnus' bottom lip. Jumping back, he ran his tongue over the small wound she'd inflicted and struck her face hard with his flat hand.

"Bitch!" he bellowed. "Do that again, and he dies! Do you understand?"

Liz looked over Magnus' shoulder to Iain, terrified of losing him. Iain gazed back at her, strong in his resolve now, to see this through to the end. Liz squirmed as Magnus forced his mouth on hers once more, knowing how Iain felt about his recent betrayal. Then stepping to one side, Magnus took hold of her long golden hair and pulled her head carefully backwards and faced Iain.

"You see? Everyone has their price Mr Lachlan? Everybody can be malleable you just have to know which button to press? But I wonder..." he paused savouring the tension of the moment. "I wonder how far she will go for you, Mr Lachlan?" he gloated as Iain remained cool and calm. "Take her down to the church!" ordered Magnus to one of the guards. "The attendants are waiting to prepare her!"

"Get your damned hands off me!" she snarled as the guard tried to grasp her arm. "Touch me again....." she threatened. Unperturbed by her aggressive protestations, the guard grabbed her and swung her firmly forwards. Spinning round to face him, Liz flicked her right leg up and kicked his chin upwards before quickly raising her foot again and pushing him sharply backwards.

"Run Liz!" Shouted Iain. "Run!"

Pausing, only for a second, to make the briefest of eye contact with Iain, she gazed anxiously into his distant pride filled eyes and nodded, before turning back towards the loch and sprinting off into the darkness.

"After her!" yelled Magnus.

Two of the nearby guards did as they were bid and set off in pursuit, disappearing quickly down the lane into the darkness, until only the sound of their clomping boots could be heard in the distance.

Iain looked up at Magnus.

"What are you planning to do to her if you catch her?"

Magnus didn't answer. He wanted nothing to spoil the surprise and horror of what he had in store for them. Then looking up at the sky, he saw the fullness of the moon as it approached its zenith, and noticed its red lined halo.

"Take them down to the church!" Magnus ordered. "It's nearly time."

"Time for what? What are you going to do? Trigger another quake?" asked Iain.

"Move!" yelled Magnus.

Two guards immediately flanked Iain on either side whilst the others flanked Fraser and Iain's younger self. Behind the safety of the curtains, several hotel residents peeped from their windows to watch the unorthodox parade march down the lane towards the village church.

Turning off the lane on to the side street leading to the church, Fraser, Iain and his younger self beheld the beauty of the brightly lit ornate stained glass windows of the church. On top of the central spire, a complex array of transmitters and receivers had been constructed, that reached far up into the night sky, masked from the village by the dense green foliage of the tall trees surrounding the churchyard.

"What's he trying to do?" whispered Iain's younger self to Fraser. "Talk to God?"

"Not quite," Fraser replied.

"He told me that the church is sitting on top of a fault

line," muttered Iain senior. "I'm guessing here, but I think he's using the church to amplify the energy signal and direct it straight into the electromagnetic field anomaly above the loch. But I don't remember seeing anything like this above or inside the mine where he constructed the last device."

"You mentioned earlier that there were explosions followed by flooding in the heart of the mine?"

"Yes. He also had a sonic Tesla device for vibrating the rock at a specific frequency," replied Iain senior.

"It's possible that the different ores within the mine would have impaired the signal. Then again, if the deepest part of the mine was below the loch, and the anomaly lies somewhere above it, he wouldn't need to direct the signal. When he triggered the quake, the seismic electromagnetic energy would radiate straight up into it. Placing his device in the church, he needs to direct the transmission from the epicentre of the fault line into the heart of the anomaly."

"So he is trying to recreate the vortex?" asked Iain's younger self.

"It's very likely," replied Fraser. "And because seismic power source is fixed and accessible, he will have a certain degree of control, fixing its co-ordinates into any equipment he uses. This isn't just a one way trip he's planning. He's organising regular expeditions."

"But why?" asked Iain's younger self.

"Why would anyone want to control where they were in time?" asked Iain senior. "Power, money and revenge!"

The guard to the left of Iain, nudged him further forward with the butt of his gun.

"Move!"

"Right, fine. I'm going," retorted Iain.

The gate leading into the churchyard was open and guarded by two of Magnus' sentries. Stepping aside and standing to attention, the sentries cleared the way for the parade to pass through. Just around the corner, the two half doors providing entry into the church itself, stood open, casting the yellow and white light from within, out into the churchyard. Magnus led the way and the rest followed behind.

Stepping through the short vestibule into the main part of the building, the three prisoners halted momentarily to take in their surroundings. The centre of the church, directly below the spire, had been completely cleared of the regimented rows of antique wooden pews, and in there place stood an eight feet long caplet shaped metal cylinder which had wires and cables attached to it. Following the cables, Fraser noticed that they radiated out across the floor and trailed up the walls to a central hub suspended below the spire. The gift shop, housed in the recess halfway down the church, had been converted into a control room, to manage all the technical equipment and ahead of them, at the far end of the church, where the altar had stood, the platform had been taken over with all manner of medical equipment including beds, scanners, heart monitors. Sentries guarded the control room and medical attendants wearing white coats and surgical gloves hovered on the platform expectantly.

"Why do I get the feeling you've been consulting Mary Shelley lately?" asked Iain senior. "I thought you wanted to control time? What's the floatation tank for?"

"Since our last encounter, I have modified my plans. Having tapped into the seismic field below the church, I no longer need to generate the quake to trigger the vortex. I can simply activate the device pulling in the power directly from the seismic fracture and feed it straight into the anomaly," explained Magnus proudly as his other self appeared from the control room.

"Why the receiver? I thought you wanted to place yourself at the heart of the vortex. You never did explain how you'd planned to do that in the mine," asked Iain senior.

"I have Miss Curran to thank for that!" replied Magnus. "You could say, her projection in the Laird's hall 'sparked' an idea in my head," he chuckled. "Similar to the detention chamber where I kept her suspended within the manmade anomalous field, my experts applied similar principles to my projection chamber. I may not have the academic prowess or technical skills to explain exactly how it was done, but put in simple terms, we created a polarity force field around the chamber's hull to deflect the rock and the water around it and to allow it to be repelled by the seismic energy field from the quake, into the anomaly, like a cork from a bottle."

Fraser shook his head.

"Damned amateurs."

"What was that?" asked Magnus.

"That's impossible! It would never have worked."

"What went wrong Magnus?" asked Iain senior. "We know you didn't have a lot of time after the first explosion was triggered, and you obviously didn't escape from the mine."

"Thanks to you, the rupture in the earth's crust occurred before I could make it to the chamber. I was caught in the field ripple and suddenly found myself here, three years ago. Not exactly where I wanted to be, but as you can see, it has given me the opportunity to work with my other self and a second chance to develop the device."

The second Magnus, who wore a medical gown beneath his lab coat, faced the three men as his counterpart replaced him in the control room.

"This time," he began. "We won't be propelling into the anomaly directly. We'll be harnessing the power of the vortex and pulling it into the isolation chamber. Lightening in a bottle, so to speak, " Magnus boasted.

"What about Liz? Where does she fit into all this?" asked Iain.

Just at that moment, there was a commotion at the back of the church behind them, and all eyes turned to see a very wet, battered and bedraggled Liz being dragged into the church. Her face and arms were bruised, and a small trickle of blood ran down the side of her mouth. Iain's eyes sparkled to see her again as she shrugged her shoulders.

"I told you not to harm her!" bellowed Magnus angrily, his voice resonating around the church.

"Yes Sir, but…."

"No excuses!" he interrupted. Then turning to the attendants he commanded, "She's all yours! Get her cleaned up and prepped now!"

"Yes Sir," they chorused and gathered around Liz before spiriting her away behind the screens in the medical area.

"Now that our last guest has arrived I can answer your question Mr Lachlan," Magnus began. "But first, a little test," he grinned sadistically. "Stand them both over their," ordered Magnus to the guards flanking both Iains and pointing to the open space in the opposite recess.

The guards pulled both of them across to the recess and stood them a short distance apart, before stepping back out of harms way with their guns poised.

"Let's see if the theory that the past, present and future do exist simultaneously, shall we?" Magnus asked as he pulled a small compact revolver from inside his jacket and fired a single shot at Iain's younger self, striking him just above his right knee. Both Iains cried out and the younger Iain clutched at his leg as a steady stream of blood flowed through his fingers. Then turning to Iain senior who was also clutching his leg, Magnus commanded,

"Straighten him up and remove the rope!"

The guard did as he was bid and Iain rubbed the

reddened raw flesh of his neck with one hand, as soon as the rope was removed, and grasped at the throbbing ache above his right knee with his other hand.

"Wound the younger one and you wound both!"

"Same goes for you Magnus! Remember that!" snapped Iain senior.

"Leave them alone!" screamed Liz as she was escorted from behind the screen wearing only a hospital gown. "I'll do whatever you want, but leave them alone!"

"Oh I have no doubt you will, Miss Curran, especially when I let you in on your lover's secret!" sniped Magnus sadistically.

"Be careful Magnus," croaked Fraser. "If you say or do anything that alters the events in Ian's past, you also run the risk of altering your own timeline too!" he warned. "Hurt Liz or kill her now and you could wind up back where you started in 1746! Do you really want that?" warned Fraser.

"Shut him up, now!" roared Magnus. "Now!!"

The guard holding Fraser pulled out a gag from his jacket pocket and fastened it around Fraser's mouth.

"He's right Magnus!" shouted Iain senior. "You're playing with a fire you don't understand!"

"Don't I?" Magnus retorted. "Perhaps you'd care to enlighten us on your experience in that area, Mr Lachlan! You know what it's like to suffer the consequences of interference. Being in close proximity with your other self, you know the effect that has on both your behaviours!" he teased.

"What's he talking about?" asked Liz mystified.

Iain senior thought about what Magnus had said, and wondered what they could have overlooked. Looking at Fraser's gagged face, he searched for clues to help him figure it out.

As soon as Iain senior made eye contact with him, Fraser

discreetly looked down at his feet and using his heel, slowly and carefully drew positive and negative symbols on the floor of the church. Iain senior puzzled for a moment as to what Fraser was trying to convey. Then the penny dropped causing a resounding splash of realisation in his mind. How could he have not seen it before? Magnus had obviously learned the drawbacks in his three years there, Iain observed, noting how Magnus maintained significant distance from his counterpart. Maybe it wasn't just direct contact with your other self that could have dire consequences. Maybe proximity was an issue too! Maybe there was a biochemical consequence of two identical people existing on the same time plain, just like identical twins. Twins! That was it!

In his studies as a researching psychologist, Iain had come across several cases of identical twins who, although they even looked identical, behaved in opposition to each other. In some cases, the first born twin had claimed seniority over the other, taking the commanding role and displaying highly competitive and ambitious tendencies whilst the latter became more submissive and introverted. Iain had considered how their lack of visible uniqueness appeared to drive them apart temperamentally, almost polarising their personalities, in their desperate battle to be different from each other. The closer they lived together, the greater the difference between their behaviours. For non-identical twins, with their visible uniqueness, opposing personalities wasn't such an issue, he'd found.

Since their arrival in this time, Iain senior had noticed that his other younger self had been noticeably moodier, darker in his attitude and less tolerant too, like himself on a once-in-a-blue-moon bad day. Then he thought back to his other self's determination to be with Liz and the deceitful way he had taken advantage of the opportunity to make his move. This was not who he was, Iain concluded. In fact, thinking back to how he had felt a year ago, Iain realised the stark difference in their personalities. He realised too, that if they were both going to get out of this situation, they would need to stay well apart but drive Magnus #1 and #2 closer together.

"Don't you think she has a right to know?" Magnus goaded.

"Know what exactly?" asked Iain.

"Will somebody please tell me what's going on?" demanded Liz.

"Ah, Miss Curran, I see it falls to me to enlighten you to your lover's darker side," Magnus began, as the attendants began to attach various wires to Liz's head and sensors to her arms and legs.

Fraser tried to speak out but his gag blocked his words.

"You're treading on icy ground Magnus," warned Iain senior.

"Then if you care, Mr Lachlan, why don't you tell her? Why don't you ask her how it felt?" Magnus snapped.

Magnus #2 strolled over to where Liz stood in her hospital gown and whispered teasingly in her ear as Iain senior look on, anxiously.

"I observed a man enter your room tonight," Magnus grinned. "I watched him make love to you and I saw how you enjoyed it."

"Is that all, you dirty peeping Tom? What's the matter, did it make you jealous? Or perhaps with your background, you think it should be a burning offence for a woman to enjoy the company of her husband in bed! You need to keep pace with the times!" she replied. "Of course Iain made love to me!"

"Yes. But which one?" he asked, knowing the answer.

"What do you mean, 'which one'?" retorted Liz as Magnus grinned gleefully.

Then, looking at both Iain's standing in the recess, other than the clothes they were wearing she noticed they seemed more identical now than they had done when she first arrived. The Iain from this time had seemed slightly older in the hotel at dinner, than the Iain she was acquainted with. But now, strangely, they looked the same. Only one thing could have changed his appearance like that, and the truth made her blood run cold. Her instincts that night had been right. There had been something different about him and the difference was the man himself.

She had to think quickly. Magnus, being the monster that he was, stood behind her, relishing the bizarre emotional triangle that now existed between herself and both Iains. She could feel his hot breath on the back of her neck and his hands, surprisingly gentle on her shoulders. She didn't have to be genius to figure out that he wanted her for himself and to get her, he had to drive her away from the man she loved. He had to destroy her trust in Iain. However wrong Iain's younger self had been, to do what he had done, she did not want to play into Magnus' hands. If they were all going to get out of this alive, Liz was going to have to take a chance and hope that Iain would pick up on her game plan.

"Stop it!" she suddenly cried. "I don't want to know!"

"Mr. Lachlan and I met up on his return to the hotel. He never returned to your room! He never returned to make love to you!" gloated Magnus.

Carefully employing the real pain she felt inside, she willed herself to stay in control whilst allowing her tears to flow for full dramatic effect.

"How could you leave me? How could you let him do it?" she cried as Magnus lay his falsely sympathetic arms around her. His touch made her feel sick inside, but she soldiered on with her performance.

"What do you want me to do?" she sobbed as Magnus walked around to face her.

"I need your help my dear," he replied softly. "I need some of your regenerative energy to protect me against the destructive aspects of the vortex. I need you to share your unique field frequency with me so that I might begin my journey."

"And how do I do that?" she asked quietly.

"Well, I can take it from you forcefully or, if you prefer, you could give it to me in a way that might even the score with those two over there," suggested Magnus. "Together we will enter the isolation chamber and we will monitor your heart rate and field energy generation during our liaison. Once you have generated your protective field around us as you did in the hotel room, the device will be activated."

Liz thought carefully for a moment.

"Okay," she sighed. "But I'll need a moment to myself to clear my thoughts and my feelings," she said as she looked into Magnus' dark and soulless eyes. "I need you to excite me," she whispered into Magnus' ear as she softly ran her fingers beneath his lab coat.

"You lay a hand on her and I swear I'll kill you!" yelled Iain senior.

Magnus looked deeply into Liz's sparkling blue eyes, searching for trickery and deceit, as he felt the soft caress of her left hand on his trousers. Her lips parted gently and he imagined the feeling of her body next to his. Closing her eyes and entering his thoughts, she provocatively walked through the darkness of his soul, shining like a candle against the blackness. In his mind, he gazed at her perfect naked form as he removed her gown. Pulling her tightly to him, he pressed his rough mouth to hers.

As Magnus #1 sat at the control panel, the thoughts of his other younger self invaded his head. Raising his head above the monitor, he could see his other self wrapped around Liz and fumed. As the images in his mind became more clear and he felt what his other self felt, his anger boiled. She belonged to him. After everything he'd been through, he had no intention of handing his victory and his prize over to his younger self. The more he seethed the more his other self weakened in Liz's embrace. His thoughts became more malleable as her image flaunted her body at him in his mind.

Distracted by her attentions, Magnus#2 failed to notice the removal of his gun until he felt the end of its barrel against his trousers.

"One wrong move," she whispered. "and I blow your nuts off!"

Suddenly Magnus#1 came rushing out of the control room shouting,

"Grab her!"

Iain smiled as she pushed Magnus around to face them and moved the gun barrel to his neck.

"Drop your weapons and get over there beside the isolation tank!" she yelled. "Move it, now!"

As the guards and the other personnel moved to wards the isolation tank, Liz backed away towards the two Iain's, pulling Magnus #2 with her as a body shield.

"One of you free Fraser. One of you get the guns off the guards," Liz instructed both Iains.

"I'll get the guns," said Iain senior, doubtful of his younger self's loyalty.

Iain's younger self marched across the church to Fraser, untied him and removed the gag from his mouth.

"Stay here with me," he whispered dryly to Iain. "We need to take a look at those controls.

Once Iain senior had collected the guns, he returned to stand beside Liz.

"I'm sorry about leaving you alone earlier on," he whispered to her. "I didn't know he was going to do that."

"It's not your fault. We can discuss it later," she replied assertively.

"Wow, you're sexy when you're in charge," he whispered into her ear.

She smiled.

"Fraser! How are you doing over there?" yelled Iain senior across the church.

"I need a few minutes to remove the panels and figure out how to disarm it," replied Fraser.

"I wouldn't do that if I were you," remarked Magnus #1. "You should know me by now Mr Lachlan! Do you seriously think I wouldn't design such a device without a few precautionary booby traps for good measure?"

"If that's the way you want to play it," replied the younger Iain. "Iain, get them into the isolation chamber!"

"But we still need to know how to disarm the device!" replied Iain senior.

"I have an idea about that one," said Liz. "Catch!"

Tossing her gun to Iain senior she dragged Magnus #2 over to the isolation chamber and tying him to a chair with a roll of electrician's tape that lay close to hand. Then, striding over to Magnus #1 she grabbed hold of his arm. Magnus resisted.

"Don't make me use this!" shouted Iain senior.

"If you shoot me, what difference do you think that will make?" he taunted, buying for time.

"There'll be one less maniac in the world!"

"Don't listen to him!" shouted Liz.

"Move it, Magnus!" yelled Iain senior. "Or do you want me to enjoy tying you up like your other half?"

"You underestimate me, Mr Lachlan!" he said as he backed towards the control room. "I have no intention of giving in to you, not this time, not ever!"

Iain senior advanced towards him.

"Iain stay where you are!" shouted Liz. "I've been inside his head I know what he's trying to do!"

"Do you my dear! Maybe you saw what I wanted you to see! Maybe I've learned a trick or two, myself, in the last three years I've been stuck here!"

Quickly fumbling in his pocket, he pressed the keys on his tiny remote.

"Like I said, you underestimate me, Mr Lachlan!"

Suddenly four of the large flat stones on the church floor lifted up on hydraulic arms and pivoted to reveal the crypt below. Nearing cautiously towards the opening, Liz peered over the edge whilst Iain senior aimed the gun at Magnus #1. Looking down she could see a familiar and extremely frightened face staring back up at her. Slightly younger than the last time Liz had seen her, there was no mistaking the bottle blond voluptuous figure of Janice, clad in a tight clinging dress with just the protrusion of a luminous pink bra through a rip in her bodice. Strapped to a metal cradle with a gag in her mouth and connected to a small cylinder of milky white liquid, Janice looked unsurprisingly puzzled when the stranger above her shouted out her name.

"Iain it's, Janice! The bastard's got Janice strapped to some kind of cylinder!"

"Let's just call her my little insurance policy, shall we?" grinned Magnus #1.

"Why did you have to involve her?" yelled Liz. "She doesn't know anything about all this!"

"Call it an unfortunate sequence of events," Magnus #1 replied. "My guards turned up too late to way-lay the younger Mr Lachlan there, but managed to bag this prize loitering in his office. I didn't think she was your type, Mr Lachlan! Or had you allowed your standards to drop over the years!"

"Let her go Magnus! Let them all go! This is between me and you!"

"Very well, Mr Lachlan," sighed Magnus #1. "Drop the guns and kick them across the floor. Now!"

"Not until, Liz, Janice, Fraser and Iain are out of here!" demanded Iain senior.

"I don't think you're in any position to make special requests Mr. Lachlan! Drop the guns!" roared Magnus defiantly or I press this button right here!"

Removing the small remote switch from his pocket, Magnus #1 held out the device and hovered his thumb over the red left hand button.

"When I press this button, the white milky liquid will be released from the cylinder and pumped into the drip that's attached to the young lady's arm. Once that begins you will have just one minute before the liquid, a fatal poison, reaches her arm. Now, drop the guns!"

Slowly, Iain senior lowered the guns to the ground and then straightened up again.

"Kick them away from you!" ordered Magnus #1.

Iain flicked the guns away across the stone floor with his foot.

"That's better Mr. Lachlan! Now I will have the pleasure of killing you in front of your friends!" Magnus grinned, as he retrieved a small gun from within his coat and aimed it at Iain.

Vaulting into Magnus' line of fire as the shot rang out, Liz screamed,

"No!" one split second before the shot struck her and blew her backwards towards Iain. The silence was overwhelming, deafening, pounding in her head to the exclusion of everything else around her. Just like that day in the science laboratory at school, the actions of those around her slowed to an almost standstill as her body impacted with the ground below her. Then, he was beside her, clambering on the ground and lifting her shattered bloody body. Magnus cursed and yelled at his attendants to fetch the medical supplies realising what her death would bring.

Iain's younger self held back in the control room as Fraser rushed over to where Liz lay. Iain senior lifted her head gently in his arms, and for one final time, he swept the golden waves of her hair from her face.

"Easy now," he whispered softly. "Try not to move."

"Iain," she whispered weakly. "I love you. I don't regret a single minute being with you."

"Ssshhh, stay quiet now. Conserve your strength," he whispered and kissed her brow.

"I need you to listen, both of you," she began, and reached out to Iain and Fraser, stroking their faces lightly with her delicate fingers. "When I am gone, time will reset. How far back for each of us, I'm uncertain. For me, it may take me back before the original vision and projection that started me on this journey. If it does, then Iain, you will return to the point of your true origin, back to your home, and this will become just a bad dream in your mind. Magnus may have undone our future together and your past with his deeds, but he will be pulled back too. The vortex will never be created. The cycle must be broken and it can only be broken by me. My ability was an accident that was never meant to happen and the balance must be restored," she coughed as the pool of dark scarlet grew on her chest and she choked on the blood in her mouth.

"Liz! Don't leave me! For God sake, somebody get some help!" Iain senior screamed at the onlookers to their plight. "Do something!" he yelled angrily, then he felt her touch and heard her softer words. Looking once more into the crystal blue depths of her sparkling eyes, he listened.

"I love you and always will. I will never forget you, no matter where we find ourselves. Never lose hope," she whispered as she used the last strength she had to pull herself up and kiss him. Fraser, supported her as she gently pressed her mouth to Iain's and this time, tasted the salt of his tears and felt his strong protective arms around her.

"It's cold, Iain. Hold me close," she said, and Iain held her tightly to his chest and felt her heart pounding close to his. As the deafening silence overcame her and she struggled to hear his last words to her, her heart slowed and then suddenly stopped. Her head slumped against his chest and her arms dropped limply by her sides. His angel of time was gone and with her the dream of a present and future happiness never destined to be. The despairing cry from his shattered soul radiated outwards into the night and touched the latent remnant energy of his ancestors. Weeping inconsolably with the savage pain of his raw grief, Iain yelled his despair and anger at the stained glass window above what had once been the church altar. The bright light of the full moon shone through the beautiful array of colours in the glass, and cast a rainbow of light down on the beautiful soul he had quested almost three centuries to find. She had saved his life and his youth so many times with her energy and now she had saved it with her fragile, physical body too.

The stars shimmered in the inky black night sky outside the church and a tremor rippled along the timeline and across multiple dimensions, spreading its impact throughout the universal wavelength and across the web of time.

CHAPTER 23

IT WAS EARLY AUTUMN AND the heather on the hills and mountains surrounding Libran's Loch resembled a patchwork quilt of mottled red and vivid purple heather blossom. The leaves on the trees had begun to turn golden and red, shining and rustling like bags of copper pennies in the afternoon breeze.

With his heart heavy laden with the grief of her departure, Iain left the Laird's mansion, just as Captain McGregor was led out of the court yard in heavy chains. Placed onboard a peasant drawn wooden cart, the Captain was flanked on either side by the sheriffs riding alongside on horseback. Recognising Iain, despite his change of dress back into his kilt and shirt, the Captain scowled bitterly as the cart clattered over the cobbles towards the main gate.

"Fear the shadows and guard your back well, shepherd," warned the Captain. ".. for we will meet again! And next time, you won't have your witch to save you, and I will have my revenge!" Then standing up in the back of the cart, struggling to keep his balance amidst the heavy shackles and creaking uneven timbers across the floor of the cart, he yelled," Make the most of every day, shepherd, because when I return, that day will be your last!" he threatened.

"Sit down Captain!" commanded the sheriff. "Or I'll make you walk all the way to Edinburgh.

"Run and hide shepherd! Run and hide far away from here," he bellowed menacingly. "…. because when I return,

I will find you!" shouted the Captain, "and when I do, be ready to die!"

There was a sudden thud as the weighted leather cosh struck the back of the Captain's head and his body collapsed unconsciously on to the floor of the cart.

Iain could barely hear the Captain's final words in the distance, above the clattering on the cobbles. Standing for a moment, he watched as the rickety cart finally disappeared through the trees, before solemnly making his descent to the loch side, to his boat. A sudden warm breeze whipped around him, stirring up the heaps of fallen golden leaves at his feet, and for just one wish filled second, he thought he heard her voice calling to him through the rustling leaves. Reluctant and unexpected tears misted his eyes turning the light from the afternoon sun into a blaze of drifting gold shining down on him through the trees, like the golden cascading tresses of her hair. The ethereal glow of her remembered face held him firmly in its grasp, as the memory of her haunted his soul. In a moment, the illusion was gone and warm bitter sweet tears fell upon his cold mournful cheeks, tracing the lines of his face like a trail of soft whispered kisses.

Though he'd barely known her for a few hours, their time spent together had etched lifetime lasting impressions in his mind. Now that he knew she existed, the detailed childhood images that had sustained his hopes and dreams through the years, now lost their meaning against the reality of her presence. Replaced by the memories of recent events and the new emotions she had invoked within him, he could find no solace in their viewing alone, only a gaping black chasm of loneliness. Not since the tragic passing of his parents two years ago, had he felt such grief, a pain so deep and so sharp that it cut through him keener than the finest French blade. Like the strong winds that blew through the perennial steadfast forest around him, she had blown into his predictable but resilient life and devastated the monotony of the only existence he'd ever known. No image could satisfy the longing he felt for her deep inside. She had opened the Pandora's box to his unknown and unspent desires and only she could quench those fires within him. She exuded life, spirit, a wealth of possibilities far beyond his humble imagination. She made him feel more alive than he'd ever felt before. She would come back to him, of that he was certain. She had to, she needed to, he had seen it in her eyes. For both of them, the alternative was unthinkable. Whatever it took, however long he had to wait, he knew she'd come back.

The golden sunlight twinkled on the gentle ripples of the loch, as Iain un-tethered his boat and rowed back towards the village and his cottage on the hill. Where the sun shone at its brightest, blinding his way forward, Iain bathed in its warmth and imagined her projection magically guiding him through the currents. For several minutes, the white light invaded his senses, blocking out all the sounds of the water and the birds around him, bleaching out too all the colours he knew to be there. He felt the sun's rays warm and soothe his body as he wondered about his future, barely caring where the boat and the currents would carry him. He would never again feel satisfied tending to his sheep on the hillside, now that his eyes and his soul had been opened to the wider, richer world around him. Beyond the village, who knew what adventures lay out there for him to encounter. Maybe she was out there somewhere, waiting and hoping too. Maybe he could find her again and if he did, he'd never let the tides of time take her away from him.

Suddenly, the white brightness faded behind the loitering storm clouds that loomed over the loch like expectant vultures ready to strike. As his eyes adjusted to the threatening gloom, he observed anew the beauty of the summery palette of deep colour that filled the landscape around him, smiling at the familiar pebbled shore line where he'd fallen at her feet and heard the music of her laughter for the first time. Moments later, he felt the dragging and scraping of the hull as the small boat struck the pebbled bottom of the shallows, bringing it to a decisive halt close to shore. After carefully climbing out and pulling the boat on to the bank side, the shepherd, unrelenting in his determined and hopeful belief of her inevitable return, hiked purposefully homewards up the hill towards his lonely lowly cottage. But as he reached the brow of the hill, he could see a fine trail of smoke drifting upwards from his home. Was it on fire? Had the Captain ordered his mercenary militia to destroy his home in revenge?

Iain sped off towards the cottage, ploughing through the long grass and thistles, oblivious to the cruel lashing of their sting against his skin. But, as the front of his cottage came into view, he stopped and gasped a breathless sigh of relief at the sight of the cottage standing serenely peaceful, undisturbed save for the unexpected smoke ascending from the chimney.

Someone was there. Someone was inside the cottage. Iain crept quietly up to the cottage shutters and peered cautiously between the timbers. He could see someone moving through the room, but the narrow gap in the wood made it hard for him to view anything clearly. His nose twitched with the smell of cooking from within, and he wondered who would take such trouble to feed him supper before retribution. Intrigued but cautious, Iain fetched his spare axe from behind the cottage and tiptoed back towards the door. Then, taking a deep breath and holding the axe poised for attack, Iain kicked open the door.

As the door flew wide and the slamming timbers reverberated off the stone wall, the afternoon sun rushed into the cottage around the shepherd's axe wielding silhouette. The young woman spun around startled, and an almost empty wooden bowl was sent clattering on to the stone floor. As she beheld the axe wielding shadow, she let forth a terrified scream.

"Who's there?" she shouted out, trembling with fear.

The voice, so unexpected and so familiar to him now, shocked the returning shepherd. His once firm and determined grip on the axe slipped, and the weapon dropped with a resounding thud on to the stone floor at his feet. Could it really be her, he mumbled to himself in excited disbelief, or was this another cruel trick of the light sent to torment him?

Rushing forwards towards the figure standing in front of the fireplace, Iain's eyes met hers peering out from the shadows. In an instant, his face broke into the broadest excited smile, as he reached out to her projection. His fingers touched the soft pale skin of her hands and he hesitated, wide-eyed. This wasn't an image. She was flesh and blood. What miracle was this, allowing her to return to him as a whole, complete person, he asked himself.

Liz held her breath, her chest pounding hard, nervously as she waited for him to speak. She recalled the previous tortured face that had filled her visible world as her life faded away in that other time and place. How much time had passed between then and now, she didn't know or care. Was this heaven or had time and the wavelength rewoven events and brought her back to that day, so long ago? His hand gently combed through her hair seconds before he swept her off her feet and into his arms. Although her clothing had changed into something far less familiar and bizarre, there was no mistaking the sound of her voice, her long golden hair and her sparkling crystal blue sapphire eyes.

"You came back to me!" he exclaimed excitedly, before

kissing her with an unreserved passion that took her breath away and left her in no doubt that this was real and so were his feelings for her.

"What happened?" he asked wildly curious. "How did you get here? How long can you stay?" he asked so quickly, he could barely get the words out clearly.

Cupping his excited beaming face gently in her delicate hands, she saw his rich brown eyes fill with an indescribable joy as he swung her around elatedly before lowering her gently to the ground. Leading her to the edge of the bed, he sat her down, eager to learn of her explanation and understanding of the miracle that had returned her to him.

"Please, tell me!" he implored. "Tell me everything!"

Liz took a deep breath and began at the beginning. Careful to exclude the references to dates, Liz told him of their adventures in the present. No timelines rippled as she recounted every fantastic detail, nor did they ripple when she spoke of their journey through the vortex to the recent past. Iain leaned back against the bedpost and listened intently with wide eyed fascination as she babbled like a bubbling brook about the dangers they had faced together. Then, when she was done, she stopped to catch her breath waiting silently for his reaction. Eventually, he gently parted his lips and whispered softly,

"So, we were together, in the future?"

"Yes."

"But we weren't ….."

"Married?" she anticipated. "No, how could we be? There was no time. Everything happened so fast back there," she began. "My world was suddenly turned upside down. I was in hiding from Magnus, though I didn't have any idea at the time, that he was behind it all. Then you turned up out of the blue and no sooner had we met than all holy hell broke loose. You managed to save me from his militia and we've been running and hiding ever since. We barely had a moment to breathe never mind think," she explained. "You did ask me though, the moment I got back from here, and the ring ....that was really strange. The ring stayed with me, ... Look!"

Iain looked down at her outstretched hand and the gleaming silver band that still adorned her finger, where he had placed it earlier that day.

"Did he come back with you? Is he here?"

"I don't know, I don't think so," Liz replied. "When I," she hesitated.".... died I honestly thought that everything would go back to the way it was before," she continued. "I thought I would find myself back home and you, ...well, I thought you'd come back here to restart your life, untouched by everything that's happened."

"So, why are you here?" he asked curiously.

"I honestly don't know, but there must be a reason for it," she replied.

"What makes you say that?" he asked.

"The Laws of the universe I guess. Balances and counter balances," she began. "I'm upsetting the balance just being here. Unless, I'm here to put that balance right some how, but I haven't any idea where to begin," she confessed.

"The Lord moves in mysterious ways, his wonders to perform," sighed Iain.

"If he does, I wish he'd give me a clue, ... or a hint even. Without Iain and Fraser to figure things out the way they do, I don't stand a chance."

Iain's face dropped with disappointment.

"What am I like?" he asked tentatively. "..... in your present."

"Just the same as you are now, I suppose. A little more worldly wise and better educated, but beneath that, he's ..... you," Liz replied with a soft sparkle in her eyes.

"You miss him don't you?" asked Iain dejectedly. "I can tell by the way you talk about him."

"He saved my life. He protected me," she answered carefully.

"That's not what I asked," remarked Iain.

"We're ..... close," Liz replied hesitantly. "Of course I miss him, I mean you. God this is confusing!" she added. "Why should it matter anyway, you're him and he's you?"

"From what you've said, we're not the same person," replied Iain. "I haven't seen what he's seen, or done what he's done. My life is summed up by everything you see here in this cottage."

"Okay, I accept that," she replied. "but underneath, he's still you. He's just older, in his mind, otherwise he looks exactly like you, more or less."

"And you're in love with him, aren't you?" he asked. "You were in love with him when you arrived here? I'm just his understudy aren't I?"

"Stop it!" she snapped. "This is insane!"

"I need to know!"

"Why? What does it matter?"

"It matters to me!" he insisted. "I won't play in someone else's shadow, ... not even mine! It's not right, and besides, if you're in love with him, you'll not stay here with me. You'll return to him and you'll probably never come back!"

"I'm here now aren't I? I came back and I'll keep coming back, I promise!"

"I have to take your word for that," he sighed despondently.

"You keep talking about yourself like he's someone else," she whispered.

"But he is. That's the whole point," replied Iain. "Like I said before, you've had adventures and experiences with him that I haven't had...."

"Yet…." she interrupted. "But they will happen."

"Look, I'm no hero like him! I'm just a shepherd! I didn't rescue you from that mine…"

"No, but you did rescue me from the Loch and Magnus! That definitely qualifies you as a hero in my book," she replied encouragingly.

"But I didn't meet you first. I'm not the one who awakened your interest."

"I know and I'm sorry," she said apologetically. "There's nothing I can do about that! You're from, ….here and I'm from the future. It's a miracle we ever met at all. So why don't we just accept that and make the most of whatever time we've got together."

Iain studied her closely for a moment, before heaving a huge sigh and saying,

"Aye, you're right. I just can't get it right in my head that you met him, my future self, first. It doesn't make sense."

"Don't worry, it hurts my head just thinking about it," she smiled.

A sudden crescendo of powerful energy radiated outwards across time, upsetting the delicate equilibrium throughout the universe. Their relationship teetered on the edge of a paradox far bigger than any that the vortex or Magnus could ever manufacture. Snapshots flashed out along the wavelength like S.O.S. signals, searching for a receptive home.

A sudden inexplicable surge of electricity flowed through the power pack in the school laboratory and in an instant, young Liz's world froze around her as she flew slowly backwards through the air. As she saw the horrified faces of her classmates suspended in time, she saw too her future, the pivotal, critical moment when the decision of a handsome stranger would make or break the eternal cycle of events that brought them to each other.

Cell by cell, orbits of positively and negatively charged atoms decayed, splitting and polarising every element in her young body. As the electricity raged through her, pushing her almost to the point of death, a sudden calmness quelled the turmoil across time.

A sudden expression of odd surprise flashed across Liz's face, as an image of Iain, identical in every way, suddenly popped up from the depths of her subconscious and superimposed itself on the reality she saw before her. As she watched the slightly time-lagged image repeated Iain's words, and she suddenly remembered where she'd seen the image before. She recalled the accident in the laboratory and she recalled the stranger's face that spoke to her during that suspended moment in time, all those years ago. More pieces of the puzzle slotted into place and the daylight of realisation dawned in her eyes. The negative thought energy generated by Iain's heart break must have transmitted a powerful negative aftershock along the wavelength, she thought to herself. Somehow, it must have been drawn to the peak of positive electricity surging through my body during the accident, she concluded.

Iain noted, the sudden odd expression on her face and wondered what strange, odd notions were going through her head.

"I think I've figured it out!" she suddenly exclaimed excitedly.

Iain stared at her, startled by her sudden excited outburst.

"I don't understand," he replied shaking his head.

"I think I know why I'm here or should I say how I'm here!" she bubbled with exasperating joy. "It's you who brought me here, and it's you who first hooked me in! It's always been you!"

Iain stared at her wide-eyed.

Gulping back her excitement and taking a deep breath, Liz willed herself to calm down and speak slowly.

"I think I better explain," she began.

"I think so too."

"Since the accident years ago, I've had dreams, brief visions of seemingly meaningless events," she explained. "But recently those events have begun to happen for real. You were in the first vision I ever had. I remember. I saw your face, exactly as you are now, saying exactly what you've just said, during the accident that changed my life, the accident that gave me the ability to find you across time," she added. "There's something else too. I should have died when the electricity blew me across the laboratory, or maybe had a heart attack or a seizure, but I didn't."

Iain looked at Liz, puzzled by the strange words and terms she used that he didn't understand.

"I think that vision of you, saved me! I think it must have blocked out or weakened the impact of the electricity passing through my body. If it hadn't, I'd be dead right now! I think you must have transmitted your thought energy somehow from this point in time and I picked it up. Your thoughts found a way to me across time and saved my life! And now we're connected to each other," she grinned. "I'm pretty sure, if it wasn't for you, I wouldn't be alive right now!"

"I'm not sure I understand everything you've just said, but it's good, yes?"

"It's not just good, it's fantastic! It's cosmic, literally!" she exclaimed excitedly. "There's just one thing I'm curious about," she added.

"And what's that?"

"What were you thinking about, just before?" she asked.

"I'd rather not say," he replied. "It's private."

"It's important," she pleaded. "It could give us a clue as to how we can tune into each other. When I saw you, during the accident, I thought I was about to die."

"That's the way I felt," he muttered. "When I thought, ….. it wasn't me you loved."

"That must be the key! If either of us are in danger or we need each other, I find you! It's just strange that I couldn't recall that vision until now. The shock of the accident must have wiped you from my short term memory and buried you deep within my subconscious," Liz explained."… and I'm here, now, to complete the cycle you began."

Iain looked into her eyes. They shone brightly, joyously with a deep sincerity that rang out to him louder than any church bells. However mad and unworldly her explanation seemed to be, she believed it, and she believed in him. Okay, so his future self had a few extra qualities which he didn't have, yet, Liz was right, he could never change who he truly was deep inside. That part of him would always stay the same.

"So, how did you manage to find me again?" he asked with a restored gleam of hope shining in his eyes.

"I'm not entirely sure, but perhaps once the connection was made, like a path once trodden, it was easier to repeat," she smiled.

"So, does that mean that you're staying?" he asked hopefully.

"Perhaps," she sighed. "At least until another storm comes or another crisis pulls me away."

"And when will that be?" he asked, concerned. "There was a storm brewing over the loch on my way here."

"I don't know," she replied softly. "Perhaps it was that storm that brought me to you," she replied.

Iain didn't respond. His mind was distracted by his

intense anxious search for the storm that threatened to cut short their happiness.

"It's gone," he replied eventually, more than a little relieved as he closed the cottage door.

"That's it then. It looks like I'm staying," Liz smiled.

"Is this what you want to happen?" he asked tentatively.

"If we hadn't wanted this to happen, do you think I'd be here now?" she asked rhetorically. "It makes a lot of sense, in a way," she added.

"Why's that?" he asked curiously.

"I've never really been happy where I come from. Life is so complicated there. People have lost sight of the important things in life, like family, friendships, just being alive and making the most of the precious time we have. There's always some meddling bureaucrat telling us what to think or do, mucking things up in the name of power or personal selfish profit."

"Nothing's changed then," Iain smiled wryly.

"I guess you're right," she smiled back. "But I think I'd still prefer it here, like moving away from the rat race of the city into the country. Yes, it might be hard and a lot less convenient, but it's a lot simpler, straight forward. You live, work, love, have children, and grow old."

"Is that what you want, Liz?" he asked curiously.

"A simple life? Definitely!" she smiled. "… with maybe just a dusting of excitement from time to time," she added, grinning broadly.

"I meant, …." he interrupted, looking directly into her eyes. "do you want… a family? Do you still want me?"

"Would I have accepted your proposal, if I didn't?" she asked. "Don't you get it? I don't care if you're twenty-eight or a thousand and twenty eight. It's you, it's always been and always will be, you. I want to …."

"Ssshhh," he interrupted, pulling her into his arms and silencing her words with a kiss. His arms felt firm and strong around her and she felt safe again as she melted into his embrace. The rich, brown, honey golden eyes that had cast their spell over her, the first time they met, now glistened brightly with renewed hope. She could feel his overwhelming joy like a warm glow radiating throughout her entire body and she felt happy. The traumas of the past few days faded into the mists of time as she looked upon his broadly smiling face.

"Liz," he whispered. "Marry me."

"But you've already asked me, and I said 'yes', remember?"

"Marry me, today."

Liz swallowed hard and looked into his excited, hopeful face.

"Why today?" she asked.

"I want you to be my wife, so that whatever happens tomorrow, nothing can change that."

Liz thought for a moment. Iain noted her hesitancy and held his breath expectant of the rejection he dreaded more than any of Magnus' menacing threats.

"Yes," she smiled.

Iain's eyes suddenly widened. Had he imagined it?

"Are you sure?" he asked in disbelief.

"It feels like the right thing do, ... and like you said, whatever happens tomorrow, wherever we find ourselves, I will always be your wife."

"Is it what you want, Liz?"

"More than anything else in the world!"

Suddenly sweeping her up in his arms, Iain leapt across the cottage towards the door. Then, flinging the door open, he stepped across the threshold into the afternoon sunshine and yelled his boundless delight across the valley.

"We're getting married!!!!"

"Congratulations, my son. Be sure you yell loud enough, now. I don't think they quite heard you in Edinburgh."

Startled, Iain turned to notice the elderly Minister clothed in his everyday vestments, staff in hand, venturing towards them across the hill.

"Sorry, Father," Iain replied repentantly.

"You need not apologise for declaring your thanks to God," smiled the Minister. "I fear only that your hearty exclamations will frighten the sheep in your care."

"Yes, Father."

"Do you perhaps wish to make a request of me?" asked the Minister.

Iain looked bemused.

"Serendipity," whispered Liz.

Iain looked at her puzzled.

"A happy accident or coincidence, perhaps?" suggested Liz. "He's asking if you need him to perform the wedding."

Iain's face suddenly broke into the broadest of grins.

"Yes, Father …….. "

The tall grass in the meadow close to the loch swayed from side to side in the warm afternoon breeze as Liz made her way down the hillside towards the surprised village congregation gathered at the foot of the hill, close to the waters edge. Dressed in a simple, white, long flowing gown, worn previously by Iain's mother, Liz waded her way through the intense carpet of tiny forget-me-nots that drifted and rippled over the luscious green pasture like a temperate blue sea. As the breeze caught her long trailing sleeves and skirt, the white cloth rippled high behind her like the wings of a dove.

Standing patiently beneath the marital bower, Iain

caught sight of the look of wonderment in his kinsmen's eyes and turned to gaze up the hill towards the miracle bound in his direction and swallowed hard. His starlight maiden, the focus of his childhood dreams and aspirations, was real and there she was, with eyes of pure sapphire blue gazing down towards him with a warmth and excitement that lifted his soul. Her long golden hair, delicately trained into soft plaits, was highlighted with sprigs of tiny wild flowers, freshly plucked from the hillside that afternoon. Suddenly, the sunlight caught her dress, casting out a radiant white aura around her as she softly and serenely approached the wedding bower. Pale pink blossoms rustled in the branches of the boughs above their heads, like a host of delicate butterflies fluttering their wings in the breeze, as Iain reached out his hand towards his bride and held his breath. Softly placing her hand in his, Iain noticed the silver ring gleaming in the sunlight and whispered a silent prayer.

As the sun began to sink towards the distant horizon, the long golden rays of light cast a veil of golden shimmering stars across the surface of the loch, and the congregation fell silent as the Minister bound the shepherd's hand to his bride's and performed the marriage rites.

"By the power invested in me, as minister of this parish, and in the sight of God and this congregation, I declare that you are now husband and wife, together," said the Minister. "May the Lord's spirit shine upon you and bless you and keep you always. Amen."

Whilst the Minister unbound them before the congregation, Iain leaned forward and swept a wayward curl from her face before sealing their betrothal with his kiss. A loud cheer went up from the gathered assembly of villagers and kinsfolk, before the cheery throng bid their congratulations and farewells.

Had she done the right thing? Would the wrath of time come crashing down on their heads because she changed what happened in Iain's past? Or had she? Liz thought back to when she asked Iain in the present, if he had ever been married. He'd said 'no'. She remembered that distinctly. Or had he lied to her, she asked herself. But then, why would he do that, unless, he wanted to be sure that she married him out of choice and not because she felt she had to. Was that what he'd meant about giving him hope, knowing that she had made her own choice? Had he known all along about her return to the cottage but said nothing to preserve the past? Liz didn't know.

Watching the last of the congregation as they disappeared into the village, Liz felt suddenly afraid and looked up at the sky expectantly, searching for the storm clouds she hoped would never return.

"The storm clouds are gone," he whispered softly. "You've nothing to fear," he added reassuringly as he tilted her face towards his. "I won't let them take you away from me again."

Liz smiled and reached out towards her new husband, whispering, "Take me home, Iain. Take me home."

Whilst the evening sun cast its dying fire upon the sky above the distant horizon and long evening shadows fell upon the hillside towards the loch, the shepherd swept his bride up into his arms and carried her back to the cottage.

As the flames crackled and danced in the open hearth, the fire cast its own long shadows across the matrimonial bed as the humble shepherd lay back against the pillows, with his bride's cheek resting gently on his chest. Carefully picking out the flowers from her hair and setting free her curls from the soft plaits that bound them, Iain watched in almost reverend silence as her hair cascaded over her bare shoulders. Ever the gentleman, Iain waited patiently as the flames of unspent desire burned within him. Sensing his hesitancy, and relegating her fears to the back of her mind, she whispered softly, and reassuringly,

"I won't break."

Turning slowly towards her, Liz held her breath as he marvelled at her delicate femininity and explored the curves of her body. A heavy silence fell over the cottage, and Iain noted a new and different sparkle twinkling in Liz's eyes as he made love to her. A sudden shiver of energy and excitement rippled through her body, and for just a moment, he saw something, an image, a strangely fashioned room, the likes of which he'd never seen or even imagined.

Suddenly a million tiny stars spread like a cloak over her body and she opened her eyes wide in fear. A single flash of lightening and a sudden crack of thunder echoed above the cottage announcing the unexpected arrival of the storm.

"No, please!" she pleaded. "Not now!" she sobbed, wrapping her arms tightly around Iain. "Don't let me go, Iain! Don't let it take me, please!" she cried.

"Fight it Liz!" Iain commanded as he clutched her tightly to him and muttered a desperate prayer vehemently under his breath, "I have never asked you for anything ever, but I'm asking you now, … don't take her away from me again! I won't let you take her, do you hear me! She's my wife and I won't let her go, ever!" Iain bellowed defiantly.

Time suddenly slowed as the stars engulfing Liz's body grew brighter and Iain kissed her desperately, bidding her to hold on. Another flash of lightening struck through the ceiling to the point on the floor where she first projected before him, lighting up the cottage as bright as day. Another heavy crack of thunder boomed overhead, causing everything in the cottage to shake. Terrified, Iain looked around him as the entire cottage threatened to crumble around them.

Abbygail Donaldson

Stretching over his frightened bride, he braced himself to take the blow that never came.

The heavy intense silence returned and the incessant shaking and rattling stopped. Looking into the dark emptiness of his own shadow laid out beneath him on the bed he realised with heart breaking despair that she was gone. Only a few loose sprigs of blossoms from her hair remained upon the pillow.

Clutching the fragile petals in his hand, he roared with anger into the shadows of the night.

Chapter 24

When the shaking stopped, Liz opened her eyes slowly. It was still dark. Where was she? As her eyes began to adjust to the new darkness lit only by the halcyon yellow glow of the streetlamps through the curtains, she realised that she was home. Everything was as she remembered it, before all the chaos began. Had she been dreaming? Was it all some elaborate cruel nightmare that had never really happened? If it had happened, had time restored events back to the way they were?

Climbing out of bed carefully, she switched on the bedside lamp. Several tiny petals fell from her hair on to the soft carpet pile at her feet. As she bent down to pick them up and examine them, she noticed the bright silver ring on her finger. She hadn't been dreaming. Everything had happened as she remembered it.

Focussing her thoughts on Iain and believing she might never see him again, Liz collapsed on the bed, gasping breathlessly as the incontrollable flood of tears poured from her heart and soul. He was gone.

Deeply devastated and unable to face the world again, she huddled beneath the covers on her bed and stared blankly into the darkness as she flicked off the light switch. Her head ached, her chest wheezed and a sickening feeling filled the pit of her stomach as she sniffed and gulped, trying to breathe.

Nothing mattered now, she thought solemnly, as she

wallowed in her grief and self pity. No energy sparked her will to find the answers that might bring her hope. Though her body was alive, though heart and lungs still pumped away to keep her engine going, her mind and soul lay dark and devoid of life and light.

Suddenly, there was the sound of hammering on the glass of her front door downstairs.

Liz didn't move, and sat undisturbed and untouched by the noise.

The hammering on the glass happened again. This time it was more determined, more aggressive and far louder too. There was a sudden metallic creaking noise as the brass letterbox opened and a mouth bellowed with a faint familiar Scottish lilt that made the hairs on her neck stand up.

"For Christ's sake Liz, let me in!"

Liz's eyes flickered in the darkness.

There was the sudden shatter of breaking glass and the front door flew open. Foot steps, two sets clomped along the hallway to the foot of the stairs.

"Fraser, stay here and watch the door. I'll go and get Liz," directed Iain.

The stairs creaked as heavy foot steps pounded up the long flight to the first floor.

"Where are you?" Iain yelled breathlessly, as he pushed open door after door until he reached the front bedroom.

As the solid white wooden door swung open, he saw her silhouette frozen in the centre of the bed like some ancient Egyptian statue, motionless and cold. Rushing to her side, Iain felt for her pulse. It was weak but she was still there, alive.

"Iain I can see torches coming up the hill!" yelled Fraser from the hallway. "We need to go now!"

Grabbing some clothes quickly from the wardrobe and throwing them into a bag which he slung over his shoulder,

Iain dashed back towards the bed. Carefully wrapping the top sheet around her, Iain picked Liz up in his arms and carried her out of the room as the first barrage of bullets struck the window.

"Hurry!" yelled Fraser.

"I'm coming, I'm coming!" replied Iain as he pounded along the landing and back down the stairs to the hallway.

"We'll leave by the back way," instructed Iain as he headed past Fraser through the dining room to the kitchen beyond.

Keeping Liz balanced in his arms, Iain handed Fraser the bag.

"Take this."

Fraser grabbed the strap of the bag and hooked it over his shoulder as Iain lifted his foot towards the lock on the back door and kicked hard. The lock sprung and Iain pulled open the door as they heard the clomping of heavy boots climbing the front steps to the house.

"Come on!" yelled Iain as he shot out into the back yard and through the adjoining wooden gate leading to the garage at the back of the house.

The house shook behind them as one after another of Magnus' militia charged into the building and searched every room looking for them.

"What's wrong with her?" whispered Fraser as they entered the garage.

"She's cold and her pulse is weak like she's in some kind of shock," explained Iain. "Get the car open, Fraser! They'll be on to us any minute!"

Fraser spotted a small brick on the ground near the wall and picked it up. Covering it with the bottom of his sweater, he thrust the brick through the driver's side window and opened the door. Placing Liz lying down on the back seat,

Iain climbed into the front and opened the front passenger door for Fraser.

"Get in!" Iain commanded as he fiddled with the ignition wires and started the engine.

A soldier suddenly yelled out from the house.

"The garage! Quick!"

Revving the engine and placing the car in reverse gear, Iain lifted the handbrake and pushed the accelerator pedal to the floor. With a sudden jolt that threw them both forwards, the car shot backwards ploughing through the wooden garage doors and into the lane beyond. Changing the gears quickly, Iain pointed the car away from the house and drove at high speed down the cobbled lane.

In the hallway, his face twisted from the bizarre side effects of the vortex he'd created, stood Captain Magnus McGregor.

"Where are they?" he bellowed as the young soldier marched towards him.

"Gone Sir! We missed them by seconds Sir!"

"I don't want excuses, get after them! Bring them back! I've a score to settle with Professor Lachlan and his witch and it will be settled tonight!" growled the vengeful tyrant.

Ten miles away from the village, down a dark and winding road, Iain pulled the car in towards the verge. Opening the doors to the back seat, and climbed in beside Liz.

"Liz, Liz," whispered Iain. "You've got to snap out of it!"

"Try this," suggested Fraser as he pulled out a small hip flask of whisky from inside his jacket. "I know it's not usually recommended in these situations but it's all we've got!"

Iain took the flask and unscrewed the lid before carefully placing it against Liz's lips. Tipping a small drop of the amber coloured liquid into her mouth, Iain waited impatiently for a response. Suddenly Liz lurched forward into his arms, coughing profusely like her lungs were on fire.

"That's it, Liz! Come back to me!"

At the sound of his voice, Liz threw herself away from him against the back of the seat, cowering in fear.

"It's alright Liz! It's me! Remember? It's Iain."

The black inky pupils of Liz's eyes suddenly enlarged as they adjusted to the darkness inside the car. She could just make out the short cropped hair, his well defined familiar facial features and the tiny unmistakable flicker of gold in his eyes. As Iain noticed her begin to relax he whispered softly,

"Hello. ….. Did you miss me then?" he asked grinning.

A resounding stinging slap across his cheek was her response.

"Ow! What was that for?"

"For frightening the hell out of me, and dragging me out here in the middle of the night with just this to wear!" she replied clutching at the bed sheet wrapped around her body.

"Sorry," he whispered. "Didn't have a lot of choice I'm afraid. But I did manage to grab a few things during our hasty departure," he added, indicating to the bag on the floor beside her.

"What are you waiting for then?" she asked. "Get out and give a girl some room to dress!"

"Yes Ma'am!" saluted Iain as he sidled his way out of the door and wandered around the front of the car to where Fraser was standing, facing the road.

Then, sticking his hands in his trouser pockets, Iain looked down at his feet and casually kicked over the roadside gravel with his shoes.

"Can you hurry up back there?" he shouted presently. "They could be here soon," he added.

"I would if I could just get, …" she hissed struggling with the zip on her trousers. "There," she sighed, as the car stopped rocking.

Climbing out the backseat wearing a pair of jeans, a t-shirt and a thick sweatshirt she stumbled towards the two men as she tried to shuffle her feet into her slip-on shoes.

"Where are we?" she asked. "What's going on? What year is this?"

"We're about ten miles from your place, … I'm not sure exactly where. It's 2009, at least it was the last time I looked at my calendar, though that will change very soon. As for what's going on, …… Magnus, …He's back and he means business. He's armed and he's got spies everywhere looking for us. We were lucky to get to you when we did!" explained Iain.

"Hang on," she replied puzzled. "2009? But that's before ….."

"The New Year when you disappeared?"

"That's right."

"When we got back, Magnus' militia were waiting for us. He must have got back earlier than we did and tried to change things. We got away by the skin of our teeth and headed up here to get you," Iain explained. "Anyway, what's with the year question? Have you only just got back? Where have you been?"

"Back to the cottage," she said then quickly qualified her answer. "Back to Libran's Loch."

"Ahhh," sighed Iain. "Did I miss anything? Anything important?"

"You knew didn't you?"

"Knew what exactly?"

"You knew, all this time that we were married and you said nothing."

"Yes," he confessed as a deep frown drew across his face. "A lot of things happened that day and they weren't all good."

"Why didn't you tell me? Why didn't you say anything?"

"He was preserving your free will, my dear," interrupted Fraser. "He wanted you to be able to make your own choices. He wanted to know that you married him for love and not because events in his past, dictated you had to."

Liz looked at Iain in the moonlight.

"What if I'd married somebody else, not knowing I was married to you? You might have turned me into bigamist," she remarked.

"That wouldn't have happened. I wouldn't have let it."

"So what would you have done, ...stood up in the church on my wedding day and said something like, 'sorry everybody – she's already married to me.'"

"That was one possibility I considered," he replied. "but, like I said, that problem didn't happen."

"And what about after I disappeared on our wedding night? What happened?"

"I don't remember," he muttered reluctantly.

"I don't believe that for a moment," Liz replied.

"Alright! What do you want me to say? That I tore my hair and heart out with grief for you? That I swore I would search the world for you, however long it took?" he retorted moodily. "Well that's exactly what happened! Satisfied?"

Liz began to shake. She'd never seen him angry like that before. She could tell he meant every word and she could sense the pain as it erupted in his apoplectic face.

"I'm sorry, Iain," she said softly.

"You didn't know and I couldn't tell you! I didn't want you loving me out of pity or guilt!"

"I didn't! I don't!" she whispered gently. "I mean, ….I love you – end of story!"

"Is it?" he asked curtly.

"Like I said back then," she began. "It doesn't matter where or when we're together, I just want to be with you whatever happens. I'm still your wife."

Iain looked straight into her crystal blue eyes shimmering with silent tears in the moonlight. Then, discarding his anger like a piece of useless rubbish, he broke into a huge gleaming wry smile.

"Well now, That's alright then!" he replied and wrapped his arms around her in a big bear like hug before kissing her passionately.

A sudden whizzing noise shot passed Iain's ear.

"Sniper! Duck!" he yelled and pushed Liz and Fraser behind the car. "Bloody hell that was quick! He must have had the car tagged!"

"What do we do?" asked Liz.

"We've got to get out of here right now!" replied Iain.

"But how? Where do we go?"

"Not where, my dear. When," suggested Fraser.

"You're kidding, right?" she asked.

"You can do it Liz! You got us out of tight spot once before, remember? The boat?" said Iain.

"I can't control it! We could wind up anywhere, anytime! We could get very lost in time!" she pleaded.

"That's still better than being very dead!" replied Iain.

"He's right Liz," added Fraser. "We need to live to fight another day! We have to stop Magnus!"

Two more bullets whistled over their heads and into the tree behind them.

"Do it Liz!" commanded Iain.

Terrified by the danger they faced yet excited to be back with Iain, Liz's heart began to pound powerfully with a deep strong energy pulse. Nothing was going to hurt them, she'd make sure of that!

As the ground beneath their feet shook with the vibration of heavy vehicles and foot patrols heading their way, a familiar green mist began to engulf them. Holding tightly on to each other, the three fugitives huddled together within the green cloud and prayed.

As the jeep drew alongside Liz's abandoned car, Magnus stepped out on to the road. Walking determinedly around the side of the car into the intense green mist with his gun ready to fire, Magnus bellowed his anger across the valley.

"Noooooooooo!!!!!!" he yelled to the sound of bullets being fired. Striding angrily from the dissipating mist, Magnus stopped and glared up at the sky. "Damn you, shepherd! You can't escape from me! I'll find you! I WILL FIND YOU!" he boomed as he extracted a small black hexagonal box from his pocket.

Holding his hand out into the residue of the green mist, Magnus watched as the digital screen lit up in the darkness and began to scan the energy cloud for its electrical frequency. Finding the frequency, a series of numbers appeared on the screen changing in rapid succession as the device plotted the signal from its point of origin to its termination. Within seconds, the numbers settled and the figures 1, 8, 7 and 9 appeared on the screen.

"Back to HQ! We've got an expedition to plan!" he commanded. "…and I've got some family ties to rekindle," he muttered with a sinister grin. "It's times like these when family really can prove to be such an asset," he added laughing heartily. "We'll find you Professor. No matter where or when you run to, we will find you!"